LIBERTY, GREED AND JUSTICE FOR ALL

Warren DeVere Stephens

2nd Edition

PUBLISHED BY DeMore

2021

ISBN 978-1-7376770-1-7

Most of us go through life seeing occasional exhibitions of greed, self-indulgence, and amorality. The Pittman family of Boston and their immediate circle each possess the entire package of major character flaws. They focus only on their individual sinister ambitions to be unshackled from any limits on personal pleasure. Lauren, Phillip, and Jane Ella Pittman, as well as Safari Guide Richard Martin and Phillip's friend and attorney Murray Eddleman find a soothing balm of depravity insulates them from any tidbit of conscience. They each seek to find a nirvana of amorality to justify greed, deceit, and infidelity. Perhaps crime does pay.

CONTENTS

INTRODUCTION

INTRODUCTION

Inspiration for this story comes from my desire to see people get their just rewards. I could not find any storytelling traction where good, decent people get fortune, fame or happiness. Instead I took the easy rabbit hole and relate this story about despicable people. The characters are wholly fictional and not replications of actual individuals (Okay. Go ahead and breathe. You're not in the book). Each character is a synthesis of bits and pieces of greed, amorality and a void of conscience. While the aforementioned character flaws are bad, it's even worse when the self-centered owner of the evil traits sees family members, so-called friends and the rest of the world simply as tools for gaining what he or she wants.

It's a pleasure to complete this project because I can leave these characters behind and be happy to smile at the angelic side of life's human scale.

Warren DeVere Stephens

June 6, 2018

CHAPTER 1

I'M LAUREN PITTMAN

Okay, I'll admit I am a sarcastic, self-centered bitch but I can turn it on and off in an instant. I only act this way to my husband and jealous women. Well, there may be a few other selective bitch-performances, but I reserve those when needed and then I call up my demons from hell and spray it out like projectile vomit. It is a natural talent and an effective defense mechanism for self- preservation.

I look terrific in every way that counts for a mature, desirable woman in today's world. I'm a long-legged five-nine, one hundred thirty pounds, ten pounds of which are my made to order boobs. I love to wear clothes that accentuate my boobs and I create male magic when I pull some of my long dark brown hair in front to make a thin hair curtain over the cleavage. I exercise to keep my butt from sagging, my calves shapely and my waist trim. And I don't have just any face. I have a face that is gorgeous by custom design, and it is absolutely age defying. I can afford it because I am Lauren Pittman. People introduced to me frequently think they've met me before but in truth my cosmetic surgeon gave me a face that's a Liz Taylor look alike albeit my face is a bit thinner. I think it's an improvement Liz may have chosen if it had been available in her earlier days. Just to be clear, I've earned everything on this body and face. I've earned it through endurance for years of subhuman treatment by my nerd-tyrant husband, Phillip.

I'm confident in my flirting because I can capture men's attention and make them think very, very naughty thoughts. My extramarital sex life has some glorious moments but, in all honesty, they have been very few and far between though some of the vicious, jealous gossip would have you believe I get laid extra-maritally three times a month- once by the Boston Bruins, once by the Red Sox and once by the Patriots. I suppose rumors are a bit like exercise. If it doesn't kill you, it makes you stronger. But that's about all there is about moi. Like my body and beauty, my surroundings are top drawer but certainly my life didn't begin like this.

I grew up in a suburb of St. Louis, Missouri originally brought into this world as Lauren Jane Copeland. I'm the product of a broken home. My father was seldom around and when he was, he was downright mean. My mother barely made ends meet and so my future depended on my own resourcefulness. I began to realize after high school I could either remain in my hand-to-mouth existence or position myself to tag onto someone else's financial comet. I focused on the latter.

I financially scraped and finagled my way into Lindenwood College outside of St. Louis and I never had any ambition of a degree but decided college was to be simply a means to an end to meet people and socialize. I'm proud of myself because I was quite successful in achieving my singular college goal, not a degree but "hooking" and marrying a promising, wealthy young man.

Phillip Pittman came from a nouveau riche Boston family who were so busy with their successful retail enterprises they simply pushed Phillip out the door to the very best schools money can buy. Phillip was very suited to academics and showed little interest in athletics. He kept himself busy enough in his nerd-like world so he missed out on romantic experience but assumed one day the right person would come along. He dreamt of someone who could fulfill all the social requirements and let him concentrate on making serious money.

The moon and the stars must have been aligned that one weekend for both Phillip and me. Phillip was visiting an aunt who was a professor at Lindenwood College. Phillip was waiting to pick up his aunt. He just happened to be waiting for her in her Jaguar convertible and I couldn't resist the opportunity to say hello. Phillip wasn't about to let the opportunity escape and so our story took off like a rocket ship that weekend.

8

My body and seductive ways hooked Phillip Pittman, but Phillip was certain he was the studly aggressor and I was the prize of a lifetime. However, my calculations were sharper than Phillip's in the sexual department and what began as a weekend tryst resulted in me quitting Lindenwood, packing up and moving with Phillip back to Harvard in Cambridge, Massachusetts. I playfully worked at a couple of part time jobs, but Phillip's family wealth kept us from any financial concerns. My focus was **control** of Phillip. Once hooked, there was to be no escape or change of heart. I smothered him in attention and sex as he diligently attended the graduate business and banking school at Harvard. I loved controlling my nerdy, well-connected, ambitious boyfriend. I knew Phillip was visualizing me as a future corporate trophy wife and my sexual proclivity assured, he stayed mesmerized with me being his one and only choice.

A formal Cape Cod wedding was everything a fairytale wedding should be except it was obvious the emptiness of my side of the church told a story of its own. The Pittman's were aghast when not a single Lauren Copeland relative was present for the wedding and reception though the Pittman's held several RSVP assurances that I had created. Though the Pittman's had their red-faced moments during the reception they were glad to see Phillip out from under foot of their own busy ambitions. Phillip seemed happy and after the "I do's" were exchanged it was too late to check for my pedigree papers.

Though the marriage took place with the speed of light after Phillip's graduation, the luster of romance wore off nearly as fast as Phillip's erections. We moved to Boston and Phillip threw his energy into the business world. It was as if the day he went to work for the first time he wanted me on a shelf at home in case he had a need to display me. Phillip saw his role as human ATM. He could and would provide money on request and my role was to not bother him. Phillip's amateurish romantic side lost all energy and began to shrivel and fade away…literally. His sexual motivation toward me was more like a checklist or calendar appointment but any unhappiness was masked by his enjoyment of work and my enjoyment to spend money.

9

Jane Ella Pittman was born a year after the wedding so one more checklist square for Phillip and one more reason for me to maintain my gorgeous body to rub under the noses of the "other" wives…and their husbands. The nearly immediate dysfunction of the marriage was handled through denial by both parties, and I no longer felt any threat of losing Phillip or a need to keep him controlled. For years, I spent most of my business-induced widowhood playing bridge and shopping. But that morphed into afternoon binge drinking as a substitute for playing cards.

And so Phillip and I, Mr. and Mrs. Pittman, continue our lives together twenty-two years later. For better or worse, I have him and he has me. It's an understatement that for years I've been very, very unhappy, and frustrated. The marriage foundation is strongly rooted in hostility and causing pain. There is neither hope nor desire to rekindle any relationship. I'm consumed daily in self-pity, rage and fantasies. Therapy by shopping and spending no longer provide any respite in my life and true happiness would require total excision of Phillip Pittman sort of like having a hideous tumor removed.

CHAPTER 2

I'M PHILLIP PITTMAN

I'm a forty-two year old Boston native. I can stretch to five feet-eleven with my shoes on but I round up and simply say I'm six feet. One might guess my ethnicity as Italian or Greek in facial features. My black rimmed glasses sit toward the tip of my Roman nose and I confess my lips are always a bit pursed as if I'm about to whistle or thinking about something to say. My black hair is graying at the temples and pattern baldness has invaded the crown of my head but the gray is only known by my barber so the gray regularly is extinguished as the sprouts appear in the garden beneath my balding head's solar panel. I religiously shave each morning so there's little chance for salt and pepper stubble to show.

I'd say I'm relatively trim at a hundred-seventy pounds but my midsection shows the natural effects of gravity and middle age. My favorite uniform is a dark, custom-tailored Armani suit, monogrammed white shirt with cufflinks, suspenders and the latest style Berluti shoes. Rarely is there a day off from work in my life but occasionally there will be a work-related event that requires smart or business casual clothes and I admit that sends me into more anxiety than it should because of the decisions over what to wear on such an occasion. I want never to be caught dead in any clothes except the very latest European executive fashions.

My best friend, Murray Eddlemann, tells me that I seldom, if ever, laugh out loud (except at his jokes) but frequently chuckle in the presence of others even though it's an expressionless chuckle. Murray says that's because I'm entertained by verbally cutting, slicing, and dicing someone in front of others and that brings my chuckle as if no harm was intended or deliberately poking it in deeper. The only time anyone hears me laugh out loud is when I'm talking privately with Murray, my longtime best friend since being schoolmates at Harvard. He was in law school and I was in business. Now talk about a real marriage! Murray remains my trusted corporate attorney and confidant. So, laughing is not my most notable quality but I pride myself in dramatically showing hair-trigger anger around employees. It is the expression most people associate with me. From irritated to angry occurs quickly and my face turns crimson at irritation but when angry, the veins stand out in a "V" –shaped pattern on my forehead and like purplish garden hoses on the sides of my neck. Why would anyone pride himself on showing anger. It means my employees walk on eggshells when in my presence. They are my employees because I need people to work and perform the tasks I assign. They are not paid to think or challenge me. I do the thinking and Murray and I reinforce the brilliance of our performance.

Of course I am preoccupied with business. No one has any idea how many balls I have to juggle and none of them will ever hit the ground. My graduate degree is from Harvard in International Banking and Finance and early on I competed, scratched and clawed very hard to get the financial success I have today. After university I was sought by prestigious international banking firms looking for my education, workaholism and brains. After three years of proving my abilities, Murray Eddlemann and I formed our own investment corporation. We acquire risky businesses and other investments, mold them into marketable assets and sell them individually or break them apart and re-group some together for sale. Highly profitable. I am the principal stockholder, Chairman of the Board and CEO of Boston's highly successful Patriot Star Investment Corporation. My concept of juggling all the balls is by brains and total control, risk is reduced to background noise. I routinely go to the office six days a week and work at home evenings and on Sundays.

Part and parcel of my duties are that I "must have business cocktails and dinner after work" two or three nights a week. Lauren must know it's not all business but she ignores it, in fact I seriously doubt that she cares. Believe me when I say the lack of care is mutual. Some evenings I arrive home very late and go right to bed. On the evenings I stay in the city I arrive home after close of business the following day. Lauren is never told about my schedule, she has no business questioning my schedule nor is she concerned enough to ask about the official nature of my schedule. Lauren and I have separate bedrooms because of my disruptive schedule, my computer activity off and on during the night, and most of all because I can't stand being near a ranting, stumbling drunk. I find her literally repulsive.

All-in-all, I am very, very wealthy but very unhappy man other than when I'm at work…controlling, directing, deciding, demanding and of course sampling the finest of my lady staff members. Lauren and I remain unhappily married for over twenty years. Divorce is not worth thinking about because I can't waste time on distractions from my business and Murray tells me it's not the right time because it could expose some of our financial games to unwanted scrutiny. But one of my long term goals frequently shared with Murray is the inevitable dissolution of the current marriage sham.

I suppose another night without sleep makes me stronger if it doesn't kill me. Or so the myth goes. My inability to sleep soundly is not about worries. As owner, Board Chairman and senior executive officer of my company I do more than any ten others. It's not about worry. I may get concerned about business, but never worried. That's because any concern I can fix, I do fix. I'm the linchpin of the entire operation. I fix anything that needs fixing day in and day out. I fix things by assessing, running legal decisions through Murray and then I direct others to do the tasks. I am the grand taskmaster. I am the ringmaster.

Nope, what keeps me awake is gnawing anger about being yoked around the neck to my blushing bride. Her I can not fix. Yet. More aptly I think of her as a middle-aged, plastic face and body, very little education, uncouth trollop. Yet she thinks she's as hot as a sixteen year old slut. God, I can hardly bare to look at her. We don't live together at home. First It's not living, it's imprisonment. Second, it's not a home, it's a house. With all her natural God-given charm and skillset it's my wealth and this luxurious house that keep her from living under a bridge somewhere. My freedom will come the day Murray says he's got everything lined up so she can be sent packing. Or perhaps it will be the day she is driving drunk and runs into a train or something. Either way is fine by me. I am incapable of violence or else I would hit her across that ignorant phony face with a full bottle of her Grey Goose Vodka.

I'm sure psychiatrists have a name for my condition but I endure this life a day at a time because I have many, many others on whom I can inflict mental abuse to alleviate my rage. And for me it works reasonably well. Murray knows exactly what I do but he never criticizes or attempts to alter my course when I'm getting vicarious revenge. It's quite simple. I abuse my employees. You know the remarkable thing? They take it. I've wondered if in some ironic way my employees then go home and commit the same on their families. But that's their problem, the puny little sheep.

So tonight I can't sleep because I'm feeling the rage. My pressure cooker is about to its limit so let's remedy that. I can't wake Lauren out of her drunken beauty sleep at this hour so I'll take it out on some weak-dick employees who call themselves managers. That's a laugh. If my thumbs will work I'll text the research teams and beat the living shit out of them…so to speak. Let's see… it's two AM.

I've just reviewed the status of proposals to acquire Delaware REIT and WILAMCO Manufacturing. I'm more than disappointed that the documentation and research details are incomplete. Our corporation's success and your paychecks are the result of having timely, accurate information necessary to make good decisions. At present our Investment

and Real Estate Research Department seems to be letting us all down. I decided to get these two proposals back on track so my workday has begun at this early hour. So has yours. Managers and supervisors of the research Department will meet with me in the boardroom at five AM prepared to identify the unfinished data for the risk analysis, responsible manager for each task and progress details. If you do not understand what's expected of you on any of the details I'll be able to clear that up very quickly. If you know what's expected but are not sure how to do it that's a training issue and I will clear that up very quickly. If you know what's expected and know how to do it but just have not done it that may be a disciplinary issue and I will clear that up quickly as well. See you at five sharp. Mr. Pittman

I feel better already.   I, shower, dress and leave home at three-thirty. At exactly at four-fifteen AM my black Mercedes S65L makes a wide sweeping turn, tires screeching on the spotless concrete of the garage floor and into the space marked "PRIVATE-PHILLIP PITTMAN". It causes me to smile every morning when I look at my name because I'm not just the president and CEO of the company, I am the pinnacle. Every action of the corporation depends on my seal of approval or it isn't done. By four-twenty I'm nearly at the door to my office at the end of the hall. I've passed Murray Eddlemann's office and of course it's still dark. Murray is my confidant in the corporation and my closest friend in life. Murray and I literally spend hours together each day. But it doesn't begin until Murray makes his grand entrance around nine, Starbucks in one hand, briefcase in the other.

I turn on the office lights. The familiar smell of cleanliness is because I demand it from the night cleaning crew. I wander over to the credenza and select a K-Cup of coffee to start my day. This is the last menial labor I'll do today. My executive assistant, Julie will be sure my silver service is full and hot for the rest of the day. Julie makes quite a production out of filling the coffee service and fussing to be sure there's not an errant drop to be found. She also does some very delicate movements and bends and twists that are unbelievably sexy and it's become like a game. She putters around, I drop my specs onto

15

my nose and stare over the top smiling. As she leaves the area she acts surprised when she catches me looking. Cat and mouse. Mouse and cat. And on discrete occasions, this cat has had that mouse and the mouse did more than just an obligatory squeak. I don't think even Murray suspects.

After standing at the credenza and ritually stirring my coffee, I walk behind my desk, boot my computer, lean toward my open day-planner on the screen, looking at the day's schedule and appointments. Next to my computer is a slotted holder for what Julie calls my "smart cards". They're four by six inch briefing cards with quick facts for upcoming appointments, meetings or anticipated phone calls. Throughout each day Julie gathers the information and if she has time she has Murray add to them before they are placed on my desk. She's amazing!

I walk to the large window that overlooks the Boston skyline. As I sip the coffee I pick up the stack of morning newspapers, Barron's, Wall Street Journal, China Daily, Pravda and of course the Boston Herald. The night security people place the papers in a neatly aligned staggered stack on my coffee table by the window each morning. After looking briefly and rapidly through the papers, I toss them on the coffee table and go to my desk. Time to get this day underway.

I open the next screen on my computer and quickly focus on the international financial markets. From bedtime the night before until I catch up in my office each morning I have international market information running on my home computer so I can glance at it throughout the night. Friday nights and part of Saturdays I must admit I feel deprived of financial information. This is what I think about all day, every day except for the amount of time wasted arguing with Lauren or the occasional six-hour intermittent coma to which I succumb a few nights a week. I am driven by finances and power. With Murray as a team mate we are like ravenous crocodiles in the world of business. We gobble up everything in sight and we make money. Lots of money. This is why I am the rock star. I am the boss. I am the leader. I am God in my company. I am the ringmaster. When I blow my whistle the sheep perform.

16

At exactly five AM I make my entrance to the Board Room. There's no need for pleasantries or formality. I called this, so let the torture begin.

"You may have surmised that there is something amiss when a meeting is called with such urgency and for some of you a dreadful hour. You'd be correct. Unfortunately when some people choose not to do their jobs correctly during regular hours we must refocus and make corrections at irregular hours. So, the purpose of this meeting is to get the risk analysis for both Delaware and WILAMCO completed so the corporate board can decide on acquisition. Let's take WILAMCO first. There's a copy of financials currently in exhibit D but these financials are nine months old. That's sloppy and ridiculous. Who's got this one?"

"Yes, Mr. Pittman, I guess that's mine. I…"

"Stop right there. You guess it's yours? Goddamn right it's yours, Charles. When were you planning to include current financials in exhibit D?"

"I can't imagine that should be a problem. I'll check as soon as…"

"Okay. That's enough. I don't need to sit here listening to a room full of managers say things like I guess or I'll check or I'll monitor. At this moment not a one of you can clear these items to my satisfaction because for starters you weren't even aware there are problems. You don't know your areas of responsibility well enough so you can eat, live and sleep the details. Yet that's what I expect. When one department slips it weakens our ability to perform as an entire corporation. Do you remember that every department agreed on the time schedule? Nod your head, blink your eyes, show me there's something living in those zombie bodies I'm looking at.

Okay I don't want to hear I'll check when WILAMCO opens this morning or I'll check with my analyst when he or she comes into work. I'm going to give you directions, so listen carefully. You all will use this Board room as your control center this morning. I expect to have all the incomplete, missing or sloppy data perfect by noon. You work from this room. I'll make sure Julie gets some coffee and rolls brought in. I will be in here to check on progress at nine AM, ten AM and eleven AM. I expect for this to be complete by noon. Each of you understand? Do you have questions of me? Okay. Do your job. I'll see you at nine."

I get up and leave the room. People hate when I do this. I call it pacing. It forces them to figure out what they must do, how to get it and work together for success. At the moment they have one rallying point. They hate me but I've just proven to them I can demand anything I want and make it happen. Yeah it's an ungodly hour to drag them out of their warm little beds but I feel energized at the moment. Santa's elves are busy in their workshop. This is why I love being at work.

"At seven-thirty I can hear Julie fidgeting around in the front office and she dutifully gives a few light raps on my door and pokes her head in with a, "Good morning, Mr. Pittman."

I motion for Julie to come into the office and glance at my watch. Plenty of time.

"You look spectacular this morning. I have to be the most fortunate man in the world to begin my morning this way."

Julie glances at the clock, "Just needed to check the time so I know whether to say oh, Mr. Pittman, you'll embarrass me or say thanks, Phillip. I think I still have time for the latter so I'll just say you're looking dashing and sexy as always."

"Julie, you're the only shining spot I have in my life. Believe me. I wish we had more time to spend together. Why does life have to be so complex and restricting? I feel like I'm trapped by everything I have to endure outside the office. I love it when we are alone and you can call me Phillip. I really love it."

"I feel the same, Phillip, but I'm always worried I'll slip and say it at an improper time and embarrass you."

"You slip up? That's got to be a joke, Miss Perfect...in every way."

18

Julie keeps looking out the partially open door, nervous that someone could walk in. I slowly rise from my desk staring into her eyes and without a word walk past Julie and gently close the door.

As I slowly return toward Julie my eyes are drinking in every detail of her beautiful pose. I gently take both of her hands in mine and breathe a sigh of desire.

CHAPTER 3

I'M JANE ELLA PITTMAN

I'm an only child and that is likely a blessing. I do not play well in the sandbox with others. I'm tall, five-ninish barefooted, and slender with disproportionately big boobs and derriere. I have long fingers with perfectly manicured nails. My longer-than-shoulder-length strawberry blond hair, not auburn appears to be sexily wind tossed but I know where every hair is at all times. One look at my mother definitely shows from whom I inherited my strikingly attractive facial features and magnificent body. I suppose to be entirely truthful it's my mom's genetics as well as her checkbook and plastic surgeon. I gladly accept the genetics and I gladly accept the available money. My big brown eyes, long lashes, and puffy lips make heads turn in most venues. I love to wear short shorts in summer but otherwise I like to wear white tights with vividly colored over-blouses. I am a flirt just like my mother, and one of my favorites is when I spot a shy voyeur staring at my boobs. I'll rapidly make eye contact , laugh, shake my hair from side to side deliberately swinging my breasts as well. I love when my performance leaves men stammering and breathless. When I walk I move my hips sending radar signals to every man nearby. I usually carry the latest color and style Coach purse slung over my shoulder and I'm seldom seen, day or night without my big round sunglasses. I'm frequently mistaken for a celebrity. If I were to pick one word that best describes me it's the word ballsy. Brass ballsy.

When I lunch at a hotel I speed up to the valet in my Audi convertible and jump from the car dangling my keys. Most valets around Boston know me by name or sight. I look and act the role of spoiled little rich girl and it's effortless because it's my natural inclination to be a brat, party girl and regular at the Boston after hours scene. I frequently allow a man to accompany me but most men who know me choose not to set themselves up for humiliation by abandonment half-way into the evening. Mostly I hang around with a couple of girls who look and act similarly. I flirt with everyone, men and women and I manage to be on lots of over-the-top social invitation lists.

I am not motivated to ever work. I've never had to work and see absolutely no reason to start. I've always had lots of money for my day to day needs but my real prize is a trust under the control of my parents or more precisely Murray Eddleman. It's like having an allowance. What I want more than anything is having my trust money without strings attached. So for now I must stay under King Phillip's roof, endure his crabby, autocratic style and endure my mother's jealousy toward me until I'm old enough to have complete control over my trust. Twenty-five is the magical age unless my mom and dad do the unthinkable and give me the trust account early. Fat chance! But even if it's twenty-five, at that point I'll travel and party wherever I want, whenever I want and with whomever I want. Total freedom with lots and lots of money. That's my career choice.

I would say I'm quick-witted and like my mother, I never back away from a spat. The more opportunity for sarcasm or demeaning someone, the better. Since primary school age I've been shoveled off to boarding schools but my resistance to dictatorial bullshit always was my undoing. I felt like school should be an escape from what went on at home so I wouldn't put up with it at school as well. I was described as having a borderline antisocial aggressive personality which resulted in schools deciding the loss of my tuition was less important than losing several tuitions from parents of the students I turned into neurotic whimpering, insecure little girls. In fifth grade I changed schools three times in the one year but that didn't bother me in the slightest. New schools were simply a challenge to see how quickly I could intimidate classmates. Finally I graduated from Montrose Girls Academy, a college preparatory school in name only.

After graduating from the prep academy I attended the exclusive women's college, Stephens College, in Columbia, Missouri. It was sheer boredom for two years. Similar to my pre-college days, I proved my casual, unmotivated approach to studies did not lend itself to a stellar academic record. My declared major was Forensic Anthropology but I never really understood or cared what that was actually about. When asked about it I'd state without any shame that I could not imagine how anyone would want to do that "boring stuff" as a career.

After two years I didn't return to college and thereafter spent my time in focused study of how to live a lifestyle of being rich and carefree. To this day, my experiential laboratory work in shopping at exclusive stores garners my greatest all-time level of achievement.

I am counting the days until my twenty-fifth birthday when I'll have full access to my multi-million dollar trust, compliments of King Phillip's success and futile appeasement of my mother over the years. I long to be independent and of course, wealthy without accountability to anyone. I worry from time to time that Phillip and Mom will explode in one of their fighting bouts and it will negatively affect my trust or the timing of it. Though I would not admit it, I hang around the house as if I could rescue my trust if it ever fell into jeopardy. I also have a longer range dream. Once I get my trust money I will put a plan in place to get the entire Pittman estate while I'm still young enough to enjoy it. I don't dare mention a future of plotting to anyone but you can't possibly know the real me without knowing I have no limits or conscience to keep me from what I want. I can't imagine how that will exactly come to pass but there's enough millions in the estate to put all the family crap or guilt aside and do whatever has to be done. I will not shy away from taking it.

CHAPTER 4

I'M MURRAY EDDLEMANN

Hairy from head to toe, the back, the front, the legs, the arms, the knuckles and the bush of hair around my schmuck should have a barber of its own. I'm stuck with the world's largest schnoz and I swear it grows bigger every time I look. Maybe a new mirror. And how come I'm blessed with nose hair like it's the garden of Eden or something. Every day…every friggin day I trim my El Paso mustachio…ya know the inch long hairs that grow from the nostrils every night. It's like having Jack in the beanstalk in my nose. My bushy gray eyebrows don't even take a break over my nose, like one continuous monobrow. I'm not kiddin. A squirrel, a friggin squirrel could actually crawl from one side of my face to the other without me ever knowing it.

And then the ears. I could braid the gray hair that grows out like clumps of Pampas grass. Oh, the hell with it. Every day I look. Every day it's the same old shit. I'm fifty-five years old and I'm still dreamin of lookin like Cary Grant one morning. Looks are important. Health is important. And money isn't everything in life but it's as important as air. Some got it. Some don't. And I do. Gals who know I got money don't stare at my nose hair. They stare at the front of my pants. Not the center front. The pockets 'cause that's where I got a big roll of cash and my ATM card. Power, baby! Pure power.

Okay. So, if anyone wants to know the real Murray they need to get past my outer shell. The outer shell is a suit of armor where I am competent, professional, smart, funny and loyal to my friend and partner Phillip. Inside, I am driven by acquiring wealth and living like royalty. That's it. I am in this game with Phillip to achieve my

23

ultimate desires. There is no such thing as too much but I will know when I am approaching the too much mark. At that point I will drop from sight with my wealth and no one will ever hear my name again. I have no children, my wife has been wonderful but unfortunately she is not part of my end game. Too bad. So sad. I happen to be smarter than anyone else I have ever met in my entire life, and I am a genius when it comes to what others call white collar crime. My difference from all others on this planet is that I will never, no never, be caught. My loyalty to Phillip is easy to playact. He is a ruthless, smart, greedy bastard but he is ultimately a tool for me and that's that.

" Ahhh. Whataya gonna do? Time to hit the ball outta the park one more time. Ya hear that Ruthie? Time to go to the gold plated salt mine. "Hey Ruthie, driver out there?"

"Murray, don't ask me that every day. Of course the kid's there. He's been there for twenty minutes waiting for you so he can speed down the street and get you a Starbucks or whatever."

"Yeah, yeah. I'm out the door. MMMwuh." I throw Ruthie a kiss from one room to the other and head out to the waiting car and driver. Just another work day for fireman Murray. Phillip's the bad guy and I'm the good guy. I have the ability to keep the natives calm and still have plenty of time for scheming with my buddy, Phillip. What will be our next big killing? It's seldom boring because Phillip's always stirring the pot with new opportunities.

He's got amazing instincts. He can sense financial blood in the water a mile away so he finds financially floundering companies before anyone else has any inkling of problems. We analyze them so much we know more about them than they know themselves. Phillip wheels and deals to acquire them by our company and then we fire, cut expenses, squeeze, squeeze and make them profitable or at least look good on paper so we can merge them with others or keep some individually and then spin them off at great profits. Ruthless and wild negotiator. No mercy. Sharks would swim away from Phillip. I should love the guy but he's my tool and I am the ultimate craftsman. He smells blood in the corporate water, I set a strategy and figure the spoils of victory. Phillip negotiates deals from my strategies, I do contracts at

24

the speed of light and I watch the legal-eze to keep everything squeaky clean. Man, are we a pair, but let's be clear who pulls the puppet strings!

I hate to brag but our little extra-legal adventures are so exciting just thinking about them or talking to Phillip about them makes my blood pressure go up fifty points. These private, confidential projects give the term wealth an astronomical plateau. Lots of money. Lots of commas and zeroes. Lots of international banking and phony foreign companies. Wonderful!

CHAPTER 5

I'M RICHARD MARTIN

My childhood and adolescence can be rolled together as formative years. I was raised in a foster home and my foster parents were in it for the money. I never knew what it was like to be surprised by a kind gesture or a surprise gift. I learned from the beginning that the enjoyable extras come from taking. I took by a little gambling, outsmarting other kids and occasionally stealing. I finished high school in Athens, Georgia and joined the U.S Army. Four years later I had improved in two areas. I was physically buff and I found I could make extra money as a gigolo.

After high school and the army, I used the GI Bill and enrolled at Washington University in St. Louis. I was marginally accepted because, shall we say, my academic projection was not strong, but I was a walk-on for football, so I was in like Flynn. It was a good deal because I got room and board and extra special football season food in the jocks' dorm.

I met Lauren Copeland and thought I might actually be in love. But alas, it was just the sex. I will admit we had quite a time together and she found some blueblood Bostonian and I was left behind. Lauren got married very quickly and I thought that would be it for us as a couple. But for Lauren marriage was simply a slight speed bump in our torrid affair. Boston was just a lot further than across St. Louis city limits.

Since academics were not my strong point or interest, Washington University showed me the exit after eighteen months.

I took a part year job with a British travel company and worked as a laborer in what is now Botswana. I was a general flunkie for luxury safaris. Years went by and I became the go to guy for so many details of the safari business I got promoted and promoted and the pay was a bit better than okay.

I have an exercise regimen to slow the aging process and so I'm somewhat of a poster boy what a middle-aged man should be. I'm six feet two inches and weigh two-hundred. I am described as ruggedly handsome and I confidently act the part as well. While graying at the temples is a give away for middle age, I have the market cornered on True Sons hair dye. It is used on any, and I do mean any, hair that attempts to betray me. This year I have been touching up an increasing amount of betrayal so it's time to develop long range plans.

I still make side money entertaining women and the safari business provides an endless stream of delightful, wealthy clients. I realize I must snag someone for the long haul and leave this whole business in the rear view mirror but frankly I have few candidates who I could possibly stand for more that a few weeks of play-acting.

I am partial to one person out of all the rest and that is a woman, Lauren Copeland who now lives in Boston. Lauren's my age and though I don't see her often I find her incredibly gorgeous and she could likely be a person I could stay with for the long term. Unfortunately, Lauren treats me like a sex toy when I pass through Boston. For several years I have a couple of meetings in New York City and I can usually wangle a day or so off the trail in Boston. When I get to Boston and call Lauren she's most accommodating. I get a luxury hotel suite and all the extras for two or three hours of actual enjoyment and performance. She got married after we had a fling twenty or so years ago and I think she's still married to the same guy, something Pittman. A corporate wheel. He's wealthy so she's not likely to pick me for any reason other than a couple hours in the sack. So, Richard, back to the shopping list and maybe you'll find someone who's as wealthy and beautiful as Lauren. Someone for the long term beauty and wealth to which you'd like to become accustomed. But the clock is ticking, old boy.

CHAPTER 6

PHILLIP IN CONTROL

Julie and I are awkwardly interrupted at the sound of the outer office door opening. Julie, the ever-ready executive protector steps back, clears her throat and launches toward my office door. I move toward my desk .

Julie's voice sounds a little disheveled, "Uh, good morning, Sir. Umm, Mr. Bolton isn't it? How may I help you?"

"Yes ma'am. Morning. I'm Francis Bolton, Director of Security. There's an emergency, an accident and I need to see Mr. Pittman immediately. I know his car's already in the garage. Is he in there?"

"Of course, I'll let him know you're here."

I straighten up at my desk in anticipation of Julie announcing Frank Bolton. As Julie opens my door Frank is on her heels and there won't be any time for formal announcement of his visit. Before Julie can say a word to me, Frank Bolton pushes past her.

"Yeah, of course, Frank. What's going on?"

 "Well, sorry to barge in on you so early and without notice but we have a situation you need to know about. As well as directly providing security for this building and our employees, I administer the security contract for our corporate aircraft over at Logan. The contractor secures the hangar, the aircraft and sees to the passengers but we always have one of my staff right there whenever we have a corporate flight scheduled. So I know details of all scheduled flights and who's supposed to be on them. In addition to one of my folks being on hand for all of our planes coming in or going out, I personally get a text of wheels up notification as one of our planes leaves or on touchdown when returning to Logan. I have no flights scheduled today. Zero scheduled flights today."

My attention is glued on Frank Bolton and Frank pauses a second and looks at his watch.

"So, eighteen minutes ago I was totally shocked when I received a notification from Logan that our twelve passenger Lear went down off the coast after takeoff. There's no word on survivors yet. I..."

"What the hell, Frank! What the hell! No scheduled flights but it crashes? C'mon here! You sure it's ours? Maybe wrong tail number?"

"I had the tower read the tail number twice. I needed to make sure you know about the accident and see if you know anything about who might have been on it."

"What the hell! You're asking me who was on it? What the shit kind of security is it when you don't know about a flight on one of our planes and then you come in here to ask me who was on it? Think, Frank. Engage brain before the mouth. You gotta get this buckled down real quick. Understand?"

"Yes Sir. Sorry Sir. I'll keep you up to date with everything as I get to the bottom of this."

"Listen to me, Frank. No more eighteen minutes ago bullshit. You tell me what's going on within the next five minutes. So chop chop, Mister Security. My clock is ticking and you've got five minutes! Do your job!"

Frank turns to leave and I turn to look at the face of a shocked Julie. "Julie, sit down here for a second. Let me figure out what I need to do. Seems our friggin security experts are in name only."

Julie sits in the chair nearest my desk and she's visibly upset. Probably thinks we've lost some friends and the uncertainty is overwhelming.

" Okay, Julie. Here's for starters. Call each department head and just ask if anyone is flying out today. At this point don't say anything about the crash. But do this quickly because you know TV and internet will be all over it. In fact I'll bet they know about this now... long before any eighteen minutes The breaking news will stir everyone quick enough. Let me know for sure."

Julie is already headed for the door, "I'll double check but I'm sure none of the seniors and board members were scheduled for any trips this morning. In fact I have no flights scheduled for either of the jets until tomorrow."

Julie leaves the inner office and closes my door. I can't believe this. That god damned Frank better have a handle on this in the next few minutes.

Suddenly I look up in surprise as my door quickly opens again and Frank and Julie come back in a rush. Frank holds his radio out in front of him as he nears my desk, " Our tail number confirmed again and I've got Logan Emergency on the air so you can hear first-hand, sir."

Frank holds the mic up to his bearded chin, "Logan, this is KQPY eight one nine four, Bolton here. Request update on niner-niner-three-four."

Over the radio, we hear the crackly response, "Command Center- this is Chief Summerfield. Bolton?"

"Affirmative. KQPY eight one nine four…Frank Bolton, Chief. Any update you can give me. I've got Mister Pittman listening."

"Okay. Morning Mister Pittman…Okay, Frank, latest and not yet for public release- though I'm sure this channel is monitored or hacked by the media so I'll give you what we know without any names. Looks like a contract maintenance crew needed a check ride. Reported three aboard. Pilot plus two aircraft mechanics. Right now it looks like an early morning F-C-F…ya know a functional check flight for engine maintenance or fuel system something like that. Just not absolutely certain at this point, No names. We've closed runway 28 left so outgoing and incoming flights are diverted from passing over the scene. FAA's on it. NTSB's notified. City and Coast Guard first responders are enroute to the site but there has not been any communications with the aircraft since it went down. You're on the Emergency notification roster so you'll get an update as soon as more comes available. I repeat though, nothing I've said is for release. Summerfield out."

Frank turns to Phillip. "Well, that's the big part of the mystery. But it doesn't look good and there will obviously be a lot of press inquiries. It's up to you Mr. Pittman but the current procedure is for all press to be routed to Mr. Eddlemann's office. If that's what you want, okay but he isn't here yet and my guys couldn't reach him by cell yet."

"Of course. Stick to the plan. And yes, I'd be surprised if Murray's in yet this morning but we should be able to reach him by phone. Julie, you try as well to reach Murray and put him through to me. Frank, just continue on with your required actions and after I've spoken with Murray I'll have him get hold of you. Alright?"

"Yes sir." Frank takes a deep breath of satisfaction and turns for the door.

But I'm not letting Bolton off the hook this easy. I find it exciting to belittle a subordinate in front of others. "And? And, Frank?"

Frank turns with a deer in the headlights look at me, "Sir?"

"I expect managers to keep me informed, be sure fires are extinguished and very, very important determine what needs to be in place to prevent a future recurrence. So, Frank what's your plan to prevent this from happening again?"

"Well, Sir, I don't really understand how I can prevent a mechanical or pilot error. Maybe I don't understand your point."

"Let me serve it to you on a platter. What was the problem other than a crash? You have no oversight when our planes, *our planes*, are taken out for an FCF. Seems the maintenance contractor would know in advance if they are working on one of the aircraft systems where an FCF is going to happen. All you have to do is get in the loop of notification of which plane, when, maybe duration...getting the idea. Jesus, Man. Do I have to do your job for you? Think. Okay?"

"Yes Sir. Got it. I'll get something in place." Frank turns once again for the door.

"And, Frank? And?"

Frank turns around to face me once again and looks like he's about to wet his pants. "Sir?"

"When you figure your something out…you'll inform me of the details. Right?"

"Oh yes, Sir. Of course, Sir."

"And you'll be informing me before the end of business today, Frank. So get out of here and do your job."

Frank hesitatingly heads for the office door once again as if he's expecting to be humiliated one more time but I've made the point and so out he goes. I'm scheduled for a short meeting with the division heads at 10:30am. That meeting is in addition to my hourly checkup meetings to keep Santa's elves on track. Yesiree. It's a good day!

Almost as if I can flip an emotional switch, I begin to thumb through the financial disclosures of the Right-Fit Automobile Parts Corporation in preparation for my meeting. Quite uncharacteristically for me I lose my concentration, briefly pause and stare straight ahead. Some poor maintenance guys and a rent-a- pilot are likely burnt to a crisp. The innocent, unexpected tragedy is terrible for some unknown families.

But I have a better idea than feeling sorry for somebody I don't even know. My practical side takes control as I smile and permit a fantasy. Just imagine how wonderful it would be if Lauren could be on the corporate jet like that and then…woops. All over. No fault, no suspicion. No more screeching to contend with. Too good to be true. And just look at yourself Phillip. You're not feeling the slightest bit of remorse or emotion if that could happen. But. Couldn't happen. At least not exactly that way. But maybe there are other ways that are just as simple, innocent in appearance and just as final. I stare at the financial reports but my thoughts are not on financial records this morning.

I look up as my door opens and a rather harried Julie comes through the door, "Mister Pittman, What else do I need to do about this plane crash?"

"Well, for one thing, take a deep breath and sit down here. We can probably expect phone calls from the media very soon so you respond for now with no comment. Keep trying to get hold of Murray. Murray needs to prepare a little script for you as one of the first things. No comment to anyone else. Got it?"

Murray Eddlemann's distinctive voice is clear as he makes a rather grand entrance in the hallway outside my office. I hear Frank Bolton nervously telling Murray what occurred. I stay at my desk knowing Murray will soon be in to see me.

"Yeah, yeah, yeah. I got it. I got it. It's a tragedy. But c'mon here, Frank. Quit with the convulsions. You weren't on the plane. I wasn't on the plane. None of us were on the plane. You hang around Julie's desk. I'm gonna go in and see the boss right now and then I'll dictate a statement for you, one for Julie and then you guys have a script. After that, regardless who calls or what is asked, you stick to the script. Okay? Jesus, Frank, quit freakin out over this."

"Sure, Mr. Eddlemann. I'll wait around.

As Murray comes into the outer office Julie is the next to grab Murray's attention. " I'm ready for the statement whenever you say."

"Okay, Okay , Gorgeous. Just give me a couple of minutes with the boss and time to flush my ulcers with this rapidly aging, cold coffee. I'll be right back out in a second and I'll give you the statement."

Murray comes unceremoniously through my door, briefcase in one hand and juggling his Starbucks in the other.

" Morning, Phillip. Anything exciting today in the world of investment banking, huh?"

"You're a trip, Murray. You've probably looked over more than I have this morning on your luxurious limo ride to work. So everything can

33

get back to business as usual as soon as you get Julie and Frank squared away with what to say and to whom they should say it. By the way, please give Julie some priorities of who she should contact immediately."

"Right-O. I'm going to leave my stuff here and I'll go get Julie laced up tight. I'll have her call the wives of the seniors and the executive secretaries of the divisions to allay any panic in our company when they see or hear something on the news but the rest of the real mess can be handled through the airport. From what Frank said and I'm betting it's correct it was the maintenance contractor, and onboard a contract pilot, couple of techs so likely none of us have ever met any of them or even know the names. Our company name may pop up that it was our jet but I'll make sure all the media attention goes straight to the contractor and keep our involvement very tangential. Of course you and I should go shopping at Neiman -Marcus for another jet this afternoon. Bring your credit card. Okay, okay. Let me get Julie fixed up. You please sit tight. Before we have the meeting at ten-thirty I have some exciting little things you and I need to discuss…need I say privately?"

"I'll wait right here. And Murray, your coffee is safe here so long as it doesn't leave a ring on my mahogany."

I hear Murray instructing Julie what to write and who to call. In a few minutes Murray is back in my office with the door closed. Murray is one incredible lawyer and friend.

CHAPTER 7

LAUREN'S RESOLVE

I pick up a nearby extension, "Hello."

"Mrs. Pittman, Please. This is Julie Harris, Mr. Pittman's Executive Secretary.

"Yes, Julie, Mister Pittman's Executive Secretary, this is Lauren and of course I know who you are, Sweetie. How are you, Julie?"

What a phony! She probably thinks she'd be happy as Mrs. Phillip Pittman. She probably thinks I don't appreciate him enough. Ha! Understatement. I hate the bastard.

"Um, I'm fine, Mrs. Pittman and I'm calling to alert you to something that has just occurred and I want to be sure you know before you hear or see anything on the news.   First let me assure you Mr. Pittman is just fine. Perfectly healthy and fine."

"What's this about? What's happened?"

"Well, Mrs. Pittman, the corporate jet was just involved in an accident after takeoff from Logan and it's not good news for the people who happened to be on the jet today…but again let me assure you Mr. Pittman was not on the jet and he is right here in the office and he's fine. Just to reassure you that when you hear the news reports you know Mr. Pittman is perfectly safe."

"Well, what happened?"

"We've just been notified so we're not sure of the details but the jet apparently went down right after the takeoff. Mr. Pittman told me to call the families of the six seniors to let them know they were not on the plane. He's afraid you'll get a call by the news stations and be caught by surprise. Mr. Pittman says for you just to refer any calls back to me here at the office. Are you okay with that?"

"Sure. But who was on the plane Julie?"

"Well, until we know for sure I can't say but AVSTAR had the jet in for maintenance and we think at this point they were taking it on a test flight either before or after the maintenance. Crazy, huh? But I haven't even been told any names and this is just to let you know Mr. Pittman is fine and if any news media or reporters call you, please just refer all questions to me here at the company. Okay?"

"Sure. Fine. That's it then?"

"Yes. Mr. Eddlemann gave me a script to read but that would have sounded pretty lame if I'd read it to you. Really, at this point we don't know any more than what I told you. So, thank you Mrs. Pittman and have a nice day."

"Okay. Bye, Julie."

"Bye bye."

I flop down on the sofa and take a long deep breath and as I hold my breath for an instant I wonder why I'm acting as if in gratitude that Phillip is okay. I realize how automatic and practiced my reactions are because truth be told I really do not care about Phillip or his health. Calmly I release my breath and a different thought , a fantasy quickly takes shape. What if Phillip had been on that plane? What if it was the ultimate casualty call that he'd been killed? What would it be like to suddenly have all the money without Phillip's manicured, hairy fingers holding the purse strings? What would it actually be like to have all the money of his empire without him being appended to it in any way shape or form? Jane Ella would be well-taken care of by releasing her trust and she would quickly go her separate way. I suck in a big breath of refreshment and close my eyes, imagining life in luxury and freedom. I feel refreshingly intoxicated as I think of living in peace and solitude with lots and lots of money. Money that doesn't have the feel of an allowance being doled out with a perceived cloud

36

that one day through hate and hostility it could be taken away in some sinister plan by Phillip.

I think I shall just sit here for a while and indulge my fantasy and glide deeper and deeper into thoughts of an unusual, but well-deserved change to my dismal world. I close my eyes and smile. It feels good! I can't imagine anything but happiness if Phillip were to be in a plane crash or if he had a heart attack and died.

My eyes still closed, smile fixed in place, I boldly talk aloud to the empty room, "I'm sure a plane crash would be sudden and effective but I'll bet there are dozens of other ways just as quick and just as effective for the asshole to bite the biz bag. God, I should be so fortunate."

I open my eyes, stand and gracefully walk across the room picturing how I would view a casket with the remains of my beloved Phillip. I dramatically fumble with my coffee cup playacting how I could publicly mourn while being secretly awash in utter happiness.

"Oh, yes. He had a good life. Oh, my dear Phillip! He worked so hard and was such a good provider…uh husband. A good… no a wonderful, caring husband. What ever will I do without him?"

And then I act out my most sinister look, focus my eyes like a glare and laugh a haunting, ghoulish laugh.

"What ever will I do without him…*indeed*! Well, for one thing I will not spend another minute with any mementos of Phillip Pittman in this house. Redecorate immediately into Lauren Pittman's house. *Free!* Do *what* I want, *when* I want and *with whom* I want."

I laugh a little more, " Oh yeah, I forgot and *where* I want! Maybe I'd do the deed with one of Jane Ella's jilted boyfriends, in the family room on the loveseat or the floor. Or maybe I'd invite Murray Eddlemann over and give him the thrill of his life on the kitchen island until he'd go comatose. Nah. Murray'd probably fall off onto the tile floor and then sue me. Hah! I love it!"

But reality has a way of dampening even the most thrilling fantasies and no matter how I try to extend the momentum of this fantasy, it fades and I drift sadly back to the here and now. My wonderful but brief happiness melts away like an icicle on a sunny day. I know it is only make believe and it's not likely ever to happen. Phillip takes no chances. He has a VIP, gold-plated medical plan and gets regular perfect health reports from head to toe. Heart attack? Pure fiction. I could never be so lucky. Nope. Plane crash? Car accident? How sad that anything short of a hired assassin is a real long shot of ever salvaging a happy life and even if I hired someone I'd probably fail and wind up in prison forever. Nope. Just get used to the misery, Lauren. Phillip having an accident has about as much chance as winning the lottery.

Unless of course I prompted the accident. Ya know, like cutting the brake lines on his Mercedes as he races down a mountain. Or, what if there was a way for me to push him into the Grand Canyon or poison him or some non-messy, untraceable way to just make him go away-for good? A sigh and another deep breath of resignation that none of my ideas are plausible. I simply can't imagine something happening to Phillip without it starting a complete hassle, ending with me getting entrapped. And worse, what if I plotted and failed? I can picture Phillip still alive, survivor of a failed attempt on his life and gloating. I'd spend my life in prison and he'd mutter to himself over his coffee for the rest of his life without me.

And what about when Jane Ella moves out? Left alone? Keep living every single day with him? Like this? I whisper to myself," There's gotta be a way. Maybe not tonight or tomorrow you son-of-a-bitch; but some day, Buddy-boy…someday very soon I'll figure all this out. I just can't stand it anymore."

I pump my fist and in a normal tone of voice, confidently affirm, "I will figure this out. I deserve to have a shot at great wealth...*and* absolute freedom."

CHAPTER 8

JANE ELLA, THE LOVING DAUGHTER

I try my best to look frightened and out of breath as I push open King Phillip's office door. Julie Harris recognizes me immediately and stands behind her desk,"Good morning, Miss Pittman. I take it you've heard at least part of the big event this morning. I'm sure you want to see Mr. Pittman so let's get you right in there."

"Oh, thanks, Julie. Yes. I was driving along the freeway and heard the name Patriot Star and very few details. It's all very frightening."

Julie opens my dad's door and he barely looks up at first and then he sees it's me and rises to his feet, "Jane Ella. What a surprise. What can I do for you, Dear?"

"First of all I'm just happy to see you here and want to know what the heck happened with the plane crash. I was just entering the Ted Williams Tunnel when they broke in with the news of a plane crash and the company name and then I lost the signal in the tunnel. I was so worried."

"Well, it's flattering to have your concern but unfortunately it was a maintenance contractor over at Logan and they took the plane out for a test and it obviously failed the test. Makes me wonder if we ought to be looking for another maintenance crew. Anyhow, it wasn't anyone any of us at the office even know. Doesn't make it better for the families of the poor schmucks who were on the plane but it wasn't anybody from here."

"I won't bother you anymore but just know I am always concerned. I try not to bother you here but I've gotten where I really don't know when to trust Mom or not. She gets into her bottle and her personal pharmacy sometimes and I wonder if she's in the real world. I seriously hate some of the arguments but I want you to know I'm concerned about you. I also don't want anything between you and

Mom to mess up my future relationship with you so it's important you know I'm on your side."

Phillip attempts to smile, "Well, thank you, I think. I'm sure you perhaps didn't mean you even suspect you aren't my real daughter. Or you feel pressure to act concerned about me so you get your trust released in a couple of years?"

"Oh heavens no. I didn't mean it that way. I'm sincerely concerned about you and my only point about my trust would be just so Mom doesn't do anything to poison the relationship I have with you."

"Nicely, diplomatically said. Thank you, Jane Ella. Wish I had time to take you to late lunch or even a cup of coffee but I have a couple of things coming up pretty quick here. You know there's no rest for the wicked."

"Yeah, Dad. I know. Glad you're okay and I'll probably see you later this evening. Ciao."

"Bye Jane Ella."

I continue on my way out of the office, "Bye Julie. Keep the corporate lid on everything."

"Yes, bye Miss Pittman."

As I'm parading through the hallway it's obvious most people on my dad's floor know I'm his daughter. They obviously go out of their way to smile and be nice instead of how they likely feel. What a bunch of phonies.

Murray enters the hallway and as he closes an office door he nearly runs into me. He quickly smiles like only Murray can. The bushy eyebrows and the nose look to me like he just dropped his Groucho glasses somewhere. Sort of a mix of executive handsomeness, perversion and comedy, but a big toothy smile nevertheless. But Murray's not a phony.

"Well hello, Mr. Murray Eddlemann Esquire. You're looking particularly dapper this fine day."

"Hey little girl. Didn't your mommy tell you not to flirt with dirty old men?"

"At the moment I don't care about her warnings. You send out vibes of true manhood and virility so given half a chance I'd like to take you into one of these fancy conference rooms and cause you to clear your calendar for the afternoon."

"Awww, Geez. Why do you do this to me Jane Ella? I feel like I should still be rocking you on my knee but then I look at you and it sure isn't rocking on my knee I'm imagining. You talk a little dirty and all my pent up sex goes straight to my head and I can't do anything except babble and drool. You shouldn't make such idle suggestions. One day I'm liable to know of a vacant conference room and see if you're all bark and no bite. Of course with your dad's permission. Gotta run everything past the boss ya know."

"Well, I'm glad to turn you on or spank you for being naughty. What do you think?"

"I can tell you I wish I was twenty years older right at this moment."

"You mean twenty years younger don't you?"

"No. Older. Cause then I'd be so old I probably wouldn't be thinking what I'm thinking right now, Sweetie."

I continue to walk leaving Murray behind. "Aww. You're no fun. Not if you've gotta get permission. Somehow that may not work out so well."

"You take care, kid. Good to see you. I mean it's really good to see you." Murray wiggles his eyebrows.

As I return to my car I think of the prim and proper Julie. I'd never thought about it much but I'll bet she's putting out to Dad and maybe even Murray. I know Murray's a dirty old man but I seriously doubt if

41

he's all bark. I suspect Murray takes care of Murray's appetites around the corporate flock of women. I can't imagine Phillip doing anybody but I suppose it's the power thing. I guess some women are blinded by the power and authority. Anyhow I'll just bet discrete sex is one of the prerequisites for being a la-tee-da executive assistant or whatever the hell they call themselves.

But all in all, I think I got my point across to dear old Phillip. He needs to know I'm on his side, if there is such a thing. I only want to be sure if he dumps mom in the next couple of years I'm not flushed along with her. Good job, Jane Ella.

CHAPTER 9

THE HOUSEGUEST

It is late in the afternoon and I have my feet comfortably elevated, reclining on a family room sofa and immersed in listening to music, sipping an afternoon martini and dreaming of life without Phillip. It would be wonderful to be rid of Phillip and have all the money. Deal with all the money? Of course! Deal with his business? Of course! Just sell it all, simple enough!

I jump a bit as my daydreams are interrupted by the ringing phone.

"Hello."

"Hey Lauren. It's Richard. It's been way too long since I've been able to see you and I'm going to be in town for a couple of days…any chance you can recommend or arrange a hotel so we can get together for old times' sake?"

What a pleasant surprise. It's my old friend, Richard Martin.

"Richard? Wow! "Well, well. If it isn't my favorite boy-toy, Richie. Just hearing your voice makes me feel like there's hope in this world. I had no idea you were anywhere near. Of course let's get together…the sooner, the better. It's been a while and of course we'll…uh…uh for old times' sake as you say. Your place or mine?"

"Is this a good time to talk, Lauren…ya know?"

"Yes, I'm home alone…as usual and I *really* could use a little inspiration and in fact as much inspiration as you can give me when you're all excited. Whatdayasay? Got any lead in that pencil of yours?"

The wonderful surprise of Richard's call immediately focuses his image in my mind. Actually two images. One with clothes and one sans clothes. He's a fortyish plus, six foot four inch, ex-college football player, Army veteran and currently a world adventurer. He fancies himself quite the ladies' man. When he meets someone for the first time it's a sure bet that within the first few minutes Richard will have covered his made up stellar background from college up to his present career of leading African safaris. He carefully picks clothes that show his biceps and pectoral muscles and likely imagines himself looking thirty. Though admittedly in good shape, the age of thirty has long since passed him by. He has a smooth, deep voice and laughs even when things aren't meant to be funny.

I don't get to see Richard often enough for my preferences, maybe once or twice a year at the most. I'm certain he's been adding color to his hair and David Niven-like moustache for the last decade. Although few would say to his face that he's a meathead, he fills that mental description to a tee. He seldom has two nickels to rub together but by wit, charm and hanging around people with money, he is able to find women in need of his temporary companionship and so he deftly pockets financial crumbs from many tables. He looks the part of handsome, rugged adventurer and bounces from woman to woman as if looking for his holy grail but always settles for a short fling with a little money attached.

Before I married Phillip, Richard and I had a torrid and steamy love affair. But I was in the male flesh market for someone with permanently deeper pockets than my lusty stud, Richard. Over the years, Richard unexpectedly shows up, calls and re-enters my life for a couple days as we revert to the lovemaking and fantasies of adventure together. Richard holds a special place deep in my heart but none of it is ever taken too seriously, particularly by Richard. With each return, the exit is equally as swift when Richard gets a few lavish gifts, some serious spending money and off he goes back to Africa leading safaris or in search of another possible conquest attached to some spending money. I easily cope with and rationalize my infidelity by believing it takes two men in my life to keep me sane. One with no place in my heart, no charm and lots of money and the other man is all he-man, lots of charm and always near and dear in my heart with no prospects of wealth.

Richard continues, "Well, I didn't want to say too much without knowing who might be listening when I called. I'm at the airport and I've successfully escaped an invitation for a threesome of flight attendants who were after my body and now I'm getting ready to get a cab…just didn't know exactly where I was heading."

"Oh, Richard. I know how you love to gigolo around nice hotels for a few days at my expense, but this time just come and spend a few nights at my house? I'll try my best to keep you entertained. "

"Wouldn't mind but how 'bout the hubby? I don't want to stir up a hornet's nest. But you know the situation better than I do so it's up to you."

"Look, Richard, the hubby, as you call him, is as predictable as the sun. He leaves early and if he comes home he's only present so he can fight with me and then cloister himself to a night of work in his private boudoir. Even when he is physically home he's not really here. He's usually off in a little computer world in his bedroom. Jane Ella is gone most every day as well. Besides it will be fun playing close to the fire. Okay?"

"Yeah. I don't mind. I can act the part while everyone's around but I'm anxious to spend some time with just you…and you know what I mean."

"Just wait until tonight. I'll…oh, you'll see. What if I assure you, Richard, that this visit will be *much* more thrilling and rewarding and in the comfort of my home instead of a hotel? Would that sound okay?"

CHAPTER 10

RICHARD FEELS WELCOMED

After paying the cabbie and dragging my luggage to the front stoop, I'm barely inside the huge doors, when Lauren grabs me and lays a passionate kiss on me. Shocking! I'm in her house so I stiffen and pull back a little, my eyes glancing from side to side during the long embrace. "Whoa there. Whew."

"Relax, Richard. No one's here but you and me…but not for too long. Phillip the great will get home soon. So we need to get our stories straight before he gets here. Come sit."

"So there's nobody here right now? No one?"

"Nope, scaredy-cat. Just you and me. C'mon, you're the big brave adventurer. So come sit."

"Lauren you're positive no one else is here?"

"Positive and…"

I grab Lauren and pull her toward me, but suddenly Lauren pulls back from me. I give her a puzzled look and reluctantly release her.

"Okay, Richard. Knock it off for a second. First things first. We have to make this work so let's review a couple of things. We're just old college friends and today's visit is purely coincidence. Since you're only going to be around for a couple of days it makes sense for you to stay here so we can reminisce about old college friends. Very innocent. You okay with that?"

"Sure. Got it. Not a problem except you said on the phone this will be a time to remember so where am I sleeping and how do I get to your room or you to mine? "

"Keep your pants on, Superman. Look I'll show you the house right now but don't worry about exactly what is where. This is a lot of house but the arrangements are simple. Phillip and I sleep in separate bedrooms and I'll show you where you'll be, but don't venture out looking for me at night. That would be way too easy to go the wrong way or bang into something and arouse suspicion. No. You just stay put and I'll come to your room when it's safe. Your room is separated from the rest. Piece of cake. Trust me."

"Can we at least have a quick practice session now before the big game later?"

"Richard! This will work very well but it's late enough Phillip will be home any minute. Later, Richard. Later."

Lauren takes me by the hand and guides me through the house and then back to the living room nearest the entry and foyer where we sit on a sofa and she playfully pushes me to a safe distance and then pushes down on my shoulders like telling a puppy to "stay".

That's actually fine because there's no reason to get hot and heavy only to get interrupted and maybe tossed out on my ear. Relax. This may be a bonanza visit. Lots of sex, lots of money and lots of extravagances in appreciation for my physical efforts. This visit may also have a glimmer of possibilities for my longer term goals. So I sit quietly, even trying to act like I'm a bit nervous as if to impress Lauren this is some moment of great importance.

We are just settled into place when this nerdy looking bald guy appears from the kitchen and stands in the foyer looking at the two of us sitting on the sofa. First impressions. All this wealth from him? Jesus, This guy looks like a hollow shell. A smug, tight-assed blue-blood, probably old money, silver spoon and all that crap. Best behavior , Richard. Curtain going up.

Lauren's quick to get the formalities out of the way, "Hi, Phillip. This is an old college friend who's visiting in Boston, Richard Martin. Richard this is Phillip."

Phillip is obviously surprised to find me at his home and he also doesn't look like a gracious host. This could be bad. I rise from the sofa in anticipation of shaking hands but Phillip doesn't move toward me in the slightest. He holds onto his briefcase like some courier and it doesn't appear there will be any hand-shaking.

"How do you do, Mr. Martin?"

"Fine, thank you. And call me Richard, please. And a pleasure to meet you, Phillip."

Lauren immediately chimes in to the icy atmosphere but I doubt her technique is very effective to soften the situation.

"Well, Phillip. Take off your coat and stay awhile. And don't be such a sour-puss. Our guest will think you're the grouch you really are. Now be a good boy and get us all some drinks."

"Yeah …and well, nice to see you, too, Lauren. Arriving to such accolades is always a highlight of day's end. Where *are* my manners? And for that matter, where are yours that you haven't already been to the bar for your guest?"

Wow! Not a pleasant atmosphere. I'm not feeling welcome and wonder just how long my visit may be. Maybe minutes not hours or days. Phillip and Lauren continue their little personal jabs at each other and Lauren makes a face and sticks her tongue out at Phillip as he passes through the sitting room on his way to make drinks, loosening his tie as he heads toward the bar area off the kitchen.

 Lauren leans over to me and whispers, "See how happy my life is with that jerk? This will be perfect with you here. Right under his sniveling nose. That way he gets screwed and so do I, Richard. The difference is my screwing will be much more fun and he'll never even feel his at all, good or bad."

Lauren's cutting remarks surprise me, "Geez, lady. Do you eat out of the same mouth you talk from?"

This could be a big mistake coming here. I suppose if they get into a full scale war I can slip out and get a taxi. But to where? Shit. Maybe I'll wind up at Motel 6 and eating at KFC. Just cool it, Richard. Be quiet and maybe all this will play out in a positive direction. I really do not want to leave this house before I absolutely have to leave.

Lauren playfully slaps at me and within moments Phillip returns with a tray of glasses and a pitcher of martinis.

I wink at Lauren out of Phillip's view and lick my lips. She jerks her head around to be sure Phillip isn't picking up on any of the not-so-subtle innuendos. She quickly gets up and heads for the kitchen. This little sexual game is about to get out of hand and Phillip's likely to spot it. I have to be a little more careful because after all I am in the master's castle with the queen. I merely have to meet and greet the master in a way that will quickly gain the master's trust. A trust that will be tossed from the tower window so Lauren and I can cavort.

CHAPTER 11

PHILLIP, MEET RICHARD

I arrive home and come in through the garage entry into the house. Seems a bit strange to already hear voices in the house but perhaps Lauren has taken up a new pathway to insanity by conversing with herself. As I continue into the front sitting room it's obvious we have company. A man. Lauren's trying to look her sexiest best for whoever this guy is and she's probably already sloshed. She doesn't take long to pipe right up with the opening swipe at me.

"Oh, here's Mr. tycoon himself."

Well, typical day, I'm two steps in the door and she starts her slashing sarcasm. I don't make any retort to her announcement of my arrival but I grant her a grunt, wrinkle my forehead and give her a disgusted looking smile with one corner of my mouth up and the eye over it pinched shut almost like an exaggerated wink. That's probably enough said at the moment since I walked right in on a stranger enjoying the company of my lovely wife. It's not the milkman or pool boy so who can this be?

With a broad smile, the visitor rises from the sofa, and Lauren introduces him as Richard Martin. I'm sure he expects me to drop my briefcase and hop over the coffee table to shake hands but I just stand my ground and exchange verbal formalities. Lauren starts in on me about being a grouch and making a batch of martinis so I slowly begin to remove my jacket, loosen my tie and listen to Lauren's continuing verbose excuse for this imposition.

"Richard was going to Washington University in St. Louis when I was going to Lindenwood but I'm pretty sure the two of you never met. I mean, maybe you did. I'm not sure but you've probably heard me speak of Richard. He was playing football at Wash U back then. He called me this afternoon and told me he is here in Boston for a couple of days so I suggested he just come stay here. I'm sure it will be boring for you and Jane Ella but I just want to indulge myself in a little of the past. You don't mind I hope?"

"No. Of course not. And where's home for you, Richard?"

"Well I travel a good bit. But for the last thirteen years I've called Botswana,Africa home. I plan and guide safaris for a five star tour company, Polamba Travel, Limited. Our specialty is luxury safari tours in the magical land of Botswana. Perhaps you've heard of us?"

I shrug my shoulders and shake my head with a minimal negative response. That's about as polite as I can be instead of admitting out loud that of course I've never heard of his little tour company and I have zero interest in hearing anymore about it. This guy looks like a real mental giant. Ya know, size twenty neck, size five hat.

"Well, never the mind, I've been mostly in one of the larger parks in Northwest Botswana and I've been fortunate in the guided tour industry. It's a really great job and I'm darn good at it if I do say so and I might as well live the exciting life while I can. Right?"

I'm fighting off the sarcastic urge with all my might but this is going to be a challenge to be civil. "Of course. I've also made my living leading the exciting life, daily battling and avoiding being eaten by big critters, so I can relate to your calling. I only wish I could wear khaki shorts and a pith helmet to the office. And some days it would be nice to have a high-powered rifle to pick off the useless employees at a distance. You'd understand...improve the herd and such. Well, let me get going to make a pitcher of martinis. Martini okay for you, Richard Martin? Was the gin and vermouth drink named for you? Martini? And you, Lauren? Mix you another as well?"

Richard tries a bit of ice breaking, "Oh, a martini will be terrific. And I can't claim naming rights for the drink but I can always get you outfitted with the helmet, shorts and rifle if you like. Sounds a fair trade for a martini and lodging. "

Lauren forces a sarcastic smile in my direction, "And, me too Phillip. I may as well have one as long as you're fixing them."

51

I toss my head, scoff aloud and sarcastically look back over my shoulder at Lauren as I leave the room. "Sure, I'll be right back. Lauren did you say you'd like yet *another* martini? Getting you a martini sounds safer for me than there being a rifle anywhere around you."

Lauren makes a face and sticks out her tongue in defiance. I leave Lauren and her guest sitting and tend to the drinks. I put the cocktails on a small tray and return to the sitting room.

"Here we go. Hope this is to your liking, Richard. And here ya go, Lauren."

"Ah, this is a terrific martini, Phillip. Now I really feel lucky to have called today. Again, thanks so much for…uh…*all* your hospitality."

I think I caught a little playfulness in his comment about my hospitality and he turned his head toward Lauren so I couldn't see the expression. So this is very unlikely a surprise visit. It's more likely my drunken wife inviting her aging boyfriend right to the house. How convenient that will be for her.

"So, Lauren, what shall we do for dinner? For some reason it seems Fanda failed to fix an evening dinner and I really don't feel much like going out anywhere and I have some work I need to do later. Maybe order something that can be delivered. Okay?"

"Sure. I can do that, Phillip. What's your *pleasure,* Richard?"

Well, this is downright entertaining. Lauren just winked at her buddy there as if I can't see her. Open flirting. A new low for the Pittman dinner hour.

"Oh, I'm not a picky eater. Just whatever you and Lauren like. I've learned to eat about anything from being in Africa. But when I'm working I always say, 'I *love* being deep in the bush' because it gives me such an appetite!"

My God. Class B, triple X, raunchy movie talk is taking place in my own house, right in front of me. This is like junior high. Try to mask comments as if no one's ever heard that sort of moronic crap before. She's drunk and thinks I'm too clueless to catch her dramatic winks at her boyfriend and he's so horny and dull he thinks I don't catch any of his crude innuendos. Murray won't believe it when I tell him. And Murray better get his ass in gear to get me split from this slut a lot quicker than he previously planned.

"Lauren can handle this sort of dinner preparation the best. She'll just hit any of a dozen speed dial numbers and whoever answers will either be a boyfriend or some food place. But the response will be the same, 'The usual, Mrs. Pittman?'

"Phillip, That's rude and disrespectful. I can handle it because I'm used to it but that would be cruel if Fanda ever heard you say such a thing. She usually fixes our dinner but she had to leave early today."

Richard and I just sit and stare blankly as Lauren walks from the room and the situation is defused at least temporarily.

Later, after a fill of Chinese food, I find this entire scene totally boring. I feel like I'm trying too hard to act interested as the three of us make small talk. I think this is the time for me to get out of here before it becomes nauseating. As Richard and Lauren sit at the kitchen island and continue their drivel, I stand, yawn and stretch. This is about as polite as I care to be in the process of disengaging so I can escape to my room for the night.

"Okay, I'll leave you two to catch up on old times and I'll say good night. I really have a lot to read tonight before a bunch of boring meetings tomorrow. Jane Ella out this evening, Lauren? I guess you haven't met her yet, have you Richard?"

"No, I haven't but Lauren tells me she's quite the independent young lady."

"I guess you could call her that. Not quite independent enough for my liking. I call her a spoiled brat. But it's time she flies out of the nest. And I almost neglected the only real motivator I know about for Jane Ella. She likes money and beyond that I'm not sure anything interests

53

her. You may catch a glimpse of her while you're visiting. Ya know, she comes in late, dashes in, dashes out. Who knows?"

"Well, I'll hope to meet her if she happens to dash in. So I suppose I'll see you tomorrow, Phillip."

"Actually I doubt it. I get out of here pretty early and unless you're a super-early riser, I'll probably be gone. But make yourself at home. If Lauren's sleeping the martinis off in the morning, just rummage through the fridge and at least have some juice until she can drag in here. But you might want to arm yourself in the morning. Even in the wildest parts of Africa, you may never encounter anything as mean and ferocious-looking as Lauren in the morning."

"Thanks, Phillip. And I thought you didn't even notice me anymore."

I turn toward the hallway and wave over my back without turning around toward Lauren and her friend. At least there won't be a full-scale battle tonight in the presence of a houseguest.

CHAPTER 12

HOSTESS WITH THE MOSTEST

Later this evening, I'm certain Phillip is asleep or at least in his room for the night so I make good on my promise to find Richard for a little fun and entertainment. I knock softly and then quickly enter our guest room where Richard is obviously expecting me. I put my hand over my mouth to silence a sudden giggle at the exhibition staged for my enjoyment. The bathroom door is slightly ajar and the bathroom light on, so there is a sliver of light spotlighting Richard sprawled on his back on top of the bed, nude, legs spread apart on top of the maroon duvet and duly prepared for our time together.

"Wow. Now that's a pose worthy of a photograph. I've been waiting to see you all evening, but I guess I underestimated how much of you I'd be seeing. And me without my camera. "

"Sorry. I didn't hear you knock. I'd have tried to be a bit more formal."

"Oh, I see no need to worry about it. I can tell at least part of you is happy to see me. Were you expecting my arrival, hear me in the hall, or do you stay like this all the time?"

"Don't tease me, Lauren. I could hardly stand it at dinner. Come here and lie down beside me. I just want to feel you close to me. "

"Listen you. When we started playing the little winking game, I know you well enough you'd never stop until it became obvious what we were doing. Fun, but...I don't think I'm quite ready to have that sort of scene just yet."

"Sorry but I was trying to talk to Phillip and trying to listen but all I could think about was being here with you like this."

Richard and I talk and gently hug. But the playful kisses and soft caresses quickly give way to passion's surrender. Complete and happy surrender.   I try to be particularly sexy and playful so Richard knows this is special. I sense Richard's eagerness from his erratic breathing and focus of his eyes. I love this but I control our intimacy. In fact, the sex is wonderful but I want to prove that I have control over Richard and I know at this very instant his brain is not functioning. He's lost in sexual deaf and dumbness imagining himself the greatest sex machine God ever made. So, go for it, Richard, because you are a sex machine **but** you shall earn your keep.

All too soon, we lay together exhausted in satisfaction, Richard from the sex and me from my domination and control over him.

 "You okay, Mr. Studley?"

"Oh God, Lauren. I hope it was good for you. I thought I could last longer but I just couldn't this time. I couldn't help myself. "

"Oh ,Richard, it's wonderful and I've missed you so much."

 "It's been way too long, Sweetheart.   We're made for each other. Always have been. It's so wonderful to be with you…playing 'close to the fire' as you say or just being anywhere with you."

"I know, Richard. Sometimes I wish…well, I wish I could be with you constantly, but I know that's not possible. If only you knew what a miserable life I have. Why can't things be different? Why can't it always be like this? Just you and me."

I know better than to suggest any sort of commitment because that will surely make Richard run terrified into the night.   But he's curious as he listens intently to me. Just his interest in me, whether pretended or real, is like a breath of fresh air. I have always felt completely comfortable telling Richard anything, the complete detailed truth. Well, at least truth from my viewpoint which is the only viewpoint and truth that's important.

Suddenly I hold my fingers up to my lips and point to the door of the guest room because I think I hear something or someone in the hallway

56

outside the door. I crawl over Richard and quietly tiptoe to the door and listen. Satisfied it was nothing at all, we resume our conversation perfectly at ease.

"Richard, I'm just saying in a perfect world, I mean if I wasn't joined by choke collar to Phillip, you and I could be together as often as we liked without sneaking around to a hotel or even like tonight. You know, the perfect world…you'd have more money than you ever imagined. You'd be able to have complete independence and of course see me whenever it suited you without sneaking around like we've had to do for the last twenty years. I'd even promise, cross my heart and hope to die, that I'd never, not ever be jealous. My gratitude and indebtedness to you would outweigh any jealousy forever. Promise and cross my heart."

"Lauren, my dear, why and how could you possibly be indebted to me? I haven't got anything to offer that could possibly influence you or have you owing me anything. Remember? I guide tourists in a hot, dusty park in Africa. At least it has job stability as long as I'm the one with the Land Rover and the gun."

"I'm just thinking and dreaming out loud, Richard. I know I could divorce that robot with the starched white shirt and silk tie. But I also know how miserable and chancy that would be. I'm sure Phillip has already thought of all that and I'll bet he's got a legal and financial plan orchestrated to a tee. I'm certain I'll come out the loser in every way. I just can't stand to be around him anymore so I know our standoffs and charade of civil harmony can't last much longer. I don't want to put off the inevitable but I'm scared to death he'll crush me like a steam roller.

"That bad, huh? And you figure he's already got his ducks in order if a split comes."

"Oh yeah, I can't just leave him…it's not that simple. I'll get slaughtered. But if somehow Phillip was to drop out of the picture. Gone. I can't imagine not being forced to listen to his muttering little comments that so entertain him…and only him. Believe me I'm ready to see dreams come to reality. I'm so ready, Richard. I wish you could see my dreams, Richard? But I'm probably scaring you."

" Scaring me? No. I think now is the time I should ask why I should be frightened. Should I assume you're talking about leaving him? Divorce? Or are you talking about him dropping out of the picture in some permanent way altogether?"

"Let me be clear, Richard. I'm not talking about me leaving him or a divorce.   Divorcing Phillip will never work. Out of the question.   I have no chance of winning. No, Richard, I'm going to take a chance here and tell you my very deepest secret wish.   I'm wishing for Phillip to be totally **removed** from the picture. Ya know…gone. **Gone!**"

"Wow, lady! That's a mouthful. Now I know what you're dreaming. I also think you know me pretty well. I'm not a vicious or vile person…at least not totally. It's as plain as the nose on my face how unhappy you are. It's also pretty plain after seeing Phillip, why you're so unhappy. What a stiff-necked asshole. I guess you've been dwelling on this for some time and it's not just a whim. Right?"

"Oh, dwelling on it, as you say, doesn't describe my thoughts. I'm obsessed with this.   I can't think of anything else. I know what I want. I just don't know how. I'm not asking you to kill him. I don't know what I expect. I'm just at my wits end and I'm desperate. Not desperate enough to be stupid and spend the rest of my life in prison…but pretty close. How could prison be much worse?   It's just if there's a way he could magically go up in a puff of smoke never to be seen again, then I'm free and …ahem…relatively wealthy."

"Say no more. I'll promise you right now I know of ways to make you happy, Angel. You've been special to me for so many years and I feel terribly, terribly sad thinking you're so unhappy."

"Oh, Richard, your visits are about all I have as hope for freedom from this insanity and daily misery. The last time I felt like this was when you visited in October and we had a couple of afternoons at the Omni downtown."

"Yeah. But let's just lay here for a bit. I'm not only talking about making you happy with sex. I can help you in the really important department as well. So relax for a sec and we'll start with baby-steps of how to get to your ultimate, perfect solution."

"Of course, Richard. Let's just relax together. I already feel better."

After a couple of minutes of cuddling Richard breaks the silence in a low voice, " It's great being able to hold you, Lauren. Now, let me just run something past you and see what you think. I'm going to tell you a little hunting story, sort of the things I do best. Sometimes a client hires me to help find a particular trophy animal, so I do the plan to be absolutely certain the client gets what he wants. My shtick for which I've got considerable experience, is setting a situation that the animal cannot resist. Of course the hunter thinks he's lucky and great risk is involved. Reality is it's not luck and there is no risk. When done correctly, my quarry comes willingly and often enthusiastically into the perfect environment and the brave hunter gets what he wants.

In the end, it's like the trophy animal assists in its own demise. I'm not the hunter. I don't do the killing. I just make the ingredients and circumstances fit in a natural, very predictable way. Now that's a little story about hunting and maybe it's a bit too abstract for you to see how it applies to your fantasy."

"I understand the story but I don't really see how it applies to me. "

"Well, here's how it relates to you. Imagine that Phillip is the trophy and some of my natural African predators are the hunters. The most difficult task is simply to get Phillip to my part of the world…let's just say, on a safari. With a little creative planning, an irresistible situation draws him, absolutely of his own volition, to walk, even run toward a very predictable demise. Africa has its dangers, ya know. Who's to blame? The innocent but foolish quarry goes into the situation of his own free will or even begs to be in the situation at best. So who's responsible for the tragedy? The victim is ultimately the only one to blame for the tragedy of his own disappearance or death. All other hands are clean. Sound a little more understandable?"

"I follow that very well. Very well indeed. But it seems like a lot, probably too many uncertainties have to fall into place. You know exactly what I'm suggesting, you handsome devil. If it's even possible like you're saying, Phillip just walks completely out of the picture by his own stupid mistake. No lawyers, no courts…he just goes away. And as you said,' hands are clean'. If I thought for a second I could get away with something like that I'd sign up tonight. But please be honest with me Richard, does this talk frighten you?"

"Frighten me? Why should it? I'll say I'm a bit surprised but not frightened. I never dreamt this afternoon when you invited me to stay that we'd be spending time discussing this instead of me simply chasing you up and down the hallways. You have to remember the mindset and now is the time to develop it. Mindset, Lauren. Mindset. Victim places himself in harm's way and nature takes its course. Things like this happen in my part of the world … simply a tragic accident. People come and go. People sometimes just plain disappear. Sometimes there are accidents. Some are simply never heard of again. I will say my company has a good track record for safety to guests but it's an understood risk that something tragic is always possible."

"Well, you make it sound like a piece of cake but my heart is about to jump out of my chest. What about getting away with it, Richard?"

"Well, there are the park rangers, province police and insurance investigators. I've seen it with accidents over the years. Investigators mean to do their jobs so they come, looking very official and take a look at things but really can't fabricate or read too much into a cut and dried accident or disappearance. Local authorities grew up around this way of life and they know how life comes and goes. The strong survive and the weak or foolish don't. There are many, many ways a foolish, tenderfoot tourist can, by his own doing, wind up in the wrong place at the wrong time and whoosh. Disappears. And I'll bet I know what you're thinking. You watch as somebody is being mauled by lions or half eaten by hyenas. But a tenderfoot tragedy doesn't have to be something messy or traumatic to anyone …except for the victim."

"Richard, I'm so afraid of planning something and getting caught. That gives me a sick feeling in the pit of my stomach. If only I could

60

somehow be sure of what would happen and it wasn't like you said…a half-eaten torso to contend with or the FBI dragging me off in chains. That's what stands between me and really making this more than a wish."

"I still don't think you're understanding the mindset of this or what I'm saying about simplicity. I've never, ever killed a person and I don't intend to start. But what I'm describing isn't about me killing a person. Not at all. I'm telling you I've seen the results of accidents and it's often the same. Someone gets introduced to surroundings he or she can't resist, inexperience or foolishness overcomes caution, the surroundings close in very quickly and kabam, it's all over, just like that. Some people unfortunately and unwittingly bring about their own tragedy and often it's a complete disappearance. Literally, nothing ever found or left behind. The police do what they can to establish what happened, but who's to blame? The poor guy who ventured too far out of safety. Oh, yes. I know what I'm talking about and it's not like pulling a trigger or putting poison in someone's food. And it certainly isn't a crime introducing someone to an irresistible situation and then they insist to take it from there…poor fools."

"So, you've done this sort of thing before?"

"Never. I've only seen it happen by unplanned chance and I've never set the table for something like this before. But I can. I can plan the menu, describe the options, let him choose the entree and then you and I are simply no where around when tragedy happens. People get excited about something and they throw all caution to the wind. They pay a lot of money for their trip and assume it's like being at the downtown zoo. "

"You seem pretty certain, Richard."

"Try this, Lauren. I *guarantee* the result is one hundred percent certain and safety for you is one hundred percent certain. How's that for certainty? You get your hubby to come on a safari and you'll have no other involvement…at all."

61

CHAPTER 13

PHILLIP'S CURIOSITY et al

I'm still putzing around reviewing some papers for tomorrow and it's about time to force myself to sleep for at least a few hours. It's around eleven-thirty and I really should get some sleep but I keep thinking about Richard Martin, houseguest. Houseguest? Does someone simply show up after twenty years and decide to spend the night to reminisce? Something a little too suspicious about Lauren's insistence he's like some long lost friend and her acting like a teasing schoolgirl. Who knows? Maybe if I caught them in the act or something it will give Murray enough fuel for the divorce. My curiosity gets the better of me so in robe and slippers I amble silently through the dark hallways toward the garage and guest wing.

Within several feet of Richard's guest room it's obvious from the sounds what's happening. Seems I missed the foreplay or any discussion of the mean old husband. This must be the main act.

But it causes me to smile at my true feelings. I'm only angry they think I'm so dull witted I couldn't guess what's going on. But as far as this slob bedding my wife, I feel less interest than if I was watching a movie. Even shocking to me is my cold, total lack of concern. But perhaps at some point I can muster enough dramatics to playact my bruised and battered feelings by my thoughtless wife who brings a safari gigolo into my house.

Suddenly I'm startled by the sound of the garage door opening, I quietly pull my ear away from the guest room door. It's got to be Jane Ella coming home. I stand quietly in the dark of the hallway listening for another instant and then I hurriedly return to my room. I'm truly surprised at my reaction of being cuckolded in my own home. Down deep I simply do not care except for how this can help me. This is a new stage in our long, dismally unhappy wedlock. I sense the end is on the horizon no matter how cautious Murray advises.

CHAPTER 14

JANE ELLA'S HAT IN THE RING

Eight-thirty. Gawd! This is too early for me to be up but my curiosity is aroused, to put it mildly. I got home last night and the guest room was abustle with steamy sounds. One thing for sure, it wasn't my dad with my mom. I suppose if he finally strangled her it may sound a bit like that but no, it wasn't the agony of strangulation I was hearing. It was just good old cooing, ooooing and romping. in bed. So who was making all the noise?

I stare out the kitchen window toward the pool as the final belches of brewing coffee announce the first cup is ready. Suddenly I jump in surprise at the movement near the kitchen entry and a hulky male frame comes into view. Maybe I should pinch myself. I'm joined in the kitchen by a strange man albeit a good looking, stranger. Wow. This has to be the source of half the sounds last night. Maybe he brought the other half along and she hasn't gotten up yet. If he's here alone it's not likely he was sticking it to Daddy Phillip so that leaves only my mother. What a horrible thought to waste this guy's body on Plastic Woman.

Oh well, I may be surprised but this happens to be my house and I'm plenty confident to take on the unexpected windfall. I smile while looking at this man through my long hair hanging over one eye. "Gee! You startled me. Should I scream or just surrender myself, body and soul? A strange man in my house has poor, defenseless me cornered in the kitchen."

"I'd say it's not at all necessary to scream. I'm harmless and in fact a smile is about all I can manage most mornings pre-coffee. And you have a very pretty smile, I might add. Pardon me for frightening you. I'm Richard Martin, a friend of your mother."

"Really? I am surprised for the second time this morning. I'm not aware that my mother has any friends. Lucky her."

" Yeah, we went to college in the St Louis area twenty years…well, twenty-plus years ago and I was just coming through town. So your mom and dad invited me to spend a couple of nights. You must be Jane?"

"I'm Jane **Ella** but since you look tan, rugged and dashing, you can call me anything you want. How about some coffee, Mr. Martin… ah, Richard?"

"Yes, please call me Richard. And coffee would be a life saver."

Richard has a look of disbelief as he watches. I continue to look at him smiling as I turn and pour him a cup of coffee. He drinks my full-body appearance before he raises the coffee cup to his mouth. I'm wearing short pajamas and the over blouse is loose enough so my magnificence is never going to allow my pajama top to touch my waist. Richard seems captivated studying my body and he's not acting as if he's about to change his focus. So let's play.

He's undressing me with his gaze and so I flutter my eyes and ask a stupid question. "So did you sleep well, Richard?"

"Yeah, just great."

"I got home late and usually I just go straight to my room from the garage. But when I drove in the driveway I noticed the bathroom light was on in the guest room. I didn't realize it then but I'm sure the guest room must be where you slept. When I got ready for bed I came to the kitchen for a Coke. If I'd known there was a strange good looking man in the house I shouldn't have paraded the hallways in this skimpy little Teddy. I probably shouldn't have worn it this morning either. But I hope it doesn't bother you."

"Oh, no. Certainly not. Quite becoming." Richard shakes his head and smiles to openly respond to my flirting as he raises his eyebrows showing he heartily approves of my outfit.

"Funniest thing though. When I left the kitchen I thought I heard little noises in the guest wing and as I got near the guest room I suppose you must have been having a nightmare or trouble sleeping. It almost sounded like people whispering and laughing. Can't imagine what that

64

was all about. Strange noises? Strange lights left on? I might have come into that spare room to turn off the light and been surprised."

Richard smiles and looks like he's so mesmerized he's about to drool. He scrunches his shoulders as if to indicate he doesn't know what to say. This is turning into fun with this guy.

I take a step toward Richard, look right into his eyes, smile and playfully squeeze his forearm, never losing my direct eye contact.

He gasps a little and when I touch him he looks like he's about to faint from the shock. He's very cute as he struggles not to be nervous but his face flushes in embarrassment.

It sounds like he is just saying words to get through this discomfort, "Gee, I dunno. Never heard a thing last night. Very tired from traveling I guess."

Richard sucks in a quick deep breath and steps back further. He nervously makes a little cough, smiles and clears his throat.

"Tell you what. I'm going to my room for a sec and then I'll be right back for that coffee. Okay?"

I know I'm hot and I love seeing men fall all over themselves. This is fun for me even this early in the morning in the kitchen. I caused his obvious sexual interest and excitement and I'm not about to de-escalate this. What a hunk of a man! Let's just see how far this can go. I put one finger to my lips, shift my hips to one side and give a dramatic innocent look as I stare at what's beginning to look like a tent pole below his waist.

"Sure, Richard. Oh my! Would you look at that? What an interesting way to say good morning. Go to your room or do whatever you think you must do so we can enjoy our coffee."

Richard doesn't respond but looks like his face is about to explode with uncharacteristically awkward embarrassment. He hobbles quickly down the hall out of my sight toward the privacy and safety of the guest room.

Suddenly it dawns on me that aside from a possible sexual encounter with Richard, he might be a perfect catalyst to make my fantasies become reality. We'll just have to play this along and see. Hmmm. The first priorities are to see if I can wrap him around my finger sexually and figure a way to get my hands on my trust money without waiting another three years. I could be free from this haunted house and these two ridiculous people I'm supposed to call Mommy and Daddy. They couldn't possibly hate me as much as I hate them.

CHAPTER 15

LADY LUCK SMILES ON RICHARD

After my encounter in the kitchen with Jane Ella I get to my room without anyone witnessing what just happened. I look in the full length mirror and realize the mess I'd have been in if Lauren or Phillip had walked into the kitchen when I was hypnotized by their daughter.

I whisper as if talking to the man in the mirror, "Ho-o-oleee Shit! So, hello, Jane Ella! You are a goddess. A tall, beautiful, Amazon, flirting, frigging goddess! Thank goodness Lauren didn't see any of that. Boy, I can't imagine what would have happened. But...oh man...I've got to be careful...but oh, man! I'm in a house filled with both heaven and hell. Youth has a special luster. That's for sure. What a great looking, sexy, treasure but, boy oh boy, do I have to be careful. This is more dangerous than any safari I've ever guided."

I look admiringly at my full image as I continue to talk to himself in a hushed tone, "Whew. Phillip...just puleeez... please stay gone out of this house as much as possible. I've really got to sort this out. My future is suddenly looking like I hit the lottery and in spades! It's dangerous enough skating around hubby and wife in the same house, now I add mother and daughter, and even more I add father and daughter   The last thing I need is the hubby-daddy jumping into the mix. Hoo-oly Shit, Richard. *Hoo-ooly shit!* What are you getting yourself into? "

After a couple of deep quivering breaths and some adjustments with my suddenly shrunken, binding underwear, I regain physical composure. But I really have to focus on something else or the same problem will occur as soon as I walk back into that kitchen. Think about flowers or mountains or God knows what. Just stop thinking about how quick she was coming onto me. She's pure animal. She could just possibly be the very best luck I've ever had. Young, gorgeous and rich. God, I liked it when she touched me. I liked it a lot! Who knows how long Lauren may sleep. I'm going back to the kitchen and just see where this can lead with Jane Ella while the opportunity exists.

As I slowly return to the kitchen, I'm trying to look nonchalant but my widened eyes are alert and taut muscles are prepared for whatever may luckily come my way from my new acquaintance, Jane Ella. Any further incursions of the young maiden go immediately on hold because as I near the kitchen I hear voices, one of whom is Lauren. I double check my composure and take a deep breath. But down deep I murmur under my breath, "Richard Martin, your future is in this house. Who will turn out to be the final pair?"

CHAPTER 16

NEW OPPORTUNITIES

I laugh and applaud as Murray enters my office. "So Murray-The-Great puts out his first fire of the day. But you also hinted about new ideas of fortune, Murray Eddlemann, Esquire?"

"Yeah, Phillip. Herculaneum Manufacturing in Cleveland is a new target acquisition you identified for us. I've reviewed your summary and as always, my friend, you are spot on. Very simple. Piece a' cake, but timing is everything. You and I are pretty well at the Phd level when it comes to doing this. We've done it before and never a hint of any impropriety. So, another operation is good for you and me money-wise and it spreads risk and liability even further afield.

I'll supervise filing everything with the Corporation Commission to rename the new corporation, set-up taxes, payroll and accounts payable and receivable for the new merged company and I have a few additional odds and ends to add into the mix while everything is chaotic. But, it only appears chaotic because I'm tightly controlling all the details. I'll set up perfectly sterile identity and background records, some will be payroll, some will be small contract companies who will regularly bill Patriot and of course Patriot will promptly pay for goods and services, some of which will be legal fees. The extra folks on payroll will have their paychecks, after taxes of course, deposited directly into bank accounts over which I have some, shall we say, influence and then squeaky clean money transfers into our offshore accounts. The contractor companies I can pass through a little more complex cleansing process but it will eventually wind up as pure untraceable cash. And as I always say, Phillip my friend, cash makes no enemies."

"So this is tax safe, can't be tracked to you or me?"

" Yeah, I'm sure. And there's more. I'm going to have our two other shill companies invest in the new company so when all the announcements begin to leak out their good fortune results from solid, long range foresight, not anything insider. So then, not you and I by name but two of our alter egos are going to make a killing when this new company goes public. That's all set. I'm using our two German identities to invest and pay the appropriate taxes. But trust me. A couple of washes and the money goes squeaky clean to Phillip and Murray offshore and secure."

"Lots of balls to juggle, Murray. I'll just be glad when we can leave this stuff behind and let time bury our little sins."

"Trust me, Phillip. We've had these little games going for what, fifteen years? Have you ever even had so much of a question asked of you? No, you haven't. Remember back in the early years when I deliberately fed the IRS a little red flag so they could get all excited and come and audit. I did that to test the water. I had to be sure one-hundred percent about the safety and insulation of our little games. Passed with flying colors. The IRS and SEC are spinning in circles chasing the Ponzi guys while you and I take hundreds of nibbles around a very safe edge of a different pie. Who's going to complain? We're basically ripping off our own company that still remains profitable. Who's to know? Who's to complain?"

"Well, you know my long range plan is to be elsewhere, sans wife and my biggest worry is living long enough to enjoy it. Lately Lauren has been driving me bug-fuck and I not only don't love her, I don't even like her. I can't stand to be in the same room with her. Emotions are cold. I think sometimes I should just cut her loose with some money and be done with it."

"Now's not the time for a divorce, Phillip. Please stick with the plan. Yes we could get you through a divorce but it might complicate things. Besides, what grounds? Don't like her? Not quite enough substance if you know what I mean."

"Yeah, Murray. I know. And every time something happens I start speculating what brass rings might be passing me by on life's carousel. Like the airplane this morning. I have no idea exactly how it could happen, but an accident, an off the books maintenance flight. Who

70

knows? Seems like any opportunity for disappearance could get rid of Lauren and give me the new life I want. "

" The IRS may not be smart enough to connect all the dots and find our accounts but some greedy lawyers, present company excluded of course, would spend years breathing down your collar and therefore mine as well. You don't want years of looking over your shoulder. Trust me. Keep this simple and follow Murray's plan. So now's not the time for divorce. Trust me. The time will come. You will be set for life and Phillip Pittman of today will be the invisible man with a totally new name and life. Be patient."

"Yeah, yeah. Okay. But I have to tell you some days Julie looks awfully good to me, Murray. Maybe if I had her...ya know...not married or any mistake like that again. Ya know just like set up in a nice condo for whenever I want and forgotten when I don't want her. "

"Did you hear anything I said after good morning? Bzzt. Bzzt. Warning lights are going off. Arms-length or whatever other body part you'd like to use to measure, but do not get involved with Julie or anyone else. Maybe a condo. Maybe maybe maybe. You're looking for freedom from wives, freedom from commitments, freedom from the rat race and oodles of money to spend. Do not complicate things. So, I have to know...no shit..., are you sliding toward serious feelings for Julie or just a little momentary panting and licking of the lips?"

I pause and look at Murray, "I'll heed your warnings but frankly, Murray, I really can't take much more of life in the big house with Lauren and as far as Julie, it may be a little more interest than just chasing a new skirt."

"Okay, Phillip, you're scaring me now but enough is enough. You know what to do and what not to do. We continue to hit home runs and we keep coming up to the plate for more. Don't screw it up...for both of us."

Murray picks up his briefcase and his coffee cup, takes a sip, looks at me and makes a grimace from the taste of the coffee. Without further comment Murray goes out the door leaving it standing wide open.

Seconds later, Julie steps into the doorway and I look up, breathe heavily and smile at her.

"Anything you need Mr. Pittman?"

"The way you're looking that's difficult for me to answer at the moment...but no. Just pull the door to and I'll finish looking over these reports before the gaggle forms and the blood-letting must begin."

I'm very proud of myself. Julie's eyes sparkle when I talk like that. She loves power.

Murray always prides himself as the thinker out ahead of everybody else but I may have hatched the beginnings of a plan by sheer luck. I planted a seed with Murray that Julie may be more than a fling. I also acknowledged to Murray I wouldn't get too involved with Julie nor get tied up in a misguided or complicated divorce with Lauren. Murray's right about grounds for divorce. But I'm thinking past Murray's plan. What if divorce isn't necessary? What if Lauren unexpectedly met with a fatal accident? A perfect sort of accident. My new life could start immediately. I have plenty to think about and I'm suddenly excited to engage a new line of very personal, very private thinking, sans Murray Eddlemann. I'm on the lookout for a carousel brass ring that could surgically remove Lauren from my life-permanently. And as long as I carefully plan it all and keep it secret who cares if Murray has to go under the bus at the same time. Just so it doesn't affect me. I mean, what are friends for? They help you, they help you , they help and when they can no longer be of use...goodbye. Total freedom and wealth. Is that too much to ask? I think not and I can do this.

CHAPTER 17

MURRAY –SEEDS OF MISTRUST

I must be getting old. I'm suspicious of everything and everybody. I even have dreams that in my own twisted fantasies that are supposed to mean nothing, my dreams include Phillip as the evil person and I'm always struggling to get loose from his evil. I know, I know. They're dreams but I notice Phillip is quieter around me than in years past. He used to gush out every secret but now I see a frequent look like he wants to share something but instead keeps it inside. I've asked him if that's the case and he denies it. He says I'm just a paranoid, guilt-ridden, aging, Jewish lawyer and my particular DNA's loaded with worry and guilt.

But all in all, my conversation with Phillip just now was very unsettling. I've known this guy long enough to know when he's got errant, private thoughts on his mental horizon. Honestly, some of Phillip's private thoughts frighten me because he gets so caught up in emotion like revenge, that he doesn't always sweep out all the corners looking for little problems that can be a trail of breadcrumbs right back to your doorstep. Like just last year we were absorbing that grain company in Kansas. The previous owner's son kept getting under Phillip's skin until Phillip told me he was actually thinking of having him killed. Some shit about hiring a couple of guys to bury this kid in one of the grain elevators and let the kid's body surprise the family a year or so later. Pure immature horseshit. Even to consider something so stupid shakes my years of faith in Phillip. But we get past it because I watch out and talk sense.

Nope, that just wasn't something I would have let happen and it's a damn good thing when I get this sort of intuition about Phillip and his brainiac ideas.

Perhaps I should examine my responsibilities from a little different viewpoint. Who must be taken care above all others on this planet? Me, of course. But in my zeal to protect my buddy Phillip and set him up with a new identity and money…well just maybe I've allowed taking care of myself to slip to a distant second in priorities.

Okay, Murray, get your thinking cap on and get this shifted in the correct direction. Maybe Phillip's operating with the usual set of plans that run parallel to mine but what if at some point his plans strike out in a direction unknown to me. I could get screwed, blued and tattooed. Maybe that's why my gut instinct that Phillip's withholding information from me has some merit to it. Murray, old boy, you didn't become the lobster with the biggest claws by being stupid or falling asleep at the switch. Get smart. Self-protection comes first, Murray.

I hope I didn't give away my feelings while Phillip was talking. He often talks about what he wishes but it's only half-serious. Today I got a gut feeling that given half a chance he'd pull the plug, take the new identities and disappear off the face of the earth so to speak. His talk about Lauren in an accident? That's new. I fear he's entered into a new and dangerous dimension. Frankly I need to have some serious thought time to be sure I haven't forgotten anything. Because if he gets caught and swings from the gallows how far behind may I be? Perish that thought. I'm gonna make this all work for me. I'll fix everything so if there is any swinging from any gallows…it'll only be Phillip swinging.

I laugh out loud at my own humor, "Like my version of the old saying …hell hath no fury like a scorned fellow crook. I like that."

So what will make me happy? Totally happy. First a long and healthy life. No pain. I don't like pain and suffering. My health should be okay but better to get more frequent checks so I know with total confidence. I mean how'd ya like to be one of these guys with an aneurysm, a big balloon vein just waiting to explode and they have no idea. I want to know about it if I have one. Well, shit. There's not a really good reason to worry about any of it…just be nice to know if something's on the horizon. Okay, check that one off the list and promise myself to get more checkups and stay abreast of the ever aging and changing body of the invincible Murray Eddlemann Esquire.

Second in importance is money. There's never enough. I want to be able to have so much I have to do a double check of all the commas and zeros. Together with Phillip I'd say that's not out of the realm of reality. I just have to install a new set of detailed plans that will separate my money and my risk out of Phillip's world. I will add yet a third set of accounts and drain my money slowly but surely into the third set that Phillip knows nothing about. The only money I'll leave connected to Phillip will be traceable legal fees by his fraudulent identities. Purely above board legal reviews of contracts. He only directed me to be sure there was legal sufficiency of the contracts not vet the companies themselves. No risk to me. Perfectly justifiable arms-length legal reviews. If the house of cards folds up Phillip will be the only one buried.

I'm starting to really enjoy this. I don't feel one iota of guilt like I'm screwin a friend and I think that's because I trust my instincts and Phillip's on a dangerous individual path. The arrogant shit thinks he's smarter than everybody and he's close to correct, except for me.

Third and final goal is to have lots of available sex. But there's one little added element and it's the ultimate coupe de grace. I will make certain that I get properly laid by Lauren Pittman and her luscious daughter, my God-daughter, Jane Ella. And if Phillip is gonna try to rip old Murray off then I'll make certain Phillip knows somehow I had them both just as a way of pissing on him.

And for this moment, I'm going to reward myself with a little single malt in a nice crystal glass, sit by my view of the beautiful city of Boston and sort through the possibilities of what my best friend is thinking. Of course I could just ask him but that would simply force him to lie to me and embarrass him that I'm onto his little escapade of independence from his wise master.

I pour a glass of scotch and sit down. Ah, feels good and tastes great.

I can't imagine what's pushing him to actually kick the false identity plan into motion before I comfortably say ,"Okay, Phillip. It's all set." Whatever it is, my self-preservation is ultimate.

I try to project myself into Phillip's twisted life and habits for a few minutes. Sometimes he reveals something that is seemingly very minor but turns out to be the absolute driving force behind a rather ill-advised view…in other words sometimes his reactions are so irrational the only way I'd have any clue is to get lucky with a stupid, fucking wild-assed guess.

Okay, Murray, figure this out. Get inside Phillip's head and figure where he's going with his hints. Very early in Phillip's meteorical rise in the financial world, Phillip and I became close friends and allies, a very natural but very unholy alliance. Phillip is the financial whiz, and me, the aging but wily and brilliant corporate lawyer whose expertise is unmatched in technology, domestic taxes and international tax accounting. As friends and confidants, we are indeed an alliance spawned by Satan himself.

As we got to know each other better, it was obvious how Phillip felt about his marriage. Phillip knew he'd been sexually seduced and probably the only time in his life when he let physical pleasure influence his decisions. What a mistake! From the start he realized Lauren was not a true trophy-wife for corporate success. He sees himself trapped with a permanent fixture with whom he is destined to be unhappy. From day two of the marriage Phillip felt as if he had a millstone around his neck.

Phillip's problem has always been the same, he has no idea how to control a wild woman like Lauren. She's lusty, competitive, fearless, everything to be the perfect woman for a very strong man. Therein lies Phillip's underlying problem. Lauren loves to be the sexy center of attention and she flirts constantly. The overt flirting excludes her from being the most popular woman among the wives in the business party circuit and when she does attend social functions, catty remarks abound. Her arrogance suits her well in dishing out sarcastic and condescending opinions and she appears insulated from comments about her.

I smile to myself because of all the men who flirt with Lauren, I'm probably the one who loves the tete-a-tete most of all. I love being at parties with her and my little schtick that works is to wait until I catch

76

Lauren a bit away from the others and I make a remark about how she looks wonderful while staring into her eyes. That's about all the encouragement Lauren needs and after a quick glance around she'll describe in intimate detail what she thinks I'd like to do to her in my raunchiest fantasies. I'm convinced given the right privacy Lauren and I would do every one of the things she's mentioned. My God, I'd do it with her until I pass out. But no matter the enjoyment of imagining what could be, there is a line I cannot and will not cross. As long as Phillip and I are joined at the hip by risk I will not cross that line with his wife. When things are different I have no problem splitting my marital blanket with Ruthie and then taking on the hot tigress herself. Some day. Some day.

C'mon, Murray, back to business. I've been toying with Phillip for the last month or so. Some of his comments I didn't exactly trust so I began just floating some little tempting balloons out in front of him to see his reaction. I have to admit his reactions struck a dark chord in my own imagination. As I tossed out exotic and risky possibilities to escape, live in freedom and above all protect his money from a bitter marital split, Phillip stopped laughing and became obsessed with deciding on a plan that would extricate him from his situation and allow him to personally gloat from the revenge. Before long Phillip's side of our dream-talks turned from whimsical ideas to formative, sadistic plans. I am convinced that if Phillip could murder Lauren and know he wouldn't be caught, he'd do it today. Nah. He'd hire somebody to do it so he wouldn't get any more involved than necessary.

Phillip's about murder almost like he was about becoming involved in our financial escapades all those years ago. Sounds good. Let's do it. He is truly a ruthless bully bastard. He can brutally mete out mental torture and laugh about it as if he's the toughest guy in the world. But ultimately he has no stomach for risk if it looks like it could actually roost on his spineless shoulders. His greatest fear is to be caught and I'm the guy who guarantees him that will not happen. He'd cry like a little girl if the cuffs were clicked on his wrists. Years ago when he was convinced that I have his back and he won't likely get caught in our little extra-legal activities, Phillip showed he has neither conscience nor morals. Fine with me. I was given neither at birth. But at least I got big brass balls instead of a penchant for whimpering.

We need to continue to be very effective financial criminals with minimum risk of being exposed. In the early days we laughed about it but as the scenarios began to fall under both sets of eyes, we both realized it was certain we are the perfect guys to actually pull it off. The secret is to be technical wizards and meticulous with details. Error and ultimate capture follow carelessness in details.

Our first fraud was when I applied for a German tax identification number for the fictitious Dieter Leithund, the President of Leithund Financial Investment and Consulting Company based in Frankfort. By the way, Leithund is a loose translation of German meaning lead dog and Phillip often refers to himself as the lead dog. As he says frequently in manager meetings, If you're not the lead dog, the view and the smell are always the same." Very demeaning but of course that's Phillip's entertainment.

But I digress… The Leithund Company became an investment client of our home office, Patriot Star Investment Corporation and I was paid on retainer by the fictitious German company. Phillip put some personal money in the Leithund Company coffers for a couple of years and established a track record of paying German taxes, both for the Leithund Company and individually for Dieter Leithund. I was paid fees from Leithund Company for legal services and paid my personal income taxes on that source of foreign income. For five years we carefully watched and fine-tuned the process. Then we moved on to replicate more fictitious companies and personal identities in South Africa, Spain, France and Sweden. In each case I applied for tax identification so we could be good citizens and pay the taxes owed. More foreign bank accounts were set up and taxes carefully and dutifully filed and paid in all the countries. The lack of any international cooperation or cross-checking for taxes by the United States, as well as the other countries keeps everything above suspicion. With very little black market help I got a series of passports, some for me and some for Phillip.

After five years of toying and tinkering to be sure of our footing, Phillip and I worked schemes to rake in millions and millions of dollars. Much of it was inside trading information because we knew of very long range plans for approaching acquisitions or mergers and magically, Leithund and the other companies invested wisely months and even a couple of years before the ultimate transactions were complete. Of course who but the President and CEO along with the senior corporate attorney would better know the level of success of investing at the right time. Millions of legitimate appearing investment profits funneled directly into the foreign accounts.   Insider trading at its finest, without ever a hint of who controlled the successful German investment company. The money went to the foreign accounts and I have been paid very generous legal fees and bonuses from the phony, shell foreign companies.

So down to brass tacks. If Phillip is itching to try his identity bail out, perhaps I need to let him think I'm being persuaded to think it's okay. I need to line everything up so if anything goes wrong with his plan, it will fall singularly on him and not a whiff on my jacket. I can do that. But I need to play him along so he thinks he's convincing me.

Well, Phillip here's a toast to you. We've had a long and profitable run. But now our friendship is set for a different path. A rocky, and likely, a one-way path.   I need to take care of myself and I believe it will work for you as well but I'll make sure all liability tracks in one direction. Sorry old boy but that's the way it is. I just can't trust you any longer. Besides, it will be nice to have my own independence and wealth. And...my old friend, who knows? Maybe a shot at your wife...or daughter...or hell, Murray, you can have them both.

CHAPTER 18

SAFARI? WHY NOT?

Jane Ella and I share an unusual moment together in the kitchen this morning. She seems to be in a very good mood, sort of like when the cat eats the canary. Well, well if it isn't my prince from last night.

Richard ducks his head into the entry to the kitchen almost like he's fearful to enter. He needs to stop worrying and relax. What we did last night is going to work out perfectly fine in this big house.

"Good morning, Richard. I hope you had pleasant dreams." Since I have my back to Jane Ella I make a kissing expression in Richard's direction.

"Yes. I can say my dreams were most pleasant. Isn't that the way dreams should be? Fantasies."

Richard sees Jane Ella looking away so he too makes an undetected kissing gesture in my direction.

All three of us stand at the kitchen island, coffees in hand.

"Jane Ella, this is probably a surprise to see a guest. This is Richard Martin, a college friend from years past. I should have left you a note so you'd know to wear appropriate clothes around the house while Richard's here. Well, anyhow, now you know he's here. And Richard, this is my daughter Jane Ella. "

"Yes Mother, I know he's here. We briefly met earlier and I got Richard a cup of coffee that seemed to really perk him up." Jane Ella smiles at Richard and though my instinct alarm goes off, I'm probably wrong so I don't react and I continue to talk.

"You'd probably never guess, but Richard is a safari guide in Africa."

Jane Ella smiles at Richard teasingly, "Oh my, goodness. Safari guide with animals and stuff."

"And after talking briefly to Richard about safaris I was thinking it might be fun and somewhat therapeutic for the Pittman family to go on an African safari sometime soon. Would you be up for that?"

"Africa? A safari? I don't know. Jungles, Dust. Animals. Tents. What's the appeal of a safari?

"Well, this is just the first thought of it and Richard says it's luxury and not anything like you think of roughing it. And of course it would be wonderful if we could make everything match up and have Richard for our guide. But the first step is to get all three of us to simply consider it. If you think it's an okay idea, Jane Ella, then I'll talk to Phillip about it."

"Yeah, I guess it's fine with me. Something to do for a bit. But fat chance big Phil will go for it. Therapeutic to him is recharging his IPad. But who knows? If it's possible for him to feel anything about anything, maybe you can catch him feeling guilty or stressing out about something and he'll agree, just to shut you up."

I give Jane Ella a look of disgust. "Thanks. Slightly supportive but always ending with a jab at me. Oh well, I'll take what I can get. Maybe this really *would* be a good thing. And Richard, maybe you could give us some information, maps, pictures about what, when, where…ya know, for reservations, and all the travel details."

"Of course. It's actually a whole lot easier than you probably think. The tour company I'm with can take care of air travel all the way to the camp and of course whatever level of room accommodations you'd require. We rival four star resorts. The prices are all inclusive of meals, tours, everything from your door to Africa and back to your door. There. That's my pitch and I'll shut up."

I try my best at cheerleading for the safari cause, "Oh, Richard. Don't be so modest. That sounds great and besides being modest doesn't fit the image of the big strong safari guide."

"Well, the first step is to determine if it's something you'd like to do. I can call the company today and have detailed information sent here to you so you'll know more about the entire experience. For most folks, a
81

safari with a good guide, like yours truly, is a once in a lifetime trip of exciting adventures. My company knows that and does a great job taking care of all the details. As I just indicated, from your door on vacation and back to your door by way of a couple of exciting, fun filled weeks in Africa."

I am shocked beyond belief but Jane Ella actually is standing up straight like she is showing some sincere interest, "I'm actually feeling this could be a good idea. I've traveled quite a lot on my own and with friends but I never considered a safari. Mom, it would be fun, particularly if the accommodations are comfortable."

"Do you think Phillip, you and I would be too dysfunctional for Richard?"

"Yeah, Mom. That's possible. But c'mon. Can you even imagine Phillip in the wilds of Africa? Him swatting flies or mosquitoes while his milky-white body is being eyed by a lion, or tiger, or hippo or whatever is running around there. "

"Don't start making fun of him just yet. He has to be convinced to go and talking about his milk-white skin or being eyed by a wild animal will certainly not sell him on it being much fun. I'll talk to Phillip this evening. Richard, the most important thing for Phillip will be air conditioning, internet access and no bugs in the rooms. Problems?"

"No, of course not. This is the twenty first century and we have unbelievable levels of top drawer lodging…no bugs or critters, two or four legged, lurking in the rooms. And there's excellent Wi-Fi throughout the base camp. I think Phillip will find the trip pleasantly up to or even exceeding his standards."

Richard continues, "And if lions and hippos seem exciting that's great because we have plenty of them, but tigers, Jane Ella? I think you're a continent or two away but the real point is *we* don't expose guests to danger. I'll admit that when we leave base camp to go out and look at animals, that's what we refer to as roughing it. But that term is rather silly because we make people very comfortable and even pampered when we're out and about. We're there to observe the wildlife close enough for excitement but avoiding risk. Then, of course there are custom adventures, ya know like private tours or even one-on-one's to accommodate people's' wildest fantasies in the ferocious lands of Africa. Some of the custom adventures are a little closer to nature. Something for everybody. Still sound good?"

"Sounding better all the time." I smile a confident smile at Richard.

"To me, too." And Richard gets another smile, this time from Jane Ella. "So when do we leave?"

"Well, don't get too far ahead. I need to talk with Phillip before we get too far into the stage of wild enthusiasm. I just have no idea what he'll say. I mean it's probably pretty expensive and trying to get him to take off work is next to impossible."

I look at Richard with a little impish smile. I can't believe how cavalier I've already become about my dream to precipitate Phillip's eternal demise.

"Why would you mention cost, Mother? That's not a consideration. You know good and well, if it's something Phillip wants to do, cost is no object...thus, no worry about the cost. On the other hand, if he doesn't want to go and says no, then cost doesn't matter because we won't be going. So I'd say forget the cost. Just work on old Phillip. You know. Just appeal to his ego...the lead dog...his narcissism. That's a good first step. You know. Don't start by pissing him off as he walks through the door. I swear, sometimes you love having him come home and he loves to get home just so the two of you can fight like cats and dogs."

"Jane Ella, that's not true. I'll talk to Phillip when he gets home but let *me* bring it up and then please don't throw any sarcastic comments into the discussion. When, and if, I need your cheerleader skills, I'll let you know. And if I need your support, please back me up. Okay?"

"Sure, Mom. Just try not to be shit-faced drunk when you bring it up to him."

"I think that's unfair and I've heard enough of your little jabs. Just stop. You don't have to show off for Richard."

The three of us stand quietly for the next few moments trying to figure a way to get back to civility and reason.

CHAPTER 19

PHILLIP'S PLAN

It's the end of the day and I hear Murray making his way into my inner sanctum, predictable mumbling as he picks up anything on Julie's desk to see if it's of interest to him. Murray taps lightly on the door frame as he opens the door. I'm sitting, looking out the window and jump a little for the drama as if surprised by Murray's presence.

"Oh, hey. I guess I didn't hear you come in at first."

"I have to say, Phillip, this is the first time in many, many years I've seen you sitting to enjoy the view. You sick?"

Leave it to Murray. Always the razor sharp, sarcastic wit, "Nah. I feel fine. And don't give me a ration of shit about enjoying the view. I earned this view. We earned this view, Murray. Why shouldn't I check on it ever so often just to make sure it's still there? Who knows? Sometimes I'm in this office so much my windows might just as well be bricked in and the view sold to somebody else."

"Of course you've earned it whiz kid. But seriously, everything okay?"

I lean back in my chair, hands behind my head and pause for a moment.

"You know me too well, Murray, my friend. I'm processing lots of crap at home. A college friend of Lauren's dropped in on us and he's apparently staying over for a couple of nights. I was suspicious of the flirting from the second I got home and then later after everyone was supposedly tucked in their little beds I decided to do a quick head count in bedrooms. I peeked in Lauren's room and whaddyaknow? Nobody home. So, I went to the guest room and listened through the door. Screwin' their brains out, Murray."

"Shit, man. I'm sorry. Right in your own house. What did you do?"

"Nothin'. Absolutely nothin'. I listened to all the moaning and groaning, and ooo-ing and and ahh-ing to be sure it was Lauren. Then I heard the garage door and figured Jane Ella was coming home so I cut the audio voyeurism short and just returned to my bedroom. You know what? I went to bed and actually slept very well. Something's wrong, Murray. Sure, I was insulted and outraged but it's why I was outraged, Murray, that's strange. It really wasn't about my blushing bride screwin some knucklehead. I *really do not* care. All the care about her is gone. What made me angry is that they'd do that in my house as if I'm too stupid to know. That makes me mad as hell."

"So what are you going to do?"

"I don't know just yet. I'm thinking and looking out my wonderful window. I think it's time to no longer ignore it and process all this into something that has importance to me. Don't worry. I'm not going to shoot them although it wouldn't bother me one bit. Cold as ice. But that's not in my best interest. We've worked too hard and come too far with our dream, you and me. Nothin's going to upset that golden applecart."

Murray shrugs his shoulder and turns to leave, "Well part of that's a relief anyhow."

Phillip pauses, "Know what, Murray? You know what?"

"Do I know what? Do I know what? How could I know what? I'm sposed to guess what? We playin twenty questions or something?"

"Maybe instead of spending so much time in anger about being shackled to this witch…maybe I should do an acid test on one of the identities just for a little excitement. Maybe we've got enough and it's time to ride off into the sunset. Maybe I should consult my favorite attorney about what evidence or documentation I need to collect for a divorce that gives her pittance and me the world. I always thought I'd be buying my way out of my yoking to psycho Lauren. Now I hate her so much I don't want her to get shit. I want everything. Jane Ella gets her trust and Lauren leaves with the aristocratic luggage she's earned and deserves …paper bags so she can carry her prized possessions-vodka and pills."

"Look my friend. A test is not something you do for entertainment. When the time comes you and I will have to tear our blanket in half and each go our own ways. Too soon, Phillip. We got more fish to fry. Fatten the coffers while the risk is still very small compared to the rewards. Listen to me when I tell you I have it all covered. Trust me. Don't jump the gun on me here."

"Okay. Okay, Murray. You're right. But maybe the time is closer than you think. Listen to this. Not that I give the slightest shit but sometimes I see a little something that makes me think just maybe, just maybe, Lauren is actually feeling a bit of guilt for how she's treated me. At first I was suspicious but I really think it's genuine."

"What the hell! C'mon here. You just finished tellin me you had a houseguest who's bangin your wife right under your nose and now you tell me you're all teary-eyed because she's feeling guilty?"

"No, don't misunderstand me. Let me make something really clear. I don't really care a nickel for her and how she feels. Okay? I want away from her without a bunch of legal strings unraveling my Armani every time I turn around. But I'm looking for opportunities, Murray. Opportunities to end this shit with her once and for all."

Murray's listening with interest, "Yeah. Okay. Don't care at all? So if you find me screwin her in my office, it's okay? If she gets hit by a car, it's okay? If she dies a long and painful death of hair cancer, you don't care? That's your bottom line with her?"

"Yep. You can screw her in *my* office for all I care and afterwards push her cancerous bald head in front of a car. I do not care. But this guilt thing from her is new and I don't want that complicating me getting loose from her. If anything I want to use it against her."

"Okay. She's actin guilty and screwin some schmuck under your nose and you don't care. I'm still not seeing any reason that will prevent her from getting half of what you've got on the legit record. You'll keep half of the legit and have all your share of the stuff off the books.

Her horse comes in to Place and you get the Daily Double. So let's just be sure you and I are on the same page with all this. We take a deep breath, keep makin money and follow our plan. Okay?"

"Sure Murray."

"Okay, then. I guess that's it for now. Just take it easy."

I twist in my seat and lean forward as I stare at Murray, "Well, there's more. I've got an idea that might turn out to be my salvation. What if I were to take Lauren and Jane Ella on a little vacation? How shall I put it? Good husband trying to reconcile with guilty wife, sort of recapture our family bonding. Me, Mister Perfect trying to do the right thing."

Murray laughs out loud, "Ahhh. Ya had me goin, The way you were staring at me I thought you were serious. Aw, Murray she's feelin guilty. That was good. But down deep you know the secret to our team, you and me, Phillip. Legal wisdom. I'm your go-to guy. Advice on why you oughta keep your pickle away from your executive secretary. I'm your go-to guy. But you start talking family vacation to Wollyworld in a station wagon? You're beyond help and on your own."

"No. Listen. This vacation has a real purpose. The guy she was screwin in my house is some tour company's African safari kingpin. Just think about it Murray. A safari with a real purpose. If she's screwin Little Abner in my house how long do you think it would take them to resume their bangin over there and then I get real evidence of infidelity among the bushes of Africa and a little foreign travel could give me a chance to at least try a phony credit card or passport or something. Ya know, just make sure it works the way you say it will. At least the thing with Lauren could give you something to work with. Right? Jane Ella gets her trust, we negotiate a settlement with Lauren and that's it. I can work a bit more, keep my only entertainment of getting into Julie's fabulous drawers whenever I want and plan the disappearing act when I want with nobody really caring to look except maybe Julie when she runs out of money. But who even really cares about Julie? She'll get over it... or not. I could care less."

Murray is expressionless and obviously thinking, "Yeah. Okay. But no more right now. Interesting, Phillip. It's why we're a good team. Creative thinking. We're always looking for the brass rings on the carousel and trying to grab them when they come by. But you're scaring me at the moment. Let me think about this."

"Okay, but let's not wait for the next ice age. Okay?"

"Yeah. Yeah. Night, Phillip."

The plan Murray and I have is that as I approach a suitable retirement age, I drift apart from Lauren, legally separate and eventually sever the marriage completely. Lots of money as a condition of being peaceful is supposed to keep Lauren from causing trouble and I would live abroad traveling around and then begin living totally under a new identity. Phillip Pittman would become more and more difficult to find until finally he'd be completely off the radar screen and truthfully not missed nor looked for by anyone. No marriage involved, no insurance, no suspicion just slowly evaporate.

With a legitimate looking record of birth, a clean record of paying taxes, and multiple passports it becomes a matter of how much Murray and I stockpile for the future. The day the plan is implemented I call Liberty Day.

Now I see light in the tunnel that I might accelerate and modify the plans Murray and I have pondered all these years. What if I do it on my own? That would avoid having an accomplice like Murray. I could have even more money if I didn't split it with Murray. I could get one more identity all on my own, strip some of the accounts, change ownership of some accounts and what could he do? Tell the authorities I stole his illegal money? Besides the excitement of pulling-off the perfect disappearance would be wonderful. Instead of slow evaporation, just a poof and gone.

Difficult to trace and already out of the USA it's easier to become a chameleon of the world. A very wealthy chameleon. A chameleon on a yacht, a private jet, a coastal mansion...Oh man, this is all too good.

I've got so many wonderful details to think through. Well, Murray, looks like this is where we begin to part being best friends.

CHAPTER 20

LAUREN'S PLAN

I feel energized about Richard's ideas. I know I have to look at this the way Richard does. I'm not involved in planning a crime even though it may very well be the perfect crime. It's not a crime. It's components of risk and danger combining purely by accident with a hundred percent effectiveness. It's a tragic accident. It's an accident that can hold up under the scrutiny of the toughest police and investigators.

I softly whisper to myself, "I can do this. I've got to make it a wonderful performance. Not too phony. I've got to show true sincerity as if I honestly feel guilty and still have a soft place in my heart for Phillip. God. If I don't throw up pulling this off it may be worthy of an Academy Award."

"P-Tttt," I make a spitting sound.

I sit up straight to regain my composure and whisper to myself, "Now I've got to stop. Stop reacting the way I really feel and get into character. Play to his need for control and introduce this a bit at a time. First I have to be able to trust that Jane Ella's on board with the safari idea."

Perhaps with Jane Ella's birthday on the horizon, just maybe I could tell her I'll broach with Phillip for us to revise Jane Ella's control of her trust account to coincide with this birthday. Great birthday present. She'll be on my side at least while I work on it for her. That is brilliant, Lauren. If I simply mention that to Jane Ella she'll be my best pal on anything else…like getting Phillip on board for a safari.

Her other motivator is men and I'd best be very, very careful. Richard's mine and I'm not about to use him as bait for her. The very thought is physically revolting.

I have to be ready to introduce this to Phillip. He will be the challenge. I've got to do it from a position of sobriety or else it will turn into a quick screaming match. I don't need a drink this afternoon. I want a drink. I want a drink very badly but do I need a drink? No. This is what's important.

CHAPTER 21

JANE ELLA'S PLAN

Well, it's one hundred percent fake but if it helps to get my mitts on the trust money, I'll be a total phony to both Lauren-the-Lush and King Phillip.

I'm idly thumbing through my closet and suddenly I stop.

I know plenty about Mom and Richard in the guest room and I might be able to put a bit of blackmail pressure on Mom to get King Phillip to agree to roll the date of the trust account forward. Why not?

I whisper a new and inspiring thought to myself, "I'll get them to agree to release the trust and then I'll be all goody-goody to go on this trip. I'll bet Richard will show me a couple of wonderful weeks. Over there is probably a good time for him to drift away from Mom because she and Dad will be residing together. God. I can't imagine both of them even living through that experience. Perfect!"

CHAPTER 22

RICHARD'S PLAN

I feel relaxed for a change. My future is getting some actual focus instead of a bunch of what ifs. At this point I have to remain the master planner and take complete advantage of favors for Lauren and Jane Ella but, God forbid, avoid some catastrophe of being caught by Phillip or Lauren or Jane Ella. Even the Wallendas never walked a tightrope like this.

I feel like I've got my seeds planted and now I have to make sure it takes shape under my control. Lauren and Jane Ella are on board with the safari so I have to be doubly careful not to cause any suspicion by overplaying or selling it too hard. Let them do the work so it's in no way like I'm pushing the idea. If something goes wrong, I can dump it all back on them. All Lauren has to do is keep her drunken mouth under control and get Phillip interested in the idea.

Once the idea seems feasible I'll simply fulfill their request for details and they'll hopefully solidify the plans. My hands are clean. It will be the Pittman's request and all I do is provide them information. When I get them all into camp, I can play to his ego and I'm sure he'll want to play big-man-in-camp and have an exotic adventure. All the plans will be at his insistence of course, for a very, very custom side trip. Clean and easy.

I'm not worried about the police in my district but here in the good old USA the insurance lawyers will be picking through all this with a comb like getting lice out of a kid's hair. Combing, looking, suspecting. That's when I must stay away from the Pittman's and the greatest risk will be that Lauren keeps her mouth shut. She simply must stick to showing all the trauma of a picked on little wife who just wants what her wonderful hubby wanted her to have. But no matter how good everybody acts their part, that insurance claim will be the sticky wicket for sure.

But I absolutely cannot appear to be involved or an influence over Lauren or Jane Ella and at the same time I've got to dig my hooks into them individually so they depend on me. At the appropriate time I want to be Johnny-on-the-spot to pick up the emotional pieces of a shattered family and give them the loving strength they'll need. Better warm up your acting skills for that one old boy! Just think of being wealthy for the rest of your pampered life.

The real long range goal is to schmoozle Jane Ella and not let her drift away. Promise whatever I have to- marriage, family and all the really convincing bullshit. Geez. She'll eat it up. And I must say, too bad for Lauren. Lauren's always been special but her physical shelf life is hastening toward its expiration date while Jane Ella has several decades. I can live with it because it sets me up for the grand prize. And guess what's behind door number three? It's winding up with Jane Ella and the entire Pittman estate. Now that's what I call retirement!

If I make a move for Jane Ella too early there will be tidal waves hit this house. I've got to get Jane Ella thinking and committed to a long future life with me and only me. Just imagine, Phillip out of the way, insurance claims cleared and then if Jane Ella got pregnant, Lauren predictably becomes a raging lunatic. At that point I can see Jane Ella being very ballsy to get Lauren out of the way. Could be that Lauren may accidently overdose on alcohol while washing down a massive dose of her bedroom pharmacy. Just keep clean hands.

It should all work. Right now I just can't get shot by the jealous husband, yet keep Lauren from talking too much, be certain she keeps up her bad habits and most of all be sure she never goes to some high-brow treatment center where they convince her to "unburden" herself. My long range plans depend on Lauren's unhealthy habits. Her bad habits are like an accident just waiting to happen. I think I've got this and I think it's solid.

Beats the prophecy of the airline stew that recently told me I'd have to gigolo some old lady out of her social security money at a KFC. How d'ya like me now, Miss Stew? If only you knew you'd be beggin for a night at the Omni. Oh well, small fish.

CHAPTER 23

MURRAY'S PLAN

I can't think about some company's financial spreadsheet at the moment. I stand up and stretch, toss the report on my desk and again admire my window view of the Boston skyline. I push my glasses onto my forehead and walk to my overstuffed chair by the window. I call this chair my "thinking zone". I scoot around in the chair and put my feet on the ottoman.

"Now let's see, Murray. What's got you bugged? Hmmm."

I take a deep breath and frown, "Admit it. I don't want to lose my friend Phillip and all the daily bullshit of him wheelin and dealin but always with me like his alter ego. My God we've made a ton of money. We have a very successful legitimate investment company that anybody would love to control. We have shill companies, multiple identities and obscene amounts of big bucks safely overseas. Phillip and I could probably blow out the national debt with our ill-gotten gains. Man, what a ride this is!"

I rub my eyes and my eyebrows bush out a half inch making a bridge across my nose, If Phillip's thinking about taking off, it's just a matter of time. And the worst part is Phillip can be impulsive. If he thinks I'm dragging my feet he's liable to do something totally stupid. When he latches onto something like this it doesn't go away. This whole thing is going to be over sooner rather than later. Face the reality and protect yourself, Murray. If it's over, it's over. Face it and be smart, you devious prick.

I mouth the words, "Encourage the safari thing and give Phillip a specific plan to test at least one of the identities. Stay close, occupy his co-pilot seat like always and keep him on a short leash so he doesn't get too far out on any solo stuff."

I breathe a sigh and groan as I get up from my chair. I'm out the door on my way home.

CHAPTER 24

EVERYBODY ON THE SAME PAGE?

Lauren and Richard decide it best if Richard leaves the house so Lauren can approach Phillip about the safari.

Later as Phillip enters the house, loosening his tie, he looks around and raises one eyebrow toward Lauren. "So, where's your friend, the great white hunter? Have enough of you or our loving family after just one night?"

"No, it was just a quick visit like I mentioned yesterday and he has some business to attend to so he left earlier today."

"Humpf. Business to attend. Big meetings, huh? Real high-level, high finance business. I can imagine a board room with everybody sitting around with their pith helmets, khaki shorts and knee-length socks. They probably discuss safari mergers like combining the rhinos with the hippos and a partridge in a pear tree. Right?"

Phillip laughs out loud at what he thinks is clever on his part. Lauren scowls and rolls her eyes in feigned disgust.

Jane Ella isn't due to be home until late, if at all, so Lauren starts in on Phillip immediately . It's unusual she hasn't even thought about drinking this entire afternoon. Too much at stake. She has to stay focused and at the top of her game.

"Phillip, I was thinking today after Richard left. We do have some wonderful memories in spite of how we have our troubles. I know I've been very hateful to you and I drink too much and I was just thinking…"

Phillip turns and doesn't have a sarcastic or irritated look as usual. He looks hurt and for a second Lauren isn't sure what he is going to say or do. Little does she realize that Phillip's thespian skills are well-honed.

"You know, Lauren, I've been thinking some of the same things today and I really don't like living in a constant war zone. We have had some good times. And, after all these years, it's very difficult for me to hear what you said that perhaps Jane Ella is not my child. But you know what? I'll get past that. I'm going to assume that was fabricated to hurt me at the moment so I'm willing just to erase it unless you tell me it's true. She's been raised by us and I'm sure she's my child. Some of my bad habits come to her too naturally for it to have been otherwise. I suppose I was just feeling sorry for myself and I really need to mend the fences so to speak."

Lauren is speechless. What could have brought this on? But knowing Phillip as she does, she has a tiny suspicion it may be a game. Phillip rarely, if ever in his life, has feelings and now he's expressing them as if he's even partly to blame. Is it possible he could even be part human? Absolutely not! That would be totally out of character for Phillip.

The anger between Phillip and Lauren will not allow either to trust the possible motives and theatrics of the other. The tete-a-tete continues.

"Oh, Phillip, I feel so bad for what I said about you and Jane Ella. I feel bad for all of the arguing. I was thinking this afternoon. After hearing all the tales from Richard about safaris…well, I was thinking a trip like that could be a dream come true, to sort of get our family back to civility once again. I realize in a couple of years Jane Ella will be on her own. Even though she can't wait to be independent and get her hands on her trust, I would just feel so much better if we could have things at least somewhat peaceful. And who knows maybe a little "family" vacation would do us all good."

"Safari, huh? Huh. Very interesting." Phillip pauses as if he's thinking in overdrive and then he smiles, " You know, Lauren, you may have a point. We've never done anything like that and I'm sure your buddy can get us some literature on it. That might be just the thing. Listen, I have some things I must do this evening so I'm a little predisposed, but I promise to think about this and let's see if we can figure something out tomorrow. At least in general terms. I'll look over what's coming up on my schedule and see if I can block out a week or two. Then when we get some info on this stuff, we can make decisions one way or the other. Okay?"

"Sure. That's fine. I just think a safari would be so much fun and Jane Ella said this morning how exciting she'd find it as well. When's the last time you saw her excited about anything? So sure, just promise you'll think about it."

"I'll do it. Promise. And you say she was excited? Did she meet your friend? Knowing Jane Ella and her friends, it's probably the bronze, tan, great white hunter that has her excited. Of course I think he's a big phony buffoon and besides, he's old enough to be her grandpappy. But who knows? Maybe she likes older guys and then we'd have a son-in-law our own age. A safari for Jane Ella. I just can't picture her getting dust on her Prada's."

Phillip laughs at his attempted joke and then looks puzzled as he faces Lauren. "What's the matter, Lauren? You're not smiling. Was it the possibility of having your friend as a son-in-law or was it visualizing dust on your daughter's Prada's?"

Phillip's comments show he's not turned over a totally compassionate leaf and he's returned to usual role of being cutting and offensive. Probably a good thing he doesn't know how Jane Ella enjoyed making fun of his milky-white body. Each family member seems to find entertainment by injuring the others. But this moment has a very different feel to it. Lauren is excited from all the positive things that Phillip said earlier and the rest needs to be ignored. Lauren feels satisfaction even with some mistrust. Her plan is edging its way toward fulfillment.

Phillip couldn't be happier to put his ideas into focus. He's fascinated by the safari idea. Wait until he tells Murray it's not going to be Wollyworld but a safari.

The time flies by and Lauren spends an alcohol-free evening and about ten o'clock she decides to go to bed. She sees through Phillip's open bedroom door that he is still at his computer and deeply engrossed in his work so without disturbing him she goes to her bedroom.

There's a soft knock at Lauren's bedroom door and Jane Ella comes in and sits on the corner of her bed.

"Well, this is a surprise. I thought you weren't coming home until very late."

"Sorry, Mom. I decided to cut this evening short and get home sooner. I'd hoped to get home a little before now to help if you got the chance to talk to King Phillip about a safari."

Lauren sits up and smiles at Jane Ella. "Yes. I brought it up."

"Oh, come on. Don't make me beg."

"Okay then. Yes. Phillip is checking his very important, executive schedule and determining if the world economy can do without him for a week or two. And, I might add, he was encouraging about a safari. So, I think this might happen. And you're really on board with this. Right?"

"Gosh yes. I think it would be very adventurous. Very, very, very adventurous. And your Richard-friend, Mother…just how adventurous is he?"

"Now what do you mean by that? Are you planning something ulterior? Phillip even thought maybe you had eyes for Richard and I hate to do it but I'm going to remind you anyhow. Richard is old enough to be your…uh, er… father and he's a very close, personal friend so please don't act like you're trying to seduce him. You have no idea how the very thought of it is absolutely out of bounds. It's unnatural and makes me physically sick just to think about it."

Jane Ella stands up from the bed and shows a serious look.

"Nope. Enough said. Just the wild animals and bears or whatever they've got.

"Well, that's good, dear. We'll have fun."

100

Ya know, Mom…I forgot my wallet when I left home today and had to come back after it a little later and at first I thought the house was empty. Then I went into the kitchen and heard you out by the pool…"

"Uhhh." Lauren gasps but doesn't say anything else. Could Jane Ella have overheard their discussion about the motive of the safari plan?

"What's the matter, Mom? It was just a wallet. Why? Is there something else you were gonna say? About my desire for adventure? About Richard? Anything else, Mom? This afternoon? Out by the pool? You look like you've seen a ghost."

Lauren is speechless and just sits in bed as Jane Ella gives a little forced, sadistic laugh and starts for the door. Lauren wants to know if Jane Ella is just toying with her. Maybe she actually heard nothing.

"Well, did you find your purse? You should have said something. I'm sure we may have helped find it.."

"Oh, Mother! I'm sure we may have helped find it? C'mon. You can do better than that. Interesting discussion. That's all."

Jane Ella goes through the door and looks back over her shoulder, laughs and winks.

Lauren feels a total failure at the cat and mouse exchange. She still can't be sure what Jane Ella heard or didn't hear.   So it's probably safer to assume the worst.   What can be worse? She'll blow this whole thing. What if she blurts something out to Phillip? Lauren can't wait to tell Richard and see what he thinks about damage control.

About mid-morning the next day, Lauren is wondering how the conversation with Phillip will go this evening. He did promise to check over his work schedule and discuss it when he gets home.

 Lauren's deep in thought about Phillip, what Jane Ella knows, and how to not act nervous. She jumps when the phone rings. It's most likely Richard.

"Hello."

101

"Hi Lauren. I was hoping to catch you." To Lauren's surprise it's Phillip. He's probably already quashed the idea. Her heart is pounding.

His voice sounds strange but she realizes that's probably because she rarely talks to him during the day. He's always too busy.

"Okay. We were talking about a safari? Let's do it!"

Lauren squeals and then feels a rush of excitement.

"Oh, God, Phillip. Do you mean it? Just like that? Oh, Phillip I'm so happy. You said you'd think about it and check but this is so wonderful. Oh thank you, thank you, thank you."

"Take it easy. It's just a trip. But you guys want to do it and I thought what the heck. So I haven't got a lot of time at this instant but here's the deal. Set it up for two weeks total and the departure date must be between the fifteenth and the twentieth of next month. I've blocked three weeks starting as early as the fifteenth but I'll only take two weeks. So, It's important whenever we leave is not before the fifteenth or after the twentieth and regardless of the date we leave, the duration must be fourteen days or less. Got that?"

"Oh, of course. How wonderful. And I can go ahead and book it?"

"Yep. Set it up. I mean we need to see the details before we put any money on it but see what they've got and tentatively block it in. Once we've looked at the fine print and approve, then you can pay for it. Oh yeah, be *sure* wherever we stay has air conditioning, private bath, nothing that bites and high speed internet. I'm not going if they can't guarantee all those things. Otherwise if they can, reserve it…and first class on the air. Okay?"

"Got it."

"Okay. See you tonight."

"Okay, see you tonight." Phillip's already hung up.

But Lauren doesn't care at this point. She's speechless. He trusts her to do it all? But yet he's so Phillip-like. He's so exact about the departure date, no earlier than one date, no later departure than another exact date. Phillip obviously carved out a very specific time to be away from the company. Oh well, he probably has to plan how to keep Santa's elves busy in the workshop so Santa can sneak away for two weeks unnoticed. Whatever the case, he's doing it. This is just way too easy.

Lauren thinks how cruel and heartless she would be judged by plotting her husband's death and he's suddenly so trusting, agreeable and easy going. But there's enough mistrust on Lauren's part to doubt Phillip's sudden sincerity. The conviction to follow her plan is not diminished in the slightest. No matter what he does at this point, she only feels hate for Phillip. If he's mean and sarcastic, she hates him. If he's suddenly nice like today, she hates him for not being that way the last twenty years.

Deep inside, Lauren's mistrust cannot be shaken. Is he planning to dump her between now and then? Maybe he's being so agreeable to this vacation just to keep her occupied in excitement until he can spring some insidious plan. Then there's Jane Ella and if she suspects Lauren's plot against Phillip. Lauren keeps thinking what can go wrong and even though she's certain Richard would say she's over-thinking it, she still worries.

She feels like she'd be fine if she could just talk to Richard. She walks briskly across the room, picks up the phone and calls Richard. After what seems like several minutes, the hotel staff locates him at poolside and Lauren can hear women's voices close by. She's certain he's holding his stylish gigolo court at the Omni but his voice is reassuring just the same.

"Hello. Martin here."

"Hi Richard, it's me. I've got to talk to you. Everything, and I mean everything, is coming together so perfectly I can't believe it and…"

"Wait a sec. You must realize how distracting all the noise can be to start discussing anything important over the hotel phone. Can you come over for a while?"

"Yeah. That's probably a good idea just to talk in person. But I can't stay long. I've got some other things to tell you as well…about Jane Ella."

"What about her? Did she say something about me? Well…uh…as I said, let's just talk about it when you get here. Okay?"

" Oh sure. Talk when I see you. You're right, Richard. I'll tell you when I see you."

"Okay. I'm in room 1015. I'll just stay in the room."

"Hey. Now listen, Richard. I'm serious about not having too much time this afternoon."

Richard laughs, "Yeah. Yeah. See ya, Lauren, my old college buddy."

"Yep. See ya."

Partly out of concern and partly his cynical curiosity, Murray stops by Phillip's office. Murray can overhear Phillip beating up on some of the underlings and he loves it when Phillip is so aggressive with the staff. Murray sits in the outer office and when the brow-beaten executives leave, Murray accepts their nods of subservient homage to him as they file out and then he quickly taps on the door frame and enters Phillip's office.

"Hey, Sport! How are things today? Give up on Boston cityscape viewing or figured out a path to revenge?"

Hey, Murray. Good to see you. Actually I'm fine with everything. I just had to think it through. It may surprise you but it looks like Lauren, Jane Ella and I will take a couple of weeks and go on vacation."

"You must be sick. You don't do vacations. What will you do without dispensing the daily terror to the junior g-men down the hall? Did you see those guys when they came out? Mental shadows of their former selves. And you love this shit. Sure you weren't an SS in a former life?"

"Aw, come on. Quit flattering me. Here's the big surprise. Not only will I dutifully take my family on a vacation, it looks like we'll go on a safari, no less. To Africa. Can you believe it?"

"Jesus, Phillip! How could that even possibly be a vacation? You've got to be kidding with the wilds of Africa thing. Sure you didn't intend a few days to the Catskills. Even the Pocono's, God forbid. But a safari? What the fuck, Phillip? You've lost it."

"Yep. Safari."

"Well. I am shocked. But I guess whatever works for you. You and I always have a lot of irons in the fire and I just like to think you're feeling good about everything…ya know here and at home. I will say, you look tons better than the other day. Jesus…a safari?"

"Yeah. I'm good with everything now. And it will be entertaining. Very entertaining!   Guess what, Murray?"

"Guess what, Murray. Guess what? How can I guess what? Okay, I'll play…what, Phillip?"

"The safari honcho for our trip is the same guy who has been in **my** house porkin' **my** wife. So, we go on this family outing and I serve her up to him on a platter. Of course they think I'm too stupid to know what they're doing and I'm gonna catch them on video, audio…living color, my friend. I have enough cameras and techno crap to make this a real expose'. How totally violated I will feel. Then your job, Murray is to get this divorce off the shelf and done once and for all. I will deliver like Cecil B. Demille."

"Geez, Phillip! At least I feel better. You're still the same conniving, heartless son-of-a-bitch. A family vacation with jagged edges. I should never have suspected you could do a family vacation for real. You're going to travel halfway around the world to take pictures of your wife and this guy and then dump it by internet on Murray to magically do a perfect divorce. What the hell? Fine. Your plan will get you a divorce but I'm tellin you sport, she'll still get half. You are sick."

"Aaa. So what? I suspect they'll get right after it again, over there. Once I catch them I want you to help me cut my joint accounts with her so I can give her half of some ridiculously diminished assets and then she can screw her great white hunter all she wants. Of course, my secondary goal is she'll be screwing him in poverty. Figure out what I'll have to do Murray."

"Sure, I'm supposed to go before some judge and jeopardize everything we've done by trying to put your wife into poverty so you can sit on the sidelines and grin like a jackass eatin cockleburrs. Brilliant. But listen to me. She'll still get half, you deaf schmuck. Diminished assets. Ha! Just repeat after me...she'll get half, fifty percent, two quarters of my legit assets."

Within forty minutes Lauren is at Richard's room and sure enough he is presentable and actually in a serious mood. Lauren can't know Richard's worry about what Jane Ella may have said, but she launches into her tale of Phillip's call and how she's excited beyond belief but very, very suspicious.

"Look, Lauren, relax. Who cares what he's thinking? Just stick to our very, very simple plan. Step one is done. He agreed. Right?"

"Yes. He told me to set it all up."

"So, okay then. What was the thing about Jane...uh, your daughter?"

"Oh God. Richard. I think maybe she heard us talk about the plan for Phillip and she's just playing cat and mouse with me. Jane Ella came back for her wallet shortly after she'd left. She may have listened to us on the patio. I am so afraid she'll say something in front of Phillip and screw all this up."

"You really think she could hear us from the kitchen? Maybe not. That's what was so important? She may be just messin' with you. Maybe she never heard anything at all but just figured she'd see your reaction. You even said she does that sometimes. Ya know, she just floats a little innuendo to see if you take the bait and to me it seems she hooks you every time.

 Guilt has a way of popping out. My guess is she's fishing for a guilty reaction from you Lauren. And so what? I don't think she would gain anything by telling Phillip. Seems he's taken care of her quite well and she can just game you to death over what you refer to as a little cat and mouse. Look. Do the safari and get your problem solved. She goes out on her own. So what? Just stay focused on the job at hand. And you've been amazingly successful up to now. Just keep it up."

"Whew. I guess I just needed to hear it again. I make mountains out of molehills sometimes. So you think I shouldn't worry about Jane Ella and just act like I have no idea?"

"Yep. Poker face, Lauren. Practice your poker face. With what will play out over the next few months the use of a good poker face to her fishing questions will probably serve you well."

"Okay. I will practice. It's just I get so nervous about all the details."

107

"I'll call our booking company and get the wheels in motion. Our company can set up the air travel as well. You want me to line that up, too?"

"Yes. Everything. Air needs to be first class and the fewer stops the better. I need to be sure about the accommodations at the camp as well. Phillip said it was a no-go unless there was air conditioning, private bath, and high speed internet. "

"Well, at least he wasn't making a fuss about what you called critters…"

Lauren starts laughing, "Oh, God, Richard. He did say that, too. You see how predictable he is?"

"I'll get it all set. Then you pay for it and that will be step two. The hard part will be waiting for the day of travel. But once that day arrives and you're all in camp, everything is in place. We'll do a few of the little daily excursions and see what he likes and doesn't like and then I'll take it from there. You won't even realize how smooth and painless everything will be…at least painless for you and me."

"Oh, stop making jokes about it , Richard. This is serious and I just want it done without a hint of suspicion. You already said the police, insurance companies and others will look at this through a microscope."

"Of course I know. Relax. I told you how different it is where my office is located. I've not seen a single investigator in a three piece suit out stomping around with the lions, rhinos and the black mambas. Nope. They begin to figure it's likely one person already lost to the wild, no need for themselves to meet the same fate. So they leave very satisfied that they've done all they need to do. But it's the third-degree questioning of all of us afterward that's the critical part. Just have to be mentally strong. But for now, just relax. This will be done in a month or so. You'll be a very, very rich lady and I hope I can be your very close friend, or prince or whatever you'd like me to be."

"Richard, what would I do without you? You're the only person in the world I trust. You've always had a special place in my life. Surely you must know." Tears roll down Lauren's cheeks.

"Yeah. Hey. Hey. Dry those eyes. Everything's fine. We've always had a special sort of thing. Haven't we? So, okay, I'll call you with the trip details and we'll be all set. So, until then, my dear, do we have time for a little of Richard's favorite game?"

"No, not this afternoon. I'm wound up like a spring and I just need to get home, get settled down and get calm again. Maybe tomorrow? Until then, I'm sure a resourceful guy like you can take the situation in hand."

"Uh, no thank you. I'll wait for tomorrow. I'm not one for occupying myself in that department."

CHAPTER 25

EXTORTION

The next day Lauren is straightening the guest room from Richard's visit, totally preoccupied about the trip and the excitement of the expected future -freedom from Phillip. Being busy helps a lot. Jane Ella pokes her head into the open doorway and smiles an unusual smile at Lauren.

"Hello, dear. You surprised me. I thought I'd just get this room straightened a bit before the house cleaners come on Friday."

"Sure, Mom. Never know what might be left behind, do you?"

"What do you mean? It's just a bedroom and bath for heaven's sakes. Richard was only here one night and he travels light. That can't be too exciting."

"Oh, if only these walls could talk."

"Okay. What is it you are trying to imply or say? About Richard…or me?"

"Oh, nothing in particular. I just hope you don't miss our safari guide too much until we can get to Africa."

Lauren looks very annoyed at Jane Ella. This is exactly what Richard was talking about-a fishing trip by Jane Ella. Lauren's prepared this time and she's not about to play.

"Well, Jane Ella I suppose you have your dirty little fantasies about my friend spending one night. I'd hate to think how you'd react if I made comments about your friends or where you go and what you do. I enjoyed seeing Richard and catching up on old times."

Lauren thinks that should clip off further comments.

"You're right, Mom."

Finally a little relief from the insinuations thinks Lauren.

Jane Ella turns slowly and starts to walk away, "Catching up on old times sure did include a lot of secretive talk about Phillip on the safari. But who knows? Guess that's what you call catching up from those old college days, huh?"

"Listen, you smart ass! I don't know what you think you heard but you're wrong. I've had it with your little snide remarks and comments. Maybe you're trying to make me angry to see what I'll do? Well, Janey-girl you're about to find out and it probably won't be very pretty. So I'll advise you…shut your filthy mouth and get out of my sight."

Unfortunately for Lauren, Jane Ella has experience in family scraps and knows all too well how to hold her own.

"Is that supposed to be a threat? Woooooo! Pretty scary. Just remember who holds the cards. C'mon, you played cards before you took up drinking. Surely you remember to watch out for the trump cards. Well, maybe I have 'em all. So, Mommy-Dearest, you may want to be a little more polite."

"Get out of my sight!"

Lauren kicks the door shut behind Jane Ella and returns to the bed, flopping face down across it. She feels like her head will explode. Maybe it's not too early for just one little glass of vodka. Maybe that will take the edge off before Phillip comes home. Lauren imagines Jane Ella trying to make Lauren dance to her tunes. Surely she has nothing to gain by telling Phillip of a plot that's not supposed to be a plot.

Lauren takes a deep breath. "I can play the game, whatever it takes. "

Maybe she'll act a little intimidated so Jane Ella stays entertained but most importantly, Jane Ella must stay away from Phillip. This only has to play out for a month and then things will change dramatically toward perfection.

Later that evening Phillip is home and relaxing with a drink. Lauren walks into the family room.

"Good day for you?"

"Yes, Phillip. It has been a good day. I am particularly excited about the trip and I can't wait to get the details of the camp and accommodations. The day trips into the bush sound wonderful."

"How would I know? I haven't *seen* anything tangible about all this. I only hear it from you, who heard it from your broken-down buddy who may or may not know what he's even talking about. I trust you didn't commit any money to all this until we've had a chance to look at the details."

Lauren is shocked. Her stomach feels like it falls to the floor. This certainly isn't starting well. "Of course not. We should have all the brochures within the next day or so and then we can review the details."

Lauren looks away from Phillip and rolls her eyes as she secretly crosses her fingers in hope. First Jane Ella with her comments and now Phillip sounds like maybe he isn't as sure about the trip as he seemed earlier. She knows she simply can't let this opportunity unravel this easily. But perhaps now is the time to leave it alone for the evening.

Phillip continues, "Yeah. We'll have to look at everything very carefully. I've got my time blocked for being away for two weeks out of a three-week window but that's as far as I'm committing at this point. If it doesn't pan out, then it doesn't pan out. I can cancel the time off and try to earn a dollar or two."

Lauren feels like screaming. He's starting to figure out a way to get out of this and there goes her freedom up in smoke. If only she could see Richard right now. But he's probably enjoying his carefree time at the

112

Omni, compliments of Lauren, and though Phillip has no idea, compliments of Phillip as well.

Jane Ella comes walking into the family room and flops down on a sofa.

"Am I missing some quality family time?"

Phillip seems amused and smiles as if appreciative of the question, "I don't think you miss much of anything. Ear to the ground. Voyeur. Lurking about the halls of mystery with an endless cascade of wise-ass sarcasm. That's my Jane Ella. Just beating on any hornets' nest in hopes of some stinging entertainment."

"Daddy, you have such a way with words. But as always, I have no idea what you mean…and though I try really hard to care about what you say, I simply don't care. Your insulting remarks fall upon deaf ears."

Lauren knows this sort of banter can't lead to anything but an entire evening of hostility and arguments. Her worst nightmare. Jane Ella can't be trusted. Her little barbs of sarcasm with Phillip might lead to the total undoing of Lauren's plans.

"Jane Ella, will you help me get something on the table for a quick dinner? I would really appreciate it."

"Sure. I can do more than you think, Mother. I can be quite the domestic. But I hope my future will not depend on my culinary skills. But sure, I'll help. What do you want me to do?"

"Well, let's go see what we can get together. You ready to eat something, Phillip? I'll give you a shout when we're ready."

"Fine."

Lauren and Jane Ella get to the kitchen and Lauren feels like at least a lit fuse has been temporarily separated from a stick of dynamite. Just to separate Phillip and Jane Ella will hopefully be enough to stop the momentum of a beginning argument. The last thing Lauren needs tonight is to irritate Phillip.

"Jane Ella, you do want to go on this trip, don't you?"

"Actually, I really, really do want to go. I've been thinking about it and I've never done anything like this. I probably will never do anything like this more than once but yes, Mother, I'm really looking forward to it."

"Well, you know how irritable and unpredictable your dad is about being away from his work and you want to go on this trip…and I want to go on this trip…so when things move too fast or he feels like he's not in total control …well, I just don't want him to spoil all this. What I'm trying to say is please don't banter with him or set me up to look bad right now."

"I wasn't aware that I was doing that. Maybe I was bantering King Phillip, but I don't have to do anything at all to make you look bad. You do enough of that without any help."

"Look, Jane Ella. You've said some things in the last day or so that insinuate I may have some insidious or off-color relationship with Richard. That's not the case at all but even if you imagine something or just want to antagonize me…well, this is not the time to rub that under Phillip's nose."

"Rub it under his nose? I'm not the one who told him he may not be my father…"

"I know what I said and I've already told him it wasn't true and I just said it in a moment of anger. He understands. In fact he was quite understanding about it when I apologized. And I owe you an apology as well."

"So none of that was true? You just said it to stick it to dear old Dad? Well, how about that? And you had me convinced. But what's the harm in a little white lie if it serves a higher purpose and is believable? Right?"

"Look. I'm sorry I said that and I'm sorry for a lot of things I've said. But it seems at least on the surface we have a peaceful co-existence going right now and I don't want to spoil that. So if you really want to go on this trip like you say you do, then help me out here. Okay?"

"Look, Mommy-Dearest. Just so you know. In the guest room and by the pool...I heard what I heard. As long as we're having an honesty session right now, I'll be honest with you. I know you and Richard are cooking up some plan and I'm sure it will have shocking results and you and your Richard are not even being clever about your romping around. The first night he was here I came home late and as I drove in by the garage, I noticed the light was on in the bath of the spare room. I thought it was on by accident and I'd be a good girl and turn it out. Well, I heard everything going on in there and your voice was very distinct. You want some details? Lots of talk of fantasies and other stuff. Boy, you were really buttering him up. Dump Phillip? Who knows? But definitely some plans with Richard. So, now you know. You and Richard are just *friends*. Friends my ass! That's one lie that won't go far with me. It doesn't pass the believability test. I *know* the truth. If you want me to be silent, I will. But believe me I know. So don't be pushing your denials at me. You can play it for Phillip all you want but remember...*I know!*"

Lauren stands and looks at Jane Ella in fear. She feels that sick feeling again. There are no words that can fix this or play like she doesn't know.

"I...I...uh..."

"Surprised are you? Just remember, Mother. *I know.* I hold all the aces of trump. I've always believed that you are a dangerous risk to me when it comes to *my* trust money. All it takes is for Phillip to go ballistic over something stupid caused by you and for him to revoke the trust. Like your little jab about him not being my father. That could have done it. So I have to worry about that right up until the day I turn twenty-five. After I get the money that's rightfully mine, then I'm home free. So, I'm not going to let anything get in the way of *me* getting that money. Least of all, you. Got it? Understand?"

115

"Jane Ella, I'm still your mother and I want you to have the very best, including that trust. Neither Phillip nor I would revoke that. Even if Phillip is furious with me, he won't take it out on you. So, I won't screw anything up for you as you say."

"Well, me knowing about you and Richard is just the insurance I need so you not only won't intentionally goof it up but that you *can't* screw it up for me. And, Mother Dear, since I hold all the cards, if I need your help with something I feel certain that I can count on your full assistance. Now *that's* insurance! And now that you say you've cleared up the mystery about my parentage, I *can* use your enthusiastic help for my own personal needs or as you whisper to Richard, 'fantasies'. I call them greener pastures and Mother, you are now my ticket to greener pastures."

"What's that supposed to mean? Blackmail? You think you can blackmail me? Don't ever threaten me or you'll be very, very sorry!"

"I'll be sorry? I'll be sorry? Oh, I think you have it all backwards. And me threaten you? What's to threaten? Let's see what happened. When you said the other night I wasn't his daughter, I almost died. I figured if Phillip really believed I'm not his daughter, then he doesn't need to be quite so generous, maybe not generous at all. I've been scared to death ever since you said that. So, I'm glad you say you repaired that little blunder. But what if Phillip throws you out the door and then divorces you at some future date for your obvious screwin' around right here in his own house? You're out in the cold. Phillip would see to that. And I'll just bet you know that, too. Not my fault what you've done or that my trust should be at risk for what you've been doing. So threaten you? I don't have to. The truth is just hanging over you like a fifty ton rock waiting to fall. I intend to win, no matter what. But you? You have a glimmer of a chance only if that rock doesn't fall but it will never go away as long as I know what happened."

"You little bitch! I can't believe the hate you have for me. You don't just want the money. You seem very pleased to be able to hurt me with no more emotion than flipping a switch on or off."

116

"Well, that's not all. I really would like to go on a safari. And next month? Perfecto! What a way to celebrate my twenty-second!

"I can't believe this. You think you're so smart having something Phillip would believe about me. Most children would already be away from home, working, but not you. Hang around to make trouble."

"Now that I think of it, this is a good time for you to see what you can do to make my life a little more comfortable, get me out of the house and who knows…remove me as a threat to you. Let's say since it's so close to my birthday …let's say you were to convince Phillip to add a nice birthday bonus."

"You must be out of your mind! Me ask Phillip for a pile of money for your birthday? That's not going to happen. I won't do it and even if I did he'd dismiss that before the question was finished. That's ridiculous."

"That's not what I'm even talking about. Just listen, Mother. You can do this. What if you convince Phillip to simply change my trust so I have full access on my twenty second birthday instead of waiting three more years until I'm an old maid of twenty-five? Then we'll be on the safari, celebrate my birthday, and come home. But the story doesn't end there. We'll come home, I'll sign some papers, pack and off I go on my own. No more boarding schools to keep me out of your way. It's all up to me at that point. Seems pretty nice for everybody. You know, Mom, I think you can make that birthday change happen if you really put your mind to it. And then I'll be out of your hair."

"Jane Ella! This is blackmail and there's no way he'll do that. I can't believe you even suggest such a ridiculous scheme."

"It's not a scheme. It's worth a try, Mother. You need to make a very, very energetic effort to get it done the way I want. What's the worst that can happen to me? You fail and I still get all the money that's currently in the trust. You just have to live with me knowing our little secret for three more years. If you're successful…which I think you can be…well, then you and I are both free. Now you, Mom are in a tough spot. If I don't think you try hard enough, I just make sure

117

Phillip knows what's been going on and your involvement and plot with Richard…and you'll be out on your ass with nothing, zero, nada, zilch. And since I would be the loving daughter who couldn't stand seeing my father suffer from an unfaithful wife, I'd be okay on the trust thing. I'd just have to wait three years until I turn twenty-five. That's seems so unnecessary, and what a horrible prospect for you."

"You wouldn't dare. You don't know what you're talking about. You're just guessing. And a plot? What plot are you trying to make up?"

Lauren is so frightened she's about to throw up.

"What plot? Well, from what I heard in the bedroom, you're planning at some point to dump Phillip for Richard. Probably just trying to get a trust of your own setup or something. Who knows? Not my concern. But please just remember who holds all the cards in this game."

Lauren and Jane Ella stand and glare at each other. The cloud of fear, greed, power and anger is so thick it fills the room like an evil fog. It's amazing Phillip can even see across the room as he enters the kitchen.

"Well, did you two get something going for dinner or are you just yapping."

"I don't feel very well. I think I'm going to lie down for a while. I'm sure Jane Ella will get something together. I don't think she needs my help."

Lauren goes to her bedroom, shuts the door and throws herself on the bed. How can this be so bad, so quickly. If only she could talk to Richard. He'd be able to figure out how to get out of all this.

CHAPTER 26
TRIP PLANS

The tentative reservations are in place for the safari and within a couple of days a Fedex truck rumbles up the Pittman's street, its unmistakable orange, blue and white markings, its throaty engine surges, idles, and squeaks as the truck turns into their circle drive, brakes squeeling to a halt. All to announce the safari brochures are delivered! Lauren unpacks the shipping box and is surprised at the extensive quantity of printed materials and DVD's. She sorts through it all and strategically stacks everything on a coffee table in the living room closest to the foyer.

"Wow! An information jackpot! Phillip will love this!"

Phillip arrives home and he immediately notices the brochures laying on the coffee table. He pauses, loosens his tie and smiles a big unusual toothy smile.

"Great. Everything is here. I'm anxious to see it all and decide on this."

Phillip gets a drink, sits down on a sofa surrounded by all the brochures. After a few glances and flipping of pages he looks over the top of his glasses at Lauren.

"Looks perfect to me. All the accommodations at the camp seem fine and I would imagine you can get two rooms and good airline reservations...so let's do this trip. I just must be sure we leave after the fifteenth and confine all the traveling and vacation time to two weeks within the specific window I gave you. I have to be certain that's understood. We're clear on that. Right?"

"Absolutely. The dates I understand very well and I already checked the times with the travel company. Now I'll just double-check that they can do everything…exactly the way you need.   I'm glad you're pleased with all this, Phillip. I'll get everything fixed up tomorrow."

"Okay and I need to know details. And I mean all details."

"That's fine. I'm sure if what you require isn't in all this information we just received, I'm sure I can call and get it quickly. Just let me know."

"I need to be sure I'm good with all the smallest details. Maybe there are maps in all this stuff that What's-His-Face sent. Looks like somebody cleaned out their brochure closet thinking quantity is more godly than quality. But I'm fine with you finalizing the trip. I don't really care about reading all this crap. Just need answers to my personal specific questions."

 Lauren removes her glasses and nods her understanding toward Phillip while masking total shock that he trusts her with finalizing the trip.

"Suit yourself, Phillip. You're always such a details-person, you usually insist on doing things like this. But that's fine, as long as you're satisfied."

"Yeah. I've seen enough pictures of the great white hunters and huntresses. I'm sure it's fine. Book 'em Dan'l!"

Lauren is shocked by Phillip's unusual reactions to this entire scenario- agreeing to a safari, not too many devil's advocate questions, trusting her to take care of things. Very unusual! He's always such a control- freak and after expressing an interest in details, he doesn't seem interested in the brochures or the details of the rooms or the expeditions once they're there.   He's only checked and double-checked the departure date and the "exact location" of the camp.

Jane Ella comes into the room while Lauren and Phillip are there. She casts a condescending look at Lauren. Then she pauses and looks back and forth at both Lauren and Phillip, judging the harmony level as if holding a wet finger in the wind.

"Well, have you two got this all figured out? I'm really looking forward to this so let's not screw it up or back out. And besides I'll need all new clothes and luggage appropriate for this first-class safari."

Neither Phillip nor Lauren say anything to Jane Ella's comment and she seems satisfied enough at their tacit approval so she shrugs her shoulders and saunters out of the living room. Lauren watches in disgust as Jane Ella walks away, knowing she would have stayed longer had a typical Pittman fight been brewing.

The next day Lauren calls the Omni hoping to arrange a meeting with Richard, talk through the blackmail threats from Jane Ella and finalize the plans.

"Sorry, Miss. Mr. Martin checked out around nine-thirty this morning."

"Well, do you happen to know his destination by any chance?"

"No, I'm sorry. I wasn't actually the clerk who checked Mr. Martin out. "

"Oh, that's okay. Bye."

Checked out of the hotel? Lauren sinks heavily into a chair next to the phone. She certainly doesn't want to be abandoned in this mess, least of all by Richard. Why would he have left so soon without letting her know?

The phone rings.

"Hello."

"Hello gorgeous."

"Richard! Where are you? I just tried to reach you at the Omni and they said you were gone. What's going on with you?"

"That's why I called, Lauren. I thought I'd best not hang out for too long at the same hotel. You were concerned about Jane Ella being suspicious. I'm also concerned about Phillip so I moved to a different hotel, the Boston Harbor. You know where it is?"

"Sure, I know where it is."

"Would you like to come and see me in my nice clean, luxurious room overlooking the harbor?"

"You certainly have good taste in hotels, Richard. What's the room number? I'll be there as soon as I shower and change clothes."

"Room 1944 and don't dally at home. I've got some things I have to attend to later.

"Great! I won't dally, as you call it. See you in a bit. By the way, I'm showering before I leave home to save time when I get there to see you. Not a dally. Just a shower and so, please be fresh as a daisy, yourself. Without dallying of course. Bye- bye, Deary."

Lauren hurries to get ready and she gets to Richard's hotel a little after noon. Her heart beats quickly as she lightly knocks on Room 1944. Richard opens the door, gently takes her by the arm and in near-formal fashion escorts her into his room.

"Gee. That was a polite way to drag me into your lair. C'mon, Caveman, do what you will. I'm defenseless. You don't know how I've missed you...how I've needed you."

"I know what you mean, Lauren."

Richard seems to want to hold the loose embrace but Lauren is excited and wants to make love.

As she begins to guide Richard toward the bed, he hesitates and pulls with a little resistance to just stay standing.

"Well, what's the matter? I thought you'd want to...you know?"

"I'm sorry, Lauren. Maybe it's a little stress. No worry, just a lot going on. I know I have to return to Botswana very soon and that alone causes mixed feelings as I'm sure you understand. I just don't

122

particularly feel like doing anything…ya know…intimacy… right now. I probably can, but you know…I just really don't feel much like it at the moment."

"Listen, buddy. We've known each other's ins and outs for so long, it's fine. Take your time. Here, let me see if I can help."

She grabs the front of Richard's pants and playfully massages him as she again kisses him. It seems to have little effect on Richard's excitement level.

"Lauren… I just can't right now. I just don't think I can. I'm sure it's very temporary and it's certainly not you. I'm sorry but I'm sure you know me well enough to know I wouldn't refuse you if I could help it."

"Well, I should hope so. I can be very patient so let's just take our time and see what happens. Come on now. Let's see my guy perform."

Richard pulls away and turns his back.

"Lauren… come on… I just can't today. I'm stressed. I'm tired. Look. I love being with you but it just isn't going to happen right now."

'Well, okay. Let's just go over and sit down. I really didn't mean to press you into something you don't want to do."

"Don't say that. You make it sound like I-I…it's nothing really. I just told you, though, I'm stressed and honestly, I'm tired."

"Well, Richard. I guess I've just never even imagined you this way…and I don't mean this way… like there's something wrong or anything. But, are you sure you're okay? I mean I'm not complaining but I think you're getting short-changed, big guy. I want a return match to show you what I can do."

"Oh, Lauren. I'm sorry. How wonderful it is when we…ya know like old times? There's just something so special about it. A real expression of feelings. "

"Richard, you don't' need to say you're sorry to me. Not after what we've had in the past and what we are *planning* to have in the very near future. Come here for now and just lay in my arms."

They lay on the bed and relax in each other's arms. Several minutes pass in silence.

"You okay, Lauren?"

"Richard, I can't stand to be away from you. There's been some of the most unbelievable things lately. I feel like there are things that happen and I can't deal with them unless I can talk to you. I think that's what real love is all about, Richard."

"I'm sure you're right and of course I guess I've always known it but there's a practical side to things, too. I mean, you're married and have been for twenty years. You're also taken care of very, very well financially. We're not getting any younger either but maybe when your plans are complete…who knows, Lauren? I just feel like my head is swimming today.

"Oh, God. Richard, this frightens me. Usually you calmly say all the right words that make me feel so safe, like there's not a thing in the world to worry about. But, it's okay. I understand, baby. The sooner I get completely free of the mess I'm in, the better off I'll be. The better off *we'll* be."

"Okay, Lauren, I'm putting on my broad shoulders. Okay, I've got them on. Go ahead and tell Richard what's been going on?"

"For starters, Jane Ella isn't bluffing me or just fishing for a guilty look. She actually *knows* a lot. She heard us the very first night you stayed at our house, the bedroom conversation about my fantasy. I can't be too sure how clearly she heard or exactly how much but it's enough that it scares me to death."

"Hmm. Okay. Of course that's not good but you aren't certain of how much or what exactly she heard? Seems obvious she heard us romping on the bed but not sure of any details about our talking?"

124

"Right, I can't be sure. I just listened to her without trying to act any guiltier than I am. And then she heard our conversation when we were by the pool. She isn't guessing about that either."

"Honestly, I find that sort of strange, Lauren. From what you describe Jane Ella isn't horrified about us making love nor is she shocked by whatever she may guess about our plans. It's like she wants to absorb the details for use as leverage more than being emotionally upset by any of it."

"Well, for me the Coup de Grace is that she cornered me in the kitchen and threatened to blackmail me with what she heard and saw. I can't believe it! My own daughter. Blackmail. And I have to tell you, she's thought this through and she's not afraid to do whatever she has to do to get exactly what she wants."

"Yeah. I'm sure it's a disappointment about her sort of pressuring you to do something for her, but to think she watched our whole escapade. Weird."

"Richard. Did you not hear what I just said? She's not being weird or her usual pain in the ass self. She's blackmailing me! From your expression I don't think you understood what I said. She's actually blackmailing me."

"Oh, I heard, Lauren. I don't think there's anything really to actually fear with the blackmail thing. And I guess…and I'm not trying to be mean but there are a few kinks in that little gal of yours."

"Richard! My little gal, huh? I thought you'd think a little differently of her by now…a little like a …oh never mind. I think she was getting turned on by you. So, I know you were being a little sarcastic about the jealousy of my treatment, but you may not be too far off the mark."

"You think so?"

"Yes, I certainly do. And that scares me…and it should scare you as well. Remember, you promised me a while back you'd be careful of her. I want you to promise me, Richard. You just can't encourage her in any way or let her tease you into anything sexual. That would be sick…twisted…sick. You know how sick that would be, don't you?"

"Yeah. Yeah. I'm not going there. Let's talk about what she wants. But I guess I do have a little different take on it than you. I think Jane Ella is spoiled and has never heard the word no in regards to anything she wants. Would that be pretty close to correct?"

"Of course. I'm sure it is. I'd rather give in to her than have to listen to her. In younger years, she pitched screaming fits, but later it was the moaning and groaning for days on end. Why do you think I was so happy when she was away at boarding schools?"

"Fine. The way I see it, she's just a little older now and has a different technique for getting what she wants. I really suspect down deep she isn't interested in your consequences or telling Phillip on us, or perpetual blackmail, or even seducing me as you may think. I believe she just wants what she wants and thinks this is the way to get it without throwing tantrums at age twenty-one . This isn't going to turn into some sort of mysterious intrigue with boiled pet rabbits or notes stuck to a door with a dagger. I think it's just another form of tantrum…she's just a little older now. She wants to get her hands on her money three years early and this is a new form of pitching a tantrum to get it. At least that's my take."

"Well, I have no idea how Phillip will even react to such an idea and I can't imagine how to justify it."

"You just did a couple of minutes ago. Just tell Phillip she's all grown up and wants to be gone…along with her inheritance or trust or whatever it is. Tell him he knows what a pain in the ass she can be and there aren't any more boarding schools to avoid tantrums. Maybe it would be a nice thing to just let her have the money at this upcoming birthday and let her move on in her life."

"Richard, you're a genius. I have been so stressed over this but you may be right. It's at least worth a try. And you think it won't be just one demand after another with Jane Ella?"

126

"Well, who can be sure? But I think once she's got her six and a half million she'll stay occupied for a long, long time."

Lauren pulls back a little from Richard, pauses but then forces a smile as if she's not reacting to his comments. First, that he would just casually talk about Jane Ella's trust account as the reason for her tantrum blackmail. Then he says a dollar figure about the account. How could he possibly know about this? But she tries to quickly change the subject rather than act suspicious.

"You may be right. If I bring up to Phillip how we can have a bit more peace and quiet with Jane Ella happy at least it's worth a try. Well, now I'm excited about getting everything on the trip confirmed and guaranteed. Just think. Phillip on safari. Jane Ella on her own. In other words, both of them gone out of my life. My future actually may have a glimmer of freedom."

"Yeah, Lauren, honey. I'm sure everything will work out in the long term."

"By the way, Richard, regarding the trip to Africa, I want to confirm all the flights, the rooms and the dates. How's the quickest way I can go about that?"

"I'll tell you the quickest way. Let's call Virginia at my company's VIP travel section and just see what's cooking."

Richard calls the travel department and puts Lauren on the phone with Virginia Wilson in the VIP Concierge Department. They go through the details of dates, times, accommodations. There are pauses while Virginia is checking all details.

"Well, that sounds just marvelous, Virginia. And yes our passports are up to date. I guess I'll just be on pins and needles until we get all the actual travel documents. Then I'll be able to relax a little."

There's a pause as Lauren listens and smiles.

"Oh. You can do that so quickly? That will be wonderful. Yes I'll stay home tomorrow so I can sign for them.

Lauren listens to Virginia's instructions.

"And then all we have to do is return the Personal Information Sheets with the passport info, social security numbers and that sort of stuff?"

Lauren listens again.

"Okay, that all sounds marvelous. And I'll call you, Virginia, as soon as we are ready to overnight our information back to you."

Lauren listens again and then closes the call, "Okay then. Thanks and bye now."

Lauren puts the phone back on the cradle and smiles at Richard.

"Virginia is printing all the documents, itinerary, luggage tags, tickets, everything right now and she's sending it to our house guaranteed overnight delivery so I'll have it tomorrow. She's even arranging a limo to pick us up at home to get to Logan Airport and the same for when we return after vacation. Isn't that wonderful?"

'See, I told you. That's all it takes. Now what else are you stressing about?"

"Actually, I think I'm okay. Thanks for everything, Richard. I wish I could help with your stress as quickly as you deal with mine. You have a way of always making everything better and I suppose part of it's because I guess I trust you. That helps a lot."

"Wow. Talk about make me feel inadequate! You *guess* you trust me? I was hoping what we had is a little stronger than a possibility that you trust me. "

"Of course it is, silly."

"Well, I really am glad you came by. I'm glad when we can talk. I hope our talks make you feel a little more confident about everything."

"Of course it does. But I guess I really should scoot. I know you're tired and need a little time. I am so excited about getting everything tomorrow and I'll see what sort of mood Phillip's in when he comes home tonight. I may even suggest the thing about Jane Ella to him tonight. Yep. I'm feelin' pretty darn good at this moment."

Lauren and Richard embrace and while she fully expects Richard to protest her departure, he seems resigned to it and casually assists her out the door of his room. Lauren shrugs as she returns to her car. Maybe Richard simply needs some time to himself. Lauren really expected for him to play the little "oh please don't go" game but Richard didn't do that at all.

Soon Lauren is pulling into her driveway at home, heading toward the garage and the garage door begins to open before she can press the button on her car display panel. Jane Ella backs out of the garage. When Jane Ella sees Lauren waiting to pull in, she pauses beside Lauren's car. Both bring their car windows down. Lauren smiles. Jane Ella lifts her sunglasses to her forehead and smiles broadly as if very happy and excited.

" Just so you know, we should get all the travel documents and tickets tomorrow, Jane Ella. Isn't that exciting? We'll be going to Africa in just a couple of weeks."

"That is exciting. By the way and in case you care, I'm going out now and I won't be home tonight."

"Oh. Okay. Of course. What are you planning to do this evening?"

"Nothing too much. I'm planning on staying over at, uh… Erin's tonight, so see you tomorrow."

Even Jane Ella looks happy to be on her way. Lauren tries to get out and about quite a bit but she can't imagine how Jane Ella can find so many places to always be away from home, morning until night, most nights returning home, but the last few days she's been spending the night with Erin. Today she seems almost in a hurry to leave. Lauren thinks it's odd because Jane Ella's very seldom in a hurry to do anything.

As Lauren pulls into the garage, shuts off the car and sits there wondering why this house always brings her mood, confidence and

129

feelings down to a low point. She was feeling so good a short while ago with Richard but now there's a foreboding feeling. Maybe it's Richard not being in the mood for sex today. Maybe it's Richard not protesting for her to stay longer today. More likely it's the comment Richard made about Jane Ella's trust being six and a half million dollars. Lauren has never mentioned that and it's not likely it's a wild guess. Lauren knows the trust is something over five million but only Phillip, and perhaps Jane Ella, would know a more precise amount. Phillip for sure didn't discuss the amount with Richard. Does Jane Ella have private contact with Richard where they discuss money?

Lauren knows down deep inside that something is badly flawed in all these little tidbits. Would Richard betray her? He certainly seems preoccupied this afternoon. First he couldn't or wouldn't have sex. Then he hurried her out of the room. Too tired! What if he has a date set up with someone else he's met? Surely Richard wouldn't be that unfaithful. Lauren gasps out loud at the very thought of Jane Ella possibly on her way to rendezvous with Richard. She quickly suppresses that from her mind. That's just too horrible to even consider. But Lauren has a difficult time shaking the doubts and insecurities she's feeling. There have to be perfectly logical explanations and she trusts Richard more than anyone else, but even so, she can't trust Richard one-hundred percent.

The day ends without fanfare. Phillip comes home but retires almost immediately to work in his room and he laughs," I have very, very , very important plans to be sure I have everything buttoned up at work so I can truly take time off on this most marvelous family vacation."

Jane Ella's gone for the night so Lauren drinks a little more than anticipated and soon finds the night is gone and she awakens in her bedroom the next morning. She didn't even remove her clothes last night and already she must recuperate to face another stressful day. As she dresses she whispers to her image in the mirror, "Why can't this just get over?"

The Fed-Ex truck appears mid-morning , bringing the documents as scheduled and Lauren lays them all out on the dining room table. Jane Ella comes home and joins Lauren in the dining room.

"Oh, great! Everything came just like they said, huh? Phillip will be impressed, Mom. You've really done a good job putting all this together. And I'm sorry for our words the other day. I know I was pretty hard but come on, I know you can talk to Phillip. I can be gone so quick it will make your head swim. That's all I want. No more tantrums about what I want, I'll have everything I want. So try, pleeeez."

Lauren is surprised by Jane Ella's sudden change of personality toward her today. From insidious blackmailer the other evening to begging daughter today. Lauren is not going to question anything that's positive, no matter how short-lived it may be. But the words Jane Ella chose..."tantrums". That's the exact word Richard repeatedly used as he and Lauren were talking yesterday and it's neither a term Lauren ever personally applied to Jane Ella nor a term Jane Ella ever applied to herself. The stress and fear return as a knot in Lauren's stomach.

"I don't want you to feel like you have to leave home, Jane Ella but I understand how you want your independence and how important that money is to your freedom. I don't see any reason why you should have to wait another three years and I promise I'll talk to Phillip about it. But please leave that discussion to me. Okay? And...please...stop with the blackmail threats."

"Sure, Mom. I can hardly wait to see Phillip start looking through all this paperwork about the trip. I'm going to take a shower and change clothes."

"Did you and Erin have a good time? You look tired. Surely you two didn't go biking or play tennis or anything athletic...did you?"

"What? ...Oh yeah. It was fine. And no, we didn't play tennis. We were up really late. That's all."

Lauren can't rid herself of the gnawing feeling that Richard is somehow secretly involved with Jane Ella She frowns and says aloud, "I'm missing a piece of the puzzle and I don't even know what the puzzle is."

131

Soon Phillip arrives home and as he gets his evening cocktail he sees everything on the dining room table.

"Oh man! This looks terrific. Let me see these tickets. Yep. Leave on the sixteenth and return on the twenty-ninth. Perfect. Just perfect. I also see the rooms have Wi-Fi and there's Wi-Fi even to the edges of the camp. Perfect. Lauren, you did a great job. This will be a vacation to beat all vacations!"

"Wow. When you're excited you talk even like the rest of us in the lower world. I'm glad you like it. Jane Ella saw it earlier and she was very happy as well."

"Okay for you. I'll practice my role of being more communicative so as we gaze upon the flora and fauna I can ooooh and aaah alongside all the lame-brain touristas with whom we'll probably be forcibly and sadistically compressed in some rusty jeep or old green school bus. I'll try."

"You've got me convinced, Phillip. Just think. Rubbing shoulders with common people."

"Ha! You slightly misunderstand, my dear. I clearly said we'll be forcibly compressed. You make it sound like it's a choice. I didn't say rubbing shoulders in the sense of having friendly little chats around the campfire with Joe-The-Plumber and Rosie-The-Pole-Dancer."

"Oops. My mistake, Mister Pack-Leader."

Phillip's head jerks around at the sound of the name but he quickly clears his throat and smiles, "Oh, how right you are! You clearly assumed an overstated level of intimacy in camp, at least on my part. Look. Now that all the details are arranged, I'm going to get right on it tonight. I have to be sure I'm not bothered while we are there. I want to be able to control what's happening in my absence without spending every waking minute having to intervene in decisions. So I'm going to make a sandwich and be scarce tonight. See you in the morning. And…well, anyhow thanks again. Good job, Lauren. By the way, where in the world did you come up with the name Pack Leader? The term I use at the office is Lead Dog…not Pack Leader. It's not the Cub Scouts."

"I have no idea. I thought I heard you use it but never mind. No harm intended." Lauren cannot believe how she's pandering to Phillip. But right at this moment it is like a different atmosphere and Lauren thinks perhaps she's lost touch with the real world as she's survived the last many years in the adversarial world of her marriage. First, Jane Ella's sudden congeniality and now Phillip actually acting happy and giving a compliment. Lauren's surprised Phillip's lips didn't crack and bleed when he smiled during her compliment. If she can catch him tomorrow night in this sort of mood perhaps she can be introduce the question about Jane Ella's trust.

Lauren is still bothered by Richard knowing the dollar figure for Jane Ella's trust account. It makes her feel sick just to consider the possibility of Jane Ella seeing Richard when Lauren's occupied elsewhere. What if yesterday Jane Ella was going to spend the night with Richard and not Erin? Could that be why Richard didn't try to keep her from leaving the hotel and he almost acted like he wanted her to leave? What if Richard wanted her to leave so he could phone Jane Ella as Lauren was leaving the hotel? That could have been where Jane Ella was going just as Lauren was driving into the driveway. Maybe Jane Ella was never at Erin's at all but spent the night with Richard. Lauren pours a very heavy martini and says, "To drive a stake through the heart of my misery…at least until tomorrow morning".

A little later in her bedroom, one martini down and one more to go. Lauren quickly falls asleep.

CHAPTER 27

EVERYTHING FALLING INTO PLACE

In the morning Lauren is recovering from her "silver bullets" but she just can't wait to call Richard. She feels fortunate as she calls and he picks up the hotel room phone.

"Good morning."

"Hi there, angel. What are you up to this morning?"

"Nothing much. I thought I might come visit you if you want."

"Of course I want you and I miss you, Lauren. Even for one night. But I really can't today. I must get hopping. I checked in with my company late last night...actually early morning in Botswana and I've got to get back. One major booking event starts week after next for one of our annual clients and my company wants me back on site a week sooner than I'd been originally scheduled. It's a British company renting the entire camp and I need to be sure everything is perfect for their arrival. Then after that safari, I'll have a week of down time after which I'm scheduled for a very special safari. You can probably guess who I'll be seeing on that second one."

"Aw. I was hoping to come see you today and pick up where we left off yesterday. You really have to leave today?"

"Yep. No two ways about it. I'm going to New York out of Logan this afternoon and then get whatever I can out of JFK tonight for London and then from London to South Africa and over to Botswana. Long trip. About twenty-four hours by the time I get to the camp. But I'd like to have a rain check on where you and I left off. Can one have a rain check for that?"

"Promise me, Richard. Promise me we are an item. We've got a thing going. Just promise me you've got my back on everything. Promise me I'm important to you and…"

"Hey. Hey. There you go again getting all down. Stop worrying, Love. You've done your job. Everybody's coming to my part of the world. My playground. I'm planning on meeting your expectations in a whole lot of ways. Okay?"

"Oh yes, Richard. I'll miss you until I see you on the seventeenth. But I want you to tell me I'm important to you and I'm not just a little entertainment on the side."

"Yes, my dear. You're very important. Now, Lauren, I've gotta run. Until the seventeenth, then. Bye, sweetheart."

"Bye, Richard."

Somehow Lauren knows she should be feeling a little better after her brief conversation with Richard, but the reality is that she doesn't feel better. It's like she had to drag everything out of him today and even then her submissive fawning didn't draw a response she liked. Perhaps she's just not as trusting as she used to be. Perhaps the planning for Phillip has her on edge.

Lauren puts her hands to the side of her head and squeezes in hard. "God. I feel like my head's going to explode. I've got to stop worrying about every little thing. Richard's fine and I think under control. I'm fine. Jane Ella's okay and I think under control for the moment. And Phillip. Poor unsuspecting Phillip. He's okay and definitely under control. We're going right down the forked path where he'll go one way on his own and I can go my separate way…for good."

Lauren thinks maybe the alcohol is leading her to depressing thoughts when there really aren't any. She laughs and says aloud, "I've got to relax. It can't possibly be the teensy-weensy bit of alcohol in my martinis."

That evening Phillip gets home, loosens his tie, flops unceremoniously on a sofa in the living room and gives Lauren an uncharacteristic smile, "I wish we could leave tomorrow. I am so ready for this…our *family* vacation."

"Wow! Sounds good to me but I think we have a few more days. How about if I fix *you* a drink for a change, Phillip? Just relax. Think of tigers and lions and elephants and zebras."

"Yes, Lauren. A big fat martini! And yes I can think of lions, elephants and zebras. I can think of dust, snakes, thorns, wild natives with curved knives but I'm having a little trouble visualizing tigers since they live in Asia…thousands of miles from where we will be."

"Oh, you know what I mean."

"Yeah. I know what you think you meant. Ha."

Lauren returns with the drinks and she thinks in the history of their terrible marriage has she never had a better opportunity to ask a favor of Phillip.

"Phillip. I'm sure you know, but just a reminder… while we are in Africa, Jane Ella turns twenty-two."

"Yeah, I know. How time flies when you're havin' fun."

"I know. Hard to believe but she is that old. I thought this may be a perfect opportunity to let her know she's appreciated…you know regardless of the rocky roads and all the times when she was sent away to boarding schools. Well, I guess I feel a little guilty for a lot of things but for once maybe we could do something really nice for her from us."

"Sorry to interrupt. I'm guessing you have a suggestion. But even without hearing it, I couldn't agree with you more. This is a grand time to rid ourselves of guilt by paying real money for our parental transgressions of the past."

"I won't cry. But I do feel guilty when you understand me and are so agreeable. Why couldn't we always have been on the same wavelength?"

"Be careful, Lauren. Don't spoil your momentum. I'm good with doing something very, very special. Let's don't talk about history and old wavelengths. Liable to wreck this magic, passionate moment. The wallet's out and open and I think I'm welling up with tears so best you blurt out your ideas before I'm engulfed in a weeping-session."

Lauren hates his sarcasm but she has to get past it for now while she's got a chance.

"I was thinking about Jane Ella being able to get full access to her trust on this birthday instead of waiting until age twenty-five. That's it. I think she'd be shocked and ecstatic. I think she's ready to be out on her own and I think a lot of her seemingly nasty disposition is that she subconsciously begs for her independence. Sure, in a perfect world she'd have a degree, a job and would be a responsible adult. Her world isn't perfect but I don't see how it helps for another three years of us keeping her at home and us...me enabling her to be a rebellious, spoiled brat...of legal age."

"I understand. No need to say more. I got it, and I agree. But, while we both agree and it's just a stroke of the pen to do it, I really have to have Murray look over it to be sure there's not something we're missing by making a change in the date. Understand?"

"Sure. But how long will that take? I mean if it's to be a birthday surprise we have to get all the answers by next week."

"I'll get Murray on it tomorrow. I guarantee this little project will go to the top of his in-basket. Okay?"

"Of course. Thanks Phillip."

Lauren is ecstatic because of the relative ease of the agreement from Phillip. But she knows better than to tell Jane Ella. This is the sort of surprise best left for Phillip to announce. That way he can get the accolades and hugs. Lauren shrugs her shoulders as she realizes how insulated she's become in her emotions for Jane Ella and Phillip. Phillip retires to work in his bedroom. Lauren retires for the night with two of her silver bullets.

Days click by without much interaction, and everybody seems at least pleasant- phony, but pleasant. Finally, it's the day before the trip, and on the kitchen island, Lauren has passports, documents, foreign currency and medications all arranged in little protective territories for final packing.

Phillip arrives home a little later than usual.

"Hello, Phillip. Can I get you a drink?"

"Sure."

Lauren senses unusual tension in Phillip but assumes it's his version of withdrawal about not being able to go to work the next day. Nothing is going to derail this now. She'll play along at whatever cost tonight.

"Thanks for the drink. I *really* need it."

"More so than usual?"

"Yeah. I hit some obstacles today that I really must take care of...no choice in the matter."

Lauren's almost afraid to ask for fear of the answer but she takes a deep breath and asks, "What's happened?"

"I'm delayed getting to the safari camp by one day, two at the very most. I've already taken care of it. I simply must travel separately from you and Jane Ella and then arrive a day later than you."

"Oh, Phillip. Will you ever be free from the rat race? I just knew this was all too good to be true. I just knew something was bound to come up and spoil all this. I'm afraid once Jane Ella and I leave tomorrow we won't see you until we get back. Tell me that won't be the case. Or shall we just go and really not expect you'll make it over at all?"

"Guarantee that will not happen. I must be here to make some commitments tomorrow and sign contract papers tomorrow afternoon. It has to be my original signature on these contracts, and the minute I sign all parties are committed and legally bound. No backing out. It's a major, major acquisition for us and there are some cold feet and indecisive mental dwarfs at Keflo…the company we're acquiring. So, I have to get this done. Otherwise it would have to be sent to the camp for me to sign and then return. All of that time would give Keflo a chance to withdraw. The minute I sign, I'm on a plane to Africa."

"Well, at least you seem very sure. So I guess that's just what we'll have to accept and move on with the plans. Sounds okay…just makes me nervous. But I guess that's what it will be."

"And I thought it might be nice to collar Jane Ella for a few minutes tonight and let her know her trust will be accessible to her at the time of her birthday next week. That should make her happy. I brought the papers home for us to sign tonight and I'll have Julie notarize them tomorrow so that will all be settled as well."

"Oh, Phillip! That's wonderful! You got it done! She'll be so excited and why shouldn't she be? By the way, how much is in her trust now? Just in round terms."

"Well, as of today there's six million, five-hundred, sixty-three thousand and some pennies."

"Does she know that?"

"She ought to unless she has a short memory. She called me at the office just within the last week or so and bugged Julie until I personally called her back to satisfy her curiosity. She can't wait to get her hands on it and why not? It's always been intended for her. I guess it's possible but I can't imagine that even Jane Ella will be able to squander that much. We'll just have to trust she won't get hooked up with some guy who's just after the money. But there are few guarantees in life I suppose."

Lauren turns away from Phillip so he can't see the grimace on her face. There has to be some link between Jane Ella and Richard. Lauren already told Richard about how wealthy he'd be for helping to gain Lauren's freedom and get rid of Phillip. Richard can be wealthy with no strings attached. What possible advantage would it be to chase after a twenty-two year old with a fraction of Lauren's future wealth? A girl who may get tired of an aging boyfriend and dump him without any remorse.

"Wow. You're sitting like you're in a trance. You're not still worried about me traveling separately are you? Because I guarantee there's nothing to worry about."

"No. No, I'm okay. Just thinking about the details and all. I'm fine."

Lauren continues to pack that evening and Jane Ella comes to her room.

"Phillip just told me what you guys are doing with my trust. Thank you, thank you, thank you. You really did it. And I know it was you. Phillip would never have thought of anything like that on his own. He says you guys will sign the papers tonight and then he'll get them filed tomorrow. Too bad he has to stay an extra day but it sounds like he'll get there after we've had a chance to unpack. That'll be okay. In fact I clearly remember the last time I traveled with him and it's not a fun thing to do. He wants to be in control of everything and you can always count on him being brutally rude to flight attendants. Well, you know how he is. But thanks again, Mom. You did it!"

"You're welcome. You know, Jane Ella, we really can have a good time on this trip. It's almost like hitting the reset button on the family meter. Everybody has lots of good things to look forward to. Right?"

"Yeah. For me. I am finally happy. You've got to deal with whatever you have going with Phillip, Richard or whoever."

"C'mon. Let's don't start all that again. Let's just have a good time."

"You're right. Sorry. I am happy. Really happy. I have no more axes to grind."

"By the way. Do you have any idea how much money is in your trust? I mean just in round figures?"

"Wh…no…not really. I have no idea. Probably five million or so. I've never really checked on it or inquired about the details. It's plenty and that's all I really need to know. Why do you want to know?"

"Just wondering. That's all. No big deal."

Lauren knows the sand under foot is ever-shifting. But the main goal is this trip and get the first step over with while staying squeaky–clean of any involvement in camp with Richard.

Lauren knows at this point she'll err on the side of caution when it comes to any side trips for Phillip. She'll make sure there are witnesses who know she's just an innocent wife and bystander. In fact, Lauren needs to publicly make certain she's not involved in encouraging Phillip to take any risks. She'll have to find a way that witnesses can say whatever side trip is concocted for Phillip is strictly a deal between Richard and Phillip. Then if the plans for Phillip backfire, she can tie Richard to it as if he was going after Jane Ella and Phillip somehow got in the way. No matter what happens she's not taking the fall for it. Now Lauren is proud of herself. She's doing the thinking. She stretches her hand in front of her, palm down, fingers extended. No shaking. Cool as a cucumber. She's got to get *everything* back under her control as far as Richard. She can control him in more ways than just sex. She's allowed herself to become too dependent. She can outsmart all these fears that keep cropping up. Control. From this point forward Lauren must control everything. ***Everything***!

Lauren knows Richard is waiting for them at the camp in Botswana, and she'd love to talk with him but that's not going to happen and besides, there's no reason to take a chance on discussing anything that can arouse suspicion. After Phillip is out of the way, Lauren needs her wits about her to connect the dots and extinguish any relationship between Jane Ella, her trust money and Richard.

"It's all about control. My control."

CHAPTER 28

WELCOME TO SAFARI 101

Departure day dawns and Lauren and Jane Ella make all their flights and connections. The last leg of the exhausting trip is from Maun, Botswana in a small plane. Finally they arrive in Camp Moremi just as scheduled. The camp is situated on the beautiful Okavango Delta in North Central Botswana. Richard is at the airstrip waiting for their Cessna to land.   The pilot circles the landing strip low enough for Lauren and Jane Ella to wave to him, standing in his element, looking exotically handsome and rugged.

As Lauren gets out of the plane, she wants so badly to kiss Richard but knows a friendly hug will have to do for now. She is shocked at Jane Ella who takes the opportunity to give Richard a kiss on the lips that has Richard pulling away in stiff embarrassment. Lauren almost reacts to Jane Ella's behavior but catches herself, takes a deep breath and glances away as if she didn't notice.   It isn't worth starting the trip on an angry note.

The room accommodations of the camp are thatched roof, individual casitas. Richard directs the porters to settle Lauren in one casita and at the far end of the lodges, Jane Ella has her own casita.   Each bedroom is ensuite, comfortable air conditioning, a desk and well-appointed sitting area. So much for roughing it. Lauren thinks Richard imagines himself quite clever to put Jane Ella so far from Phillip and her. He probably assumes he's above suspicion in Lauren's eyes. But she is bound and determined to get what she wants out of this adventure and at the same time make sure Richard doesn't have some twisted relationship with Jane Ella. Lauren knows she owes it to them both to say the truth out loud, in the open, just once and for all, but not quite yet. If she has to put an end to something best leave the big bomb for the finale.

Lauren and Jane Ella change into what they believe are fashionable safari clothes and show up at the camp lobby to meet Richard.   The camp is bustling with activity. There are staff people buzzing around, small planes coming and going, shuttles full of tourists and luggage; and just as Richard said, he is in charge and for sure the go-to guy for the staff members.

"Ladies, I know it's been a long trip and I'll understand if you just want to curl up in your rooms. But I have a little time and I thought I might give the two of you a little short half-hour private excursion. Not far but maybe we'll see some surprises before dark. Anybody up for it?"

"Oh, of course. How about you Jane Ella?"

"Yeah. It just feels good not to be sitting on an airplane. A little outing will be great!"

"Good. Wait right here in front and I'll bring a rover around. We won't be gone too long but if you need to use the facilities before we leave, please do so here in the Lobby restroom. Much more civilized than out where the grass is tall and tickly."

"Oh great. So now all modesty is gone. We're down to talking about body functions and squatting in the desert."

Richard doesn't answer but heads out to get the vehicle.

Soon they go speeding down the gravel road out of camp and then to a dirt road that begins cutting this way and that through scrub trees. Richard slows and puts his finger to his lips to be silent. He stops the Land Rover, points and whispers to them.

"Over there is a pride of lions. See them by the trees? They're on a little mound of dirt."

"Oh my gosh. Aren't they beautiful. Is this safe to be this close?"

"Very. I wouldn't put you two in any danger. This pride comes the closest to camp and they are as used to vehicles as any wild animals can probably be. But big cats can be unpredictable and I know the safe

144

distance so we're not alarming them. And I always have a little extra help right here on my door."

He pats the butt of a rifle, holstered on the driver's door.

"Did you bring cameras or are they yet to be found in luggage?"

"I think we both just changed clothes and met you. I guess there will be more photo ops?"

"For sure. Tomorrow and every day after that we go mornings and afternoons like this. You'll see plenty. And there's always time for some individual excursions. Generally shorter but I can arrange that if anybody is ever interested."

Jane Ella is looking off toward the lions and Richard looks at Lauren and gives a big smile and wink.

Lauren smiles, then she turns her head slightly and peers through her sunglasses as if she too is looking at the lions, but she's really watching to see if Richard does any flirting with Jane Ella. She's not sure what she'll do if she sees it but at least it will confirm her growing suspicions.

Richard starts driving again and soon they are headed back to camp.

"I'll drop you two off at the lobby where you'll find our bar's well-stocked and friendly so maybe it's cocktail time. I've got a few things yet to do with the new arrivals so you probably won't see me again until tomorrow morning. Okay? And I assume Phillip will be along at some time later tomorrow."

"Sure."

"That's fine."

A drink sounds very good but Lauren is on her best behavior and she refocuses on her real purpose of the trip. Now they simply need one additional player for the game to begin.

Exhausted from the trip and time zone change Lauren and Jane Ella turn in early.

~

The next morning begins with breakfast and hustle bustle around the front lobby area as nervous travelers take out their anxieties on the staff.

After spending the entire morning driving around and taking dozens of photos, the guide for Lauren and Jane Ella heads back to camp for lunch. They've been cooped up with six other tourists and the guide for the better part of three hours. The vehicles aren't very comfortable but they are well-stocked with water and some quick energy snacks. They see lots of animals and take lots of photos so the morning flies by.

The oversized Land Rover turns the final corner and pulls up next to the lobby. There stands a familiar face and figure in khaki shirt, shorts, knee-length khaki socks and a newly purchased pith helmet. Smiling and waving is Phillip.

"Oh my God, Mom. Look at him. He's trying to look like he's straight out of a 1940's black and white movie. The great explorer!" Jane Ella is laughing.

Lauren feels a twinge of sorrow for Phillip. She's so intent on setting him up to be killed and he's trying so hard. So innocent.

"Hello! Hello, dear. I love the outfit. You'll have plenty of time to break in your clothes riding in this thing. Want to go this afternoon after lunch?"

"Well, of course. That's why we're here. The trip over here is a longer trip than I care for but it's over now. You two left home mid-morning day before yesterday and I was on my way as soon as I could break

146

free. Not bad. I'm famished and I could sure use a cocktail. Suppose I can get one this early?"

"As far as I can see they accommodate whatever you want. This is a fun place. You'll like it."

Phillip nods and turns his head facing the sun and he immediately winces from the bright sun, sneezes a couple of times and looks up as if injured. Lauren stares at him momentarily. Innocent. Vulnerable. Defenseless when outside the corporate world of the city.

Lauren smiles but it turns to a sadistic grin. That's right. Defenseless. Vulnerable. But not innocent. In fact *Guilty*! Guilty of being the self-appointed menace who controls and brutalizes her self-esteem. Her smile continues as she stares at Phillip and her heart races at the excitement of the days ahead. She has no doubts about what she wants or remorse for an accident that will surely happen. Lauren thinks she's just beginning to appreciate what people mean about the importance of freedom. Freedom from Phillip and justice for Phillip because he's become such a detestable human being.

All three of the Pittman's are on the afternoon excursion and Lauren notices that Phillip's smile is no longer a permanent fixture. He smiles less and less. At first when he looks at Lauren, she smiles and he smiles back. Now he just looks blankly at her. Surely he's not bored already. Probably just the bumps and the dust. But there are no verbal complaints and that night there's a quiet dinner in the lobby dining room and everyone turns in at an early hour and falls exhausted asleep from the day's events and the effects of time zone differences.

The next day there are two sessions of trips to look at wildlife and take pictures. As they wait to be picked up from the lobby area, Jane Ella comes walking up, sunglasses in place, looking like the cat that ate the canary. Lauren wonders if perhaps Jane Ella didn't tumble exhausted into her own bed but may have had company. The very thought makes Lauren irritable. She could end whatever has begun between Richard and Jane Ella but that would likely screw up Richard's part with Phillip. Best to force a smile and let everything alone.

"Good morning, Jane Ella. Sleep tight?"

"Well, of course, Daddy-Dearest. How else would an innocent maiden sleep in the wilds of Africa?"

"Ha ha. I hate to burst your bubble, kitten but this isn't exactly roughing it in the wilds and you are probably pushing the little innocent thing beyond the comedic realm."

"God, Dad. I don't know why you don't just loosen your Jockey shorts and talk nice once in awhile like everybody else."

"Oh, come on. Let's enjoy the day."

As the first tour proceeds, there are zebras and giraffes up close and walking around the Land Rover as if they are very used to it. Everyone is standing, leaning, pressing to get the best views and clicking cameras in a never-ending whir of shutter clicks. It seems thrilling to every single person except Phillip.

"No wonder these natives look like they're starved to death. It's not the food, it's the God damned dirt roads that shake every ounce of fat off your bones. Good God. This is like torture. Why can't they just parade the beasts past the camp so the Ansel Adams Fan Club here can take pictures with their Brownie Hawkeyes."

A little later as they bounce slowly along a deeply rutted road, Phillip is being his usual sarcastic self again.

"Oh, for heaven's sake. You all missed it. A prairie dog or whatever they are in deepest, darkest Africa , just ducked in a hole in the hundred degree sand. Shouldn't we all get out and try to capture the little bugger for posterity? Might never get a chance like this again. Pretty intense…those little prairie dogs. Might be able to bite."

One older gentleman tourist reacts a bit.

"C'mon, mate. We're just trying to have a little fun here. Loosen it up a bit, huh?"

148

"Sure, *mate*. Mindless or not, let's just all have a little fun. We rock and roll over the gullies and washboard roads, probably intentionally created and left this way to rough us up. Give us the real Africa experience of shaking our kidneys until we're urinating pure blood. And then we see some zebras, a couple of giraffes and a couple of lions as if they know the routine of parading close to our Land Rover. The so-called wild animals all look to me like they've had Ritalin this morning and are just cruising along in their drug-induced fog through another day of moronic tourists come to record their every move. But of course, that's the natural world. It's made up of protons, neutrons and morons. So it seems to me there should be little surprise when it comes to gullibility of tourists."

A woman tourist doesn't address Phillip directly but makes her comment loud enough to be heard.

"Maybe it would be more pleasant if people who don't enjoy what we're doing would just stay in camp. And I don't feel like a moron. Do you?"

"Here, here."

Phillip smiles. He's gotten a reaction but this is child's play and this is his playground. He sits quietly and smiles an expressionless smile as he bounces along on the morning's journey; but he's just waiting for anything else where he can jump in and belittle someone. The young guide, Jonathan, and his running-narrative are the next target for Phillip's venom.

"What was that you said, young man? The Cape Lion is extinct? Have you ever heard of cryptozoology? Do you know there are Cape Lions found in Siberia that are now in a zoo in South Africa...just South of here if I'm not mistaken."

"Well, of course, there are those who suggest the newest lions in the Johannesburg Zoo may be related to the Cape Lion but it's never been..."

"Proven? Only by DNA . But you're a guide and I'm sure you've studied Zoology and you're up on your facts and you've memorized the drivel the owners of this wild Africa farm here have given to you to spit out to tourists. So you'd be ever so smart enough to know I'm wrong and you're right."

"Oh, no sir. I wouldn't say that. I've never studied formally. But I know these animals and I know these parts pretty darn good, I'd say."

"Well, I rest my case. There are indeed Cape Lions living today in the zoo in Johannesburg.   I simply can't boil the zoological proof down to three and four letter words so Mark Trail up here can try to understand it. "

A muffled comment, "Why don't you just shut up."

But Phillip's on a roll with his cruel sarcasm and in a hillbilly twang, "Ewwww. Mustn't question the guide. No, I ain't been to school none but I bought a magazine and that makes me one 'a them Smithsonian guides. Who'll ever know the difference?"

"Really, sir. This is too much. I'm sorry this isn't your cup of tea."

Phillip's venom rolls on, "Oh, I say old man. I think you've hit the nail on its crown. I've just had a capital idea.   I think I will spend more time in camp than out having my kidneys thrown amuck. "

Lauren and Jane Ella have seen it all before and they just sit silently.

They arrive back at the camp and go in for lunch. It's obvious to Lauren that people who have been with them on the morning excursion now carefully avoid sitting anywhere close during the meal.   Lauren just rolls her eyes in disgust. Phillip certainly isn't doing anything to alter her plan.

At lunch, Phillip is just as disagreeable.

"A buffet lunch? Come on. With what we're paying they can bend a little. Hey! Garcon! Come here."

"Sir? Is something wrong?"

"I don't know yet if anything is wrong. I haven't ask my question yet. I'd like something from the grill. A filet, medium rare. I don't want a buffet. Life can be so simple for you if you'll simply bring me a small…"

"Sir, the buffet is open for lunch. It has most everything guests prefer and if you'd care to…"

"Look, little man, get me somebody out here who can make a decision. I'm not asking for the keys to the safe. I'm asking to get something from the kitchen. C'mon. Hubba hubba. Chop, chop. Get a move on."

Richard quickly appears at the table.

"Hello, Phillip. Can I get the kitchen to fix you something?"

"Yes. A breath of air. Thank you, Richard. Sorry they had to call you but I wasn't connecting with Mister Zulu, if you know what I mean."

"I'm going to have the kitchen manager come out and take your order. Gladly take your order, Phillip. We really do pride ourselves in taking care of guests and I most sincerely want you to be pleased. He'll be right out."

Soon everything is sorted out and Phillip gets exactly what he wants and he crows to Lauren and Jane Ella that this is how things are done.

"You ask politely for what you want. If that doesn't get immediate results you demand what you want in a tone that shows you're not going away until you get what you want. And when you chew your way through the underlings and you get to the right person, it happens. Lesson for the day brought to you compliments of your dull but very successful corporate husband otherwise known as 'Lead-Dog'."

Of course it's a lesson both Lauren and Jane Ella could quote many times from the last two decades.

Richard comes back after the meal is finished. He asks if he can join them. Phillip now feels like he has a willing patsy so he's all too glad to have Richard at the table. It also demonstrates a power trip to the other guests.

"Ya know, Richard. This is quite a going operation you run here. I assume you like constructive criticism? I don't want to beat you up after only two days on site, but the food is vastly overrated for the prices paid. I mean it's good and prepared well but when I look at the overall price, it seems pretty skimpy…price wise."

"Actually, I have not heard that before. But I do know how important it is to listen. We pride ourselves in being a top drawer camp and if the food needs a bit of tweaking to be a little more upscale, than it needs to be looked into. I thank you for being candid."

"The other thing I notice is that this camp is like Grand Central Station. I assume all the guests are here by now.   It's busy, of course , on the first couple of days when guests arrive but there are delivery people, and God knows who all, coming and going, planes taking off and landing, trucks hauling God knows what. It just doesn't seem to capture a 'camp' sort of atmosphere in the middle of Africa."

"Again, I thank you for being candid. We do have a lot of activity from the airstrip. It takes a big staff to have modern convenience where none was really intended by nature. The airstrip is two miles away but I know depending on direction of landings and takeoffs it can seem pretty busy. You'd probably guess, jobs are scarce in Africa and so the bush pilots catch a trip anytime they can, whether it's hauling a passenger or two, some mail, supplies or an occasional injury or illness. I hear what you're saying but that's a little harder to tackle than kicking the food up a notch or two."

 Phillip listens, rolls his eyes, as if he's ignoring the long explanation, gets up, quietly excuses himself and walks outside. Being rudely abandoned by Phillip, Richard's face turns red from embarrassment but he recovers quickly, "Well, we sometimes can't please everybody…but don't worry. I've got a little time yet to charm him into loving this place. So, how about the rest of the family? Are the two of you enjoying yourselves?"

152

"Oh yes. It's fun. Phillip's just being Phillip. My guess is he'll curl up with a book and not bug anybody this afternoon. He's had his fun getting everybody walking around on eggshells like something's amiss. But yes. This is wonderful."

Jane Ella looks through her sunglasses directly at Richard and smiles a little sexy smile almost as if she's ignoring Lauren, "Richard? Maybe you can think of something for an individual, Jane Ella sort of tour, something with a little excitement. I think by tomorrow I might be ready for something on my own. Maybe you can be my guide."

Lauren stands up, tosses her napkin on the table in disgust. She's trying not to explode in anger at the nerve of Jane Ella's request, not to mention how distracting it can be to her plans for Phillip, "Do you really suppose Richard is the only person to take you on an individual tour? There are lots of guides who would probably love to do that for you…of course it would be the ones who haven't met you yet."

Lauren walks outside and heads for her room. Phillip is already in the room.

"I think I'm going to skip being with the Mickey Mouse Club this afternoon. Having my kidneys and stomach on solid ground for a few hours will do me good. I may even splurge and take a nap. Okay?"

"Absolutely. Phillip, this is to be a vacation. Do what is fun and enjoyable to you. You deserve it."

Lauren thinks how Phillip deserves a whole lot more than a nap. And if everything plays out in the next couple of days Phillip may get a longer nap than he thought.

CHAPTER 29

THE MOTH FLIES FOR THE FLAME

The following day Phillip, Lauren and Jane Ella are in the lobby after breakfast.

"Well, what great wonders of Africa will we see today? Maybe I have it all wrong. Maybe I should just seek comedic relief from the idiots on these little excursions. Their astute comments are hard to take but just watching them bouncing around may be the real entertainment. We could wager between the three of us who we think is suffering the most from hemorrhoids or something like that. What do you say?"

"Come on, Phillip. The people we've been with are just trying to have a good time and you picking at them doesn't make that very easy to do."

"Right-O. Then perhaps I'll do something else today. Maybe I'll say cheerio and just read some more today. In fact now that we're standing here with a few minutes to spare, that sounds like a capital idea old chaps. So ta-ta."

Phillip waves over his shoulder and leaves Lauren and Jane Ella standing alone.

"Why does he always have to be such a miserable SOB and make everybody else miserable as well?"

"I'm not the one to ask, Jane Ella. I've been with him for the best part of twenty-five years of my life and I've never figured it out. He's just a permanent and naturally miserable SOB. That's just Phillip."

Lauren can't help but think how Phillip's isolation and irritation of the other guests should make it easier for Richard to offer some optional private side-trip for Phillip. She's getting antsy about when this will play out.

The day wears on and when lunch is served, Phillip comes sauntering into the dining room to meet up with the returning group.

"Well, Hello all you campers. I see you're back in one piece from the dangerous morning session? Any excitement?"

"Probably nothing you'd want to hear. But we saw a herd of wildebeests and there were hyenas following the herd trying to cull out one of the young calves. But the bulls kept charging the hyenas and so they never attacked while we could see. That was about it. Oh, there was a snake across our road and it was huge. The guide said it's not poisonous, but I wouldn't want to meet up with it I'm sure. But I have to admit, Jane Ella didn't look all that frightened."

Jane Ella seems to be in a captivated mood, "It really scared me at first but I thought it was pretty exciting when the guide got out and picked up the snake's tail and just dragged it off to the side. I kept thinking if the guide got bitten we may be stuck or have to try to find our way back."

Phillip can't resist making a loud comment, "Ha! They got ya! They probably pull all the teeth of the animals they show on these trips. Likely no one could get hurt so it makes the guides look brave and strong. And you know I was a day late leaving Boston? Well, good old Patriot Star, the Boston investment firm with gifted leadership was like the hyenas but instead of looking for one little weak guy, we devoured the whole herd. We finalized the buyout of Keflac Manufacturing. That's what puts food on the table at the Pittman's and that's what I did, nearly single-handedly the day before I left town. Quite a deal!"

"Dad. Come on. Mom and I are enjoying ourselves. I just wish you'd try a little harder to have fun. You never take a vacation and I hate to see you doing stuff you can always do at home. Well, anyhow. I just hope you have a good time while we're here."

"That's nice of you to say and I appreciate your concern. I'll try a bit harder. I've still got my grump-face on from work."

"Hello, everybody."

"Hi, Richard."

"Hi, everybody. Hello, Phillip. How's everything today?"

"Well, hello, Richard. The girls were just trying to get me out of the grumps so I was wondering...you mentioned or maybe it was in the brochures that there are possibilities for a little individual escapade or two. That possible?"

Lauren's stomach does a flip from excitement. Phillip just put his neck in the noose.

"Absolutely. What did you have in mind, Phillip?"

"Right. Well, how about a grand adventure for Phillip? I'm a complainer so let's get old Phillip out on some dismal swamp to fish or take pictures by himself. Tell me, are the mosquitoes any bigger at the swamp than in the casita? Maybe I shouldn't bug you about something special and out of the ordinary, and instead just quietly spend the remainder of this great vacation grumping in my casita. "

Lauren can hardly believe her ears. Richard didn't even have to suggest anything. This is the opportunity and it's being served up on a silver platter. Phillip's doing it all. If this pans out, she'll figure a way to let other tourists overhear that it's Phillip wanting to do this. How perfect!

"So what do you say, Richard? Maybe it's not possible... but does anybody fish in any of those lakes I saw when we flew in here?"

"Oh there's excellent fishing. We are delighted to do small excursions and let you tailor it to exactly what you want; not what we have sitting on some stodgy old shelf for the less adventurous tourists. You tell me what you'd like to do. We have all the gear and if you're interested I could set something up yet this afternoon or tomorrow. Actually the best time would be to get an early start and so maybe tomorrow morning would be best. But it's whatever you want, Phillip."

"No, not quite that soon. You just think over some options so I can have a little peace, quiet and solitude. If I do this I'd like to simply be left alone, if it's safe, and that would make me happy. But tomorrow's too soon…err uh you just take until tomorrow afternoon to come up with a couple ideas and then I'll see. If I can choose one of your options, then I probably will be ready by day after tomorrow and you're right about early morning. An early start will be good."

"Really it's no trouble to do it soon…"

"No. You come up with some ideas and we'll plan at the earliest for day after tomorrow. But depending how I feel it may even be the day after that. But I want to know all the details…exactly…you know maps, all that sort of detail. Okay?"

"Sure, Phillip. It will be a pleasure and I'll attend to the details. You can decide the best choice tomorrow afternoon and then just let me know when you want to do it."

"Sounds good. In the meantime, I've got some things I really should attend to this afternoon so Wifi, here I come."

Later that evening at dinner, Richard comes by the Pittman's table.

"How was this afternoon? Have fun?"

Lauren and Jane Ella both nod attentively. Phillip just looks at Richard and purses his lips as if he's about to whistle, "Any ideas yet Richard?"

"As a matter of fact that's why I dropped by hoping to catch you. Tomorrow afternoon I'll give you several options but let me fill in the blanks a little with a couple of questions for you. That okay?"

"Sure. Fire away."

"Okay. If fishing is the chosen option would you like to fly fish or fish for something a little more substantial? There are a lot of different fish and we can get you to lake fishing or river fishing. I have a terrific assortment of rods, reels and tackle. So it's entirely your choice."

"Let's try for something on the bigger side than fly fishing. Spincast equipment will be good for me and is there anything out there in the ten to twenty pound range? Or something in that neighborhood? Nothing

157

fifty pounds or bigger. God it would be like hooking a crocodile. I also don't want to spend the day with little bait-stealers. I'm not an experienced fisherman beyond what I've learned from reading about it, but I'm a quick learner."

"Sure. Got it. I'm getting excited for you, Phillip. You'll love some of the whistles and bells you can have with you. And if you catch something good, we'll clean it and serve it with all the trimmings just for you and your family"

Just as Lauren had hoped, a couple at a nearby table are intently listening and obviously thinking maybe they can try something similar. They lean toward the Pittman table, "Excuse us. We didn't mean to be eavesdropping but we couldn't help but overhear what your husband is planning. Would you mind if we just scoot a bit closer and listen? Promise not to interfere. It just sounds so wonderful. A private outing."

   Lauren thinks this just couldn't be better. "Sure. It's entirely my husband's idea and the camp seems to have all sorts of options. Here join us so you can hear because I have no idea about any of it and it's just in the planning stage."

Phillip looks at Lauren in disgust because of her suggestion for the neighboring table to join them. But he's actually pushing to do this. It's exactly as Richard had described on that first night's discussion of this plan. Phillip is doing the insisting on what he wants. Richard simply is being a good host. Clean hands! Phillip is dancing solo in a dance that will be the end of him.

The next day as Lauren and Jane Ella return from the afternoon exploration session, Richard is talking over plans with Phillip. It sounds as if Phillip made up his mind for what he's going to do. Lauren can't believe her good luck in how smoothly this seems to be working. Again at this meeting of Richard and Phillip, two couples ask if they can just listen, in case they want to do something similar. Richard is very accommodating and Phillip's big ego is making sure all those within earshot know it's Phillip making all the requests and decisions. Lauren thinks how safe the plan is turning out to be. Just like Richard said a month ago. People do this all the time and an accident is the last thing on an excited tourist's mind.

"That sounds really good. Now I'll be able to carry all the stuff without a packhorse right?"

Richard laughs out loud.

"Guarantee it Phillip. We put everything in a couple of backpacks and the packs are balanced so you'll be just fine. It's like a luxury dream day all packed in a couple of travel bags. So first, we'll head over to the Zakanahi Lagoon and I'd recommend leaving camp around six-thirty or seven unless that's too early for you. We only have to go about a mile on the other side of the airstrip and we'll be there. I can't wait for you to see the lake in the morning. It's gorgeous. Birds, fish, likely some of the bigger animals on the far bank. They'll spot you real quick and only come to drink at a distance."

" Sure. Early is fine. Let's say six-thirty. By myself. Don't need anyone with whom I must hold hands all day. Ah, peace and quiet. One with nature. That's me the natural outdoorsman. Ha. But it does sound good. By the way, how about food? Do I get something above the cheese and crackers or energy bar routine?"

"Well, part of it's a surprise but there's a breakfast that will shock you and about six cups of coffee just the way you prefer it, a very, very gourmet lunch because you'll be famished from hauling all the big fish to shore and there are a few martinis packed ready to drink, your brand and made just the way you like them-three olives each. Then we'll come snatch you from paradise when the afternoon tour is complete. I thought I'd make sure when we pick you up I'll have Lauren and Jane Ella's group in tow. I'll personally take their group out tomorrow afternoon so we can all meet you, take some pictures and hear all about your adventure. And you think this seems pretty close to what you had in mind? "

"Absolutely! By the way, do you have a detailed map for me . You know. I just want to be sure I know exactly where I'll be in relation to

159

the camp and everything else. I can't imagine it could happen but if I wanted to come back and I suppose I'd have to hoof it…"

"Well, I doubt if you'll be bored but if for any reason you wanted to get back before we pick you up, you only need to walk a bit. From the landing strip to the camp there are staff coming by fairly often and any one of them would give you a ride to camp. And I brought you a copy of a detailed map that shows everything around here, the camp, the airstrip, the photo destinations we usually go and it even has GPS coordinates. No more secrets when you see that map."

"Actually, it all sounds like it may be just what the doctor ordered. What Doctor L-l-leit…uh, uh well just what the doctor ordered."

Lauren almost gags as she listens to Phillip use his cocky, louder voice now that he's attracted an audience of other guests. She can't help but think how Phillip is being almost as agreeable as the night she introduced taking the safari. Lauren's a bit confused by Richard telling Phillip how easy it is to get back to camp. This fishing spot must not be very far away from camp. Maybe this isn't the real time for the accident. Maybe another time after this. Lauren takes a deep breath. She'll just have to trust Richard. He certainly seems to know what he's doing.

Then, in another similarity to an evening at home in Boston, Phillip stays up half this night as well, his face close to the screen of his laptop, engrossed in something apparently very important. The couple of times Lauren walks close to Phillip he turns and acts like what he's doing he may not want her to see. Lauren goes to bed, reads a little and eventually drops off to sleep.

160

CHAPTER 30

THE DAY

At exactly six thirty the next morning, Richard pulls a Land Rover in front of the Pittman's casita. Lauren gets out of bed and looks through the window as Phillip goes out the door exactly on time. Richard begins describing all the equipment and food he has for Phillip. Phillip seems uninterested in details of the two large red backpacks' contents but he's very animated in his excitement to get going. Typical Phillip. He is checking and double-checking the time on his watch as if this is some important business meeting. Lauren thinks he's pathetic. Only Phillip turns something fun into a tightly scheduled appointment..

"I really wish you'd let me show you how all this gear works, Phillip. I just want you to be comfortable with it so you don't get out there and then can't figure out how to use something."

"Look. I consider myself pretty damn techno-savvy. I can figure it out so let's don't waste a lot of time here. I'm ready to get going. I'm anxious to do this. Okay?"

"Sure. Mount up and let's go."

"Okay…but first I'm going to just sneak back into the room and say goodbye to my wife if she's awake. Be right back."

"Sure, take your time." Richard turns his head and smirks in a whisper too quiet for Phillip to hear," Good idea to say goodbye to the faithful little woman."

Phillip sort of jogs to the casita door, opens it quietly and finds Lauren standing at the window looking out.

"Oh, I didn't know if you were awake yet and I just wanted to say goodbye, Lauren."

"Yes. Goodbye, Phillip. You have a good time today."

Lauren thinks it's strange Phillip stands silently looking at her. Lauren gets a cold chill down her back. Could he be having a premonition that he'll never see her again. Her heart sinks and she has a sudden sad, guilty feeling.

Phillip breaks his stare, spins around and out the door to the vehicle. Lauren continues to watch through the window of the casita.

"All set? Goodbyes for the day? Ready for some real fishing?"

"You bet! Beautiful day, Richard. I can't wait to get started. No more dalliance, now. Drive-on, Cabbie."

 Lauren thinks how typical of Phillip. On the other hand she thinks this may be the last time she'll see him, but her shallow feelings of remorse a few moments ago, quickly vanish.   She smiles a mean-spirited smile as she thinks how Phillip will at least be happy as he's eaten or mauled by hyenas or lions or whatever might be the jungle's weapon of choice. Lauren gives a little wave as Phillip and Richard drive off through the camp.

"Au revoir, Phillip. Ciao. Bon voyage'."

Richard and Phillip leave the camp and a couple of miles later go past the airstrip and continue on for almost another mile to the edge of the beautiful lagoon. Richard drives along the edge and points ahead to a rock Jetty that extends out into the lake two hundred yards or so like a skinny peninsula. Picture perfect.

"Okay, Phillip. This should be some of the best fishing you will ever find. The best fishing is at the tip-end of the rock jetty. Just fish right off the end of it. All the way at the end.   It's a couple hundred meters hike with all this gear but I'm sure you'll find it well worth the short trek. Don't even mess around along the banks here cause I don't want you running into a snake. That's why the tip of the jetty is so good.

Just go straight out to the tip with the two red bags and make yourself comfortable. Nothing will bother you out there. Okay, now listen carefully to my next instruction. Okay?"

"Sure, go ahead, Mister Boss-man. I'm all ears."

"Okay, take both red packs with you out to the end. There's food mixed into both packs so leaving one of those here on the bank could attract animals so it's best just to take both packs at the same time. Total weight of both packs is about forty pounds so it shouldn't be too bad . Okay, Phillip?"

"Yep. I'm listening. I'm fine with what you're saying."

" Alright. When I come to get you this afternoon I'll carry the stuff you have left over back here to the bank. So get out to the jetty point, set up your chair and just relax and take in the beauty. If you sit there for a while and focus your attention across the lake with the binoculars you'll likely see some interesting animals coming to drink. I'm sure you'll really enjoy the scenery of the lake. Just relax. All this okay?"

"Yeah, yeah. Of course. Sounds good. Thanks. I'll watch for you, after say two or so? Not before then, okay? Give me a chance to really enjoy this."

"Yeah. Sure. Around two or a little after. I'll be back with Lauren and Jane Ella at the end of our early afternoon session. I'll honk when we arrive but I'm sure you'll see us driving up."

"This will be just fine. I think I'll do as you say and get set up out on the tip out there. I can relax in peace. This is perfect. Now I'm glad you packed all this stuff the way you did. Yep. I'm going to get out there, maybe start with a little breakfast and coffee and then look across the lake for a while to see what turns up. Thanks. Don't worry about me. This is exactly what I want. I'll see you this afternoon."

"Okay. See ya."

Richard drives off and Phillip watches him drive away as he's beginning to gather up the backpacks. Richard watches Phillip in the

163

mirror to be sure he's starting toward the jetty and Phillip is doing as he's been told. In fact, Phillip is hurrying onto the jetty with both packs in tow. Richard confidently smiles and hurries back to camp so he can personally guide Lauren and Jane Ella's group today.

During both the morning and afternoon photo sessions Richard steals an occasional glance at Lauren and smiles a confident smile. Lauren winks once or twice. Everything is in the works. Her heart pounds when she thinks of what might be happening at the very instant and the time slips away.

Right on schedule, at a few minutes after two o'clock the after-lunch photo group is returning to camp and Richard pauses the land Rover on the outskirts.

"Listen, everybody. Lauren's husband, Phillip, went on a solo fishing trip today and it's a good time to pick him up. I left the two empty spaces in the Rover today so we'd have enough room for Phillip and whatever is left of the food and gear he took. Unless anybody has an objection we'll just drive over there and pick him up at the big lagoon. It won't take long and it's beautiful over there. That okay?"

A few grumbles obviously about the prospects of riding with Phillip but overall a chorus of grunts and "un huh's" are all the approval Richard needs as he heads through camp and straight out the other side toward the airstrip.

Richard drives slowly up to the lake. He pauses the vehicle and looks up and down the shore.

"Awright, Phillip. Where are ya? Where'd you go?"

"What's the matter?"

"Oh nothing, Roberta, he's not where I dropped him and probably simply hard to spot down by the bank. I'm sure he wouldn't... nah."

Everyone in the truck is thrown a little back as Richard takes off rather quickly and drives with some haste toward the rock jetty. He pulls to about the location where he'd dropped Phillip and comes quickly to a stop.

"Henry? If you don't mind. Take these binoculars and scan the shoreline and particularly out on that jetty...mostly the shoreline. He wouldn't have gone out there, but I want to be sure after I specifically warned him and he repeated to me he understood that jetty was totally off limits for him. "

Richard jumps out of the vehicle and grabs the rifle holstered on his car door. He has another pair of binoculars as he starts for the rock jetty, rifle under one arm, holding the binoculars up to his eyes with the other hand and nervously scanning one direction, then another.

"Holy shit! Ho-oly shit! Just scan the shoreline and look close out on that jetty. Look for anything. Terry, would you honk the horn three blasts and then hold off and everybody listen in case he's yelling we can hear him. C'mon let's find Phillip. I don't like this! Ho-oly shit! I don't like this at all!"

Richard turns toward the vehicle. Henry is standing up looking through the binoculars and everyone else is in uncomfortable positions straining to be as high up as possible and see anything that moves.

"Lauren, Jane Ella, please stay in the Rover for now. I have to tell you I don't like this one bit. I gave Phillip two absolute critical instructions to stay back five feet from the water's edge and whatever he did to *not* under any circumstances go out on that jetty. I know he understood. He was getting a little irritated with me for treating him, as he said like a fourth-grader. He promised me. Surely he wouldn't have gone out there."

Everyone climbs from the Land Rover and begins milling around looking up and down the banks of the lagoon. Whispers of worry by the other tourists are the background for Lauren's dramatic pose, just staring at the lake, her hand over her heart. Jane Ella is pacing back and forth taking one deep breath of disbelief after another.

"Mother, what's happening? I can't believe this. What could have happened?"

165

"I don't know dear. I don't know. Just keep looking. He's just got to be here. Oh, God. I feel like I'm going to be sick."

One of the other tourists takes Lauren's arm in support and tries to walk her back to a seat in the vehicle. Lauren resists.

"I'll be okay. Just please spot him. Phillip, where are you? Oh, God. This can't happen. It can't!"

"Just everyone keep looking and listening. It's better if we can spot him from here than to start driving around the whole edge of the lagoon."

Richard takes out his radio and turns his back to the group.

"Base, this is Mantus two four. Mantus twenty-four."

"Base. Hey Richard. What's up?"

"I need you to call the Ranger station and tell them we may have a missing man... and get a couple of our vehicles out here at the lagoon real quick. I can't find Phillip Pittman. Have one vehicle check the shoreline going around the east side and the other drive the shore from west to east. I'm parked right here on the south at the jetty. Get a move on. I want to find him before it gets dark. He didn't hitch a ride back earlier, did he? "

"I copy, Richard, and negative on Mr. Pittman returning to camp. Not a peep from him all day. Let me get on this if that's all for now?"

"Yep. Get our guys out here pronto! Mantus two-four, out."

Richard turns a little toward the anxious tourists.

"Crocodiles are around here but not a bother unless you get too close to the water or walk out there. For sure you don't want to get out there and get cut off from behind by crocs and have no way to escape. I *know* he understood me because I told him several times and in no uncertain terms about the certain danger and he said...he assured me he understood and even said he wasn't about to take any chances."

Suddenly Henry yells out, "Hey! There's something out on the end of that rock thing that sticks out into the lake. Look just out by the tip and left a bit. Something red. There by the water."

Richard takes the binoculars and looks. "Oh, God! I told him. He understood. I *know* he understood! I can't believe this! Looks like part of a red backpack, fishing equipment and a tackle box or something else. Phillip, don't do this."

Richard radios again for assistance and everyone waits in silence. It takes about fifteen minutes for the first of the Park Rangers to arrive. Soon after the Rangers arrive another vehicle pulls up to the site. The car is clearly marked as Botswana Police Service (BPS). The Rangers, the policeman and Richard all seem to know each other.

"Hello, Richard. Any sign?"

"Yeah, Andrew. We just spotted something out on the jetty end. Could be fishing tackle or something. Take a look. Out by the end and off to the left."

The policeman and the two rangers all look through their binoculars.

"Yeah. If that's his, he either abandoned it or well…we'd better take a closer look. What's the man's name?"

"Pittman. Phillip Pittman. This is his wife, Lauren and daughter, Jane Ella."

"Hello, Mrs. and Miss Pittman. I'm Sergeant Andrew William Ludoku, Botswana Police Service. Are you two okay for a few more minutes? We need to get this sorted out pretty quick. If he's not here, we need to get looking elsewhere and find him. Please stay by the vehicle."

Sergeant Ludoku turns abruptly and looks agitated at the guests who are beginning to drift closer to the lake bank for a better view, "Everyone! Please, please stay away from the shore. For your safety…please! Okay?"

Lauren, Jane Ella and the other tourists look toward the Sergeant and nod in understanding. Lauren surveys the police sergeant from head to toe. He's very black and his skin looks shiny, maybe from the sweat glistening like little sparkly crystals on his face. He's wearing a short sleeve, very wrinkled white shirt and heavy, gray wool slacks. His brown shoes are scuffed and dusty. Lauren would never have guessed him a policeman from his unkempt appearance.

The Sergeant motions for Richard and the Rangers to come with him a few steps away from the group.

Two of the rangers take rifles out of their vehicle and position themselves on each side of the jetty. Richard, with revolver in hand, begins walking as fast as he can and then speeds to a jog out to the tip. Within a minute crocodiles begin to surface on each side of the rocks. They're cruising in the water at first and then quickly begin to climb out onto the rocks just about the time Richard is nearly to the jetty tip.

"KABOOM! KABOOM!" shots ring out and water splashes by the crocs. All the tourists gasp in surprise. The huge reptiles quickly retreat into the water and then beneath the water surface. Finally Richard picks up some items and begins the return trip from the point back to the vehicles. The crocodiles are easily seen lurking by the edges and looking at Richard go past them. Richard spreads the retrieved items on the grass next to the Rangers' vehicle. The Sergeant, Richard and the Rangers look at the leftovers of the apparent tragedy.

Lauren walks over to the small group.

Sergeant Ludoku is unaware of Lauren's proximity as he examines the remnants, "I'm afraid not too much mystery here, Mister. Look. The fishing pole, a tackle box full of big, sharp teeth marks and some shreds of clothes or backpack or whatever it was. That's all. I'm sorry to say, Mister. I think your tourist, Mr. Pittman is likely lost. You see how aggressive these croc's are right now. They're looking for more of the same. I'm sad to say, unless we spot him somewhere else around the lagoon I think he's lost. You have some people driving the shore line ? I hear honking so I assume that's what they're doing. If we don't find him before dark, I need information on him from your camp and his passport for paperwork. But I, too will drive the lake and the road back to camp just to be sure. Richard, check once more that he's not sitting in camp and we are goose-chasing."

"Sure Andrew. Can I get The Pittman ladies and the other tourists back to camp?"

 Lauren shrieks, "Oh, Phillip. What have you done? What's happened to him?" Then she breaks down crying and she and Jane Ella hug. One of the tourists comes over and put his arm around the pair and gently guides them to the Land Rover.

"Here, sit down in the car. Can I get you some water?"

Lauren and Jane Ella sit stone-faced in the Land Rover. Sergeant Ludoku looks embarrassed that Lauren overheard his comments but continues with Richard.

"Sure, Richard. You may take everyone back to camp. But call camp first before I drive around the lagoon. Have everyone on the staff take another look and see if he's there. Tell them to use pass keys and be sure he's not in his room, check the bathrooms, lodge …let's be sure. Check *everywhere*. But if he's not in camp and he's not here at the lagoon, then I think he didn't follow instructions very well and it's a shame. A real shame. Then Richard, you and I need to be very clear why he was out here alone and what instructions you gave him. I will need a signed statement from you if you were involved with dropping him here on the lake by himself. I know. I know. I see your look but you and I know this land is not very forgiving of carelessness. And we must know whose carelessness was at fault.   But I feel so sorry for his wife and daughter. When you get them back, please have everyone who's on the vehicle with you just stay in the lobby so I can speak with them. I'll try not to keep them too long. What a shame. Damn shame."

Lauren sobs into a borrowed handkerchief and with eyes hidden she can't help but think how her practice at home led to her star performance now as the crushed, grieving wife.

CHAPTER 31

TIME TO RETURN HOME

Slowly Lauren and Jane Ella lead the small procession into the camp lobby area. Shocked tourists who witnessed the recent unfortunate event file solemnly into the lobby, find a seat in one of the many overstuffed lobby chairs and quietly whisper to each other. Two Aussie couples sit closest to Lauren but their attempts to be discreet are a failure.

"I can't believe it."

"Yeaaah. I reckon he just got in over his head."

"Yeaaah. He was pushin the boss …that Richar… to let him go out by himself but he was an arrogant know-it-all. Who'd a' reckoned he be stupid on top of being arrogant. But it looks to me like he cocked-up his little private fishing time and it literally bit him in the arse."

"Shhh. Be a little more quiet. That's his Missus right over there. Accident, yeaah. But as careful as this place is, I'm sure Richard was very clear about the do's and don'ts. That Pittman was an arse first class and it's terrible what happened, but what a 'know-it-all'. Sod and a wanker."

"Yeaah. I'd say you got 'em pegged but too bad for the missus and the daughter."

"Yeaah."

Lauren keeps her face hidden as if crying but she's concentrating on listening to the comments and feeling good about her marvelous performance up to this point. After twenty minutes or so, Sergeant Ludoku enters the lobby.

"Excuse, please. Your attention to me, please. I met some of you a while ago today but for the rest I'm Sergeant Ludoku, Botswana Police. I need to talk with each of you briefly . I'll try to be as brief as possible but you must realize this is tragic and I need to be sure of any conclusions. I'll sit over at that table and please come one-by-one."

And as he asks, people move as he motions for the next person to join him. One by one, the sergeant talks with them and makes notes. He politely stands after each interview, smiles and shakes hands or slightly embraces the women. Then he motions for the next person to join him.

 After the interviews,   guests respectfully file by and express concern to Lauren and Jane Ella and then they quietly exit the lobby, apparently returning to their rooms. As the sergeant continues his interviews the group being interviewed gets smaller and smaller, until finally it's just Jane Ella, Lauren and Richard.

"Yes, Miss. If you would come over to join me for a moment or two, I'll try to be brief. I know it's been a terrifying and exhausting day for you all. I am so very sorry about what we think took place."

As he motions to Jane Ella, she follows him to the other side of the room.

"Well, Richard. Just two little birdies sittin' on the fence. What do you suppose he'll want to know?"

"Keep looking sad when you talk and I will simply look like I am consoling you. Yeah, perfect."

As Richard speaks quietly and undetected by others, Lauren dabs at her eyes with a tissue as if still in total despair.

"I know from the rare times we've been involved with accident investigations the police simply want to know what you saw this afternoon. You really can just tell the entire truth just as it happened. There wasn't much to see. And of course, the horrible shock of it all that Phillip would not heed my advice and go venturing out on the

171

rocks. I know Andrew…er Sergeant Ludoku and he'll believe me. But the accident is terrible. Don't you think so, Mrs. Pittman?"

"Stop making jokes, Richard. I'm afraid you'll make me laugh."

Lauren pauses and glances at Richard, You know, I really should feel something sad right now but I have to tell you, I don't. I don't feel sad at all. I have to really work at this…"

"Now you're trying to make me laugh. Oops. Quiet now. Looks like Jane Ella is already finished."

"Okay, Richard, but I want to see you later. You know. Really see you and be with you tonight. Your place or…oh hello dear. Are you finished with the Sergeant? I suppose now I must recount this horrible afternoon. I can't believe this. "

"He just wants to know what I saw and what if anything I remember Phillip may have said. But honestly I know I couldn't have been much help. I think the cop was shocked that I refer to him as Phillip but that's what I call him, soooo. I mean he even made a note of me calling him Phillip. He acted like it was just routine notes but I know that's what he was writing. Weird, huh? I sort of think he's lost in the tall weeds, ya know, not the brightest bulb. Oh well. I guess you're up next cause everyone else is gone. I just can't believe how Phillip could be taken away like this. I mean, he isn't perfect but good God, he doesn't deserve this. Nobody should have this happen. It's like getting hit by lightning. So unexpected."

Lauren doesn't answer but rises and gestures with her index finger to her chest and then back in the direction of the Sergeant to see if he's ready for her. And he is. As she takes a seat across the table from Sergeant Ludoku she notices his shirt is soaked from perspiration and his slick black skin glistens as if it's oiled. The rivulets of sweat start on his forehead and trail unchecked down his face. He's totally oblivious of the sweat and apparently comfortable with his appearance, as if unfazed by the heat, humidity, wrinkles and stress. He smiles a big toothy smile as he looks directly into Lauren's eyes. His broad flat nose looks even larger up close as his oversized nostrils flare and retract with each breath. The smell is overpowering. A mixture of tobacco and coffee on his breath and a very unpleasant musty body and clothing odor from the saturated, dried and re-saturated layers of perspiration. Lauren is unnerved by his smile. It's not innocent or naive. Somehow she knows the smile is a phony, dramatic flair to throw her off guard, as if talking to an old chum. She knows he's very focused on her and she thinks how Jane Ella obviously misread his likely capabilities as a policeman. She quickly collects her thoughts. She can't be distracted by his appearance or his smile. This is the police. Curtain's up! Time to perform.

"Yes, Ms. Pittman. I am so sorry to have to talk with you at a time like this. But could you just tell me about today. Anything out of the ordinary?"
"Well, it's all just such a horrible shock. I still can't believe it. I keep looking at the door hoping he'll just walk through it."

"Mmmm. "

"It's so tragic because Phillip asked Richard to set something up for him that would be private and he was so excited about going alone. If only he wasn't so stubborn and had someone else with him. Maybe none of this would ever have happened."

Lauren begins to sob out loud.

"So, Miss, you *think* it was his idea to go all alone to fish?"

"Oh, yes. In fact he just blurted it out to Richard at lunch the other day that it would give him the peace and quiet he wanted. He was so sure it's what he wanted to do and he got even more sure when he found that some of the other guests overheard and were anxious to do the same thing. It's like he wanted to be first to do it. But Phillip just wanted to go by himself…just be alone. He was being sort of a pain in the rear with some of the other guests and I'm sure he knew it. Sometimes he gets things in his head and that's just the way it's going to be. I just can't believe it. Him insisting to have a day to himself turned out terribly wrong."

"Do you know where on the lake your husband was planning to fish? I mean, did he mention fishing from the bank or did he mention the jetty or any place around the lake?"

"No, I never heard him mention anything about the lake at all. I'm sure he only knows about fishing from reading about it. He told Richard he wanted to catch fish that were maybe ten to twenty pounds. That's all I recall. Oh. Phillip had Richard give him a detailed map of the lake but I never saw what it even looked like. I just remember him asking for it. Maybe he knew where on the lake he wanted to go but I never heard him mention it. Sorry, I didn't mean to ramble on and on. I'm just upset."

"No, no, Miss. That's okay. And I'm sorry. I know you've had a very, very sad day."

"It's just so innocent and tragic. Poor Phillip. He only wanted to have fun and not bother anyone else. Oh why did this have to happen?"

"Again, I'm sorry for you. I find accidents are often difficult to figure out the 'why' after they happen. A lot of times we can look afterwards and say, 'if only…' but who knows why that isn't what actually took place. Tell me, Miss, was your husband a person who may not heed another person's warnings or cautions? Like Richard's warnings, if they were given as Richard says?"

"Well, he certainly wouldn't do anything if *he* thought it was dangerous but he's a very determined man. Phillip thinks he's smarter than everyone else. And Richard and the other guides are so careful in our outings I have no reason to doubt what Richard says he told Phillip is true. I'd have no reason to doubt him. I feel sorry for him because I imagine he gave safe instructions and now this has happened. They seem so safe and cautious about everything here in the camp. But if you know Phillip, he is the sort of guy who listens but then does things his way regardless of what is said, particularly if he underestimates the risk. It's so horrible. I can't stand it. I still hope he's just lost and still out there. We've got to keep looking. We've got to find him."

Sergeant Ludoku looks directly into Lauren's eyes, reaches over and squeezes her hands and smiles at her. Lauren feels his sweaty hand on hers and she is certain he's more touchy-friendly than necessary. Her first gut reaction is the very thought of him hitting on her is revolting. On the other hand, maybe he's hitting on her because he thinks she's the forbidden fruit, the vulnerable and defenseless white woman maybe attracted to the virile sweaty African stud. Perhaps with all the excitement Lauren's own perspiration and sexual vibes are radiating a strong primal message to the Sergeant. Lauren is amused at her thought that even in the human slime category, she has Ludoku beat because in reality he's flirting with a guilty but successful conspirator to murder. Lauren mentally stops short and tries to focus on Richard's early instructions. You not only must act innocent. You must believe you're innocent.

"Is there anything at all you can think of that could help me in any way, Miss?"

"No. I really can't think very clearly at all at the moment."

"Well, Ms. Pittman. I won't keep you here any longer tonight. I may want to talk with you a little more tomorrow but for now we've got the entire lagoon off limits and we are combing the shoreline. Of course it's dark now and that will have to continue tomorrow so none of our searchers get caught in the same problem as what may have happened to your husband. But I'll let you know tomorrow if anything turns up. And then maybe we'll talk a little more later in the day. If something comes up tonight, I'll contact you through the hotel staff."

"Okay. Anything I can do to help, I certainly will do my best."

"Okay. Thank you and good night, Mrs. Pittman."

As Lauren walks toward the door she's aware that Richard is going over to join Sergeant Ludoku. There's something about Sergeant Ludoku she doesn't trust. Lauren can't quite get over his crude touching and the playful little squeeze of her hand. Sweaty, greasy-looking black cop fantasizing about the white woman. But the mixed emotion is that Lauren's also excited somehow that she's the

175

irresistible white beauty. Jane Ella didn't get that treatment from him, and that makes Lauren feel good. It seems as time passes and circumstances develop, Lauren is more confident about the power and control she can channel to control others…specifically men. She likes this fantasy, or reality, whichever it is. This is all falling into place and seems way too easy, Lauren thinks as she heads for her room.

Once in her room, Lauren picks up the phone and calls Jane Ella's room thinking perhaps she'll like some company.

"Hello."

"Jane Ella. I finished with the Sergeant for the night and I wondered if you wanted me to come to your room to talk or just be together for a while."

"Mother, I'm in shock. I can't believe it. I'm tired, I'm filthy dirty from the day and I only want to take a bath and be alone if that's okay. I mean, if you want me to come to your room I certainly will. I feel terrible and I'm sure you do, too. If you'd like company or anything, I'll come right over."

"No, I think what you said sounds pretty good right now. I can't believe all this. It's like it's not real and I expect to see Phillip come walking in the room grumbling about something. I feel worn out and dirty. So I'll see you around seven or so in the morning. I'll call you before I head out of the room. Okay? We'll probably feel a little more like talking tomorrow anyhow. This has been a brutal day, hasn't it?"

"Yes. It sure has. Yeah. And please do give me a call in the morning. This is so unreal. I can't believe this day even happened. What do you think we'll do now? Stay here a while? Go home?"

"I don't know, dear. Let's see what happens with the search tonight. Then we'll see what tomorrow brings and after we'll talk about it. I just can't think anymore today."

"Okay, Good night, Mother."

"Good night."

176

As Lauren hangs up the phone she feels a wave of excitement. It's the first time in years that she can really and truly smile in freedom. Well, almost. There's still the Botswana police and then insurance investigations but this is looking very, very controllable. Her control. She takes a big deep breath and sits on the bed. She whispers to herself as she looks straight into the mirror facing her, "Hold on here, lady. Don't relax too quickly. You are the grieving wife following a tragic mishap. Act like it! Now's not the time to bring suspicion."

Lauren imagines the Police Sergeant probably still around camp tonight having non-stop coffee and cigarettes with the staff and just hanging around talking, snooping to see if anything suspicious happens to jump out.

Lauren's heart is pounding. Murder. Phillip dead. She's not **going to be** an accomplice, she **is** an accomplice! Maybe she should have just divorced Phillip and the hell with the money. No, that's a stupid thought. The whole reason to stay with him this long was to secure a free and wealthy future. And now she has it, or at least it's so close she can breathe it in with every breath. She has to play the role and believe the role as the grieving, innocent wife and give no one the slightest reason for suspicion. She must stoically accept all the pity from the concerned, well-meaning guests who are probably now cowering in their rooms trying to visualize if they had taken a private excursion and been eaten by a crocodile, or alligator, or whatever is in that swampy lagoon.

Lauren undresses wondering if Sergeant Ludoku is outside visualizing what she looks like in her current state of nakedness. What would he do if she opened the door of the casita, saw him and motioned for him to come in for a romp? She's no longer judgmental about a policeman taking advantage of a poor innocent widow as earlier and the very fantasy of his black body frantically moving atop of her causes her to take short quick breaths and tingle.

She shakes her head as if to rid her thoughts of the errant fantasy and moves deliberately into the bathroom for her bath. As she climbs from the tub she stands, total-frontal nude facing the full length mirror. Lauren moves her hands gently over her breasts and down her body until she gently and admiringly pulls at some of her pubic hair. There's not a hint of gray to be seen! She takes a deep breath and thinks how she looks so good for fortyish. Her body appears to be in prime condition for many more years of ageless good health and lots of sexual exploits. Within just a few months or maybe weeks, she will be totally free of even the investigations. She has to stay focused to control circumstances and people around her instead of vice versa, and above all, stay confident. Then she will be totally free to do whatever she wants , with whomever she wants and no strings attached. She walks from the bathroom, turns back the bed covers and slides into bed still naked.   Her last conscious thought is how she'd rather spend this night celebrating with Richard but now's not the time and there's a lifetime of those nights ahead.

The next morning, Lauren slowly walks from her casita to the lobby area and she notices Sergeant Ludoku talking with some staff members under a tree across the lot from the lobby. The hot morning sun, the musk of humidity and the grit of dust in her teeth are a bit more rugged than she cares to endure too much longer. It will be nice to get back to Boston.

Lauren's assessment of Ludoku's activities last night were likely spot on correct.
She thinks he actually may have been outside her casita hoping she'd open the door and motion for him to join her.   He's wearing the same wrinkled clothes and has probably been here all night hanging around. He waves and gestures for Lauren to wait outside the lobby as he moves toward her.

"Hello, Ms. Pittman. I want to tell I do not plan to search further today for your husband. I'm so sorry. But based on information from people I interviewed, what was found and a thorough search of the shoreline, I am going to close the report at my headquarters. I have your husband's passport but I will return that to you when my report is completed, approved and recorded by the magistrate. When you get to the United States you should go to your police and tell them what happened. They will contact my district court and then my report will be sent to your police. If you have a solicitor you should let the solicitor file the necessary claim forms for insurance and legal death certificate in your province or state, whatever it is. Do you understand?"

"Yes, of course. I just need your contact information so I can give it to my police."

"Of course. Here's my card with all the contact information. I am so sorry for your loss. It's not a usual event that a fatal accident happens in my country, but it does happen from time to time and it's never easy to cope with the personal tragedy. Tell me, how is young miss? She's okay?"

"Jane Ella? Yes, yes. She'll be okay. It will be good to get back home but it will all be so different."

Sergeant Ludoku takes a business card from his shirt pocket and hands it to Lauren. She cringes at the feel of the damp, limp paper card.

"Well I feel so bad. Your young miss is so pretty and you, Miss are *so* pretty. I feel sad that you feel sad."

"Thank you for your concern, Sergeant and thanks for the card." She gingerly holds the card between her index finger and thumb as if it's poison.

Lauren begins to cry as a fitting performance for the Sergeant. He puts his arms around her, at first polite, but then he increases the hug into a very tight, bear hug, pressing his body to hers, particularly in the tummy and pelvic areas-close and hard. The smell of cigarette smoke and perspiration is almost more than Lauren can bear even to be polite. Just as quickly, she pulls away, repulsed by the Sergeant this time because of his physical smell and he awkwardly lets go of her and gives her a sympathetic look. He smiles broadly and Lauren suddenly realizes he wanted to keep hugging her in that position for a lot longer, appearing innocent but tightly pressing the front of his body with hers. She feels the corners of her mouth droop in disgust.

But she takes a deep breath and decides the show must go on. She feels the curtain rising. "Oh, Sergeant, you are *so* sweet! You've been so

179

good in all this. I thank you for your understanding. Tell me, are you married?"

"Yes, Miss. Why do you ask?"

"Well, your wife's a lucky woman to have such an understanding man for her husband."

"Oh, thank you, Miss."

The sergeant is obviously a bit speechless and looks a little disappointed at the mention of his wife. But Lauren is pleased at her handling of this as it puts him gently back in his proper role. Easy control. Just like all the rest.

But investigating is apparently over as far as the African authorities are concerned so now she and Jane Ella should make preparations to go home. Besides, Lauren thinks she's seen about all the animals she wants to see. Back to civilization.

The next two days Lauren encounters the other tourists in the camp and they are all very subdued. Every nook and cranny is quiet as if laughing or having fun might be construed as disrespectful.   Lauren and Jane Ella are busy trying to get arrangements to leave and yet they are surprised at the brevity of the police investigation and lack of red tape. Condolences are given by the guides and camp staff and Lauren thinks how perfectly Richard pegged this from start to finish.

Richard is careful to keep his distance from Lauren and Jane Ella throughout their last days in camp but he finds ways to stealthily look directly into Lauren's eyes and give a little smile. She returns the acknowledgements when she is sure no one can notice. Jane Ella attempts to capture Richard's eyes but it seems to Lauren that Richard isn't acknowledging her advances.   Lauren figures Richard has plenty on his mind at this point without complications from Jane Ella.

Then on Thursday morning their luggage is loaded in a van out in front of the lobby. A dozen of the camp staff line up to give hugs and handshakes.

"Let me thank you both for coming on safari with us and accept our deepest sympathy for your loss. I trust it may not dampen your desire to visit our beautiful country again one day. Have a pleasant trip to your home. It's been our pleasure to serve you."

"Thank you, Mister Martin…uh Richard, and thanks to the entire staff. You've all been very kind and understanding. I just can't talk about it anymore right now."

Lauren wipes tears from her eyes and hides her face but she can hardly keep from laughing as she finishes her formal goodbye in front of the staff and other guests who are bidding farewell. Lauren and Jane Ella shake hands with the staff and guides. A few of the staff members are emotional and give a short hug or kiss on the cheek. When Lauren gets to Richard she gives him a restrained short hug and whispers, "See you soon, Richard."

He doesn't respond. Lauren steps up to get into the van and as she turns to wave she notices Jane Ella hugging Richard and crying out loud. His participation in Jane Ella's hug is certainly not as restrained as the one he shared with Lauren a moment earlier. At first Lauren feels a rush of anger and jealousy but then as the other staff members huddle around and pat Jane Ella on the back and comfort her with words, she releases her grip on Richard, turns and quickly walks to the van.

"I just suddenly feel so sad, Mom. I can't believe we are leaving my father in Africa. I know I'm not very sentimental or sensitive about most things, but I'm not sure I'll ever quite get over this. This is so sad! I can't believe this is real."

"Oh, it's *real* alright. I've never, ever felt this bad. I feel guilty. I feel sad. I feel frightened. But somehow we have to get home and try to sort through all this."

"I know, Mom. I just can't imagine, at this point, how we'll ever do it."

Lauren takes Jane Ella's hand and gently squeezes it. They both smile at each other and Lauren thinks for a second she's never seen this look
181

that passes between them at this moment. Lauren quickly suppresses a smile and any reciprocity of tender feelings toward Jane Ella. She thinks this is the logical and practical outcome for a soul-less, arrogant husband and a money-grubbing, spoiled daughter and a foxy, though grieving and well-deserving widow.

The van lurches forward and off they go to catch the plane for the first leg of their long, grueling flight home.

CHAPTER 32

GOOD MOURNING, WIDOW PITTMAN

As soon as they return to Boston and unpack, Lauren calls Murray. It will be reassuring to hear Murray's voice and let him take care of any details. She waits on hold for Murray to answer.

"Is this Lauren?"

"Yes, Murray. It's me."

"God, Lauren, are you okay? I mean under the circumstances? God, I'm just crushed. I'm so sorry for you and Jane Ella. I wasn't quite sure when you'd get back so I was hoping you'd call. Is there anything you need? Anything at all? Can I help with anything? Oh, God."

"Thanks, but it's all such a shock. And another part of the shock is to get home to a dark, empty house and know Phillip will never be here again. Of course jet-lag doesn't help at the moment but the depression of not being able to say goodbye, never seeing him again after that morning he left to go fishing and just nothing more."

"Oh God, Dear. I can't believe what you've been through."

"I can assure you it will be better now that we're home from Africa. I have to figure out what all to do now. Everything's just so strange and different."

"Well, I figured you'll want to have a little memorial service or something. Ya know. It's not something you have to deal with at the moment but something to just allow people to get together in honor of Phillip's life. He knows lots and lots of people…influential people in the financial world. "

Lauren is happy she's on the phone and not talking to Murray in person because then she wouldn't be able to make the faces she's making while he's talking about Phillip. First she rolls her eyes, then comes the dramatic mouthing of words and then the finale acting like she's sticking her finger down her throat.

"Sure. We'll have a memorial. I just haven't had time to think through everything yet. But I need to know what I should do first, now that I'm…we're back home?"

"I've spoken with the Boston Police and so they have already sent for the police report from Africa. Where were you? Botswana or somewhere? I have it all written down correctly from Phillip's itinerary. The Boston PD knows your phone number and when they get the report they'll give you a call. Not to worry. They call, you drive down to their office and they have you read the report to tell them it's accurate from your perspective. That's it. Then the report goes to the coroner and the coroner does a presumptive death review. That may take a week or two. Once the coroner produces a death certificate, then you 'll be busy for a while with all the ridiculous details of stuff, but don't worry about any of that right now. All you need to do is when the police call just go take a look at the report for them. That's all. It could be a week or so before you even hear from them."

"Yeah, I'm sure there are a lot of things to do but right at the moment I just don't feel like doing much of anything."

"Well, you just take your time, Dear. I wouldn't worry about anything or plan on doing anything until you review the police report."

"Okay, but I expect you need to go with me to review the report. Right?"

"Nah. It's just bureaucratic formality. Just go when they call you."

"Okay, Murray. I'm glad I called. At least I feel better about things after hearing your voice. It will be good to talk to you in person. This is all so confusing."

"Well, uh…I'm just sort of telling you the events. Nothing earth shattering. Just sort of what will take place. Look, I'll be talking with you soon. Okay, Sweetie? Bye now."

Lauren thinks that was somewhat of a strange conversation. First he's heartbroken to talk, then it's like he's hurrying her off the phone. Oh well, he's probably got three calls waiting.

One morning a few days later, Lauren is having coffee and reading the morning paper when she's surprised by the phone ringing.

"Hello."

"Good morning, Ma'am, this is Detective Seachrist, Boston Police. I'd like to speak with Mrs. Lauren Pittman."

"This is Lauren Pittman."

"Yes, ma'am. My condolences, Mrs. Pittman. I understand your husband, Phillip Pittman was involved in a fatal accident in Africa and we received the police report from over there. At your earliest convenience, we need you to come down to our office and review the report . Then we'll send it over to the County Medical Examiner. There was a note on the file that an attorney, a Mr. Eddlemann, had called originally and said you would be expecting us to get in touch so I hope this isn't a big surprise to you."

"No, not really. I was expecting the call at some point. Do I just show up or do I need an appointment?"

"Just come at your convenience. Come to our main downtown precinct. We're on 40 New Sudbury Street, downtown. If you can come during an early afternoon it would probably be least crowded. If you just come to the main desk on the first floor and ask for me, I'll spell it for you."

"Okay, go ahead. I have a pen."

"I'm detective Seachrist, S-E-A-C-H-R-I-S-T."

"Okay. I think I'll come down this afternoon if that's okay with you. I'll try to get there, parked and all so I get to your office about one or one-thirty. How's that?"

"Great . It shouldn't take very long and I really appreciate your cooperation in taking care of this. And I guess that's about it, then."

"Sure. Bye."

Lauren struggles through the after-lunch traffic of downtown Boston but arrives in the Boston City parking garage and winds her way around , finally parking fairly close to the elevator that has an arrow indicating the direction to the Boston Police Department. Once inside the lobby, it's just like Detective Seachrist said. She gives his name to the woman at the information counter and is directed to wait in the lobby. A few minutes later, Detective Seachrist steps off the elevator and escorts Lauren to the third floor. The detective asks her patience while he arranges for a room where she can privately review the report. Her irritation grows after several minutes and what seems like an unnecessary delay. Then another officer comes in and asks her to accompany him down a hall and into yet another dingy, waiting room with uncomfortable wooden chairs. She watches in amazement as officers and detectives have plenty of time to walk about, coffee cups in hand, sleeves rolled to the elbow as if busy but mostly involved in kibitzing about who knows what. It appears to her to be very informal and lazily bureaucratic. Cops acting like how they think cops are supposed to act. Apparently there's a lot of inside jokes and male camaraderie. Lauren fidgets. She looks at her watch. She checks her cell phone. She twists on the hard seat. Nearly two o'clock.

"Mrs. Pittman?"

Lauren jumps a little as she turns and looks up at the tall slender man standing right next to her. Where did he come from? He looks every bit the handsome, dashing detective with his crew cut, square jaw, trim physique and actually a real badge hanging on a leather flap over his belt. Lauren rises from her seat to shake hands and she's greeted with a pleasant smile, a firm handshake and a man who towers over her by several inches. He appears to be in his mid-thirties and very well-preserved. She sees no evidence of gray hair and his deep green eyes are so emerald looking contrasting with his tan face she wonders for a second if he's wearing color contact lenses. Not a chance! This guy's for real and all man. His knit polo shirt shows a broad chest with no evidence of man-boobs or belly flab. How nice! Lauren thinks it's a treat to see this young man so close because even though she loves Richard, he is showing signs that his forty plus years look a little on the fiftyish side, more than the thirties. Richard also sports a smattering of gray hair and a couple of soft spots protruding in his mid-section. Sex is terrific with Richard, so Lauren wonders what it would be with an athletic young tiger like this detective. She knows she must say something and stop gawking.

"I'm Mrs. Pittman."

He firmly but gently continues to hold her hand and smile.

"How do you do, Mrs. Pittman? I'm Lieutenant Jess O'Halloran. I first want to tell you how sorry I am. I apologize for the wait. Lacey…uh, I mean Detective Seachrist said he brought you up here but instead of seeing him, I guess I'll have to do. I hope you won't mind to verify information in the report we received from Africa. If it's not too much trouble, could you step into my office and have a seat for just a minute?"

Too much trouble? As the Lieutenant turns to lead the way to his office, Lauren can't help check out his butt. The snug gabardine trousers with no obvious lines of underwear make her interest peak if this guy is going commando and showing his wares. He carves a fine figure of two symmetrical halves filling his snug fitting slacks. Lauren finds this is no trouble at all.

"Sure. Lead the way, Lieutenant."

They go into a small office and the lieutenant closes the door. Lauren thinks calling this an office is a stretch because it's more like a closet and not a very big one at that.   His desk is cheap looking with what appears to be a finish of contact paper and aluminum legs. His wall is filled with plaques probably from his heroics in the military and while climbing the police promotion ladder. If the chaos of papers strewn about his desk is any indicator of his ability to solve crimes, Lauren figures he's very lucky to be where he is. The room smells of perspiration, coffee and pine-scented cleaning solvent.

"Mrs. Pittman, we asked you to come in today to look over the police report and be as sure as you can of dates, names, places, that sort of thing. I'm not asking you to critique how thorough or anything else. I've had Detective Seachrist look over it and he made a couple of comments, not particularly complimentary of the local African Police but just look past that. Just names and so forth. Okay?"

"Sure. What's the purpose of this, Lieutenant…I'm sorry your name again?"

"Jess O'Halloran. Once you've looked it over, I'll take one more look at it later today and make a couple of comments and then forward it to the County Medical Examiner. I'm sorry you have to talk about this again and I'm sure it doesn't get any easier each time it comes up. "

"It's okay. I understand. It's so difficult because there was never any closure with saying goodbye. It seems unreal and almost like he'll just come walking through that door but I know that isn't reality. No, it's okay. Ask whatever you like."

"Some of this you may know and maybe not. I just like to make certain you understand the process that's taking place.   I don't mean to be cold about it but since there are no remains, the coroner must review the information available and make a determination that your husband is officially presumed deceased. If there's evidence or suspicion of foul play or other indications of negligent or intentional responsibility for the disappearance or death then the coroner has the duty to ask more questions. In the case of your husband, there's doesn't seem to be much mystery as to what happened. In the past when I've seen this sort of report the coroner will act promptly so you can move on with the estate and legalities to get this behind you. "

"Sure. I'll do whatever you need. I have to tell you this is like a process of constant reminders of that horrible day. I've never been apart from my husband and I can't tell you how much I miss him. I miss his touch. His tenderness. "

Lauren lets tears roll from under her sunglasses down her cheeks. She fumbles in her handbag for a tissue and finding one she stands and turns her back to the Lieutenant at his desk. She walks toward the window of his office and sees no less than three of the cops in the squad room looking at her. She's amused that they are obviously checking her out. Facing the squad room she smiles because she figures the Lieutenant is checking out her backside from the waist down and the knees up. Lauren decides to catch the "little boy" peeking. She abruptly turns back toward the Lieutenant and of course she was right. His mouth is slightly open and he must reluctantly raise his eyes to hers.

"I'm sorry, Lieutenant. Sometimes, I just can't escape the loneliness or the sadness of the moment."

"Oh, I understand." He rises and respectfully stands behind his desk waiting for her to resume her seat.

"Okay, let me have the report and shall I just sit here and read through it or do you want me to take it elsewhere?"

"No...no, please just stay right where you are. May I get you something to drink? Coffee? Coke? Water?"

"No, I'm fine. I'll just read this report. On second thought, a bottle of water would be really good."

"I'm afraid we have a water cooler and paper cups. No bottles. Is that okay or can I get you something else?"

189

"A cup is fine. But surely our Massachusetts taxpayers can do better than that for our men in blue."

They both smile politely but his eyes are looking directly into hers. He's very, very attractive.

"And women in blue as well. Who knows, maybe someday modern conveniences like bottled water. So today you'll be able to handle a cup of water?"

"Sure, Lieutenant. I'll **handle** whatever you've got. I'm under the spell of a handsome, young police lieutenant. I'm powerless."

Lauren bats her eyes dramatically and playfully.

Lieutenant O'Halloran blushes, coughs nervously a couple of times and drops his eyes to his desk.

Lauren knows she can wrap this guy around her pinky. But he's so cute she may want to see later where this could really lead. He really turns her on.

Lauren confidently reaches over and takes the police report from the Lieutenant's desk. She looks at him without saying anything else and he quickly stands to go for the cup of water. She reads quickly looking at names and reading the comments of Sergeant Ludoku. She notices in two or three spots where the good Sergeant expresses that the "family is above any suspicion in this accident" and the lodge has procedures in place to insure tourists are not at risk" and then the comment she loves, "the victim obviously used poor judgment and did not heed repeated instructions that would have most certainly prevented the accident". There was only one loose end she could see, and if she sees it she's certain others will as well. The report says they have only Richard's word that Phillip was dropped off at an area far away from the jetty and that he instructed Phillip not to go near the bank or the jetty. But the police were unable to identify any tire tracks that indicated otherwise since all the police and camp rescue vehicles went over and over the lake bank areas. All in all, it seems there shouldn't be any problems. Lauren doesn't smile but she sure feels like it. She hands the report back to the Lieutenant.

"I see nothing that is out of the ordinary in the report. The names all seem correct although the police must have interviewed several people at the lodge who I don't know by name. So those names I can only assume are okay."

"Alright, Mrs. Pittman. I know this may seem a lot of inconvenience for just looking over a report but it is one of the steps I have to take. I need for you to acknowledge that you've read it and to the best of your knowledge it is true and correct. Just sign right here."

Lauren stands and moves toward the desk, bending over to give the Lieutenant a little show of her anatomy by way of her blouse top button being undone. After she signs she looks up directly into his eyes and she can tell he's still focused on what he's seeing right in front of him.

"I thank you for your time, Mrs. Pittman. Do you have any questions of me?"

"No, I don't think so. This is just such a nightmare. Will it ever be over?"

"I'm sure it's very difficult and I hope you have brighter days ahead. By the way, did you drive yourself here today?"

"Yes. I parked downstairs."

"I have a parking validation for you to give to the attendant as you exit but I was just wondering if I may walk you downstairs to the parking lot for your car?"

"Oh, that would be nice, Jess...uh ...oops. I shouldn't be so casual. We barely know each other...yet." Lauren can see he reacts to the "yet" as if a light bulb comes on and a door opens.

As they exit the elevator on the parking level, Lauren steps out and she abruptly pauses as if she suddenly has to find something in her purse, but it's a well-designed move, even if somewhat obvious as the Lieutenant bumps into her slightly.

"Oh, I'm sorry, Mrs. Pittman. I am clumsy sometimes."

"Look, Lieutenant, I'll skip formalities and call you Jess and why don't you call me Lauren? That would be nice. I am so alone without my husband, it's nice to just have a man's touch… or be up close…oh, sorry…that's inappropriate and embarrassing. I only mean I miss my husband being close and his touch and I may be acting way too forward with you but it's so comforting just to be touched. I'm sorry if that's over the edge for you but my emotions are so raw and craving right now. Sorry."

"Look, Mrs.…Lauren. You don't need to apologize. I may respond a little embarrassed because it is quite the sort of thing I am trained to avoid. But I must tell you, I'm flattered and I can tell you I only hope your husband knew what a treasure he had for a wife. People have to deal with loss and grief in their own personal way. So I guess what I'm trying to say is that you need not feel ashamed for anything at all today. Words. Actions."

Jess takes a deep breath and keeps his gaze locked on Lauren. "Now, which way to your car?"

"It's this one over here, The Cayenne."

"Woo. Nice car."

Lauren unlocks the door and Jess moves quickly to open it for her. She backs toward the driver seat, sits and pauses looking at her chivalrous police Lieutenant. She's got this guy drooling and wondering what might be. She slides her legs around inside her car and he closes the door. He's lost the whole cop mentality for the moment. He's just staring at her like he'll never see her again. Or maybe he's mentally undressing her and simply being a fantasizing man. Lauren knows she hasn't lost any of her sex appeal. Jess motions for Lauren to put her window down and she does while looking inquisitively at him.

"Sorry, Lauren. I meant to give you my card…ya know…in case you remember anything you want me to know or anything. I mean…*anything*. I wrote my cell number on the back. Call me for *anything*. Just call direct to me on my cell. It's much quicker and private. So, if you need anything or I can be of assistance to you in any way shape or form, I hope you'll call. In fact, I hope you'll find a reason to call. Geez. Now I guess it's me who's somewhat stepped over the boundaries. Anyhow, here's my card."

"Okay, give me your card but why should I need your card, silly. If I need anything I'll call nine-one-one and ask for Jess. Goodbye."

Lauren rubs Jess' card between her fingers. It's crisp, smooth, professional and dry unlike Sergeant Ludoku's. She raises her window and starts the engine. She backs out, leaving Jess standing like a forlorn little boy lost in the country, so she gives a little wave and smile as she drives off. As Lauren glances into her rearview mirror, she sees Jess still standing watching the car pull away. Smitten, the poor boy.

" Well, well. We'll see what the future holds for Lauren and Jess."

CHAPTER 33
MURRAY BAILS

A short distance away from Police Headquarters Lauren enters the O'Brien Building, home of Patriot Star Investments and she takes the elevator to the sixteenth floor, to see Murray Eddlemann. Lauren is stopping into his office without an appointment and she hopes he will be in this afternoon so she can get through yet another step in this "tragedy".

As she enters his office, Murray's secretary, Janet, immediately jumps up from her chair. Janet is a tall, buxom thirtyish woman with fiery red hair. Today all her glitzy, but professional wardrobe is on display and Lauren thinks how attractive she looks. She's the perfect receptionist for a successful lawyer. Janet scurries from behind her huge mahogany desk and before Lauren can react, Janet has her in a big bear hug and kisses her on both cheeks with a vibrant ," Mwaah. Mwaah."

Lauren can't identify Janet's perfume but it smells wonderfully exotic.

"Oh my God! Mrs. Pittman. I am so sorry about what happened. We are still in shock. I've never seen Mr. Eddlemann cry before but when he was told, he looked like he was going to have a heart attack and then he just buried his head in his hands and sobbed. I've never, ever seen that before. We all loved Mr. Pittman."

"Yes. Thanks, Janet. It's been devastating and that doesn't express nearly enough. My daughter and I are just getting through each day, one at a time. We are so alone and sad. But I'm sorry to hear about Murray. Is he okay now?"

"Yes. I think so. He's still upset about Mr. Pittman but physically Mr. Eddlemann seems to have recovered. I'd just never seen him so upset. Come over here and please sit for just a second and let me make sure

Mr. Eddlemann knows you're here. Can I get you a water or soft drink? Coffee? Tea?"

"No. Thanks. I'm fine. Actually, on second thought, may I have a bottle of water?"

"Sure. Let's see, I have Evian, Perrier or Voss and of course still water. I can put a twist of lemon or lime in if you like."

"A Perrier would be wonderful…and no lemon or lime."

"Sure. Let me check on Mr. Eddlemann and then I'll bring your drink to you here or in his office."

The secretary disappears quickly down the hall and Lauren can hear Murray's voice almost instantly. He appears from the hallway with both arms open for a hug.

"Laau-rennnn! Lauren! Oh my God, dear. This is just the worst! Please come to my office. Come."

As Lauren settles into a big leather barrel-back chair in front of Murray's desk, she takes a deep breath. Janet pops in and carefully places a little silver tray on a small coffee table just to the side of Lauren's chair. It contains the Perrier along with a crystal glass and ice cubes. What an office! Everything except Murray seems to be made of oxblood leather, crystal or glossy mahogany.

"Thanks, Janet. Would you hold all calls and interruptions while Mrs. Pittman and I are visiting?"

"Yes, Mr. Eddlemann." Janet leaves, quietly closing the massive office double-doors to leave Lauren and Murray in his huge private office with the killer view of the entire city.

Murray looks like he should be a lawyer. With his well-coiffed gray hair and distinguished looks. Lauren thinks she's never seen Murray in anything except a gray pinstripe suit except once on the golf course when he was wearing white polyester pants and a red polo shirt, looking a lot older in the golfing gear. But today, typical Murray. His bushy, gray eyebrows hang over the front of his black rimmed reading glasses that are well-anchored to his face by that big nose of his. He's about Lauren's height so that's relatively short in a male-dominated business world. But he obviously makes up for it with his smarts and high-powered reputation. Murray waddles a little as he scoots back behind his desk and takes his seat. He removes his glasses and holds them thoughtfully in one hand.

 Ah, the great legal mind of the corporation, Murray Eddlemann, Esquire! The highest paid lawyer Phillip has and Lauren feels comfortable with Murray as a welcome friend and trusted ally. His whole office exudes success starting with Janet out front, and the absolute luxury of this inner sanctum. Windows from floor to ceiling and sheer drapes that only slightly mask the Boston downtown cityscape. The only thing that looks out of place is a table on one side of Murray's office. It looks like he's in the computer repair business. There are six desktop computers and two open and running laptops. The multiple computer screens are a bit distracting as they flicker and flash, each portraying information from a variety of sources. Probably the main difference in Phillip's super-sized success in business is that Phillip and Murray are always one step ahead of competitors in their investment projects and negotiations. Lauren takes a deep breath. This feels like friendly territory. She's relieved.

 But Murray doesn't take long to dash her comfort to smithereens.

"Now, Lauren, before we begin talking or dealing with any questions you may have, I need to explain a couple of things very clearly. As you know, I'm a partner and also I've legally represented this company since Phillip and I gave birth to it many years ago. I've seen the phenomenal growth, and I might add, exponential financial success. It's been like riding a rocket, a trip to the moon. And I've been with Phillip every step of the way. Though from that historical description and day to day business it may seem I'm Phillip's personal attorney, that is incorrect. I am right now, today, and as I mentioned, since the beginning, legally representing the company. I represent the Board of Directors and their interests. I also over the years have handled some of Phillip's legal questions and issues that would come up with him personally but those matters were marginally allowed in my capacity to protect and preserve the interests of the Board of Directors and Phillip as Chairman. That would happen from time to time and up to this point in our professional relationship that's never presented a potential fiduciary conflict. I've always judged my involvement in an 'arm's-length' test. I'm sure you probably have ten thousand questions about where to start in picking up the personal pieces of Lauren Pittman. Am I right? "

"Sure."

" Okay, good. Ultimately there will be insurance proceeds and of course stock held by you and Phillip. I know the stock is held in joint tenancy which means that passes straight to you on his death. And, nothing happens with that at all until there is an official declaration of death from the coroner. Until then everything just keeps going on as if it was a month ago. Okay so far? "

"Yes."

" Okay. Nothing legally changes until the death is official, as if he were still right here or still on vacation. And Lauren I hope you know me well enough to know I mean no disrespect or am being insensitive by using that little analogy. Now once he is declared legally dead by the County Medical Examiner, then a lot of things are kicked into motion. Decisions may come pretty fast and you will want someone who can represent you and …"

"What? I have someone to represent me, Murray…don't I? You?"

"Well, Lauren that's why we're having this little conversati…"

"Whoa. Hold on here. What are you saying, Murray? What do you mean I'll need someone to represent me? I thought that's your job. Are you telling me that *you* won't take care of things for me, Murray?"

"Honey, I represent the Corporation and the Board of Directors and you must realize that without Phillip personally present to beat the living shit out of these chameleons every day, there is going to be one hell of a power struggle extraordinaire'. You will eventually be personally

197

holding the stock majority and that complicates the struggle. I represent them as a board and must not do anything in terms of legal representation or advice for any of them as individuals or you for that matter. I cannot. Plain and simple. I have to try to keep the corporation and its board functioning until all the dust settles."

"I'm speechless, Murray. I never imagined I'd have to deal with anybody but you. You've been a family friend for twenty years. And..."

"You have to understand, Lauren. I represent the board and no matter what Mr. Murray Eddlemann wants, *attorney* Murray Eddlemann has to walk the straight path here. You need a good personal attorney. Ethically, I can't even recommend anyone but if you stop by Jan's desk, you'll find a couple of names lying on the corner of her desk. Just take the list. I wrote it and left it there for you because I figured I'd see you soon. Don't ask Jan anything, just take the list and call one of them. Okay?"

"Sure. I have no choice. Boy. After all I've been through and I feel like I just got tossed out your sixteenth story window onto the street. No wonder you told me if the police called it would probably just be routine and you never made any effort to accompany me. Very sly way to let me down, Murray. I thought that a little strange, but I trusted you. Well, I wouldn't consider it routine and I felt very uncomfortable not even knowing what I should be careful of or mistakes I could make. So that's the way I get treated by you? Well, I don't like being hung out to dry that way, Murray. One Bit! But why am I telling you this? You don't give a flyin' shit. I'm not *your* client. Right, Murray? Well, thanks for all your sympathy. Ya know, years ago I said something to my own dad about having sympathy on me for something that happened. Ya know what he did? Huh?"

"No. Lauren, I don't know what he did but I ..."

Well, I'll tell you. He laughed and then he said, 'Lauren you find sympathy in the dictionary between shit and syphilis. And that's right where it belongs. Just get over it.' So Murray, I think he may have been right. And I'll get over it without all your friendship and help."

"Please, Lauren. There just isn't anything I can do."

"Okay, Murray. Don't whine. You don't need to repeat your legal mumbo jumbo all of which boils down to 'see ya around, good luck to ya and fuck you. Being abandoned is one thing, and I'll deal with that. But I hope this doesn't mean you are going to go overboard in the other direction and make my life miserable or somehow screw me out of what I have a right to…'"

"Oh, God, Lauren. Please don't do this. I love you and Phillip. But I have to be up front about this and I can't imagine how this can cause you a problem at all. I just can't handle your *personal* end of it. That's really all. I mean my representation of the Board of Directors is to try to get all this settled without anyone being negatively impacted in legal matters. If I were to represent your personal interests and one of the asshole directors thinks I'm pandering to undermine him or the board in some way, then it all becomes a legal nightmare."

"Say no more, Murray. Certainly no negative impact. I keep you on the Christmas and Hanukkah list but you legally throw me under a fuckin' bus from your sixteenth story office. So I'm real clear, I'm not a client and I'm certainly not a friend…but no, Murray, it's supposed to be just fine. Nobody's negatively impacted. Clean hands, huh Murray? Sounds like somebody else I know."

Lauren turns abruptly and walks from Murray's office leaving him standing there apologizing. As she walks by Janet's desk there's Murray's handwritten paper lying by itself on the corner. Obviously Janet knows the meeting with Murray didn't go well. Probably listening devices so she can be an outer ring of defense should Murray, the scumbag, be threatened. So, when Lauren comes back through the office lobby, Janet is busying herself and trying not to make eye contact. Lauren angrily snatches the piece of paper and pauses. Why not give a performance finale. Lauren takes a tissue from her purse. Her hands are trembling so badly she drops her handbag on the floor with the contents scattering about. She stamps her foot and sobs out loud.

"Fuckin' Judas. God damned fuckin' Judas. " Lauren turns and glares at Janet as she sneers her sarcastic, cutting remark.

"C'mon, Janet, let me hear some more of your 'Oh, Lauren, I'm so sorry" sympathetic bullshit. C'mon, Janet. Speechless now?"

Janet gasps in horror and puts her hands over her mouth as if to protest the harsh words. Lauren dramatically gives her the finger and grabs the scattered contents, shoves them back in her purse and nearly runs from the office still sobbing hysterically. As she closes the door into the hall she stops sobbing and wipes away the tears. Lauren looks around to be sure no one is around. She smiles and pumps her fist as if she's won the final match point at the French Open.

"I'm really, really getting good at this. Tears, charm, angry outbursts and a little wiggle here and there- it's all part of control. Actually I'm damn good. I am damn fucking good and I think I like this more and more all the time. First, the African cop, then Jess, then Murray and Janet. I wonder who will be in the executive washroom changing their Depends first, Murray or Janet? God, I love this! But what could I do but react?

"God-damned Murray! Thought he could sell me all that bullshit. Fucking Judas!"

Lauren takes the elevator to the parking level and walks toward her car with a stride like a model from a Vidal Sassoon Advertisement. Long, confident steps and, hair flying to the right and to the left. Finally she reaches her car.

"I'm just a fragile, innocent widow. But guess who's in control? I'll get my chance to have Murray on his knees begging to help me anyway he can. I'll get a chance meeting and turn on the sex for him. The trusted attorney will jump for the chance to have a go with me and I'll put the ring in his nose right then and there. Arms length…bullshit. He'll be begging."

Lauren smiles as she starts her car and drives home still relishing the moments of pure power this afternoon.

200

CHAPTER 34

SORTING REALITY

The following week Lauren is surprised by a mid-morning call.

"Hello?"

"Mrs. Phillip Pittman, please."

"Yes, this is Lauren Pittman."

"Mrs. Pittman, the Suffolk County Medical Examiner, Dr. Michael Brancowicz, completed the case of the presumptive death of Phillip Daniel Pittman. You can pick up copies of the official death certificate at the M.E.'s office or we can mail them. Do you have a preference?"

"Uh, Yes. Let me pick them up so I can take them to my attorney. Is there one official copy or can I get extras?"

"Well, if you have some idea of how many you'd like, we can make certified copies with the raised seal and you can pick all of them up at once. They are five-dollars for each certified true copy with the raised seal. How many copies would you like?"

"Can you make ten?"

"Yes , of course. I'll make them this morning so if you come anytime after noon today they'll all be waiting. You will need to pay for them at the time of pick up. We can take cash, check or credit cards. That okay then, Mrs. Pittman?"

"Yes, very good. Thanks."

"Okay, bye."

"Bye."

Lauren hangs up, fumbles for the crumpled paper with attorney "recommendations" from Murray. She dials the first name on the list.

"Good Morning, Mr. Sacks office, how may I direct your call?"

"Yes, my name is Lauren Pittman and my corporate attorney, Murray Eddlemann referred me to Mr. Sacks. I'd like to speak to Mr. Sacks if he's available, please."

"Just one moment."

After a short pause, "Hello, Mrs. Pittman, this is John Sacks. Murray told me you may call and I'm glad to be of service to you. How in the world are you coping with all you've been through?"

"I'm doing okay, I suppose, under the circumstances. Lots of loose ends yet to fall into place and I guess I got one of the big pieces just a few minutes ago. The coroner's office called and said the death certificate is available. I wasn't sure exactly how many I'll need so I told them to make ten of the certified copies. Will that be enough?"

"Should be. At least we can always get more if we need them. Listen. Are they mailing them to you?"

"No. I told them I'd pick them up this afternoon about one."

"Super. That's what I was going to suggest. Is it possible for you to bring them to my office after you pick them up?"

"Sure. I can do that. I'll guess I can be there at your office about two."

"That's fine. I will go ahead right now and begin a list of what we need to take care of, like the house, cars, bank accounts, stock transfer into your sole ownership. I'll also file the life insurance claim. So when you come to my office we'll get acquainted and then hopefully, by the time you get here my secretary, Betty, will have lots for you review. I hope it will take some stress from you as we get this all under control."

"Wow. That sounds good. See you then."

"Okay. Bye bye."

By two that afternoon Lauren picks up the death certificates and parks in the underground garage in John Sacks' office building. She steps off the elevator on the third floor and enters John's office. It seems obvious to Lauren that John is just commencing his own law practice and his office is much less elaborate and plain than Murray Eddlemann's office.

"May I help you?"

"Yes. I'm Lauren Pittman here to see John Sacks."

"Oh, yes. I'm Cindy, Mr. Sack's secretary. I'll take you to the conference room. I think Mr. Sacks and Betty have several things in there for you to review."

Lauren enters the conference room and the receptionist was certainly correct. There are six labeled sticky notes arranged on the table top likely waiting for papers. Lauren walks to the window and parts the drapes enough to see out.   John must still be living off the crumbs left by Murray and other big shot attorneys with their cityscape views. John's view is of a lower rooftop and what must be all the air conditioners for the building. Oh well, he has to start somewhere.

The young man is pleasantly smiling as he approaches with outstretched hand, "Hi Mrs. Pittman. I'm John. Are you enjoying my view of Boston.?"

"Oh, I was just looking out to see where we are in Boston."

"Well, I will say you're diplomatic. It would have been better to have bricked in that space and faked a window. Pretty dismal. Well, anyhow, we've been organizing where there will soon be stacks of papers for you to review and sign. This will clear up a lot of things."

"Good. It actually is moving along faster than I expected, John, and I'm happy about that. It's certainly frustrating not being able to guess how long some of the bureaucracy takes."

"Depends. A lot of people do this on their own and I guarantee that always takes longer. You haven't met Betty yet. She's my legal assistant and she will get started with some basics for ownership transfer. Some of those papers can go straight over to the courthouse this afternoon or tomorrow morning and get recorded. Then that's about it for today. We'll do as many of the simple issues of ownership - for cars, some bank accounts...that sort of thing. Easy stuff first."

"Oh, that sounds like the way to do it. That's for sure. I appreciate it, John…until at least you're better paid."

" The two matters I want to let you know about right now are the life insurance and the shares of stock in your late husband's Corporation…actually, your corporation as of right now. You're the queen and you can decide what you want to do with your controlling interest in the corporation. Murray's been very helpful this morning in having a runner bring some of the documents we need."

"John, I have no interest in doing anything in that company except getting as much money out of it as I can and being done with it."

"Okay, that's fine. But please say that only to me. It stays in this room. Please don't say anything one way or the other about the corporation or your intentions until you and I have an official meeting with the Board of Directors . And we can talk strategy before then. But I don't know if you know about the life insurance…"

"Well, I' remember Phillip saying there was a life policy on him that would make me a millionaire. I suppose you're going to tell me. Please make it be true, John. I can't handle too many more nasty surprises."

"First of all, no more nasty surprises. Okay? Now, sit down because this will likely be shocking but not unpleasant in any sense of the word. I think it will be quite a good surprise for you."

"Okay. That I can probably handle."

"Okay, Lauren. There turns out to be not just one policy, but two life insurance policies, both through the same insurance company.   One personal policy is for $5 million and that's likely the one Phillip told you about. That certainly will fulfill the millionaire prediction plus a substantial amount more. The second policy is a "key-man" policy through the corporation that will pay $10 million to you as Phillip's heir and $30 million to the company to help fill in the gap of leadership left by the Chairman of the Board. What do you think of that?"

"I'm speechless. Fifteen million dollars?"

"No. Not fifteen million. Here's the real surprise for you. Since Phillip's death was an accident, both policies are double indemnity in case of accidental death and so they pay double. That's right, thirty million. Glad you're sitting down?"

"John, I had no idea. Not a clue. I mean we have always had plenty of money and I just never really thought about anything like that."

"Good. I like what you just said. You're going to need to remember that. With this significant amount of money being claimed, the insurance company will be buzzing around and investigating to the fullest extent. The investigation will likely be drawn out and get a little contentious and insensitive to your feelings. You can bet they'll try to turn up anything that is contrary to an accident. "

"Well, what about the coroner? Doesn't the coroner's ruling of accidental death count for anything?"

"I wish I could tell you it does but the truth is they will still try their best to prove differently. Just be honest and don't give them any innocent, off-hand remarks or actions that could lead them to anything other than accidental death. Okay?"

"God. You're scaring me. Sounds like they'll be snooping and watching and who knows what all? Oh, why should I care? I have nothing to hide and I suppose we have no choice but to play their game."

"Yes, Mrs. Pittman, that's correct and I already know they will want depositions from you and your daughter. They may go to Africa and talk to the people there as well. As I said it will likely be long and drawn out. So don't spend that thirty million just yet."

"Please call me Lauren and it's not like I need it all at once. But then I still have a shit load of company stock to unload. Oops. That's just between you and me." Lauren winks at John.

"Yep. And I'll attend all of the insurance depositions with you and your daughter. We'll discuss the conduct of a deposition before we go to one so don't worry until they set up a time for you. I hope you don't mind, I asked them to have all communications through me and not you or your daughter directly. Once I know when they want to meet , I'll let you know. Then we'll get together and rehearse a few questions and responses so the whole thing will be a little more familiar to you and your daughter."

"Okay, counselor. Sounds fine to me. Now where do I sign all this stuff.?"

Lauren spends the better part of an hour signing and looking over the legal papers to transfer ownership of property to her.

Later in the week, John informs Lauren that the insurance investigators want to meet with both Lauren and Jane Ella. Lauren advises Jane Ella about the request and how John will meet with each of them before the deposition. Jane Ella is irritated about being questioned once again and her tone of voice vividly portrays the displeasure, "What is it with these people? They insure you. Something happens. You have a death certificate and then they don't want to pay. Weasels! Not that any of it will benefit me. How shall I say…I got mine already. I just find it so ridiculous telling the same things to people over and over again. Oh well, I guess the lawyer wants to instruct us so I don't say something stupid and screw it up for you. Right, Mom?"

"I have no idea what you mean, Jane Ella. Just tell them what you know. The truth. That's all. It'll be over soon, I'm sure."

"Well, you don't really mean to tell them *everything* do you?"

There's that icy feeling again. It's like life comes to a screeching stop when certain things are said. Lauren's stomach does a flip flop. Here it comes again.

"What do you mean?"

"Oh, Mother. C'mon. I know the tragedy was an accident and really horrible. I really do know that. It's just I'll bet nobody has so far connected the dots between you and Richard and then the safari and then Phillip, and of course poor Phillip doesn't make it back. Look. I know it was an accident and if anybody was at fault it was certainly Phillip himself. But your close *friendship* with Richard is…well, you say it's harmless but I don't think it will be good when the investigators stumble onto the truth. They'd probably dig up enough to just keep everything under a microscope for the next twenty years. And you know they'll find out everything, don't you? But don't worry. Anything they find out won't be from me."

"Stop it! God dammit! What we've been through is a horrible tragedy and there's no need to make it worse. I haven't even heard from Richard since we left the camp. So, stop it. You are so dangerous and you don't even know it. You make up things and shoot your mouth off and it only takes one comment to the wrong person and you're right…we have done nothing wrong but we'd be living under a microscope for the next twenty years. So, just shut your trap."

CHAPTER 35

RICHARD RETURNS

Later that day the phone rings and Lauren reluctantly answers it.

"Hello."

"Hey, Lauren. Been a while."

"Richard! Oh, it's so good just to hear your voice. Where are you?"

"I'm at the good old Omni, right here in Boston. Thought I'd stay here. I'd love to catch up on how you've been but you know how I hate to talk to you on the phone. We've been friends for so long and I'm just concerned about how you and your daughter are doing."

"What? My *daughter*? I can't…"

"Lauren. Sorry to interrupt you but you know… You *know…* I hate to talk on the phone and I'd rather just sit down over a cup of coffee and catch up. If you could pick me up at six we can find a spot to just chat for a while. Okay, Lauren?"

"Sure. Six. Out front."

Suddenly Lauren knows why Richard sounds so stilted and strange. He suspects her phones may be tapped. He mentioned that a long time ago and now he must believe it may be a reality. Good thing she didn't blurt out any of her real thoughts and what she wants to do with him. Lauren gets ready and drives to the Omni. There stands Richard. He politely waves, then as she rolls to a stop, he opens the door and slides into the passenger seat.

Lauren sees Richard in a slightly different image at this meeting. Of course he's still attractive but he does look older. He's still the dashing

Richard but Lauren can't keep from comparing him to Jess. Lauren feels powerful and confident that she has plenty of activities from which to choose. Now if she could do a little fling with John Sacks and Murray she'll have partners from innocent youth to robust handsome stud, to defibrillator-ready maturity. It's wonderfully exciting just thinking about it.

"Whew. I was afraid to even call you this afternoon. I've no reason to think they've done so, but the police or insurance people could tap your phone or have us tailed. Hey. You look like you're a million miles away. Are you okay, Lauren? What are you thinking about?"

"Oh, sorry. Just preoccupied over all this. But wiretapping and spying...are those legal?"

Richard takes a deep breath, "From what I understand it's probably not legal to the extent they can use any taped conversations in court but it sure is a good way to get them onto the scent of an active trail. We'll just be careful until this all blows over. Better safe than sorry."

"But what about us? Like today? Can't we just…"

Richard is obviously cautious, "Best not. A little celibacy won't hurt, and the payoff is a handsome one, right?"

"Yeah. I guess it's even more than I'd thought. I mean it was an accident so the life policies are double indemnity for an accident. That's millions in payoff. And the stock value is even bigger. Lots bigger. It's much, much more than I'd ever even imagined. Well over a hundred million total. Lots of money but there are people who scare me. Phillip's trusted friend and attorney, Murray turns out to wiggle his way clear of representing me. He only represents the glorious company. I've always trusted him but with this much money involved who knows? Then there's an Irish cop, a Lieutenant at Boston PD and he's very, very nice but being a cop I'm also sure he's naturally wired to be suspicious even when he has no reason to be. He said one of his detectives was not complimentary of the African police investigation and report. I just can't trust any of them one hundred percent. Then, of course there are the insurance people. I'm expecting the third degree from them and if what you say about phone tapping there are lots of eyes and ears paying attention to this entire fiasco. "

"Well, while I was still in Botswana I got a formal request to give a deposition to the insurance company and they offered to send their attorney over to the camp. I told them I was due for about a thirty day break so I'd just come back to the states and appear at their place. As long as you and I play the 'old college' buddy routine we should be okay. Just so we don't get our legs wrapped around each other until this is done we should be able just to stay on the straight and narrow."

"Why can't we can go to a drive-in movie or someplace and park or something. Ya know. Jump in the back seat like dear old school days. Are there still drive-ins? God, come to think of it are there back seats that can even accommodate two full-sized, pretzeled bodies without causing leg cramps?"

"I have no idea but let's just act as casual friends and not arouse suspicions. Believe me it won't be much longer if they are already taking depositions. We talk. They analyze, they look for inconsistencies and unless they find something, which they won't, then that should be it. But believe me they will not be friendly people. Just remember. We did nothing. Your family went on a safari and I just happened to be the manager. Phillip, after being a pain in the ass to everybody, wanted to go off on his own. The camp gave him everything known to man including clear instructions of what to do and not do and he ignored all the warnings. End of story and beginning of a new story. Right? You still mean what you said all those weeks ago when I was here? Ya know…sort of that I won't have to worry about my financial future?"

"More now than ever, Richard. You will have more money than you ever dreamed and I will wait for the day we can be together without any third party being around."

Richard snaps a glance of fear at her when she mentions the words "third party".

"Why? What do you mean, Lauren?"

"In case you don't remember, that third party's **not** around any longer. Clean hands all around. Now we just have to play the little game and ka-ching ka-ching…collect."

Lauren continues, "Oh, by the way, I was thinking we ought to include Jane Ella in some of our platonic lunches or coffees. Ya know. Just to make it a casual, nothing to hide, just friends sort of thing. We can maybe hear how she does in her deposition just to be on the safe side."

"She really doesn't know anything to cause a problem so I can't imagine her doing or saying anything stupid but, I agree, it's a good idea to include her."

Later Richard and Lauren part company and Lauren drives home.

CHAPTER 36

LET THE INQUISITIONS BEGIN

The next day, mid-morning, Lauren is in the family room, looking out toward the pool.

"Whatcha lookin' at, Mom? Hoping your friend is outside on the chaise lounge ready for action?"

"I won't even dignify that with a comment. In fact, I'll show true civility and offer an olive branch. How about going to lunch with me?"

"Moi? Lunch? The two of us? How different would that be? Actually, I will do it. Sounds good. Where do you want to go?"

"Let me surprise you, Jane Ella. I'll just bet you'll like my surprise."

"Right. This will be a first if you surprise me with anything."

"C'mon. Be nice."

They get in Lauren's SUV and drive into downtown Boston. Lauren pulls up to the front of the Omni Hotel and there stands Richard.

"Look! It's Richard! Well, you did it, Mom! This is a surprise and I'd say a great way to start lunch."

Richard scoots into the back seat and as they drive off, he and Jane Ella make a chatter of small talk and laughing that lasts the entire trip to the restaurant. Lauren pulls up to the Rialto Restaurant valet parking and all three climb out of her Cayenne. They get seated at a table together and Lauren is facing a large mirrored wall. She's always prefers sitting facing mirrored walls in restaurants. The reflections are never crystal clear and subconsciously the images are more exciting and have a touch of fantasy. Here at the Rialto she can see the reflection of their table in the mirror and she thinks how perfect, the image of the three of them together. It's the way things are meant to be. It's a perfect family. It's a natural family…except there's too much water under the bridge for these three to ever be a truly functional family.

"So ladies, I'm here in Boston to give a deposition to the Madison Insurance Company this Friday. Have they called you yet?"

"Oh, yeah. I'm supposed to go talk to them tomorrow and I go talk to Mom's attorney this afternoon so he can tell me what to say or not say. No biggie."

Lauren cringes at Jane Ella's cavalier attitude but Richard actually squirms and gives a nervous cough.

"Well, of course not. No biggie, as you say. We were all there. You two as guests and me as the Operations Manager. Basically we all know the same things and that's about it. Just so we all have the same story. Maybe here at lunch would be a great time just for each of us to run through the whole vacation time frame again just to see how it all sounds. Ya know, those guys are always looking for a way to try to worm into anything inconsistent in stories. And depositions are all recorded, so they listen and re-listen. I'm sure they'll also read the transcripts over and over with their beady little bloodshot eyes and…"

"God, Richard. If I didn't know better, I'd think you and Mom are worried about getting stories straight and stuff, like you're guilty or worried about something. What's the deal?"

Richard may have thought he was being very clever to preview how the depositions would go but Jane Ella's quip and direct eye contact catches him off guard. Almost like a nervous tick, Richard blinks rapidly and then shoots a fearful look at Lauren as she returns one of the same to him. Jane Ella looks back and forth at their edgy glances and her mouth drops open in a half-smile, "gotcha" expression.

"Whoa! Ho. Ho. Ho. Holy smokes. Those looks are priceless! What's this all about? Do I even want to know? You wanta tell little
213

'ol Jane Ella? Or do I have to play twenty-questions and try to pry it out?"

"I have no idea what you're talking about. Stop trying to make more out of an innocent comment than is intended. You did this once before to me and it's not fair. It's cruel. We have just been through a tragedy and I can't believe it's somehow entertaining for you to try to torture me. Richard's suggestion was simply to try to make this process shorter but apparently you want to play games and you'll see what will happen. This mess and the questioning will keep going on and on and on. I really hate when you try to act so smart. "

"Chill out, Mom. I told you something yesterday and I'll repeat it. Chill. I got mine. Listen to me. I *got* mine. You pulled off the early access to my trust account or God forbid I'd be sitting here penniless sweating out what the hell is going to happen to my meager money. I got mine. What that means to you is I'm not gonna cause you any trouble. So whatever it takes for you to get whatever is coming to you, I'm on board. Just chill. I'm messin' with ya. I won't do it anymore."

"Okay, fine. But Richard's suggestion might really be..."

" Really. Suggestion? Seems to me more like the planned, orchestrated lunch to pump Jane Ella for her 'story'. Really! What a terrific idea for a lunch for a mother and daughter and the handsome third party. I should have known. I think I have other things I'd rather do. Besides, I'm supposed to see Mr. Sacks this afternoon to go over my story so I think pouring over the boring story once today will be plenty for me . I'm really getting sick of this!"

Jane Ella stands up and gets her purse off the back of her chair.

"Where are you going? Don't get into such a huff. Sit down and have lunch and we'll find more pleasant things to talk about. C'mon."

"No thanks. I'm not very hungry and you two can sit here and dissect your salads, stories and scripts. I'll get a cab from here and go see Mr. Sacks. Tell me he's younger than the old letch, Murray. I'll just go now. In the meantime, just chill. I got your back, Mother."

214

Lauren and Richard sit in silence after the ripple with Jane Ella. Neither can eat so they quickly pay and leave. Both Lauren and Richard know their nerves have gotten the better of them this afternoon so they decide to part with a handshake, Richard returning quietly to the Omni and Lauren to her empty house.

Two days later, the morning after Jane Ella was deposed she saunters into the kitchen for morning coffee. Richard is at the house for an early visit and he and Lauren are sitting quietly at the kitchen island.

"So, how did the deposition go?"

"First of all, wait until you meet with John Sacks. He's young, good-looking and killer-sharp! He taught me exactly how to sit and how to be absolutely iron-faced regardless what sort of questions they may ask. We went over my story and then he peppered me with questions he said would be tougher than the insurance guys would ask, so I think meeting with John was very helpful. "

"That's good to hear, but what sort of things did they ask at the actual deposition?"

"Well, I got to Madison Insurance and met John there about one o'clock. We went up to the Conference room and there were eight people waiting for us. That's a little unnerving. Can you imagine going into something like that cold…no attorney? They'd devour you just by intimidation. Everybody in their top drawer suits, women included. Not a hair out of place on any of them. They are all smiles as they begin introducing themselves like it's a family reunion…not that I've ever been to one. But John had told me that's what they'd likely do and to just put up with it because they're all two-faced schmucks who the next minute want to rip you apart. "

"Yeah. Sounds about right."

"What do you mean sounds about right, Richard? How many depositions have you attended?"

"Well, none. So, actually I'm just guessing."

"Go ahead Jane Ella. What happened?"

"Then we all sat at a huge conference room table with big high-back, leather chairs. I sat on one side with John and the rest sat across from us. There were two microphones set up in front of my designated spot to sit. As they all began to rummage through their reams of paper I notice their expressions changed dramatically. One woman, 'Miz Sandoval' looked like she'd seen the worst part of a bitter lemon lunch. She's sort of Hispanic looking and she has an accent and zits. She started the questions. Then a Mr. Steinauer or something like that took up the chase and he looked like this may have been his first rodeo. I mean he looked like a college nerd and he was nervous and he had little drops of white spittle in the corners of his mouth. He probably had a pen protector in his Gucci shirt pocket inside the coat of his custom-tailored suit. He didn't last long and his questions were so general I just stared at him on a couple of questions until someone else rephrased them for me. Then there was this really good looking guy, I can't remember his name but he's the killer jackal. He sneers when he talks but geez! I swear he was so good looking I just smiled at him and pushed my chair back enough from the table so I could flash a little leg at him. Cool huh? There wasn't a smile within one-hundred feet of that room except mine. It got really tense and then they ask a lot of questions and that's about it. How's that?"

She is obviously tortuously baiting Lauren and Richard.

"Jane Ella! Richard and I have been sitting here while you tell painstakingly about the table, the suits, the zits and everything except what we wanted to hear. Can't you just tell us what they asked and what you said and if any red flags came up? What did they ask? C'mon."

"Nothing much. Actually, their questions were boring. Well, they did ask why we selected Richard's company for a safari and if there was any relationship between Richard and Phillip. They asked two or three times how Richard knew Phillip. I almost thought for a while maybe they thought there was something unusual about the relationship between Richard and Phillip. A little funny-guy, gay action. Just kidding. Then the good looking guy really was getting excited about

216

his questions on what relationship you and Richard have. I realized how important it was because the guy kept asking the same question just using different words...trying to trip me up. But I was so cool."

Richard and Lauren are leaning forward , hanging on every word of Jane Ella's deposition saga.

" So, I pictured in my mind the afternoon pool and the bedroom fantasy talk ...but in the end I thought once again how helpful you were to me, Mother. You made the supreme effort with Phillip and I got my money. So, I told them the real truth. I said and I quote ' If you are suggesting some sort of romantic relationship between my mother and Richard Morgan, you must be looney or at the very least, joking. He's nothing more than a casual acquaintance, an old college friend and he just happened to mention a safari and that seemed to be just what our whole family needed at the moment. So, primarily it was my dad, but we all agreed and picked Richard's company. Even more important, if you were seriously implying some sort of romantic involvement between my mother and Richard Morgan, just look at Richard Martin and then look at my mother. He's rugged and very handsome. What would he possibly find attractive about my mother? You'd have to be joking! Tell me you were joking. They laughed, we all took a ten minute break and when we returned, they didn't have any more questions. I'm done. You guys are home free...at least from my end of it. That's all I can do to help. "

Lauren stands straight up, her eyes glaring in rage at Jane Ella's cruelty; and then she does an exaggerated about face and walks briskly and silently to her room.

"Gee, Mommy –Dearest, was it something I said?"

"C'mon, lighten up on your mother just a bit. She's having a hard time with all this."

"Yeah, I know. But I know what I know, Richard. Don't worry. Those insurance lawyers are done with me and I didn't say anything incriminating. And yes, I told them almost word for word what I just said to Mother. Got her nose out of joint to hear it, but for them a good laugh and it certainly isn't incriminating or even suspicious. It's simply the absolute truth. I gave those nerdy lawyers a little glimpse of me here and there and they were licking their lips so it ended with a good laugh. I think even one of the women was licking her lips. So, you'd better watch out, Big Boy. You have competition at every turn of the road. But as far as the deposition, it's all up to you and Mommy Dearest."

"I'm not worried about my deposition in the least. Lauren only knows what she heard and saw and there's no reason for anyone to be suspicious about any of it. It was confirmed over and over by employees of the camp what Phillip requested and I know the staff went to a lot of extra trouble to be sure it was a safe and perfect day for him. My own personal instructions on safety were heard and understood by Phillip. Phillip ignored or thought he was smarter than any of our explicit instructions and advice. So I know what happened and that's all there is to it. Nothing mysterious or dramatic on my part. But, c'mon, you really slammed your mom and actually said that stuff about Lauren to those lawyers?"

"Of course I did. It's true, Richard. I know you tolerate being around her as a part of our charade. I see the boredom in your eyes and the boredom is sincere, not acting. What's the excitement watching her try her best to wiggle as she walks. I think the booze and plastic surgery have come home to roost. Pretty soon she'll look like a broken down old mannequin , mouth open catching flies, leaning forward, body parts detaching and falling in a sad contrail along her path. No, Richard, I know who you watch and I expect for it to stay that way."

Jane Ella hangs her index finger in the corner of her mouth like Little Miss Innocent and then she sucks on it for a second or two.

Richard likes Jane Ella's edgy flirting, "So, you think I'm all about taking care of the inner needs of younger women and…?"

"Be careful, Richard. Don't misunderstand. The promises you've made to me and our plans bind us together forever. That took you out of the girl-chasing game. Besides we still have some roll-up-your-sleeves dirty work before our fairy-tale life becomes reality. Except for an

218

occasional sacrificial fuck of Mommy Dearest you just keep your doohickey inside your stretch-waist, Sansabelt, polyester old guy pants."

"I know. I know.."

" And honestly, Richard, as soon as this insurance thing clears, we need to move quickly with the rest of our plans. Right now my mother is suspicious of everything…or maybe paranoid is the correct term. All we need is for her to get totally nutsy jealous and concoct some story just to get even with you or me. You just keep an eye on her and make sure she isn't going to get snagged by those lawyers over dear old Phillip.

"Quit messin' with me, Jane Ella. We simply need to be patient. The insurance money really needs to be entirely settled before you and I get too publicly chummy. Lauren's own choice of booze and pills are simply a natural, predictable tragic end for her. That's it. Hands clean, my love. All that matters is that you and I stick to our plan. No worries. Clean hands. She'll do it to herself. And in the meantime I'll make her feel like a queen, a relatively happy and satisfied queen."

"Well, don't give me the patience bullshit too much. I'm a woman of action and I'm not afraid to do what I need to do. I really don't know why you waste so much time on my mom, Richard. I don't give a shit if she's happy or satisfied. My dad's accident was unexpected and horrible for the official record but I refuse to let it disrupt our plans. I just don't want her to get out of control. We have this all figured out and I'm certainly not going to shy away from my role nor the results. You repeat your little clean hands mantra all you want if it makes you feel better. But I think you're a big chicken, you're afraid we're going to get caught or that I'll change my mind and leave you hanging out in the cold. So part of this game you play with Mom is to play both of us at the same time for your own sort of personal insurance. Well, Richard, I suggest you pay the most of your attention to me. All the eggs gathering into one basket. If I have to have the balls in our future, then so be it."

"Don't say those kind of things. I'm not afraid so long as I know one day we'll be together without anyone else's interference. Anyone. This is not the time or the place to have any sort of blowup. I need to keep some focus on your mom for the time being until we get all the loose ends settled. After that it's just us. "

Jane Ella gets up, walks straight to Richard bends over and kisses him with a mouth open passionate kiss and then pulls away quickly.

"I don't want to complicate your need to focus so I'm going out for a while and you can enjoy your time alone with the old lady.

Jane Ella walks to the kitchen, picks up her purse and out into the garage she goes. Richard still sits in semi-shock until he's stirred by the sound of Jane Ella's car starting and pulling from the garage.

He mouths the inaudible words to himself, "What a little banshee. Oh, man. Oh, maaan! I know now there is a heaven and hell and they're both right under this roof. Great sex, unlimited money, murder, lies ...and for poor old me it's all multiplied times two. Gotta keep stories straight. Richard, keep your strength up...your future's certainly looking brighter than hanging around in the dusty deserts of Africa."

This same afternoon Lauren is undergoing her deposition at the insurance company. A nearly identical greeting happens in Madison Insurance's conference room. After the brief, smiley and totally phony introductions Lauren and John sit on one side of the conference table and on the other side are four attorneys representing Madison. Lauren whispers to John, "Jane Ella said a couple of these people are real barracudas. Do any of the people across from us fit that description?"

John cups his hand over his mouth and whispers in her ear, " Jack Gleason...on the end is a nasty rat but that's why I'm here. The others weren't here for Jane Ella's deposition and I don't know anything about them. Just try to relax, if that's possible."

Lauren looks directly at John and gives him a confident smile.

Lauren thinks it's too soon to decide of the two women and two men who will be friendly and who may not. A few basic questions about address, dates of the trip, people involved in the safari and Lauren knows there must be more. They're surely just lulling her down the primrose path. She feels poised and up to the task at hand. She thinks to herself, "C'mon boys and girls…bring it on."

"Just another question or two, Mrs. Pittman. Are you okay?"

"Sure, I'm okay. I'm happy to help any way I can. I know you're only doing your job."

"Okay, then. Let's continue. I'm sure you've thought and re-thought about the day Mr. Pittman went missing. How long had Mr. Pittman known about the *'private'* fishing trip that was planned for him? Would you say months, weeks, days, hours or was it a spur of the moment suggestion and plan for him?"

"First, it wasn't planned *for* him or even a suggestion *to* him. Phillip brought up the idea to Mr. Martin…Richard Martin within a couple of days of being in the camp. He was bored and wanted to do something away from everybody."

"Did you know he was going fishing all alone? Or did you have reason to think a guide would be with him?"

"Phillip brought up the idea to go and he kept insisting that he wanted to be alone. So, yes, I knew he was going to be alone."

"Didn't you think it might be dangerous to go away from the camp alone?"

"I never really thought about it. Everything was so controlled around the camp, I assumed there wasn't any likely danger or they wouldn't have allowed it."

"So, it sounds like what you're saying is that you **trusted** the camp to take care of him and assumed they would. Do you feel like they could have and should have prevented your husband's death?"

"I said everything was controlled and I assume they allowed him to go because it would not be too dangerous. You have to understand Phillip. A day or so before his accident, he made comments to the other guests that he thought the whole camp was like a hoax with animals teeth pulled and that sort of thing. He really was not afraid in the slightest and he was not expecting anyone to take care of him. He kept telling Richard that he just wanted to be alone."

"Did your husband like being alone in other activities? For example, did he take vacations by himself or weekend fishing trips around here by himself?"

"Never. I don't think Phillip's taken a total of a week off from work in the last twenty years. But he wasn't a loner, if that's what you mean."

"Mrs. Pittman, did you ask your husband to **not** go by himself?"

"No, he really expressed his interest to do the day trip and I really wasn't ask for an opinion…and I really never thought twice about it one way or the other. I mean, I wasn't worried."

" If you could turn back the clock and be given three wishes about that day, what do you think those wishes would be?"

"Oh, God. Are you serious? What an ignorant question! I thought you wanted facts…so you want to know my wishes? Really! Okay, I'll play your 'wish' game. My first wish is to have Phillip back …and"

Lauren begins to sob. She claws at her handbag for a tissue and finally gets one and sneaks a peek over the tissue at the attorney who asked the question. His expression shows he clearly wasn't expecting such a dramatic, great answer.

"I'm sorry, Mrs. Pittman. I can see how difficult it is for you. Let me rephrase the question a little bit. What do you think anyone could have done-you, your daughter, the guide, the camp staff, the rangers...anyone...do you think anyone could have done anything differently and prevented this?"

"Are you mocking me now? That's a terrible question to ask me and I can't imagine how this helps us all resolve whatever it is you think you have to resolve. But I'll answer you. If Phillip hadn't asked to go on a private outing none of this would have ever happened. If Phillip hadn't insisted his day trip was so he'd be alone and if Phillip just listened to the guide and if my family hadn't even gone on a vacation at all, life would be different right now. But that didn't happen, did it? Now he's gone and you ask me if anything could have changed the outcome? I think that's a moronic question. But I guess you have to scratch around in the dust as if you're doing something important. You're so worried about covering the insurance. This just make me sick. I suppose you're having fun harassing me?"

John Sacks leans forward and puts his hand over Lauren's as if to stop her from talking any longer.

"Ladies and Gentlemen, please. This is difficult for my client and she's doing her best to be responsive but you can tell her nerves are very fragile from the tragic death of her husband. I'm asking for you to make the questions more direct and less hypothetical, please. And maybe a little break would help."

The other male attorney who has been sitting quietly and looking at Lauren, no smiles, no expression scoots forward and leans on the table toward Lauren. Oh, this must be the bulldog. He's been wearing his law-school nasty-face ever since we came in here. Lauren simply wants to get this over.

"Of course. We can take a short break if you like. But, Mrs. Pittman, we are not here to harass you and though you accuse of us of harassment in so many words instead of just answering the questions, your lack of cooperation will only drag this out. We will eventually need clear answers from you, not accusations toward us or our questions. If some of our questions touch a raw nerve, I apologize in advance, but your purpose in being here is to simply listen to the questions, answer truthfully and perhaps leave out your personal preferences about the question. The sooner we ask and you reply, the sooner we'll be finished. Understood?"

Lauren nods and glances at her attorney, John Sacks, and she thinks he looks outwardly worried as if she can't hold her emotions together. He doesn't know her very well or he'd more likely be on the edge of his seat for possible fireworks. Lauren lifts her tissue next to her mouth, looks into John's eyes and whispers, "Prick."

One of the women attorneys could see Lauren's mouth, knew what she said and snickered out loud.

"Very well, Mrs. Pittman, would you like a short break?"

Lauren squeezes John's hand and shakes her head "no" about taking a break.

Jack Gleason continues as he glares at her, "Very well, then, Please describe for me your relationship with Richard Martin."

Lauren's heart picks up speed involuntarily. So here is finally the crux of the suspicions about Lauren and Richard.

"Mr. Martin…uh, Richard Martin, I have known since college days. That's longer than I care to remember exactly, but well over twenty years. He's always been a friend. Just a friend. He came through Boston, called, and we…my husband and I decided to take a family vacation through Richard's company. Richard is some sort of head manager of the safari camp where we decided to go on vacation. That's about all."

"How well did your husband know Mr. Martin? Were they also friends in college? Did they have a friendship for twenty years?"

"Well, I'm sure Phillip met Richard as well as many of my other friends in college but it wasn't like they were pals and stayed in touch or anything. So, were they good friends? I wouldn't say friends. More like distant acquaintances. Did they talk? I doubt it until Richard came to visit in Boston and we decided to take the trip."

"How about from the time you decided to go on the trip until the accident? Did your husband and Mr. Martin seem to be on good terms? Any words or troubles between them? Arguments?"

"No, not that I ever heard…and in fact I'd say even more directly the word "no" is an appropriate answer. I'm sure there were never any arguments or troubles as you put it."

" Is Mr. Martin gay?"

"What? Gay? No, I don't think so from some of his stories about his single lifestyle. No. I wouldn't suspect it. How would I really know?"

"Did you ever suspect your husband of being gay?"

"Please. For heaven's sake. No! And that's about as responsive as I can get.

"As a wife of twenty years, I can understand how you can be sure about your husband's sexuality but how can you be so sure of Mr. Martin? Ever know from personal experience, Mrs. Pittman?"

"Nope. Just friends for twenty years. And I think that's an uncalled-for insinuation."

Lauren tries her best glare to show how insulted she is by Jack Gleason's question.

"What's Richard Martin's connection to your daughter, Jane?"

"What do you mean connection? Jane Ella met Richard for the first time when he came to Boston before our trip. She knew him during the planning of the trip up until the day of…well, the tragedy."

"Mrs. Pittman. Let me remind you that you promised to tell the truth and the *whole truth* today under penalty of perjury. Think carefully of my admonition before you make vague answers to my questions."

"Well, I'll…"

225

Lauren's attorney, John Sacks, interrupts and speaks over her, " Hold on, here. This is a deposition and my client understands her obligations. I resent you asking vague questions and then trying to intimidate her by belittling her responses. If you ask direct questions, my client gives direct answers. She mentioned the word hypothetical questions while ago. I think she's right. Don't try to bully her into thinking somehow she's on trial here. She's not. We are here voluntarily at least as long as the atmosphere remains professional."

The bulldog attorney smiles sarcastically and looks at Lauren. There's a long silence and then, "Well, certainly. I intend for my questions to be direct and professional…but I will ask questions that may be more direct than your client wants to answer. I will not back off my questioning to be gentle. Now, Mrs. Pittman, tell me any relationship of which you are aware that involves your daughter, Jane, and Mr. Martin."

"I understood your question the first time. It's just you seem to have such a condescending, nasty tone of voice that I find I must take a deep breath to remain civil before I respond. That said, my response is the same. There's no 'connection' as you call it. She's seen Richard when he was in our home when my husband was still alive. She knows who he is. We went on a safari together and Richard was in charge. That's all."

"What if I told you that your good friend, Mr. Martin and your daughter, Jane are intimately and sexually involved? Connections that in no way, shape or form could be dismissed as just casually knowing who he is. Are you aware of the relationship between Mr. Martin and your daughter, Jane."

Lauren recalls Richard saying her phones could get tapped but likely they couldn't use that in court but she suddenly wonders if Richard's betrayed her trust. Then Lauren realizes how the question was posed and she recalls John's admonition during the coaching. Gleason never said they were facts, he just said 'what if I told you that…'

Lauren lowers her voice as she stares directly at Mr. Gleason, "Pardon me. I have to take three deep breaths to remain civil this time. I'll repeat my answer. I know of no connection beyond what I already said. I believe you've fabricated a hypothetical situation to see if I'm lying. Well, I'm **not** lying."

"Honestly, Mrs. Pittman. I'm going to lay cards on the table here. I **know** there's more than a casual friendship between your friend and your daughter. I believe your husband found out and may have confronted Mr. Martin over chasing both your daughter and her trust account. Mr. Pittman was last known alive and alone with Mr. Martin. If your husband stood between Mr. Martin and your daughter's money, it is possible Mr. Martin had the opportunity to do him harm and make it appear accidental. After hearing what I just explained, is it **possible** Mr. Richard Martin may have had motive and opportunity to have caused the death of your husband, Phillip?"

"How dare you! It makes me sick to my stomach how you fabricate stories about a horrible, horrible accident. Is that what your cheap-assed company pays you to do? You take my husband's money all these years and then when he's involved in a tragedy you try to find a way…whether true or not… to weasel out of paying. You've put me through the worst possible reminders of my husband's death and insinuate someone in my family…my own daughter… and a friend are somehow at fault for Phillip's accident. What a memorable experience this has been. Now, what else do you want? Hmmm?"

Jack Gleason stares at Lauren without flinching. He's not intimidated in the slightest.

"Well, well, Mrs. Pittman. That was quite a spirited response **but** you failed to answer my question. Let me repeat it for you? First question. Is it **possible** …possible your friend, Mr. Martin could have reason and opportunity to cause your husband's death?"

"No." Lauren stares eye to eye with Mr. Gleason.

"Then, Mrs. Pittman, tell me…what reason do you have for protecting **Mr. Richard Martin**?"

Lauren gasps. Gleason's going to tie her into this after all as an accomplice to murder. Lauren prepares to speak knowing her voice
227

will likely give away her fear that he's very close to the truth. But before she can say anything, Mr. Gleason continues, "Mrs. Pittman, could you possibly be protective of Mr. Martin to ultimately protect your daughter? You know, Mrs. Pittman, even the toughest lawyers understand maternal instinct. So, even if your daughter is not suspected of being culpable in any way, shape or form...do you not see how her involvement with Mr. Martin could lead *you* to say it's *possible* Mr. Richard Martin *could* have some responsibility for the death of your husband?"

Oh my God! Home free! How wrong could I be? He was just trying to lay some of this at Richard's feet, not mine, at all. Lauren takes a deep breath and now her voice is clear and calm.

"No. And I will add, I see no reason to protect anyone. I do not believe my husband had any connection or communication with Richard other than to go on safari and go fishing...just something he wanted to do. I also do not believe there is *anything* going on between my daughter and Mr. Martin."

Lauren lets her voice trail off and drops her head, sobbing quietly.

There's silence in the conference room. John Sacks puts his hand on her shoulder, "Want to take a break, Lauren?"

Lauren dries her eyes and looks calmly at the attorneys on the other side of the table.

"As far as my daughter being involved intimately with Richard Martin, I'll say for the record that there were times Jane Ella flirted with him. When I noticed it I told her it's sad when an attractive girl in her twenties flirts with someone who is old enough to be her father. She seemed crestfallen about my comment so I figured that was enough to make the point with her. I also told Richard in no uncertain terms the way to ruin twenty years of friendship would be to encourage her silliness. Richard assured me he had no interest at all and was mature enough to never give me cause for concern. I believe him and as far as I'm concerned, that's it. Now, if you have evidence to share with me...and I mean factual evidence that I'm mistaken and have been

228

misled…then I want to know right now at this moment. If it's a hypothetical fishing expedition, then I do not want to hear another word about it. Is that clear enough and responsive enough?"

Lauren's attorney looks at her in admiration.

"Ladies and gentlemen, I believe my client has been open and honest in your inquiry. I'd like to wrap up her deposition today and not have to return, so can you finalize your questions to Mrs. Pittman?"

Jack Gleason pushes back from the table and begins to rise, " Let us take a five minute break and be sure we can give you a definitive answer, Mr. Sacks. That okay with everybody?"

Lauren nods and the other attorneys assent to the suggestion by pushing back from the table. The attorneys for the insurance company file silently out of the conference room.

"Wow, Lauren! Your missed your calling. Shoulda' been an attorney. I'm really sorry for the tone of some of the questions but it's their show and literally they can ask anything. I think your last comment about a fishing expedition called a spade a spade and even Gleason wasn't prepared to have his hand called like that. Right now, I'm guessing they are trying to find a way to save face and end this for you. So, hopefully, you'll be out of here shortly and for good. Maybe you'll be able to start putting some of this whole ordeal behind you."

"You can probably tell I don't like being here and that Gleason is an asshole. I wouldn't mind talking one-on-one to him in a little more descriptive terms to tell him what I think of him. Shithead."

John doesn't reply but joins Lauren in looking at the conference room door as two of the four attorneys re-enter the room. Gleason is not among them. They stand behind their chairs.

"We're going to conclude the deposition, Mrs. Pittman. I apologize for upsetting you and having to re-visit the tragedy. So, unless you have any questions for us we are finished for now and we thank you for coming as requested. After you leave, if you have any questions of us, please pass them through your attorney. Okay?"

"Sure."

"If you'll collect your things, I'll be happy to accompany you downstairs and to your car if you like."

"I can find my way without any of your assistance... I have to now. Don't I? Phillip isn't here to help me anymore. And I can assure you if Phillip had heard this deposition, there would be some repercussions from him you'd not likely want. Thanks for making another lonely, crappy day even shittier!"

Lauren gets up from her seat and makes no effort to smile, shake hands or even politely bid a farewell. She slings the strap of her purse over her left shoulder, dons her big round-framed white sunglasses and heads straight for the doorway.

Just before she reaches the door she, pauses, fumbles momentarily in her purse, pulls out a tissue and dabs at her eyes. As she enters the hallway and heads toward the elevator she can't help but think that the lawyers were probably glad to get rid of her so her tears wouldn't stain their beautiful polished conference room table. As she steps onto the elevator she smiles and thinks to herself that she's getting pretty convincing at this. It's not play acting if you just live the character you're trying to be and she's played the poor, grieving, innocent wife who's justifiably outraged when questioned about ridiculous suspicions. Just hold the character and let the responses be natural. Tears, at the proper moment of opportunity seem to be very useful.

She feels a burst of energy as she starts for home, thinking it's probably just the relief of having the deposition over. It's all so mysterious. The comments about Jane Ella and Richard still haunt her the most.

Perhaps this is a good time for Lauren to stop by John Sack's office and see how he thinks the deposition went. John said he was going straight to his office from the insurance deposition and he didn't seem concerned about her statement otherwise she's sure he'd have remained with her out of the room as she left or interrupted her during the testimony. On second thought, Lauren thinks it will be good to get

230

home, put her feet up and have a big martini. She'll skip going by John's office today. She may as well let the insurance play out as long as it takes and anyhow she can generate a huge sum of money by simply selling her corporate shares of stock.

Shortly after Lauren gets home, John Sacks calls to tell Lauren he's sorry for the stress of the deposition.

"Even though it was painful, I think it went very, very well and you may be finished with any further inquiries. I stayed a few minutes after you left and beat up on the inquisitors a little, hoping they'll be reluctant to repeat any of this."

"I really don't want to have to do this again, John."

"I know and hopefully we won't. But I also wanted to tell you I arranged for you to meet with the corporate board whenever it's convenient for you. We just need to let them know a couple of dates and times so they can schedule a get together and certainly I'll attend that meeting with you. I can sense the board of directors is more than a little nervous regarding what role you'll want to play, if any. I mean you have the controlling shares of stock. Want to be Chairman of the Board? This would be your chance. They are anxious to clear up the future control of the board. And as always, once we have a date and time I'm available to do a pre-meeting session with you. I believe preparation for any face to face meeting is helpful to you and to me as well."

"I agree, and John, please get the board meeting scheduled, the sooner the better. Rather than me pick a few dates and times, you just set it up and let me know. I'll be there."

"Fine. Just so you know, when we get together we'll discuss options you have and how settlements are done. I mean, these guys can be gruff and rough. You can be sure each director has a strategy that only favors him individually. They look like they act in concert as a board but down deep they are all self-centered sharks looking only for their own individual interests.I'm sure you have a kinder view of them but I'm just giving you a heads up about the illustrious board."

"No. Actually I wouldn't expect any less. I'm fine. I wouldn't mind if you want to drop by the house for the pre-meeting. We can share a martini. Oh, forget I said that. You probably think I'm old enough to be your mother. But I really appreciate how you handle yourself, John. Good looking attorney like you probably has a line outside your door inviting you to have a drink."

"Not really, Lauren. And don't put yourself down. You are a beautiful, confident woman and your husband was a lucky man."

"Wow, John, you'd best be careful talking like that or I'm liable to want to hear that in person rather than over the phone."

"Ya know, Lauren, I really need to stay squeaky clean to work for you in a client relationship. You have a lot of important things on your plate right now. So, let me get back to business."

"Sure, you're right. No mixing business and pleasure. Okay. Regarding the meeting with the corporate board, I would like for you to be there and if I have a question, I assume I can call a time-out and take you aside?"

"Of course."

"Well, then I'm not too worried. I'm just anxious to get this moving and I'm pretty sure I can make my points very clear. They have to understand it's not me there on bended knee defending myself against what they want. I want them on bended knee defending themselves to satisfy me. It's about what I want. How's that, John?"

"I love it! I'm assuming you're just offering to make available to them your stake in the corporation. It will likely look like dogs fighting over a bone. Just remember I'm here to represent you and you can ask me anything and I'll give you my very best advice."

"Yes, John. Thanks. I appreciate it. I'm fine. And John?"

"Yes?"

"Maybe one day we will have a drink over here at the Pittman Ranch. But until then, TaTa."

"Bye, Lauren."

CHAPTER 37

GETTING STRONGER EVERY DAY

A day later, Richard meets with the insurance company and he returns to Lauren's house afterward. Lauren gets them each a drink and they walk in silence to the family room. Lauren turns on a lamp and sits in the chair next to it. Richard takes a seat in an overstuffed chair across from Lauren. Lauren smiles, takes a deep breath and scoots forward on her chair looking in anticipation at Richard. Richard takes a drink, nods his approval of the taste, smiles but remains silent.

"So, you're not going to say a word? Stop with the performance. I'm dying to know. How'd it go?"

"How'd what…"

"Richard, stop messing with me and tell me about the deposition. I'm too stressed for any of this to be cute or funny."

"Okay. Sorry. All in all I'd say it went almost exactly like the way you described it with all the phony introductions in their fancy conference room. After what you told me, I think I had the same lawyers you had. That guy, Jack Gleason's a piece of work all right. I kept wanting to make some remark about Jackie Gleason and the Honeymooner show but he didn't appear to be the joking sort of guy."

"Did they ask if you are gay?"

"Nope. Never ask. Never implied anything like it. They asked immediately about you and me. "

"Like what, Richard?"

"Well, they ask me some general questions about you and if,   from being friends , I would have any suspicions about you and Phillip's death. Ridiculous. There were plenty of guests that heard and swore in their statements to the local police that Phillip was the one pushing to set up something special just for him alone. I glared across the table and told them Phillip's tragic accident was just that, an accident, and the tone in which the question was asked implied it was something other than an accident. I made sure they heard the whole song and dance about safety of guests and I really gave them my best look of being hurt by the insinuation."

"And, then what?"

"Well, they wanted to know if we…you and I had continued being sexually intimate for the last few years and the level of Phillip's suspicion or jealousy. They knew details of several visits I've made to the Boston area and wanted to know if those were for continuing our intimate liaisons."

"Jesus! They knew you'd been here in Boston?"

"Yep. Even which hotels. So I figured with as much as they already know I'd best give in and be truthful. Very truthful."

"God, Richard, what did you tell them?"

" I looked Jackie Gleason in the eye and I said we'd been screwin' our brains out since college and got tired of using the Boston hotels so we decided to let the old man play voyeur under his own roof and then become crocodile bait so we can continue future humpin' marathons."

Richard! That's not even funny. Don't be so careless. What if the house is bugged.?"

"Unless you've let somebody besides the three of us in your house, how would it be bugged for us talking? They can listen in on phone calls but how would they get into the house? Just kiddin though. The guy who asked if our intimacy continued…I looked at him like he was from Mars and told him his question sounded like the old 'when did you stop beating your wife' question. You're guilty regardless of any answer. I said we never started being intimate so how could it continue? We are just plain good friends but some people who aren't capable of friendship would find that difficult to understand."

235

"Sometimes you surprise me, Richard. Smart. But the bugging of the house scares me. Think about it. What if someone got in here and roamed all over the house? Who's to say someone wasn't in here while we were all gone to lunch."

"Shit! Now you're scaring me. But I don't think that ever happened. More importantly it sounds as if you're shocked that I have half a brain. Never expected me to be smart, huh?"

"I didn't mean it that way. What else?"

"Oh, lots of questions of what I told Phillip about the risks, what I told him to do that morning and how sure I am that he understood my instructions. "

Richard reassures Lauren the lawyers seemed more like they were a bit desperate, fishing for anything that might jump out as opposed to having any real suspicions. He seems very confident about it.

" So now, my dear Lauren, it is just a waiting game."

Two days later, Lauren and John Sacks meet with the Patriot Star Board of Directors. Lauren and John make the rounds of handshakes and introductions. Lauren is struck by the average age of the board members. She guesses the average age is mid-sixties about the same vintage as her ex-buddy, Murray Eddlemann. Eventually Murray enters the room and cautiously approaches Lauren with a rather formal handshake and smile. Lauren squeezes Murray's hand and flits her eyebrows which causes an instant ear-to-ear smile from Murray.

"I hope you're doing well, Lauren. We've been anxious to get this end of the mundane duties of business wrapped up as soon as possible."

"I'm sure, Murray…"

A distinguished looking gentleman that Lauren only remembers as William begins to lightly tap on his glass at the conference table, "Good morning everyone. Morning. Let's be seated so we may get the meeting underway. Mrs. Pittman, would you and your attorney sit here by me at the table?"

As everyone gathers at the large conference table, Lauren is struck that the names now connected to real faces are totally different than what she always pictured. Phillip was the youngest member of the board and most of these aging veterans of the business world look very pleasant. The stories Phillip used to tell and gloat about when he had this one or that one embarrassed to nearly the point of self-destruction. Among all his other bad qualities Lauren sees that Phillip was also a very sadistic boss beyond what she'd imagined. Of course there's Murray sitting quietly smiling at her. Murray probably feels like all is forgiven after Lauren's little greeting to him. But Lauren manages to lock eyes with Murray and do what only Lauren can do. She smiles coldly at Murray, more like a sneer, until the aging lawyer drops his eyes and re-enters his self-imposed doghouse once again.

William Malmoe clears his throat and pushes some papers around in front of him. All the other board members take that as a signal he's going to speak.

"The board meeting will come to order."

There's a few coughs, cleared throats, sips of coffee and scooting of chairs. Lauren suddenly sees this group as frightened old men nervously acting as if the ghost of Phillip is standing in the ante room and could at any moment pop through the door and begin a mass execution.

William begins, "Lauren, uh, uh, Mrs. Pittman. I want to welcome you to this meeting of the board. Unless you or your attorney have any objections, I'm going to get down to the business at hand. With Phillip declared, uh deceased, his shares, the majority of company stock moved directly to your ownership and we would like to know what role you see yourself playing in the company. I mean do you want to passively sit on the stock as a long term investment? Do you want a role on the board? Do you want to sell part or all of your shares? We would like to know how you see things so we can move on with some rather important investments and acquisitions the corporation is currently negotiating."

Lauren glances at John but figures this is her chance to get things moving for her financial success and for her freedom. Lauren looks down at the table, pushes back her chair and stands. She knows she looks gorgeous and confident.

"Well, it's a pleasure to meet all of you. I've heard the names many times and it's genuinely nice to connect names and faces. I know you are all on your very best behavior because I'm here and I thank you for that. I can assure you I have no intentions to make you stay in that uncomfortable role of corporate sweetie pies any longer than absolutely necessary."

A few stiff laughs around the table. John Sacks looks at Lauren and has absolutely no clue what's she's going to say or do next.

Lauren continues, "I'm pretty sure your pulses are a little more rapid than usual and you're all playing the little 'what if' games about the frightening results of me wanting and taking an active role in shall I say *our* company. That probably has you scared to death, and gentlemen, it should scare you to death."

Lauren pauses and everyone leans forward in anticipation.

"It *should* scare you to death, that is, *if* I had any desire to step into Phillip's shoes. And I can tell you with all confidence if I wanted to fill Phillip's shoes, I could. But I'm more comfortable in my own shoes but have no misunderstanding, gentlemen, if needed I can run around here like my late husband, Little Hitler, kicking your asses with these shoes. But, Gentlemen, have *no* fear. I want to be very clear and point blank with you that I have *no* interest in any role whatsoever in this or any other company. Okay? Everybody please just take a second and begin breathing again. C'mon. Take a deep breath. That's probably your biggest worry out of the way."

Lauren looks in near disgust as they all immediately put on smiley, angelic, innocent faces like dutiful lemmings. They did take deep breaths and scoot around in their big leather chairs. She wonders how any company could be masterfully run by a bunch like this. But time to get what she wants.

" Second, my wonderful attorney, John Sacks reviewed with me a copy of the key man policy payouts and that's a lot of money for me, and it's not just a lot of money for me but *a ton* of money for the corporation. I imagine it can't hurt to get that in the old company coffers to do your high flying investments and acquisitions. Sorry. I mean no disrespect or sarcasm. I want to be very clear when I say to you, I will sell all my shares to the corporation as soon as I get the insurance settlement. Sooo, bottom line, gentlemen…you get the insurance company to end all this crap and pay out what they rightfully owe to me and to you, I'll sell you guys the stock and I'm gone. But, I won't sell it one minute sooner than when I receive the insurance settlement. So the word *sooner* is good for you to remember. A woman's prerogative is always to change her mind. And I want to be real clear about something. I say with all honesty that I have no interest in being on this board but a long delay in wrapping up this insurance settlement would force me to reconsider. Ya know, based on the board's inability to make this happen. A little oomph in the priority department…okay? So now you've got something to work on and get done."

The room is quiet. Lauren looks at John and he's smiling. Lauren turns her head back to the board members.

"That's about it for me. What else do we need to discuss today for the good of my…I mean *our* corporation?"

Bill Malmoe clears his throat and smiles at Lauren, "Well, that's indeed straightforward and forgive me for saying this, I mean no disrespect but you sound almost like Phillip. Wam, bam thank you ma'am…well you know what I mean. "

John Sacks jumps right in, " Okay then. Gentlemen, I suggest if you have questions, now's the time, so we can field them. My client has cut to the chase a bit faster than you probably expected. She's obviously thought this through and what do you say?"

Malmoe furrows his brow, "Well, that all sounds fine. I mean speeding up an insurance payout sounds fine but there's realism of which you need to be aware. My experience tells me not to get hopes too high about speeding-up an insurance payout. But having said that bit of cynicism I will also tell you we *will* have a conversation with our legal staff about bringing to bear whatever *encouragement* we can for an expeditious settlement, right Murray?"

"Sure, William. This corporation has paid huge premiums for insurance over many years duration and we've gotten our corporate family of companies to do the same. I'd be pretty certain with bigger policies like this that our insurer has subsequently insured itself against risk of large lump sum payouts. Insurance on insurance, if you will. My thinking is that It would probably be in the insurance company's best long term interests to review just how important our future business will be to them. They've apparently been too busy to deal with the reality of how important it is to have a good paying customer. So, we'll just remind them of that point and hint if they don't get their asses in gear our insurance business may wind up somewhere else. Ya know… a little extortion never hurts but I'll keep it all legal and just say officially we'll tighten the thumbscrews as encouragement to complete their review quickly."

Later when Lauren tells Richard what happened he's quite amused, "Wow! You missed your calling, Lauren. Maybe you *should* be the chairman of the board. Very smart to get the company to fight the battle with the insurance company. All the pressure they bring takes any possible suspicion away from you from being in a hurry for the money. So eventually the insurance company caves in, closes the issue and pays the money. Very, very smart. "

A few days later, Lauren answers the phone and it's John Sacks.

"Hello, John. I know it's way too soon to expect it, but any good news for me?"

"Lauren, it's the best news. It's done. Murray Eddlemann called to tell me that Madison Insurance has completed their inquiry and they are paying the benefits. You and I should have a discussion about options you have and maybe some advice on how to receive the funds and deposit it. I mean it's not like having a check for twenty-five dollars mailed to you. So if you can come to my office tomorrow we'll get it all figured out. Can you do that?"

"Sure. I suppose that's safer than meeting here over a martini. I'd hate to use a five million dollar check as a coaster for a drink. So sure, I'll come to your office. What time?"

"How about ten?"

"Fine. That it?"

" Not at all. I have some papers for you to review and discuss with me. The sale of the corporate stock can be done and I want to have it ready. When the insurance money is in hand, we'll be ready to immediately execute the stock sale. That's still what you want to do, right?"

"That's exactly correct. Okay see you tomorrow at ten. Bye, John."

True to her word and much to the relief of Phillip's partners, Lauren receives the insurance proceeds and she promptly sells her stock to the company. She has no desire to be involved in the business. The proceeds from the stock sale are large enough that John Sacks puts together a team of specialized accountants and legal assistance to tie up details and take care that the proper taxes are declared and paid and best of all the money is deposited into Lauren's accounts. She looks at the numbers in amazement; the total is over one-hundred-thirty-three million dollars.

One morning soon after, Lauren is sitting at the dining room table, stacks of papers arranged in neat piles around the table and a laptop of her very own at the ready. She takes a deep breath and begins to look page by page at the numbers.

"Mother, I'm going. I may see you later today but I might not get home tonight from Erin's."

"Oh sure, Erin's. Erin, Erin, Erin. Ya know, I don't think I've ever met Erin, even once. So when did the two of you become such close friends? Last night at Erin's. Tonight at Erin's. One of these days I'll just have to meet Erin for sure and talk about how much you enjoy all the overnight trips to *Erin's*."

"Mother, I have no idea how your paranoid little mind works but never fear, one of these days I really will be gone and you won't have to worry whether I come home late or whether I come at all. Honestly, you're more of a pain in the ass than you used to be when Phillip was here. At least the two of you were entertaining with your fighting. Now without him I guess I've become your target. "

"Jane Ella, just go. I am trying to enjoy a first cup of coffee and so far it's not very pleasant."

" Not very pleasant? Apparently a few hours passed out followed by strong coffee aren't enough to cure your massive hangovers?"

Jane Ella grabs her purse and defiantly strolls toward the garage. Lauren hears the car start and back from the garage. Before she can get back to her slow morning recovery she hears the garage door go up and apparently Jane Ella returns. She must have forgotten something…like the day she came back for her purse and watched the pool antics. Jane Ella comes back into the house and into the kitchen just as the front doorbell rings.

"Surprise, surprise, Mother! It's Richard. He's come to nest."

"What?" Lauren and Jane Ella walk briskly toward the door and as Lauren opens it, there stands Richard, two suitcases beside him.

"Richard! I am surprised to see you this morning. Looks like you've come for a visit at the old Pittman homestead."

"Well, I figured it might be nice to have a little closer visit than having you drive to the hotel so much. That is , if you want me to stay."

"Of course, silly. That driving to and from the hotel just for chaperoned lunch or coffee is straining us all…isn't it Mom?"

"Ignore her. Come on in, Richard."

Richard enters, politely closes the door and when he looks up toward Lauren and Jane Ella he appears a little nervous.

"Relax, Richard. We're alone. Just the three of us. You look a little frayed. You okay?"

"Yeah. I'm okay. I don't want to impose on the two of you if you need more private time. I just thought it would be nice to be closer."

"Yes. Closer. That will be wonderful, Richard." Jane Ella winks at Richard.

After her comment, Richard nervously looks at Jane Ella as if he's not sure what's coming next. Lauren misunderstands Jane Ella playing on the edge with the little hints about her time with Richard. Lauren naively thinks Jane Ella is picking at Lauren and Richard's relationship.

"Don't pay any attention to her, Richard. She just got home from spending the night with Erin Whoever-That-Is and she was immediately on her way back to see Erin Whoever-That-Is once again but seeing you arrive Erin Whoever-That-Is lost out on the visit. Too complex for me so just come on in, Richard, and have some coffee."

Lauren turns her back and heads for the kitchen. Jane Ella points to Richard, silently laughs and dramatically mouths the word " Hi Erin". Richard motions to Jane Ella with his hands to stop the charade. They join Lauren in the Kitchen.

243

"So, I guess you are still going to Erin's but would you like a cup of coffee before you leave?"

"No…I think it's so nice to have Richard here with us, I'll call Erin later and tell her I can't make it. Unless of course that complicates your plans for the day, Mother."

"No, suit yourself. You're always so quick to get out the door to Erin's, I'm surprised you just cancel your plans with her."

When Lauren turns her back, Jane Ella looks devilishly at Richard and licks the edge of her coffee cup. Richard shakes his head "no" and looks away, carefully watching Lauren to be sure she hasn't caught on to any of the games.

"You certainly pack light, Richard. I mean, two suitcases, the clothes on your back and I guess that's all your worldly possessions? Or does your steamer trunk and moving van arrive later today?"

"No, I have some other things still in Botswana. Depending on what happens over the next short while, I'm going to decide if I really want to do any more safaris. This has been a tragic, devastating experience. So, for now it's just a visit with the Pittman ladies. I really hate being suspected of something, like those insurance sharks probably thought and so I guess I'm still a little uncomfortable with the feeling. It's terrible to be absolutely innocent of a tragedy and still have people looking at you like you've done some terrible thing. I suppose for the time being I'm a little afraid to be anything but careful."

"Honestly, Richard. You walk around like you're the guilty little boy and Mom is strung so tight she is about to explode all the time. You're innocent so no worry. Everything will settle and that will be that. In fact, I'd say from what I heard with the insurance and all, it's done now. My Jane Ella advice is to stop worrying. Let yourself go. Who knows, it may be affecting your performance in a lot of things like woo hoo."

God, Jane Ella! Can't you just stop with the comments. It's wearing very thin on me and I'm sure Richard gets tired of it, too."

Jane Ella steps in front of Lauren and looks at Richard so her face is blocked from Lauren's view. She raises and lowers her eyebrows.

"So sorry. Richard, you just tell me if you get tired of it, okay?"

With that last comment, Jane Ella leaves the kitchen with her coffee and heads to the family room where she sprawls on the nearest sofa.

Richard speaks in a quiet tone of voice, "Actually, it's great to be here, Lauren. I guess I am a little tense. This is only the second time I've been back in the house since the trip and the first time was only for a few hours."

"Come on, sailor, tell me your troubles. Old Lauren will fix you another cuppa Joe."

" I'm sorry if I seem overly careful. I want to act as a visitor…like the old friend and also to uh…uh, be sure that Jane Ella isn't suspicious.

"Ha! Who are you kidding? She knows way too much already. Remember? You're acting this visitor part so Jane Ella won't be suspicious? Why would you even worry, *or care*, about *her* being suspicious? I don't understand that at all. It's over, Richard. Remember, they released the claim and I've got the money. The investigations are over so just relax. Right? Or am I misunderstanding something about this whole claims and investigation process?"

Richard's tone sounds serious, "If possible, Lauren, I want to act like a house guest. Now understand, this is tough to do. I'm simply trying to err on the side of caution and that's the main reason I'm suggesting that we act this way…sort of formally, inside and outside the actual house. So it's for Jane Ella. It's for the police. It's for the insurance guys. Okay?"

"I don't really see the need to worry at all, Richard. Isn't it over?"

"Look. The way I see it is that time is the best insulator for all that's happened. We act the parts and eventually it is like a natural thing that's blossomed. I don't trust these insurance people. Yes, they paid the claim but I'd be willing to bet they still watch and listen. Insurance fraud has a long memory and I think we just need to be careful for a few months. That's all."

"Well, if you think that's important."

"I think it's important that we even live it in here, in your house. Let me take Phillip's old room and you keep your separate one. Just for a while. We can make room visits when the coast is clear…if you get my drift."

Lauren snaps her head at Richard, irritated that he cares about being careful in her own house. But she reluctantly agrees to maintain a relaxed, but guarded relationship. She and Richard agree they will be careful not to outwardly act lovey-dovey when Jane Ella, or anyone else is present. Somehow life isn't as exciting as it had been during the secret liaisons. The worst part for Lauren is that she wonders if this play-acting lifestyle and physical arrangement could open possible opportunity for a Jane Ella and Richard liaison. The very thought makes Lauren wretch.

There will be a right time to sit and calmly talk through all this. The three of them. Perhaps Lauren can still make this a storybook family. For now, just keep Jane Ella and Richard apart sexually. Lauren imagines the three of them sitting at the dining room table openly discussing the satisfaction now that the three peas are rightfully sharing the same pod. And for the time being, Lauren feels a little safety in believing that surely Richard must know the truth about Jane Ella or suspects it at the very least. This playful activity with Jane Ella isn't sexual but just Richard trying to figure out a subtle path to a new, more fatherly role.

One evening, Jane Ella is out of the house so Lauren thinks this might be a good time to be a little more amorous with her flame.

"Hey, Sailor, buy me a drink?"

Richard's dozed off but snaps his head up , a little confused. "Wha…huh?"

"Okay, plain English. Richard, do you want a drink?"

246

"Sure. I guess so."

Lauren brings a couple of drinks into the family room and as Richard takes a first sip and what sounds like a relaxing deep breath, " Feeling like a little adult activity, Richard? Little Miss Muffet is out for a while and speaking of a while, it's been a while since we got up close and personal. So whatdayasay?"

"Yeah. I guess. I'm a little tired but if you want, I guess we can."

"Wow! What a romantic! 'I guess…if you want…I'm a little tired'… doesn't exactly sound like this is something you're excited about doing. And I certainly don't want to force you. No problem. You go get your warm milk and go to bed. I'll take my version of warm milk and do something else besides bother you."

"Oh, c'mon, Lauren. I didn't mean for it to sound like that. I'm just tired and actually maybe I will just hit the hay a little early tonight. Don't think anything more than it is. I'm just tired."

"Fine."

The next morning Jane Ella and Lauren saunter into the kitchen around eight-thirty and the eggshell -walking goes into full swing.

 Lauren stares into her coffee cup and her raspy voice begins, "Good morning, Jane Ella. I'm surprised to see you this morning. Did you come home this morning or last night? I was so tired I guess I didn't hear you come home.".

"Uh...yeah, I came in very late last night. Everything was dark and I assumed everybody was asleep so I just went to bed."

Richard comes into the kitchen and both women look at him. Lauren notices Jane Ella's look of admiration and assumes it's more of Jane Ella's silly crush on Richard. Jane Ella assumes Lauren's admiring smile is to gauge Richard's possible ability for sex later on today. Richard smiles but looks like he doesn't pick up on any clues from either woman.

"Want some coffee?"

"Yeah...that'd be terrific. I need it. Didn't sleep all that well."

Lauren begins pouring Richard's coffee, " Well, I slept like I was drugged and didn't even hear Jane Ella come in last night. Did she wake you, Richard?"

" Uh... nope. Never heard a thing. "

Jane Ella turns to Richard, "You be sure to get your beauty rest, Richard. You're one lucky guy to have **both** Mom and me watching over you. How do you **handle** all the stress?"

"To tell you the truth, I feel honored and appreciated."

Richard 's bland comment about being honored and appreciated seems to squelch any further talking and they each just smile pleasantly and drink their coffee together in a rare moment of civility.

But there are other changes as well. Since they returned from Africa, Lauren has a better relationship with Jane Ella than she can ever recall. It's like a peaceful dream to Lauren in part because Jane Ella seems happy and adjusting to the changes as if she's in no hurry to leave home. To Lauren it feels a little more like a real family home now.

But dreams like Lauren's can't help but be on the endangered species list as they continue to be eroded by deceit and reality. The reality, whether unseen or denied includes what happened to Phillip, the flirting, the blackmail, and the complicated infidelity. This hodge-podge family group of Richard, Lauren and Jane Ella is perhaps more dysfunctional than Phillip, Lauren and Jane Ella had ever been. Old suspicions haunt Lauren. Her mistrust is fueled by boredom at night

248

because, at Richard's continued insistence, she doesn't share a bedroom with him. Lately she doesn't object when, as an evening routine, Richard mixes Lauren a little pitcher of martinis and brings the "nightcap" to her room. It's just what she needs to be able to relax and fall asleep…alone. Just another night that "could have been" turns out to be another night without love as the calendar moves steadily along.

CHAPTER 38

THE SUSPICIOUS FINANCE QUEEN

Within weeks of the final settlements and deposits Richard seems comfortable in his quarters at the Pittman house. Excuse after excuse bring Richard no closer to sharing Lauren's room as long as Jane Ella is still at home. So, Lauren, Richard, and Jane Ella continue the charade of keeping separate bedrooms.

Lauren develops a new routine, bordering on completely obsessive behavior. New routine but same old usual hangover that wakes her between eight and nine most mornings, demanding a Coke or orange juice, trying to remedy the alcohol dehydration. Morning exercises are no longer part of the obsession, she simply bathes and dresses for the day by ten o'clock. That's about the time the phone begins to ring a near steady stream of calls from John Sacks and the financial advisors he's assembled. Lauren's new interest is her laptop with a separate oversized screen set up on the dining room table. Strategically placed around the laptop are folders and neatly stacked piles of papers. Today she's spread financial statements all over the dining room table. With her pre-noon martini in hand, she lets her half-glasses slide onto the bridge of her nose. She looks over the top of them, appearing a bit annoyed at the interruption as Richard strolls into the dining room.

Richard breaks the silence, "What are you up to? Is this the den of high finance again today?"

"I've got to stay comfortable with all these numbers. Do you have any idea how many people know my finances better than I? That seems ripe for pilferage, if you know what I mean. So my goal is to change that. The least I can do is understand the numbers, be part of an informed decision process and watch where all the little piles of money wind up. John, along with the financial guys and accountants he got for me, call virtually every day with questions about options for what I want to do with large chunks of investment money. I know they are trying to think ahead to make money and avoid unnecessary taxes. That's good as long as they're looking out for my interests. John says no matter how careful all of us are, it's too much money for the IRS just to accept the filings. So, chances are pretty good I'll get audited and re-audited by the IRS. I think it's important I get to know this quite a bit better. Phillip and Murray always took care of all this stuff so I'm at a disadvantage trying to learn in a month or two what they worked on for twenty years ."

"You should be getting pretty good at it yourself. You spend nearly every waking minute doing this…this… whatever it is you're doing."

Lauren drops her glasses onto her nose, her body language showing sarcasm, "I'd say I'm sorry but I'm merely occupying my time since there certainly hasn't been any other activity of great interest lately. I'm beginning to think you took a vow of celibacy."

"C'mon, Lauren. That's not very fair. I don't think I…"

"I know. I know. I'm too tired. We have to be careful. What if Jane Ella saw us? What if Jane Ella heard us? Ya know, Richard, I'm beginning to think you've completely lost interest in me…or lost your manly drive …or lost something."

Richard's voice reeks with disgust, "Geez. That's really cold. I suppose I need to relax and be thankful for your romantic contribution to our romantic relationship. Every day you count your money, drink a martini, ever so often you ring a bell and I'm supposed to run in with my pants around my ankles and service your bearded clam. After completion of my five or six minute duty I'm supposed to zip up my pants, quietly exit and stay the hell out of the way but listen for the bell to ring. Yup. That's about the way I see it. Sounds fascinating."

"Oh, poor little Richard. You pride yourself as a super-stud but I think you exaggerate when you say you're always on the ready. From what I've seen lately your little helmeted man has taken early retirement. And by the way, don't make fun of what I'm doing. This is very, very important for everybody under this roof. I'm trying to keep up with everything and keep problems from happening. And I'm insulted when you talk in such vulgar terms about our physical relationship. I think that's disgusting."

" Sorry. I admit that wasn't very nice but I also get frustrated. Don't get me wrong, Lauren. What you have is a good problem? Most people don't have enough money to worry about and that causes them to worry. You have more money than God, and that causes you to worry. I have no money, no property but I have a beautiful girlfriend and zero worries."

Lauren continues, looking over her glasses that rest on the very tip of her nose, "It's been a while but a few times I actually checked to be sure you were in your room alone at night. Finally gave up on that. I go to sleep immediately when my head hits the pillow. But when I did check it was like seeing Phillip's back because from that pose you looked almost like him, sitting on his computer at all hours. Although I must admit, it looked to me like you play FreeCell all the time. Do you do anything else ?"

"I know how to turn on the computer and I know how to open FreeCell. Other than that, no. I don't care about email, Facebook or any of that sort of stuff. I also don't know whistle, tweet or any of that either. So, I'm not computer smart by any stretch of the imagination. Besides, isn't that Phillip's old computer?"

"Of course. That computer was more of a child to him than Jane Ella. I never touched it after we got back. But, yep, that was his alright."

"That's what I thought and I know enough about a computer to know when one's totally empty. I thought that was a little strange. Maybe he only used his laptop here at home."

"That's ridiculous. Maybe it's password protected or something. That's the computer he used at home for all his office records and financial and tax work. Let's have a look at it."

Lauren and Richard walk to Richard's bedroom as they continue their conversation.

Lauren sits in front of Phillip's old computer, reboots it and begins to look at the installed programs.

"Sure, here are the programs so let's just see if we can open some of them."

Lauren has no trouble opening the financial programs but there is no data in any of them."

"This is the weirdest thing. There are no passwords on these programs at all but yet there's also no data. It's like everything's been deleted, including the password protection. I am shocked. You sure you didn't mess around with anything?"

"Cross my heart. You've explored more than I ever have. I found the program for games and that's about it. I admit, out of curiosity, I tried to look at Phillip's email but it's totally blank. I figured there would be some emails waiting for Phillip upon his return but zero. There were no emails when I first opened it and there haven't been any since then. Weird, huh? Who would have done all that? Think about it. Either Phillip deliberately wiped it clean before you left on the trip or someone has gotten in here and wiped it out since."

"None of that makes sense. He was expecting to be back. I'm going to ask Jane Ella if she's been here diddling with Phillip's computer. She'd better not have been in this room diddling with anything else. Right Richard?"

"Nope. I've never seen her in this room or even show the slightest interest what's in this room…including me. Okay, your ladyship?"

"Good, that's the way it should remain."

"Well, who knows about the computer mystery? Aside from that, this is a period of adjustment for us all and you spend so much time now on your laptop, studying your accounts and everything. A *lot* of time. And I wonder, Lauren, when you look through all those numbers and Fort Knox accounts will there someday be a few shekels for poor Richard?"

"Of course. I'm going to set up something so you'll have your own independent account and it will be filled to the brim for you. I…uh we have to still be a bit careful with the timing. I'll have to have John's help to set up an account but I want to wait long enough it doesn't arouse any suspicions even with him. Probably another month or so."

"I know, these things take time and besides, I certainly don't want to put you into any financial strain. By the way, you never mentioned…what was the grand total…just in round numbers when all the dust settled from insurance and selling the company stock? I'm just curious. I mean, I've never known a millionaire or millionairess so I'm just curious if I know one now. Or how much of a millionairess? Multi? Hundreds of? Billionairess?"

Lauren bristles momentarily. There's that nagging suspicion that somehow Richard knew more about Jane Ella's trust than even what Lauren had known. Now he's prying ever so innocently to find out the amount of her personal wealth. Lauren finds herself with a desire to be generous to Richard but on her terms, the amount, when, where, how to be dictated by Lauren.

"Oh, Richard, I'm sure you've hopped around the globe with many wealthy women. You don't need to worry about me. I should never have expressed concern about taxes or any of that. I'm fine with things and appreciate your concern. You will certainly be a well-off benefactor of me knowing the details."

"C'mon, Lauren. Humor me. I'm curious and that's all. Don't you trust me?"

"Trust you? Well, of course. And I will set you up very, very well, financially. You'll just have to trust me on that. And you can certainly trust me. I am so very appreciative of everything. None of this would have been possible without you. I am so happy…at least I think I'm happy."

"What does that mean?"

"I wish Jane Ella would make up her mind what she wants to do. I really don't plan on her staying here forever and I hope she doesn't either. When she moves it will be a giant-step toward us having everything we want …just the two of us. Then I'll really feel free. Free as a bird. That's what all this is about Richard."

"Yeah, but Jane Ella being around here at home doesn't really bother you that much, does she?"

"No, I suppose not really. I would feel better though if we had our own privacy. Ya know, the whole house for just the two of us."

Lauren doesn't look up but if she had she would have seen a somber looking Richard. He's at a dead end about the total amount of money. He's delayed in having his hands on any actual money to call his own. But most of all the words "just the two of us" doesn't mean the same to Richard.

Lauren thinks perhaps her dwelling on all the money, accounts and investments really is boring and maybe he just wants to share more of her interests. Maybe his curiosity is more about being a part of her life than sneaking around with greedy motives. Maybe she's been too hard on Richard. But Lauren still harbors a nagging feeling that there's some piece of the puzzle still missing. She seems to have everything she ever wanted but still something is amiss. Maybe getting rid of Phillip and having all the money aren't the entire solutions for all of the woes of this house and the people within the walls.

CHAPTER 39

STRESS WITHOUT SOLUTIONS

Lauren awakens confused. She sleeps so soundly and without dreams. Time means nothing during sleep and when she awakens it could be an hour, a day or a week. This morning her thinking and reactions are paralytically slow and muddled. Slowly she swings her feet over the edge of the bed and leans forward, head in hands. She looks up, struggles to her feet and clumsily steps toward the bathroom.

What's that noise? Clearly she hears laughter and talking. She glances at her clock on the nightstand. Ten o'clock. How can she sleep so soundly and so long. How depressing. What's making her so tired? Lately it's like being in a coma.

Lauren smiles, " Surely it can't be my silver bullets. It's got to be the unfathomable stress of being filthy rich."

She continues to think about the stresses as she prepares to meet the morning, hungover or not. It seems reasonable that the money issues and the tracking of all the numbers have been much more taxing than she'd ever thought it could be. She's got to get this under control. Once she has that ultimate power-trip of control over this segment of her life, things will just get better and better. Nothing like being in control. Nothing like freedom, at total liberty to do what she wants, with whom she wants and when it pleases her. It's good to be the queen. It's wonderful! Her past seems like a horror show and always the worst part of it was not being in control. Chaos is not something Lauren can tolerate any longer.

Lauren knows she must focus more on controlling the finances and investments. Jane Ella's contentious attitude and sarcasm have been of no positive help and Jane Ella seems to have abandoned her threat to leave home very soon. Maybe it's time to subtly or even aggressively push her to live on her own. Once Jane Ella's gone, Lauren and

Richard can do the settling down and relationship building, if indeed that still strikes Lauren's fancy. That's the beauty of being the queen. Absolute control of everything and everybody. If she changes her mind about something, the disruption falls to someone else, not Lauren.

Having everything get a little more settled will probably improve Richard's sexual drive and his performance. Lauren smiles as she thinks of poor, simple Richard. Hanging around for money, still trying to get past the worry over Phillip and living in the house with Jane Ella flirting with him and sniping at Lauren. He'll probably get right back on the he-man track after things settle down. For now, the best he can do is role play as if he's a doting husband, with platonic hugs and his special caring for Lauren as he brings a small pitcher of mixed cocktails to her room each night, gives lots of hugs only, and then quickly takes leave.

This morning Lauren emerges from her room and she clearly hears laughing. It's obviously not coming from the kitchen or family room and as she looks out the kitchen window toward the pool area the mystery is over. She's just in time to see Richard with both arms around Jane Ella's midsection as she feigns a stumble and a feeble attempt to escape his bearhug clutches. Lauren watches and Jane Ella doesn't escape Richard's grasp but takes some obvious physical actions toward Richard. Richard is turned facing the pool with his back to Lauren's view as he holds Jane Ella in front of him. Jane Ella escapes Richards's bear hug and now has her arms around his waist from behind as if to throw him into the pool.

Lauren instinctively knows this has gone too far and Richard's got to stop this horseplay with Jane Ella. Suddenly Richard stands straight and though Lauren can't see his front, she's certain where Jane Ella has her hands. Jane Ella's attempting to do something to Richard that he's loving and as Jane Ella continues she flips her hair over one shoulder and in doing so happens to turn her head toward the house. She sees Lauren's face staring out the window toward the two on the pool deck.

Jane Ella quickly releases her grip, laughs out loud and dives past Richard into the pool. Richard stands motionless and dumbfounded until Jane Ella surfaces and points to the kitchen window. Jane Ella swims to the side of the pool, looks at Lauren and waves, "Hi, Mom!"

Lauren doesn't return the wave but grunts disgustedly and heads to the refrigerator for a much needed drink of orange juice. Somehow she must make Richard understand once and for all that Jane Ella will do whatever she thinks is edgy or exotic but Richard needs to have enough discipline to stay clear. It seems pretty certain from the way he was standing there he hasn't lost all his sexual drive. He sure wasn't the aggressor. Jane Ella must do this just to embarrass her but yet Lauren isn't sure where the horseplay may have led if she hadn't been spotted in the window.

With orange juice in hand, Lauren walks out by the pool and sits in a chaise lounge. She stares silently but angrily at the pair.

"Gee, Mom, I know you need your beauty rest but I've got to tell you it isn't working so hot today. That face in the window was frightening."

"Shut up! For once don't say anything. Your silence will be just fine."

"Sure. Whatever you say."

Lauren glares at Jane Ella, ignores her response and turns her attention to Richard. She takes a deep breath as if to regain control over anger, "Richard, after you finish out here by the pool, I have some things I'd like to discuss with you. No hurry, just when you have time later."

"Sure. I'm going in to dress right now. Shouldn't take long."

"Oh, Richard, are you in trouble with the mommy? Better watch out 'cause she's liable to spank you or maybe the punishment will be worse and she'll want you to spank her. Ewww. There's an image that I'll not want to witness."

"Jane Ella, your filthy mind continues to overload your mouth. It's time you shut up…for your own good. You've pressed this morning about as far as it's going to go."

258

Lauren gets up from the chair, stares one last time at Jane Ella and steps toward the house.

"Ooooo. For my own good, huh? Now you've taken to threats? Watch your step, Mommy-Dearest."

Lauren freezes. She spins around and without a word throws her glass and remaining juice at Jane Ella. The glass misses by a few feet but smashes on the pool deck.

"God, Mother. You're insane! What's wrong with you? Are you losing it? What if that had hit me or broken here and cut me? Are you nuts? Now there's probably glass in the pool. Really Brilliant!"

Jane Ella quickly heads for the safety of the house.

"Why can't you just shut up? You think I'm nuts. You're about to find out if you say one more thing. Richard, clean that up before you come in…please."

Richard stands speechless, then he picks up a towel and heads in the general direction of the broken glass.

Lauren returns to the kitchen, elbows on the island, face in hands.

"What did I do to deserve her? She's impossible and dangerous. Just as I thought she was acting half-civilized it all goes up in smoke. Jane Ella is a complete mutation. She has an evil heart. Keep Richard away from her and get her to leave. I've got to do it."

Lauren continues to feel the pangs of embarrassment for the next two days and says nothing to Jane Ella and only polite, vague small talk to Richard. Perhaps she can clear the air this week and get the household back to normal-whatever that may be. All the signs of deceit have been there but maybe it's time to quit trying to be so suspicious and just start living. Lauren sets her mind to be more pleasant, try not to be suspicious and keep up with the infernal finances and their daily requirements. Making money by using money is a full-press sport and she can't afford to get sloppy. She'll make an effort to get along for the time being.

More days pass and the piles of financial papers are growing larger on the dining room table. When Lauren isn't scrutinizing a piece of paper, she has her head focused on the laptop screens. She pours over paper after paper virtually from mid-morning until bedtime. She drinks more and more during her financial efforts, whatever they might be. There hasn't been a prepared meal in the house in weeks since Fanda simply left one afternoon and never returned to work. Fast food is delivered and then left in various stages of breakdown until no one can stand the mess.

Slowly over the next several days Lauren feels as though she's behind on everything. She hasn't talked to Richard about Jane Ella. Investment decisions she promised her counseling army sit on hold. Her bed hasn't been made in a week. The kitchen looks like a sty with pizza boxes and food cartons piled high. The euphoric state of control is fading as her world swirls around her and her frustrations nag on and on.

"Alrighty, then. Let's talk. Sit down, Richard."

Richard sits on a kitchen stool and puts one elbow on the island. He appears attentive but not overly fearful.

"Back when Phillip and I were first married, remember when you used to be in Boston on occasion?"

"Sure. How can I forget. We were an item, Lauren."

"Yes, we were an item. Then do you remember when I got pregnant and we cooled our jets for a couple of years?"

"Sure, I remember that as well. I visited once and all we could do was mess around a little. Am I gonna be tested on this history class?"

"Please. Don't make jokes. There's a point. Listen Richard…"

The front door opens and the distinct humming of Jane Ella is heard all the way into the kitchen.

"Hold it, Richard. I might as well get Jane Ella in on this right now. She needs to hear this."

Jane Ella walks into the kitchen, stops humming and looks at Richard and Lauren.

"Am I interrupting something? "

"No, in fact I want to talk to you and Richard at the same time."

"Talk? Please. You're crackin' up, Mom. You don't talk. You try to get someone to listen to your goofy conspiracies. I think you'll say anything to try to get your way and frankly I'm not in the mood to listen to any of your convoluted shit this afternoon. See ya'."

"Stop. I need you to listen and I think it will prevent some major problems for the future of the three of us."

"Don't care. Don't care. Don't care. Won't listen to your paranoid conspiracies." Jane Ella puts her hands cupped over her ears and walks straight to the hallway leading to her room.

"Well, I should have expected as much. I'll continue with just us, Richard. I'm sure Jane Ella is your daughter. That's why I've tried my best to keep you from having some sort of perverted relationship with your own daughter. Now I've said it. Now you know."

Richard sits patiently while Lauren finishes but he shows very little outward reaction.

"Did you hear what I just said? Do you understand?"

"Yeah. I understand what you said and don't get me wrong. I'm not pickin' an argument. But how do you know Jane Ella's mine? And why would you wait until now to say something? And even *if* it is true, how many times do I have to tell you nothing has happened. Just relax.

I think you build stuff up in your mind and then kaboom, you think it's the end of the world. I personally think you're stressing out over the money, way too much."

"Stressing out. You say nothing's happened between you and Jane Ella, your daughter. You question how I know she's your child? So, you think I'm going bonkers? Huh, Richard?"

Richard shrugs and raises his eyebrows as if in total innocence, "It's not what you think. That's all I need to say right now. I know how upset you are at the moment and I don't want to make it worse. It's not what you think."

Richard stands, forces a smile, touches Lauren on the arm, turns and walks out by the pool. Lauren is furious and she needs something to calm her nerves. She quickly pours a tumbler three-quarters full of vodka. No time for ice. She needs this one. Lauren drinks the entire glass contents in four giant swallows. She heavily clanks the glass onto the island and walks outside joining Richard.

"Richard, I don't know how I can express to you how much I love you and always have. You've just got to believe what I've just told you. I know this has been a zoo living here but we've come too far with everything to let go of each other. I see a future for us. A wealthy future. I even fantasize about a future for the three of us. A sort of family future. But everyone has to understand the proper roles."

Richard seems a little preoccupied but smiles at Lauren.

"Yeah, Lauren, me too."

"Well, I guess that's as good an answer as I can get...so I'll take it and hope we can get everything on the right track."

Richard has a funny look on his face and though he is smiling, his thoughts are somewhere else. Not on the pool deck at this moment. Lauren turns and walks back into the house. She goes to the family room and reclines on the sofa. It's been an exhausting afternoon for Lauren.

CHAPTER 40

THE BREAKING POINT

After a fridge-grazing session and no formal meal, Lauren takes a book and retires to her bedroom. Around nine there's a soft knocking and Richard peeks around the edge of the door. He seems to have recaptured his old familiar smile and Lauren feels like this is already better. Perhaps the air is more clear. And, if not, at least Richard looks and acts like the old Richard, attentive, kind, Richard.

Richard sits on the edge of the bed and gives his best look of sincerity and concern, "I know you've had a tough day and I haven't been any help. I brought you the martini pitcher for your nightcap and hope you don't give up on my domestication process. It's been the hardest on you but I sincerely hope you'll just stick with me. I think you'll find everything with all of us will be on the right course to happiness for all of us. Trust me?"

Lying seems to be the best for now and Lauren tries to dramatize a bit of sincerity to be convincing. "Sure, Richard. I'm sure everything will get better and better. Thanks for the drink."

"Okay, sweet dreams."

Lauren instinctively knows things will not get better but she needs to get this whole day in the past. Strangely she's not interested in drinking anymore today and after reading a while she falls asleep around nine o'clock. Tonight she sleeps but after a dream she awakens. Even in her sleepy condition she's surprised she even awakened because she's been sleeping so soundly through the entire night, every night for the past few weeks. Maybe she's returning to at least one element of normalcy. Lauren feels thirsty so she sits up on the side of the bed and turns on her bedside lamp. She feels somewhat of a sense of pride when she notices she failed to drink any of the usual "nightcap" cocktail Richard brings faithfully each evening. Well, tonight her thirst calls for a Coke or orange juice far in advance of her usual morning routine. At the moment, more alcohol or water is not the answer.

Lauren doesn't turn on any lights but feels with an outstretched hand and leads with her right foot almost as if she's about to touch her toes into freezing cold water. Slowly but accurately she edges her way through the dark hallway to the kitchen.

As she nears the kitchen Lauren hears what sounds like indistinct, muffled talking. The noise doesn't seem to be coming from any of the bedrooms down the hall behind her so it must be someone near the front of the house. As she enters the kitchen the soft glow of a shelf light seems bright enough to get what she needs from the refrigerator. But she still hears the noises. Lauren withdraws her arm that was reaching for the refrigerator handle and gingerly proceeds out the other end of the kitchen toward the dark front of the house. Still puzzled and the darkness of the front area is somewhat surreal from the street light nearly a hundred yards away and shimmering it's best through the sheer curtains. She stands at the front door looking back at the path she just came and she can still hear the sounds so she's certain it's not outside in front of the house.

Slowly she retraces her steps back through the kitchen and stops in the large cove entry that leads to one end of the massive family room. Turning the corner into the family room her vision is drawn to the far end of the room and the flickering fire in the fireplace but there doesn't appear to be anyone in here either. But Lauren freezes and tilts her head trying to place the direction of the sounds., There are the voices again. Clearly it's voices, quietly talking. She moves toward the fireplace and closer to the source of the voices. As she takes three more steps into the dark family room, she pauses at the top step and her eyes are drawn to the fire in the fireplace. The muffled voices become clear now.

First it's Richard, "…yeah and I'm just glad we got lucky after we abandoned your original plan…or we might both be sitting in jail. That was way too soon while everything about the inheritance was up in the air. Hiring violence, no matter how careful the layering just brings morons hanging around your neck as dangerous partners. Thank

264

God we didn't do that. No matter how carefully someone would have been hired if there was ever any connection to us it would be over for you and me right now…but it's not."

Richard continues, "But, my darling, I feel so fortunate that you are so brilliant."

"Nothing brilliant about it Richard. I happen to think we are perfect together. Your idea to simply let her kill herself with booze and pills…clean hands. That's the way to do it. I should have trusted your more masterful, calm approach. Clean hands. Even to the point of getting her fingerprints on the pill bottles after she's passed out. And the way she's sucking down the stuff every night it really becomes whatever night we choose. Ramp up the mix and she chooses to do it to herself. End of game. Clean hands. Just think, Richard, no more drunken, harpy, slut stumbling from one pile of money to another. It is *our* money."

Lauren is dumbstruck. Richard and Jane Ella are talking about killing her. Then Lauren's eyes become adjusted to the darkened room. She suddenly focuses over the back of the sofa and onto the floor a few feet back from the fire, clearly exposing the mystery hidden until now from her view.

Lauren stumbles back a step and puts her hand to her mouth in horror. There are the unmistakable naked figures of Richard and Jane Ella in the flickering light.

The shocking scene jerks Lauren out of any sleepy head-muddle. Jane Ella and Richard are on the floor totally naked and kissing passionately between whispers and giggles. Jane Ella pushes Richard over onto his back and quickly straddles him. Lauren is momentarily frozen in shock and then she involuntarily gasps out loud, stumbling backward. Richard and Jane Ella are so involved in their chosen entertainment they don't even hear Lauren's gasp or notice her presence. But Lauren isn't about to watch this performance a split-second longer.

Lauren shrieks with the volume of a bomb going off in the room. *"My God! Stop it! Goddamn son-of-a-bitch! Oh, Jesus! I can't believe this!"*

Jane Ella screams in fright from the shocking interruption. She rolls away from Richard and looks in fear toward the family room entry and seeing Lauren's face in the flickering firelight she screams again.

"Mother! Get out of here! Get out! God damn it! Get out of here!"

"So this is what happens? How *dare* you tell me to get out. Get up! Both of you. This makes me want to throw up. *Get up*!" Lauren's voice clearly drips with hysteria and a white-hot rage.

Richard rolls sideways next to the sofa, temporarily hidden from Lauren's view, as he claws to retrieve his pants from the sofa. His legs begin flying frantically up in the air as he awkwardly pulls his pants over one leg. He's not successful but he continues writhing around wildly.

"God damn you, Richard! You sick, perverted son-of-a-bitch! How could you? With Jane Ella? Your own daughter! Oh God. How could you? This is too much to bear. Get up! Both of you. Get out of my sight! Richard. I want you out of this house tonight. Do you hear me? I don't care where you go or how you get there. Just leave! And young lady, you go to your roo…"

"You can't tell me what to do! I'm outta here tomorrow. That's what you've wanted anyhow. Isn't it, you drunken bitch!"

" Shut your mouth and get to your room. I don't want to hear another word out of your filthy mouth."

Jane Ella holds her clothes crumpled together just enough she covers the lower part of her body with one clump and her upper area with another. She squeezes past Lauren without a word and disappears into the kitchen and down the hall to her room.

"Look, Lauren. Maybe if we just talk through this. I'm so sorry. It just happened and I never intended to hurt you in any way."

Lauren snaps a lamp on and it presents a scared, barefoot, bare-chested Richard looking like the proverbial kid with his hand in the cookie jar.

"Richard, I told you to get out and I mean it. I'm not talking about this. And I don't ever want to see you or talk to you again. Take whatever you need, call a cab but get out! I want you out in fifteen minutes. *Fifteen minutes! Just get out*!"

Lauren stomps toward the front living room and as she passes through the kitchen she turns on the overhead lights. The fluorescent lights are so bright she squints at first and everything looks cold and stark. Lauren does a double-take and looks directly at three prescription bottles and a small plastic bag of white powder next to a half-empty vodka bottle on the island. She picks up the plastic bottles one at a time and can hardly believe her eyes. She reads the prescriptions.

LAUREN PITTMAN
ZOLPIDEM TARTRATE

Lauren reads the instructions, "take one before bedtime for sleep assistance". Lauren recognizes the name of this medicine. It's the formal name for Ambien, the sleeping pills and she knows all too well because she used to take them sometimes but her doctor told her they are dangerous if taken in combination with alcohol. At the time it didn't seem like a difficult choice to make. Lauren immediately gave up Ambien, in favor of extra vodka. She threw away the remainder of the Ambien she had in the house because she knew how dangerous it could be. Lauren looks a little closer at the bottle. This prescription was filled just a week ago. The next bottle reads:

LAUREN PITTMAN

OXYCODONE

Percocet, also an old prescription months ago but recently refilled.

The third reads:

267

LAUREN PITTMAN

CYCLOBENZAPRINE

Another old prescription, a very strong muscle relaxant used very sparingly when she'd injured a muscle in her back. She certainly remembers this one even though it was a year ago. It knocked her for a loop and she was warned absolutely no alcohol within eight hours of taking the last one. Now she's apparently getting a steady dose in her nightly vodka.

So, her little nightcap from sweet-Richard has contained enough drugs to make her sleep very soundly and when the chosen time came they would just give Lauren a bigger dose so she'd slip away permanently. It seems clear the murder of Lauren was the plan so the Richard and Jane Ella could live in wealthy incest to their heart's content. This can't be any more perverted and sick. It's also so typically Richard. The prescriptions are in Lauren's name and she's drinking the near-lethal combination nightly. One night she would just get a little too much.

Richard is a cold, calculating killer and so is Jane Ella. Lauren can imagine hearing Richard say the chilling words, "clean hands".

Lauren shoves the pill bottles in a kitchen drawer, turns and walks to the living room where she sits on a sofa waiting for Richard to leave.

Within a very few minutes, Lauren can hear Richard on the phone and then he comes past her in the living room, looks at her without smiling and he starts out the front door apparently leaving his other clothes and belongings behind.

"I guess I really screwed up your party tonight, you fuckin' pervert. And trying to murder me and keep your hands clean…again…huh, Richard? Every night, sweet Richard brings a little nightcap cocktail for Lauren. Vodka laced with enough tranquilizers to kill a horse. Except tonight I found the little bottles, Richard. Trying to kill me, huh? Such hate and cold, calculated violence. Where does that come from? Probably in your genes you low life."

Lauren pauses but isn't finished, "Just looking at you right now makes me want to puke. You're a liar, a cheater and a murderer. So you thought you could worm your way sexually into our daughter's inheritance and have me out of the way as a bonus. Well, Buster, it didn't work out so well did it? I'd say you're out on your ass in the cold. I still can't imagine how you could have sex with *our* own daughter. You're the absolute worst. Any port in the storm. Huh, Richard? Even if it's your own daughter. You sick fuckin' pervert. *Pervert!"*

BANG!

Richard hits his fist on the door and glares at Lauren.

"Shut up! Just shut up! You'll keep your mouth shut if you know what's good for you and you'll stay quiet about this and everything else. I do have a breaking point and you've reached it. So, careful, Lady! Jane Ella was absolutely right. She said you'd come up with the father-daughter thing just like when you apparently told Phillip Jane Ella wasn't his but then told Jane Ella later it was a lie and you did it just to control him. Your daughter's a very smart girl, and she knows your conniving ways to a tee. She said you'd pull the incest rabbit out of the hat just to keep good old Richard with the ring in his nose and a short leash until you could get her to leave. I guess you thought you and I could be a permanent couple. I can hardly stand to think of that as my future. Particularly when the younger member of this household is so perfect. And compared to you? Well, just look in a mirror sometime. But I guess in the end, you might see all this as a draw. My little plan didn't work completely and neither did yours. But the real end result is that I get the grand prize-Jane Ella. "

Spittle drops fly as Lauren sneers, "You pathetic, weak piece of shit. When was to be my final night? Tonight? When were the grieving boyfriend and his daughter to tearfully tell the police that the old drunk mixed sleeping pills, drugs and alcohol and it was just too much? Then Jane Ella inherits all of my money and property and the two of you split it up. Boy, Richard. You're something. Sorry I goofed up your plans, you callous… *fucking* pervert! Just get out! I have a gun and if it was in my hand at this moment you'd already have lead poisoning. Lucky for you, I guess. So don't even attempt to threaten me with your 'breaking point' bullshit. Get the fuck out of my house!"

"You are one dangerous woman. And it's not because of any gun. You're crackin up. You still think you're some gorgeous rich gal and you're only foolin' yourself. You're a hopeless, delusional drunk. I'm only sorry I ever got involved with you before the Phillip thing and I can only hope you don't take me down the whirlpool with you just from stupidity. I hope you like your wealthy life because all you've got is your money. Just don't look in the mirror. You'll die of fright."

Richard closes the door behind him as he quickly walks out and Lauren soon hears a car pull up and then hurry off down the street. The house is very, very quiet. Lauren figures Jane Ella's probably in a rage of her own, partially frightened about being caught and she's probably throwing clothes into a suitcase so she too can leave. At any rate, the quiet seems peaceful for a change.

Eventually Lauren returns to her bedroom and picks up the glass pitcher and contents of what she's sure is the dangerous mixture and carefully places it under the sink in her bathroom. She'll hang onto the liquid in case she needs it for a little leverage of her own. Then she says out loud, "Wait a second. I don't need leverage. I have enough money to bury Richard and any of his stories. I have enough money to *buy* any man I choose…if I even choose to do it. For once, I shouldn't have to worry. Nah, wait a second. Shouldn't have to worry isn't quite good enough, Lauren. *I am the queen! I will not worry! End of sentence. Period."*

She looks in the mirror and tosses her hair to one side and it feels so good, " Ah ha. Maybe at this moment, more than ever before, I am closer to being totally free. And Richard, you lied once again tonight. I am looking in the mirror and I look great!"

The house is huge, silent and cold again only this time without Phillip...or Richard. Lauren expects Richard to call with some phony excuse and try to return to her on bended knee, attempting in his shallow, feeble way to reconcile. After all, he'll want *his* money and he's been caught once again giving his prey the opportunity to kill itself only this time it didn't work quite so well. But knowing Richard, Lauren figures he'll spend endless hours trying to concoct a story that will make it all seem so innocent. Jane Ella will probably try to help Richard with his story because creativity isn't Richard's strong suit.

Another day passes. Richard doesn't call. He doesn't return. Lauren just closes the door to his bedroom and doesn't go in. What a creep! It still makes her feel sick just the sight of the two of them writhing around on the floor. She's got to come partially clean with John Sacks so he can put a stop to any of Lauren's estate passing to Jane Ella. That's the best insurance policy Lauren can have at this point.

When she thinks of Richard and his bruised ego and empty pockets she gets a ripple down her body that frightens her. He's so convincing that he's above being involved in anything too violent but reality shows him differently. His true character mirrors some of the amoral jungle predators he's been around for so many years. She checks and double-checks the locks and alarm system.

Since Richard left last night, Jane Ella and Lauren carefully avoid each other. They each lock themselves into their bedrooms at night. Stone silence between mother and daughter, killer and quarry. It stays that way for another day and then a small moving van pulls up outside the house. Jane Ella comes through the house talking on her cell phone.

"Yep. You're in the right place. I'll be out in a sec."

The moving van is for Jane Ella and her belongings. Movers come in and as they go through the house they give each other glances that Lauren isn't sure how to interpret. Lauren is suspicious. She wonders if they are simply curious or if they're casing the house to come back later for burglary or worse.

It seems like a flash in time but within an hour Jane Ella's belongings are in the truck and she's coming at a fast pace through the house carrying a small carry on type suitcase. Wearing sunglasses and twirling her car keys, Jane Ella comes into the room where Lauren is looking out the window at the van.

In the most sarcastic and venomous voice she can muster Jane Ella glares at Lauren, "Ciao. And that's ciao for good. It's been a real experience being *your* daughter. But it is over with a capital "O"! Now you shouldn't have to worry…too much… about me ever again. Enjoy your life, Mother, as long or short as it may last. May it be the painful, shitty life you deserve."

As the door slams shut Jane Ella's final insult to Lauren, " Keep looking over your shoulder. You never know when or where…but in the meantime I hope you die in your own vomit, you fucking bitch!"

Down the front steps and around to the open garage she goes, suitcase in hand. As she drives out of the driveway ahead of the van, Lauren realizes she is truly alone. It will likely remain this way. So this is total freedom. It's not too early…perhaps a martini or two.

CHAPTER 41

MURRAY'S DISCOVERY

Murray Eddlemann works feverishly, three computers powered on and set up among the mass of other computers and cables on a huge work table in a corner of his office.   Though one may think he may be remorseful for wanting to dip into his friend's money, in reality he does not feel the slightest twinge of guilt. Murray is not a man to leave money lying on the table. With Phillip dead, the overseas money will just languish for eternity.   Murray reminisces about all the great times with Phillip. In retrospect he believes he wasn't such a good friend to Phillip nor was Phillip a good friend to him. Instead Murray liked Phillip's qualities of being edgy and abusive to employees. He liked that Phillip was creative, gutsy, bold and absolutely fearless unless he was to get caught by the authorities. Then Murray knew Phillip would melt into a whiny heap and try to stick it all on Murray or anyone else. Murray smiles as he thinks of Phillip's strongest characteristic, he was absolutely devoid of a conscience. He knew he was smarter than most and wasn't afraid to treat financial and tax fraud as nothing more than a game. Murray was the perfect so-called friend and accomplice in crime.

Murray remembers the time and effort he and Phillip spent, for over a decade, setting up the elaborate fake identities, shill companies and bank accounts so one day Phillip could divorce, take a new identity and live very, very well in secrecy for the rest of his life.   Murray set up the proper foreign government's taxation registration so there was little risk of being caught for fraud. Murray doesn't quite have Phillip's wealth but certainly isn't far behind. He continues to be paid legal retainers and bonus money compliments of Patriot Star Investments that has among its many lucrative investment clients those with fake identities created by Phillip and Murray.

Murray knew Phillip's ultimate plans and he feels bad that Phillip was prematurely taken in the tragedy. So Murray's challenge today and tomorrow and the day after is to find a way to get access to the money only known about by Phillip and Murray. Murray must figure out a way to break the passwords that will give him access into Phillip's accounts.

Then Murray can drain the accounts, let the income and taxes flow to the dead false identity and Murray becomes perhaps the wealthiest and untaxed Boston lawyer. But he has to find the passwords. For the last two weeks Murray's studied everything he can get his hands on about code breaking and computer hacking. Some of the techniques are pure logic but a lot is discovering personal facts about the code-setter. There are several dark web cryptographic techniques and programs, but the vast majority of Murray's work is pure trial and error to feed information about Phillip into the programs.

This afternoon he is running dark web hacking software and diligently working through all the possibilities of passwords that represent the inside thoughts and distaste Phillip had for Lauren. Murray has a growing list and is trying endless variations of each entry.

He tries dozens more and reassures himself he'll stay at this as long as it takes. He feverishly jots down his brainstorming ideas of terms Phillip used trying to hit the right combination. Then the hacking software identifies an entry that could make sense. Murray takes a deep breath and slowly types the suggestion, hoping, watching for success. As he hits the enter button on the keyboard… there's a pause. That's it! "liberty&Justice 4all." Murray hit it! Complete access to Phillip's foreign bank accounts. Murray feels a fleeting sadness as he begins to access the actual data of Phillip's secret accounts.

"What the…?"

Murray sits straight up in his chair and puts his face within inches of the screen.

"What's going on here?"

Surprise turns to shock as Murray sits with eyes and mouth wide open. Of course it's the mother- lode, millions of dollars. But within the last several days there's regular withdrawal activity on the accounts and the activity is coming from Nice, France.

"Well, Phillip, old friend, what have you done? What are you up to? Couldn't even trust old Murray? Not like you weren't planning this for a while but didn't want your old friend Murray to know, huh? Screw Murray, huh? Hardly seems fair."

Murray leans back in his huge leather chair and turns to face the view of Boston.

"I've got to think about this. C'mon, Murray. Whatcha gonna do?"

Later and across town Lauren places a phone call.

"You've reached Lieutenant Jess O'Halloran, Boston Police Department. Leave a message starting with your name and phone number."

Lauren waits for the signal.

"Hi, Jess. It's Lauren. I've missed seeing you. Maybe we could get together and have a drink or something. I am living all alone in this big old house so there aren't any possible distractions. Give me a call."

It would be fun to get Jess to come over and maybe entice him into a little fun and games. It doesn't have to last forever or get serious but he's exciting in a sort of innocent way. He's such a big studly guy but pretty awkward with his technique. Maybe Lauren can teach him to relax and let that inner beast out to roam the halls of Pittman. Besides, Richard is never coming back and good riddance. Jess might make a good substitute for a once-in-a-while fling.

Lauren doesn't get a response to her call.

She drinks more and earlier in the day than ever before and she has literally everything she's dreamt of having. Freedom. But she can't quell the demons that plague her no matter how much she drinks or where she travels. She's personally torn apart any semblance of family life. She dreamed one day of having a long time relationship with Richard but he's gone for good and never surfaced again after the night she threw him out. It still makes here sick to think of Richard making love to Jane Ella. She gets a knot in her stomach when she thinks of those days just a short time ago when she plotted and manipulated with her lover to kill Phillip and now she knows she was to be the next victim. As she lapses into another night of alcohol induced coma she thinks of a good time ahead for the next three weeks as she plans her trip to the French Riviera.

CHAPTER 42

WHEN PATHS CROSS

It's a beautiful day on the Mediterranean of southern France, in Nice. The bar and waiting area of the swank Riviera Le Padouk Restaurant in the Le Palais de la Mediterranee Hotel is very crowded and a harried maître d announces dinner reservations and seats people as quickly as he physically can.

"Monsieur Veloux, … Réservation… S'il vous plaît… Monsieur Veloux? "

A gentleman and lady excitedly stand at the sound of their name being called. "Oui, Monsieur. Oui! Je suis Veloux."

One more person ahead of her. Impatiently Lauren waits at the bar for her table. She glances at the man sitting next to her.

"I think sometimes a table for one takes longer. But I suppose I should get used to it. I generally dine alone. You?"

He smiles but says nothing. Lauren supposes he doesn't speak English or just didn't take the bait. At any rate, she thinks to herself, who cares? But sadly even her bravado can't overcome her crestfallen self-image. It seems lately when she tries her best to flirt, it simply doesn't work. She receives a lot of polite smiles that clearly communicate a lack of interest. Thank goodness the bartender doesn't let her down as he drops another martini in front of her and gives her a big smile. Lauren smiles at him nodding her approval. "Merci beaucoup."

Like an ice cube dropped down her back Lauren stiffens and sits up straight looking in the mirror over the bar. There's not enough light to be certain and the mirror has a smoky reflection. Her eyes frantically search the mirror again for details of what she thought she saw but she can't see clearly enough in the mirror of the dimly lit bar area. But Lauren knows that voice. She'd know it anywhere. It has to be Jane Ella. But it can't be. What would she be doing in this restaurant, at this exact time, in Nice? Without turning around, Lauren continues to peer into the dark reflection, scanning the people crowded behind her in the bar area. And then she sees Jane Ella. It is Jane Ella, round, chubby face but it's Jane Ella for certain. Lauren's heart begins to pound.

Lauren turns her body slowly on the bar stool as she pushes her sunglasses up onto her forehead. It takes a second for her to be absolutely certain the tall, very chubby and very pregnant lady just a few feet away is indeed Jane Ella. Standing next to her is a middle aged, grey haired man in a sport coat…it's Richard. She focuses for another second to be sure that's who it is and the unmistakable, irritating, ever-complaining voice confirms it.

"I don't care, Richard. Just give some money to the Maître d and get us in there. Now, Richard! I can't stand here forever. I *won't* stand here forever. What do you want me to do? Have this baby right here?"

Fueled by the alcohol and shock of Jane Ella and Richard's appearance, Lauren screams at them in the top of her raspy voice. Her screams of rage cause the patrons to gasp in choir-like unison.

"You murdering son-of-a-bitch, Richard! How could you? Couldn't leave your daughter alone, could ya'…ya' fuckin' pervert! "

Jane Ella and Richard freeze in fear as they frantically look around to see who's screaming.

"You can't do this…You can't have a baby by your own father! Oh, Jane Ella! You can't have a baby!"

Jane Ella zeros in on Lauren and twists her face in shock, mouth gaping as she stares in horror at her mother.

There's sudden and absolute silence as shocked patrons suck in their breaths and look around wondering what is taking place. Jane Ella

278

spins around facing Richard and buries her face against his chest. He puts his arms around her as if to protect her but Lauren, now free from her seat, is striding toward them in a rage.

"Richard you son-of-a-bitch! How could you do this to your own daughter? Huh? How can any person stoop so low? And our slut of a daughter? Did you like it, you fat pig?"

Jane Ella pulls free of Richard and faces Lauren, *"Shut your drunken mouth! I'll have you arrested you drunken bitch!"*

" Me arrested? Ha! Me? I don't think so. But maybe you should have your father arrested. What is it called when a father and daughter do what you've done? The two of you are disgusting! Why don't you say something Richard? Cat got your tongue you filthy pervert? Slut and pervert with a baby. What a family picture that'll make."

Richard is speechless and stares at Lauren in disbelief.

"You knew, Richard, and all these years you played your little game by not talking about it. But she's your child and you know it. You and your gutter upbringing …you probably think that's just fine for a father to give his daughter a baby. But it makes me want to throw up. She can't have a baby by her father. Whatever I have to do, I'll do. "

Lauren winds her arm back and throws a haymaker punch intended for Richard but it catches Jane Ella on the side of her face and continues on to Richard's eye. Jane Ella grunts from the punch and loosens her hug of Richard and sinks awkwardly to one knee. Lauren's unintended hit of Jane Ella focuses her rage on Richard and she grabs a wine glass from a nearby table and hurls it toward Richard. It misses its mark and its smashing sound against the wall is drowned out by screams of the other patrons. Chaos reigns.

In the midst of the uncontrollable scene, many hardly notice a gray-bearded, distinguished-looking, gentleman who stares in disbelief at the participants of the fight. He says something to the gentleman he's with and they both leap to their feet and push waiting diners aside in near panic, as they both head for the exit door.

279

The maître d takes two or three steps in the direction of the two men and loudly calls to them as he tries to prevent their exit.

"Wait! Monsieur Doctor Leithund. Do not leave Monsieur. Gentlemen, your table is ready. Let me take you from this madness. The police will attend to them. Do not leave. Come with me to safety, Monsieur Doctor Leithund...please! Do not leave, Doctor Leithund." The exasperated maître d is apparently trying to control what he can in his restaurant.

It's as if a higher power suddenly pauses the action between Lauren, Jane Ella and Richard. The "Leithund " term is way too familiar and Lauren, Jane Ella and Richard freeze and then turn in one movement to look at the two men hastening for the doorway.

"Phillip! My God! Murray!"

The two men look at the three with an unmistakable deer in the headlights shock, frozen momentarily. Suddenly the bearded man lunges toward them striking Lauren on the side of her head with his cane. Lauren falls directly to the floor and the cane is drawn back to strike Richard but Jane Ella grabs the assailant's leg and in desperation the cane is launched in Richard's direction. He falls on top of Lauren and grabs her with both hands around her throat and they roll around the floor amidst grunts, groans and some muffled curses. Jane Ella tugs at them screaming as Richard is still nursing his eye from Lauren's first punch. He pulls at Jane Ella and Phillip.

 Murray Eddlemann looked more like an innocent bystander fleeing the scene as he quickly goes out the exit door and runs down the street. Patrons are trying to leave and stumbling over each other and the maître d finally gives up on having any control or decorum and flees to the dining room to await the arrival of the Gendarmes.

The police arrive, quickly pull the participants apart and take them away in handcuffs. The fighting family members may have had a long silent ride to the police station except there was only one paddy wagon so they continued to hurl the nastiest of curses and screams at each other which people on the street could hear above the wavering tone of the siren.

Murray was detained at the airport but released. The police kept his passport so he couldn't leave until they sorted out the altercation. But Murray was well-prepared to go off the grid with the aid of his multiple identities and was out of France within a few hours of originally being detained. His forwarding address-parts unknown.

CHAPTER 43
EULOGY OF GREED

At Boston Police headquarters a tall, Irish-looking Lieutenant smiles as he holds a file in his hand and walks quickly through the hallway to the squad room. He comes through the door and interrupts two men who are talking.

"Jimbo! Man you will never believe what I've got here. I just got it and man, it's too much. Jimbo, some days, the world just seems a little better when justice is truly served."

What d'ya have that's got you so fired up, Loo?"

"Just got it a few minutes ago from Interpol. There must be ten agencies lookin at copies of this at this very moment and I'm guessin' they're all shaking their heads and hollerin' 'gotcha'!"

"Okay. You gotta tell me."

"Listen to this, Jimbo. Remember last year some big exec from Patriot Star Investments went on a safari and supposedly got eaten by the alligators or some such bullshit? Remember? His widow came in here right after they got home. I really couldn't put my finger on it at the time and I had no reason to do anything other than just enjoy the eye candy from the rear view. I had one of those gut instincts that everything may not be kosher about her. It was that cops' sixth sense to be suspicious. I mean, she's great lookin', but a real cold side that could come out in a millisecond. After being around her a bit I figured her husband willingly jumped into a bunch of crocs just to get away from her."

"Yeah, I remember seein' her around here. She was swinging her back bumper and you staring like a dog in heat and out of professional courtesy you even turned around and winked at us. Yeah I remember her. So what happened?"

" Their name is Pittman. Anyhow, this Mrs. Pittman was having a fling with a guy, Richard Martin.   So she and this Richard Martin started their affair twenty or twenty-five years ago while she was engaged to her future husband, Phillip Pittman. After the Pittman's got married, she was still doing this Martin guy and he knocks her up. She has a daughter but never told a soul…not her husband, not the daughter, not even Richard Martin.

Over the next twenty or so years since marriage Mrs. Pittman and Martin are havin' a thing every time he came through Boston. Fast forward…the Pittmans didn't have a storybook marriage…big surprise, huh…and now the daughter is twenty something years old. This daughter gets a trust of several million bucks when she turned twenty one or twenty-two…aw well that doesn't really matter much in this story. "

Jess shakes his head as if in disbelief and continues, "Well, now listen to this. Somehow this Richard Martin guy gets Mr. Pittman, the Missus and the daughter to sign up for a safari in Africa. Now remember I told ya this Richard has been bangin' the Missus for many, many years and so Richard and the Missus cook up this scheme to get rid of Mr. Pittman while they're on the safari.   As far as it seems, the daughter didn't originally know or even suspect anything about it. Anyway, the plan was pretty clever. On a safari it's easy to drop somebody off all alone or in a small group for a little more private excursion. I guess it's common as long as the drop off is not at the mouth of a lions' den. In this case, this Richard guy sets up Mr. Pittman to go fishing on some lake…by himself.   The plan was simply to drop him off at a spot where he'd get in trouble real quick-crocodiles no less.   I guess there were rocks that went out into the lake and Richard Martin got Mr. Pittman to go out there to fish, knowing the crocs would cut him off from getting back to shore and then they'd have a good meal of Boston white meat. So the Missus and this Richard are full on for conspiracy to commit murder. Richard was to get beaucoup bucks from the Missus for doing the deed. The witch thought she'd be done with hubby and have her long time squeeze and all the money in the world. I gotta tell ya Jimbo, we're talkin many millions this gal was to get. Mr. Pittman was one rich dude.

But it just so happens Mr. Pittman had independent plans of his own. For several years Pittman and his big Boston attorney, Eddlemann, set up phony identities and phony foreign corporations, did insider trading through the fake companies and stockpiled millions of dollars in offshore accounts.

Pittman had absolutely no idea he was being set up to be the croc's meal on that certain day, but that was the very day he'd already planned to drop out of life as Phillip Eugene Pittman and take up one of a number of new identities he and his lawyer had been cooking all those many, many years."

"Alright, Lieutenant, I'm guessing the Mister didn't die. He must have been one great swimmer to get outta that mess."

"Na. Here's what's so cool when everybody's only paying attention to trying to screw somebody else. Pittman had the fake identities and phony passports for many years... just waiting for the right moment for the lawyer to say it was safe, pull the ripcord and land out of sight with his new identity…a liberated, wealthy man. With the fake identity always at the ready the lure of the future became irresistible when he was coaxed onto the safari and it was actually Pittman who wanted to be dropped by himself for a fishing trip. The day before all this happened Pittman made arrangements for a bush pilot pickup at the airstrip near their camp. No sooner did Martin drop him off and was out of sight, Pittman ran out onto the rock Jetty with his own plan to stage his death. He threw a shirt on the rocks next to the water, tossed his fishing gear around and threw his backpack with the days sandwiches down by the water hoping animals would tear it up. He ran back to the shore and the crocodiles were already coming from the water and climbing up onto the jetty where he'd just been. Apparently he didn't really realize it was going to be such a close call with the crocs but close call or not, he made it and it fit his plans to a tee.

He ran to the air strip, handed cash to a hungry bush pilot and took off. He'd arrived a day later than his family at the start. He'd carefully planned that so he could be by himself and first travel from the States into Cape Town as Phillip Pittman. Then he booked a one-way flight into Botswana as Doctor Heinrich Leithund, his new identity, passport from South Africa. That way when he made his great escape at the end he had no passport problems leaving Botswana in his new identity. He flew back to Cape Town as Leithund and checked into a hotel , this time with the new name permanently. From there he began his life of freedom and wealth.

I don't think the lawyer would have ever been caught up in all this except for one fatal flaw of all crooks. Just being a little greedy is never enough. They have to go for even more. This lawyer, Eddlemann thought Pittman was dead and was going to pilfer Pittman's foreign bank accounts. I mean isn't that just like a greedy friggin' lawyer. Why let a dead crook's money go to waste? It might as well be enjoyed by a live crook.

Then he discovered Pittman was very much alive and using the accounts so Eddlemann decided to meet him, probably for blackmail.

Pittman, now Dr. Leithund, kept searching the internet for all the details in the news of about his untimely death. What he found was that The Botswana Police Service with the assistance of the Park Rangers determined he'd been fishing alone on a lagoon and they concluded he ventured too close to the water , where he was attacked, killed and devoured by crocodiles. The investigation was closed, though understandably they were unable to locate any remains.

How perfect. Not even a suspicious drowning as he had personally planned for his fake accident. He figured he was really lucky. A murder plot in which he willingly took part.

But listen to this, Jimbo. Remember this safari -guy Martin's doin' the Missus…well he was also bangin' her daughter…his daughter…but of course as I said the sick twit says he never knew it. Anyhow Martin tells the daughter the whole plan to get rid of her supposed dad, Pittman. She was fine with it. The daughter sits idly by to let Mr. Pittman get the ax in Africa and apparently as soon as she got home wanted to have her mother killed. The daughter and her boyfriend, Richard Martin...who's also her real father, wanted all the estate money. So then, Martin and the daughter start slipping the Missus a mickey every night and they're pretty sure they'll keep upping the dose until she'll croak. So their nightly fun is slip the old lady the drugs and booze and then they orgy all over the house. One night…oops. She doesn't drink it and catches them. She throws Martin out of the house and the daughter packs it in and leaves soon after.

"Well, that's understandable. Incest and fightin's okay as long as ya keep it in the family. Is that their twisted motto instead of a home-sweet-home sign over the door?"

" Probably right. A father and daughter! I mean, man! How sick is that? That Martin was smart enough to not come back and get mixed up anymore with the Missus. But he was stupid enough to continue to chase the tail of his own daughter. Well, he gets the girly, his own daughter, prego.

By some weird chance the Missus, Pittman, flew over to France for a little holiday…probably on her broomstick.

Then Jimbo, *real* justice! This one fine day on the Mediterranean…the perfect storm! Mr. Pittman, alias Doctor Leithund planning dinner with his crooked-assed lawyer to discuss the terms of blackmail, the Missus on her broomstick, the daughter Jane, alias prego-mother-to-be and her quality boyfriend Richard Martin, Seventy IQ Martin, alias Daddy, all met up waiting to be seated at the same top shelf, foo-foo restaurant, at the exact same time.

Anyhow it was a perfect storm! They all show up to the same place at the same time. Total surprise. Anyhow, the Missus came unglued to see her daughter knocked up by her own father and she starts screamin at her old boyfriend, Martin. Mr. Pittman sees who it is and heads for the door but overhears the yelling about Richard being the real father. So Mr. Pittman loses it-I mean totally goes bezerk… and runs back, whacks his wife with his cane and starts choking her. The French cops came and hauled them all into the pokey to sort it out.

When all of the ruckus started, the lawyer took off. But he wasn't difficult to find later. When Pittman went down, he tried to blame everything on the fuckin' ambulance chaser, Eddlemann. Interpol got the lawyer at the airport in Nice, trying to leave the country but they

286

really didn't have anything to hold him but they took his passport until they could get it all sorted. Eddlemann apparently had other means of identity and took off the same night they detained him. Who knows where he went?

And that's their story.

Hey, Loo, I can't keep up with all the names but it sounds to me like these people should never have been allowed to be on the same planet with each other. The story's too good to be true. When you have a chance, I'd like to read all the report myself. Great story, huh?"

"Yeah, I'd say so. Can you spell FBI, IRS, SEC, Justice Department, French police, German Police, South African Police, Botswana Police, Interpol, Boston Police, and the Insurance company? I have to laugh when I see the list of agencies where this report is sent. When the prosecutors, insurance companies and the lawyers are done with this mess I'll bet the financial reset button will have been thoroughly pressed.

Ya know, Jimbo, after they were all caught, each say they only plotted to get free of at least one of the others in all this tangled mess and of course they were all chasing money. Loads of money!"

Jess pauses and then makes an angelic face loaded with sarcasm, "Ah, *freedom*. Like our pledge of allegiance says…'liberty and justice for all'. Has a nice ring to it. Actually, there was plenty of legitimate money for all the freedom any of them could have wanted but oh, no. Gotta have it all. So then they get caught and now they are getting spanked with a full measure of justice. Seems fair for these folks, don't ya think? "

"What I wanta know, Loo, did anything ever happen between you and the Pittman gal, huh, Loo?"

"You know there's some things a good cop can't talk about. Undercover stuff, ya know. I just can't get over it. She seemed so nice but baby was she ever evil to the core. She thought she was smarter than everybody else. Then halfway around the world, they all land in the same restaurant on the same day at the same time. Perfect storm
287

and judgement day all rolled into one. Of course this will take years to unwind because you know that insurance company is going to try to recover all their money, but they'll probably have to get in line behind the IRS with all the offshore crap and fake identity stuff. Yep, everybody's gonna get a chunk of these folks by the time it's all done. And that spoiled brat kid is soon to be the proud Momma to a kid sired by her own father. Maybe the kid will get to visit his grandmother in jail. Maybe they'll name Phillip Pittman, as godfather. Should be interesting to watch justice meted out on these creeps."

www.ingramcontent.com/pod-product-compliance
Lightning Source LLC
Chambersburg PA
CBHW060858250626
47159CB00008B/2791